THIS IS THE WAY THE WORLD ENDS

AN ORAL HISTORY OF THE ZOMBIE WAR

KEITH TAYLOR

::::-:::

About the Author

Keith Taylor is the true identity of the million plus selling author behind the pen names Aya Fukunishi and K A Taylor, who toiled for years writing trashy but bizarrely popular romance novels that you absolutely shouldn't ever read, not even to satisfy your curiosity. Not even on a dare. Just don't do it. You'll never get that time back.

Throughout those long, cold years in the romance trenches Taylor secretly longed to return to his first love and true calling: post-apocalyptic fiction. The bestselling Last Man Standing series was written in the months after he finally realized he couldn't write one more damned love story. He moved back to his writing bunker in Mongolia, disconnected from the world and returned with HUNGER, CORDYCEPS and VACCINE.

Taylor hails from the rainy suburbs of Manchester in the north of England. He lives with his wife, Otgontsetseg, and splits his time between Ulaanbaatar, Mongolia and Bangkok, Thailand. He's been deported from more than one country, once spent two months living in his car, has crapped in the wilderness everywhere from the Gobi Desert to the Pamir mountains on the Afghan border and survives on a diet of meat, cheese, beer and cigarettes. He probably shouldn't still be alive, but for now appears to be unkillable.

∷-∷

Preface

In 2014 a team of researchers from the National Center for Scientific Research in Marseille, France carried out a deep survey of the coastal permafrost in Kolyma, a remote region in the northeast of Siberia. They recovered samples from thirty meters beneath the surface that had remained untouched, frozen in time, for tens of thousands of years, and in those samples they found something unusual: an ancient virus previously unknown to science.

Pithovirus sibericum was a virus larger and more genetically complex than any known in the modern day, containing more than 500 genes and large enough to be visible under a standard microscope, and the team, led by Jean-Michel Claverie and Chantal Abergel, returned the sample to their laboratory eager to investigate further. There they made a startling discovery.

The virus was still alive.

After 30,000 years laying dormant beneath the Siberian permafrost *sibericum* awoke, and when exposed to single-celled organisms the virus began to reproduce and aggressively infect the host cells. The sample was quickly destroyed as a precaution.

When news of this discovery caused alarm among the general public scientists rushed to reassure them that the risk of human infection from ancient viruses was minimal. Edward Mocarski, professor of microbiology at Emory University, said that only "a very small proportion represent viruses that can infect mammals, and an even smaller proportion pose any risk to humans." He dismissed the suggestion that humanity had anything to fear from beneath the frozen wastes of Siberia.

Claverie and Abergel, however, remained unconvinced. They argued that a combination of climate change and industrial activity could lead to the accelerated melting of the permafrost and the reemergence of ancient viruses that had remained trapped for millennia; viruses against which we have no natural defenses, and for which there exist no vaccines.

"At the moment these regions are deserted and the deep permafrost layers are left alone," said Claverie. "However, mining and drilling means digging through these ancient layers for the first time in millions of years. If viable particles are still there, this is a recipe for disaster."

In 2018, they were proved right.

∷∶O∶∷

For Those We Lost

I'll begin with an apology.

In the years before the war, in that blissful, innocent time when the living dead were still the stuff of comic books and poorly scripted movies, back when the very idea of zombies lived only in the vast cultural wasteland between harmless entertainment and childish nonsense, I made a handsome living writing novels that told of an apocalypse at the hands of the walking dead. I reveled in the absurdity of the subject, gleefully portraying mass murder and the made-for-Hollywood destruction of our greatest cities as a spectacle to be enjoyed, fun for all ages. Each day I slaughtered countless thousands in prose before heading out to a light lunch, and for this I was rewarded with a home in a tropical paradise, a healthy bank balance and a loyal fan club.

My *Last Man Standing* trilogy in particular was as popular as it was scientifically inaccurate. *Hunger, Cordyceps* and *Vaccine* featured zombies that could run and fight with the speed and strength of the living and, in some cases, even retained scattered memories of their pre-infection lives, all abilities we now know to be fantasy.

These novels – bordering on offensive in light of the reality we have all since come to know – afforded me the freedom and wealth to live out humanity's years under siege in relative safety and comfort, shielded to an enviable degree from the dangers we faced. Unlike most of my readers I never feared for my life. I was never forced flee my home, go hungry or wait for salvation in a festering, overcrowded refugee camp, and I was spared the dull, aching torment of grief, a blessing that places me among a vanishingly small minority of survivors.

Those readers familiar with my pre-war body of work may find it odd to see my name attached to a project such as this, a sober, serious and unembellished account of the collapse of early 21st century human civilization. Some may even find it in extreme poor taste, a point of view I can understand entirely, and for this I can only beg your forgiveness and ask for your trust. It's certainly not my intent to make light of the horrors humanity faced, nor to use the crushing loss of mothers and fathers, husbands and wives, sons and daughters and, indeed, our very innocence as titillating fodder to feather my own nest.

Instead I see this book as reparations, or at least the first step on a journey of atonement I expect to occupy the rest of my life, for the role I played in weakening humanity's collective resolve to recognize and face head on a threat that drove our species to the verge of extinction. This book is intended to serve as both penance and apology.

For years I profited from portraying the living dead as entertainment, a carnival sideshow that should not be taken seriously. In fact, in those critical early months of the crisis I quietly celebrated as each new report of an attack pushed my backlist further up the bestseller charts. I cheered as the Shibuya footage triggered a resurgence of interest in the stagnant post-apocalyptic fiction genre, and I watched with glee as my debut novel, *Hunger*, became a surprise New York Times bestseller several years after its first print run.

Make no mistake, the industry in which I made my fortune played a central role in delaying and softening our response to the crisis. We forced the public into a needless battle to disentangle fact from fiction, and even when the severity of the threat finally became undeniable our novels, TV shows and movies left many fatally poisoned with misinformation, their minds awash with survival strategies conceived not by professionals but by authors and screenwriters who cared only that their vision of the apocalypse was more spectacular and destructive than the last.

The twin scourges of disbelief and ignorance we engendered and encouraged set back the fight by months at a time when we could scarcely afford hours, and while it would be impossible to accurately quantify the harm we caused I'm certain that, spared our negative influence, millions who died would still be alive today.

Let this, then, be my legacy. Let my frivolous works of fiction fade from memory, and let the following collection of personal stories help future generations better understand the mistakes we made.

I should note before you begin that there is no moral to be found here, no overarching message to be divined from these pages because, quite simply, I have none to offer. I don't pretend to any unique insight or wisdom, nor do I offer a path forward that hasn't already been hashed out a thousand times in a thousand ways by authorities much more qualified than my own. This is simply a collection of experiences, stories told by a handful of those fortunate enough to have survived to tell them. If nothing else they should serve as a stark reminder of all those stories that will now remain forever untold; a reminder of the knowledge lost and futures stolen by the scourge of the undead, and by our own seemingly boundless hubris.

This volume was printed in part using pulped and recycled copies of my own fiction. The extensive travel required to gather these interviews was funded by the profits from my novels, and all proceeds from the sale of this book will be used to aid rebuilding efforts in the United States and beyond.

For the part I played in this tragedy, I am truly sorry.

Keith Taylor
Banda Aceh, Indonesia
February 8, 2031

::: 1 :::

Monroe, Washington

I recognize his face the moment he looks up at me through the cracked, dust-scoured panes of his greenhouse, and as he wipes his hands on a rag and shuffles slowly towards the door I try not to stare at the stooped, fragile figure who was once a nightly fixture and a comforting presence on TV screens across the nation. Gone is the perfectly coiffed head of salt and pepper hair. The tailored Brioni suit and immaculate silk tie have been replaced with a dirty, oversized gray t-shirt and a pair of unflattering cargo pants.

As he reaches out to shake my hand I notice his sunken cheeks and pallid skin, and – perhaps I'm not hiding my shock as well as I'd hoped – he's quick to inform me that he'll be lucky if he has six months at best. He blames the cigarettes he snuck at the anchor desk during ad breaks, but he doesn't seem at all bitter about his prognosis. He tells me he'll be happy if he gets to see just one more harvest, and jokes that the moment he plucks the last tomato from his greenhouse he'll be racing to leave before the long winter sets in.

Despite his illness there's at least one thing unchanged about James McIntyre, the lead anchor of CNN's nightly news broadcast for the fifteen years leading up to the war. From beneath his gaunt visage and deeply creased brow he still looks out at the world with the same cool, piercing blue eyes that won him his reputation as

a 'silver fox', melting the hearts of female fans around the country with an arch of an eyebrow. After he lowers himself slowly to a sun-bleached plastic chair and covers his balding pate with a frayed Yankees cap he settles into the same easy, comfortable fireside tones I remember so well, punctuated with his trademark soft chuckle.

Nobody wanted to be the first to use the word, obviously. I mean, can you imagine the embarrassment? Can you imagine trying to get anyone to take you seriously ever again? There's just no way. The Internet would turn you into a damned *piñata* before you even got off the air.

No, it wasn't going to happen, at least not to one of us. There was just too much to lose. You spend your entire career trying to build a solid reputation, working to position yourself as the next Murrow... the next Cronkite. You want your name spoken in the same breath as the greats after they put you out to pasture, and you don't want to jeopardize your spot in the hall of fame.

And deep down that's where all of us believed we were headed, don't you doubt it for a second. Nobody ever dreamed of sitting in that anchor chair without an ego the size of a city bus. Even the guys who reported school closures on the graveyard shift of a Wichita affiliate were sure they were just paying their dues before they got the call up to the big leagues, so nobody was eager to volunteer for such an obvious career killer.

OK, cards on the table, kid, here's what it was. I didn't want to be the next Dan Rather. You remember that guy? The way they treated him? *Jesus.* One dumb mistake after a lifetime as an honest to God newsman, one of the all time greats, and they dragged his name so far through the muck he couldn't find work checking for typos at a high school paper. That's just the way things were in the Internet age. It's no wonder we were all a little gun shy.

So yeah, I guess that's why we all waited for the tabloids to start calling them zombies before we dared say the word out loud. Let someone else take the fall if it turned out to be some kind of hoax or... I don't know, a viral marketing campaign for some energy drink or web startup, know what I mean? That's what we were all thinking. Call me a coward if you want, I just didn't want to be the subject of a damned Leno monologue. I didn't want people laughing at me.

That's why I called them 'the attackers' in my broadcast rather than anything specific, but to be honest the notion that these attacks were something new had already been in the air supply for a couple of months, bouncing around social media and the conspiracy sites. People had been whispering about unusual incidents everywhere from Central Asia to South America since the start of the summer, but the Tokyo attack finally brought everything out into the open. Tokyo finally forced the idea out of the world of movies and into the mainstream.

My memory isn't quite what it used to be, but I think we were in the middle of a pretty dry segment on Medicaid when the news broke. My producer jumped in through my earpiece and gave me the signal to wrap it up ASAP, and the first thing I noticed was the edge in her voice. I couldn't tell if it was panic or excitement, but if you ever met Sarah you'd know that her emotional gamut ran all the way from A halfway to B. That woman had steel rebar running through her bones. In five years of running our control room she'd never once so much as raised her voice, so when I heard that nervous energy I knew something serious was going down. Anything that flapped Sarah was a big deal.

She fed me cold copy through my earpiece as we cut to the footage from Tokyo, delayed from live by about five minutes. There was a shot of... well, I'm sure you know the footage I'm talking about, it's iconic. It was the Shibuya film, the first clear, unambiguous attack ever caught on camera. Beautiful, perfectly framed and lit high def shots, a producer's dream.

Some second string BBC crew just happened to be filming B-roll for a travel show with one of those old Monty Python guys. Palin, I think. It was just blind luck that the cameraman was standing there in front of those towering neon signs at the exact right moment, and that he had the stones to keep rolling when anyone else would have sprinted as fast as they could in the other direction.

McIntyre pulls a crumpled soft pack of Lucky Strikes from his pocket and moves to light one. When he notices my expression he simply shrugs. "A little late to close the barn door now, kid."

Do you know Shibuya? Did you ever see it in person? No? You missed out. It's quite... I mean it *was* quite a sight, especially at night in the rain. It was like stepping inside the kind of video game that came with a warning sticker for epileptic kids, and beneath those massive, hypnotic neon signs hundreds of people crossed the street every time the lights changed. It was like nowhere else in the world. Quite beautiful when you think about it, in a *Blade Runner* kind of way. We'll never see a sight like that again.

The cameraman was standing just by the entrance to Shibuya station when it started, facing north west to catch the sea of commuters crossing the street on the diagonal. That crosswalk always ran like clockwork, with total

Japanese efficiency, so I guess that's why he decided to bring the shot in tight when people suddenly started to scatter into the traffic.

My first thought was that maybe a small sinkhole had opened up in the street. That alone would have been big news at such an iconic location, so as I watched the footage I was already trying to dredge up a few facts and figures I could toss out while I waited for a script to appear on the prompter.

That's when Sarah said it: "Jim, watch the man in the blue suit."

I spotted him right away. An older guy, I think. It's hard to tell with the Japanese – they don't seem to really start aging until they hit sixty – but I'd guess he was somewhere around late middle age. He was down on the ground and seemed to be convulsing, his back arched and his weight resting on the back of his head, but his hand was tightly gripping the pink sweater of some young woman beside him, stretching it out behind her as she tried to pull away. *That's* why people started to scatter. I think they must have seen something the camera didn't pick up, and the girl was... I've never seen such a look of horror outside a movie. Mouth and eyes wide, screaming, tears streaming down her cheeks. The girl was *terrified*.

We caught the bite perfectly. I mean *perfectly*, like something from a nature documentary. The guy lunged out and closed his teeth over the girl's calf as she tried to twist her way out of her sweater. He shook his head and pulled away a strip of flesh from the back of her knee down to her ankle, and as she fell to the ground she let out this awful scream that rose above the sound of the crowd. That's when the concern turned into panic, and the crowd turned into a stampede. Hundreds of people scattered every which way.

The problem was that most of them couldn't see the guy and didn't have a clue what they were running from, or in which direction they should run. They just heard screams and figured it made sense to get out of there. Some of them tripped right over the guy in their rush to get away, scrambling on hands and knees to stay out of reach. I tugged the earpiece from my ear and just watched, my mouth hanging open like some kind of yokel.

The cameraman, God bless him, held his nerve like a pro. As everyone ran he actually *approached*, bringing us to within maybe ten yards of the guy in the blue suit. No sense of self preservation whatsoever. He got close enough that we could see the guy's right hand wrapped tight in a dirty gray bandage. Poor bastard must have had been one of the slow burners. He could have been simmering for days before he finally went under.

Our guy got in even closer as the crosswalk finally emptied, close enough to catch the reflection of the neon lights on the asphalt. It was... sorry, I know this sounds heartless, but the camerawork was *beautiful*. The way he framed the shot to catch that flashing yellow Nikon sign shimmering in the blood pool? It was just *stunning*.

By then the only people left on the crosswalk were the man in blue, hunkered down over the body of the young girl with his face buried ears deep in her stomach, and a young guy in shorts and t-shirt who looked like he'd caught a bite before he collapsed a few yards away, clutching his neck. That's when Sarah cut the feed and came back to the studio. Can you believe it? She was worried we'd have Standards and Practices on our ass for airing murders in prime time. Seems crazy now, but I guess at the time it made sense.

Anyway, I was sitting there staring at my monitor beneath the anchor desk, where the feed was still coming through. I didn't even realize I was back on the air until I heard a tinny voice coming from my dangling earpiece. I forget what I said next, it's all a bit of a blur. I think I just sat in silence for a few seconds, trying to tear my eyes away from what was happening on the monitor, then I pushed the earpiece back in and heard Sarah screaming at me. "Camera two! *Jim, turn to camera two!*"

That snapped me back into it. I closed my mouth and composed myself long enough to trot out a quick recap of what we knew so far, which at the time was the square root of zip, and then I rolled off the standard filler about the harrowing images we'd just seen.

The first thing that came to me at the time was the dreaded Z word, but I sure as heck wasn't going to suggest that this guy was a zombie. Of course we'd all heard the rumors by then. You'd have to have been living under a rock to miss them, but there was nothing about the footage to suggest the guy in the blue suit was anything but mentally ill, or maybe on drugs, and I didn't want my name within a million miles of a suggestion that he might be undead or some other wacky horror movie nonsense.

That's when I started swearing. I'm sure you saw the broadcast later on YouTube just like everyone else, right? That's why the show was seen by around two hundred million people rather than our usual seven. Hell, if I'd known I could bump the ratings that easily I'd have started cursing like a sailor years ago.

What the viewers didn't know – and the reason a lot of them thought I was having some kind of mental breakdown – was that my monitor showing the feed from Tokyo was beneath the lip of my desk between my legs, just out of shot. The viewers couldn't see anything, but just at the edge of my vision I was still watching what was going on while I desperately vamped my way to the next ad break, and when I saw what happened next...

Well, there's no need to go into the gory details. I'm sure we've all seen much worse in real life in the years since, but suffice to say it shook me. The cameraman was still hovering over the man in the blue suit, trying to document as much as he could, no doubt dreaming of the awards he'd win for catching such incredible footage. He was too tightly focused on his work. He didn't notice the young guy in shorts pull himself back to his feet until it was too late.

I jumped from my seat and just yelled out without thinking. I don't even know what I said – I could never bring myself to watch the video – but I remember screaming at him to run as if he could somehow hear me. I mean, the feed was delayed by five minutes. The guy was already long dead before it ever reached my screen.

I think I was sobbing by the time the image dropped out. Sarah had the presence of mind to cut to commercials after about thirty seconds but by then, of course, the damage was already done.

McIntyre drops his cigarette and crushes it into the soil.

A few weeks later and it wouldn't have mattered. Nobody would have given a damn about a few curse words on a live newscast, but back then it was enough to force the network to 'invite' me to take early retirement. I can't say I blamed them. More than ever before they needed a steady voice the nation trusted, and once the video went viral... well, it was obvious I was no longer their man. You can't trust an anchor who jumps out of his seat and starts cursing like a lunatic while staring at something between his legs. I was an early Christmas present to the makers of Internet memes, wrapped up in a neat little bow.

You know what, though? I'm glad it happened. At the time it felt like the end of the world, but looking back I know I dodged a bullet. I don't think I could have forgiven myself if I'd taken part in the massive – *massive* – dereliction of duty from the media in those final few months. And of course it meant I didn't need to be in Manhattan every night for the live show, which I guess is the only reason I'm sitting here today.

I don't know if I believe in heaven and hell anymore. I just don't know, but what I *do* know is that if I ever fall into that fiery pit the first people I'll see will be the anchors, producers and network heads who decided to treat the outbreak like old news just a few weeks after Tokyo. The way they dumped the story in the D block the moment the advertisers started complaining, because it's tough to sell Ensure and adult diapers to people worried about a zombie apocalypse? *Jesus.* They let us all sleepwalk to the end of the world for the sake of ad revenue.

Don't get me wrong, I know it's not just the media who should shoulder the blame, far from it. It's all of us. It was our entire damned short attention span culture that sent us marching towards disaster. It was our complacency. Our arrogance. The shared delusion that our place at the top of the food chain was ordained by God and could never be challenged.

If we'd just been a little more on the ball we might have avoided this nightmare. But we all decided it was easier to change the channel.

•▼•

:::2:::

Ulaanbaatar, Mongolia

Munkhbaatar 'Mike' Dugarsuren insists on picking up the check for our second meal of the day, cheerfully waving away my protests as he pours us both another measure of Chinggis Platinum vodka. A famously hospitable people even before the crisis, my Mongolian hosts are acutely aware that their country has become almost embarrassingly prosperous in recent years, unaffordable to foreigners who rely on the anemic Dollar, Euro and Pound, and the newly wealthy locals are more than happy to share what they have. It's become something of a running joke among foreign visitors that you could leave your wallet behind on your arrival at Ulaanbaatar's Chinggis Khan International Airport and you'd still leave fatter than you arrived.

As recently as 2019 Mongolia teetered on the brink of bankruptcy, reliant on IMF bailouts and high interest Chinese loans to stay afloat after years of economic mismanagement, corruption, protectionist policies and the flight of foreign investment. Today the nation is transformed. The once rundown capital is now a thriving haven of prosperity, an urban oasis of beautifully landscaped public parks, modern skyscrapers and comfortable homes, all of them built using the national investment fund that has made each of Mongolia's three million citizens paper millionaires, shareholders in their nation's future.

While few would be so tactless as to brag about their astounding turn of fortune there is, naturally, a belief among the people that Mongolia is one of the few countries it could be argued 'won' the war. The physical isolation of this sparsely populated nation, hemmed in by Siberia to the north and the arid expanse of the Gobi Desert to the south, gave Mongolia unparalleled protection from the roving swarms that swept across much of Asia, and the vast deposits of coal, copper and rare metals waiting beneath the steppe left the country perfectly placed to profit as the world began to recover from the devastation.

Mike raises his glass and empties it with one gulp, spilling a little on the expensively embroidered silk sleeve of his *deel*, the traditional wraparound robe of his people. As fine as his tailoring may be there's no mistaking the thick, calloused skin and scarred knuckles of his hands, nor the deep lines scored into his face that hint at the rigors of his former profession.

It was your sanctions that forced his hand. Did you know that? That was what triggered the Siberian expansion. Of course Putin would never have admitted it even to his closest allies, but he was deeply worried that his... what's a nice way to put it, his *Crimean adventure*? He was terrified that would be the beginning of the end for him.

In the west you used to go on and on about hearts and minds whenever you went on one of your jaunts into the

Middle East. Right or wrong – and for what it's worth we usually thought you were wrong – you understood that victory was impossible unless you had the people on your side, helping you win in little ways every day. Bullets, bombs and Predator drones could blast the enemy into a million pieces, but you knew that you also needed the support of the people or you'd already have lost before the first boots hit the ground. Without the support of the people, for every enemy you destroyed two more would rise up in their place.

Putin understood this better than most, and that's what kept him awake through those long nights at the Kremlin. He knew his popular support couldn't last forever in the face of the sanctions. He knew the people would eventually grow tired of the economic pain. They'd become frustrated by the empty grocery store shelves that used to be filled with their favorite western brands. They'd remember the dark days of the bread lines and their anger would begin to turn inwards, against the leaders. It happened before, remember?

So Putin knew he needed a long term plan. He needed something bright and shiny to serve as a distraction. "See?" he wanted to say. "We're prospering despite the sanctions! They'll never defeat Mother Russia! Be proud, my friends, be proud!" Typical flag waving nationalist crap, but he knew it was effective.

And so he looked to the east, to the vast untapped mineral wealth of Siberia. That was Putin's piggy bank, just as it had been for all those leaders who came before him. There were billions of dollars waiting to be pulled from beneath the frozen ground all the way from the shores of Baikal to the Bering Strait. Just like us they had coal, copper, gold, silver, uranium... Everything you need to heat your home, build an iPhone and fuel a nuclear power station, just waiting to be dug out and sold, and Putin fired the starter pistol.

Mike smiles as he refills our glasses.

Actually, it might be more accurate to say he swung the pickax. He actually carried one over his shoulder during his New Year speech at the end of... what, 2017? One hundred forty million proud Russians watched him loft it high in the air – you remember what a showman he always was – and declare a new age of prosperity from his office in Red Square. All international environmental accords were to be abandoned, all carbon targets scrapped. Fuck the rest of the world. Russia would once again grow rich and reclaim its rightful place as an economic superpower despite the best efforts of the traitorous west.

I think his approval rating rose as high as ninety percent after that speech. It was a firm ninety, too, not a number massaged by the state media. The Russians *loved* him for it, and it was *real* love. It wasn't just respect or admiration, like your own politicians aspire to. After that speech the people would have given him their last loaf of bread, even if it meant their own children went hungry.

Of course Vlad was smart enough to know that Russia didn't have the numbers to exploit Siberia. They simply didn't have the manpower, nor the strength. In Moscow they'd grown soft and fat in their office blocks and merchant banks, and there just weren't enough people willing or able to carry a shovel or swing an ax, and that's where we came into the picture.

Mongolia has always bred strong men, hardened to teak by the long, cold winters, and there were almost a million of us unemployed, just waiting for the opportunity for honest work. My country was almost bankrupt, and we'd grown tired of holding out our hands and begging our neighbors for scraps. It was no way for proud men to live.

The alien worker program changed everything. Putin threw open Russia's borders to *everyone*. No work visa required for any man or woman holding a Mongolian passport. No paperwork, no fees, no needless bureaucracy. He simply opened the gates and invited us in, as many as wanted hot meals, a solid roof and a guaranteed job, and the same deal was offered to all of the neighboring states, all the struggling old satellite republics.

Within two months Ulaanbaatar was virtually deserted. I was one of the last to leave. I didn't want to leave my wife and our baby daughter before the winter was over, but by the beginning of March UB was a ghost town. This was a city of one and a half million people drained to just six hundred thousand by the time the winter snow began to melt, and even more left from Darkhan, Erdenet, Olgii... anywhere there were more men than jobs. The line of buses and trucks waiting to cross the northern border trailed back thirty miles at the height of the exodus, and I found myself at the very back of that line.

I can still remember every crumbling brick and fleck of peeling green paint on the walls of the office where we were given our work assignments. It was in an old schoolhouse in Ulan-Ude, the Buryat capital to the east of Lake Baikal. The corridors smelled of bleach, damp and musty sweat. We were told to wait in the cold outside, huddling for warmth around burning oil drums until our numbers were called and we were finally allowed to join the long line indoors.

I waited for hours, watching the men at the head of the queue leave the office with their little red work chits in hand, and after a while I was able to guess which assignments they'd been given just by looking at their faces. Some were dispatched to Mirny to restart the old open cast diamond mine. That was an OK job, I guess. A little remote, maybe, but at least the town had bars and women. The guys who were going to Mirny came out of the office with the kind of faces you used to see on game show contestants who won the consolation prize, like an 'I'm just happy to be on TV' kind of expression, know what I mean?

Others came out like they'd just been given a steak and a blowjob in there, and I soon learned that these were the guys who were heading to the coal seams close to Baikal. A perfect job. The weather in the region would be beautiful as soon as the spring arrived, and the workers there could spend their downtime at the lake, or even head home to UB to see their families. Most of the guys who took these jobs were well connected, I think. I'm guessing lots of envelopes were slipped under the table.

Finally there were the guys who looked like they wanted to take a knife to their wrists. They trudged back along the line staring at their shoes, their work chit held loose in their hands as if they wished the wind would pick it up and snatch it away. These were the men who were going to Kupol, the gold mine all the way up in the far north east at Chukotka, above the Arctic Circle.

Kupol was... not desirable. *Nobody* wanted to go there. The winter temperatures that far north fell to minus forty degrees, just like Ulaanbaatar, but it was a wet, harsh cold. Our own winters are so dry you could leave your apartment for a short time in just a thick sweater, but up at Kupol... no. You'd feel the cold down to your bones after just a few seconds, and you'd only last a few minutes before you'd feel the first signs of frostbite set in.

My heart was racing by the time I finally made it to the front of the line. I was sweating despite the chill, and I could feel a lump in my throat. Somehow I already knew even before I reached the desk. I felt it in the pit of my stomach, and I started protesting as soon as I looked at the work chit.

It wasn't even Kupol. At least at the mine I'd be underground and protected from the worst of the weather, but my assignment was on the *road* to Kupol. My job would be to help replace the two hundred mile ice track to the port of Pevek north of the mine with a permanent gravel road, so that the trucks could have access all year round rather than just in the spring. I couldn't imagine a more difficult job, nor a more inhospitable location. "You should have come earlier," they said, waving away my protest without the slightest hint of sympathy. "This is all we have left. Take it or leave it."

I almost turned around and went straight back home to UB. At least there I'd have my wife and my little girl, if not money or pride. For two days and nights I drank myself into a stupor at the local bars, always on the verge of going home. I even tried to wrestle one man for his chit. He was bound for a construction assignment in Irkutsk – a dream job any man would step over his own mother to take – and I bet him for a trade. I win, he goes to Kupol. He wins, I give him a million Tugrik.

A million was around $400 back then, equal to a little more than two months of salary at my last construction job. That's how desperate I was to avoid being sent north, but I was too drunk to notice his friends laughing behind him as he agreed to the bet, nor did I notice how quickly and confidently he accepted it. How was I to know he'd taken the wrestling silver at the last Naadam festival?

Mike chuckles and shakes his head.

I met that bastard again, you know, a couple of years ago right here in the city, and he told me he'd spent two weeks in Ulan-Ude pulling the same dirty trick on everyone who was bound for Kupol and desperate for a way out. By the end he made so much money he didn't even bother to go to Irkutsk. He gave his work chit to the final loser, got on a bus back to Ulaanbaatar and bought himself a new car, with cash. I still hate him now, but I can't say I wouldn't have done the same thing if I could fight like that.

Anyway, after losing my money the decision was made for me. I only had a few thousand Tugrik left in my pocket, not even enough to pay for the bus ticket back home, so the next morning I hitched a ride to the airport and boarded a rusty old Tupolev to Pevek, still nursing a hangover from the cheap Russian vodka and a sprained shoulder from the fight, loaded down with the cold weather gear we'd been issued by the Russians. When we landed in Pevek we were each given a shitty two season tent, a pack of survival rations and a shovel, and we were put straight to work.

The work was... it was just *brutal*. There was a reason Kupol had been mined by political prisoners in the Soviet days, and there was a reason the Russian road layers already working there were paid four times our wage. The cold was unrelenting in March, and even as the brief summer approached and the temperature finally climbed towards zero the constant snowstorms made life a living hell.

Each morning we'd break into teams of a hundred men to tackle another mile long stretch, chipping away at the ice with shovels and picks until we reached the permafrost beneath, and once that was exposed we'd move on to the next stretch while another team moved in behind us to grade the road and lay the gravel. It was backbreaking work, harder than anything I'd ever had to do in my life, and more than once I considered just dropping my tools and leaving.

What's worse, as soon as we arrived we realized we'd been sold a lie. Back in Ulan-Ude we'd been told we'd be working in shifts: two weeks on, one week off. This much was true, but what they hadn't told us was that there was absolutely nothing to do and nowhere to go during our downtime but back to our ice cold tents, and our limited supply of heating fuel was reserved for the nights. All of us, every last man, decided to abandon the shifts and work without a break until the road was completed. We also promised to hunt down and kill the recruiters who'd sent us to that icy hell, and I don't think a single one of us was joking.

Somehow we survived. By the end of April we'd reached the hundred mile mark, and suddenly it felt as if there was a new optimism among the workers. We'd passed the halfway point, and every day drew us closer to escaping that frozen hell. The end was almost in sight, and for the first time I began to see smiles back at camp at the end of the day. *We can get through this*, we all thought. Soon we'd be back home with full pockets, and we'd get to enjoy the long Mongolian summer with our families. One night I heard laughter coming from one of the tents, and I realized I hadn't heard that sound in two months. It was... strange.

The storm came in the second week of May, just as the

sun finally began to set after twenty two hours circling the horizon. I remember we all stopped working and just stared when we saw the massive front approach from the west. Black, angry clouds that looked like a tsunami about to crash over us and leave nothing but destruction in its wake. One of the supervisors back at the camp called out with a foghorn, and we all dropped tools and started to run. We made it back to camp just as the clouds arrived overhead and the first heavy drops began to fall on the canvas.

For two days we huddled together for warmth in our tents, praying for the weather to pass. The wind took a handful of tents each night, and flash floods took many more. About a dozen people died in the blink of an eye when the dry creek where they'd pitched suddenly flooded and carried them away in a torrent of black water. We couldn't go out to recover the bodies, the weather was so bad. Couldn't even leave to go to the bathroom. All we could do was huddle four men to a tent, each of us laying in a corner stewing in our own piss and shit, praying that our weight would be enough to keep us on the ground. The smell was horrific.

There were a lot of empty tents. Two of the work crews hadn't made it back before the storm hit, and we hadn't been able to reach them by radio. We were missing almost two hundred men in total, and for the two days the heavens hammered us we all prayed they'd made it to shelter. Of course we didn't hold out much hope. Siberia is no place to be caught outdoors at the best of times. Two days outside in a storm like this was nothing short of a death sentence.

On the morning of the third day the worst of it finally passed, and as we crawled from the broken remains of our tents we all looked at each other with expressions that said *can you believe we survived that?* The first thing we found was that the road to the north as far as the eye could see – the road we'd spent the last two months laying down – had been stripped back down to the permafrost. Two feet of compacted gravel has simply vanished, countless tons of it washed away in the torrent. We couldn't spare much time to dwell on that, though, and none of us wanted to think about the extra weeks we'd need to stay on to repeat the job. No, we needed to find our missing crews, so about a hundred of us volunteered to form a search party and set out on the melting ice track to the south.

They were nowhere to be found. After fighting our way through six miles of knee deep slush and sucking mud we found tools, rations, a few tattered personal items, even a few half-pitched emergency tents that had survived the storm, but no men. It was as if the Rapture had arrived, and they'd simply been lifted from the earth. For two days we searched the dense forest on either side of the road, scouring the landscape for caves where they might have taken shelter, but by that point we knew we were no longer a search party. After so long out in the open we knew we'd only find bodies, if we found anything at all.

Darkness was approaching on the second day of our search when a message arrived by radio from the camp. It was... confusing. The voice on the other end sounded excited. He kept yelling the same words: *"They're back! They're back!"* I couldn't really understand his dialect – he sounded like a Kazakh Mongol from Bayan-Olgii out in the far west, and I was from Khentii – but he seemed to be saying that our lost men were coming out of the forest from the north.

I didn't understand. *The north?* We'd been searching only to the south of the camp, close to where the men had been working. It didn't make any sense that they'd come from the north. Surely they couldn't have missed the camp on their walk back, could they? It was directly beside the road, the only landmark for miles around. Even if they'd been blinded by the storm it was impossible to miss. I could see the line it cut through the forest from where I was standing, and I wasn't even particularly high.

I was confused, but I didn't care. I was just relieved that at least *some* of the men had survived, and even more relieved that we could finally return to the warmth of the camp, put on dry clothes and eat something more nourishing than hard Russian biscuits and stale black bread. We gathered our men, found the road and set off at a fast pace to the north.

We were halfway to the camp when we saw him, a man running on his own, splashing through the half flooded remains of the ice road, covered in mud from head to toe. His clothes were torn and blood was streaming down his sleeve and dripping from his fingers, flowing from a deep wound in his shoulder that looked like he'd been savaged by a damned wolf. Even before he reached us I could see the whites of his eyes, they were so wide. He was crazed. Frantic. It took a firm slap to get him to stop struggling as the men tried to hold him still, and even when he finally calmed down a little he still seemed to be talking gibberish.

I was standing on the edge of the group, struggling to hear the madness pouring from his mouth, but I managed to get the gist of it. He told us the returning men had begun to attack the workers without warning or provocation. They'd walked into the camp and lunged for any man who came close. Biting. *Clawing.* He said they moved as if they were sleepwalking, slow and without direction, and when the men in the camp tried to fight back the attackers simply wouldn't fall.

"Where are the men? *Where are the men from the camp?*", one of ours demanded, shaking the lunatic like a rag doll. The man looked up at him with tears in his eyes, shaking his head, and spoke just a few more words before his mind gave up on him entirely.

"Dead. They're all dead."

Mike pours the last of the vodka into my glass, and as he slips a sterling silver snuff bottle from a hidden pocket within his *deel* he looks ruefully out at the snow falling beyond the window of the restaurant, the flakes whipped up by a harsh, frigid wind that keeps them from settling on the sidewalk of Peace Avenue.

We argued amongst ourselves for an hour about what to do next. Some of the men wanted to set out south for Kupol. At the mine they'd have food, water, and a radio we could use to call for help, but we argued it would be suicide to walk seventy miles through the forest, especially since the storm may return at any moment. And where would we go from there? Kupol had no airstrip, and the only road leading back to civilization was the very road we were building. The only way to escape was by air or sea from Pevek, so eventually we agreed – some more reluctantly than others – to trek back to the closest supply site twenty miles north of the camp where there were trucks that could take us back to Pevek. The only problem with our plan was that it would take us past the camp, and none of us were eager to see what awaited us there.

Just before we departed the crazed man slipped away – from blood loss, I assumed – and three of our men volunteered to stay behind and bury the poor soul. We left them with spare rations and extra clothing and promised to send a truck back to collect them, but... well, the fact that we never returned for them is one of the many regrets I'll take to my grave.

We reached the camp an hour later to find it torn to shreds. Barely a single tent remained standing, and most of those destroyed on the ground were covered in blood and some sort of thick, brown liquid, almost like treacle. There were a few bodies, or at least what was left of them. Most were just parts. An arm here, a trail of trampled offal there. Not enough left to identify the victims, and none of us wished to take a closer look.

I... I'll never forget the noise I heard from the other side of the camp. It wasn't a scream, not really. It was more of a mournful, hopeless wail. Even today when I think about it my lip trembles a little. It was the sound of a man who'd had his world ripped out from beneath him in an instant, a pain we'd each come to understand all too well soon enough. I never learned the man's name. He was an old Buryat, Russian born, and we tended not to mix with them. They were shunned in the camp because as native Russians they were paid more than us, but we forgot our envy when we saw what he'd discovered.

It barely looked like a man any more. Naked from the waist up and dressed in tattered rags from the waist down. The skin was mottled and pale, and the veins were almost black, thick like ropes pulled taut beneath the surface. He looked like he'd been attacked by a bear, with what looked like claw marks dragged down his torso in deep lines, but the wounds looked like they hadn't bled. Beneath the torn skin the gashes were black and glistening, as if someone had poured hot pitch into his wounds and allowed it to set. His left arm was nothing more than a sharp gray spur of dirty bone broken off at the elbow, and he was pinned to the ground with a shovel that had been driven into his throat, almost severing the head. But even *that* wasn't the most horrifying thing.

A few of the men gathered around the old Buryat and tried to console him, and it took me a moment to figure out from their strange Russian-Mongol lingo that the body on the ground was this man's son, one of those who'd gone missing in the storm. I thought for a moment that I'd misunderstood the language, but I swore the man was insisting we must help carry his boy back to the trucks. He kept yelling out, "*Where is the doctor? Fetch the fucking doctor!*", as if anyone but God could heal those horrific wounds and bring his son back to him.

And then I saw the boy *move*. I had no idea how anyone could possibly survive those injuries, but he was alive! The poor bastard reached up with his remaining arm and tried to grab at his father's leg. He looked up at us and stared out through milky eyes, his jaw moving back and forth as if he was trying to speak. I couldn't believe what I was seeing!

The old Buryat lowered himself down towards him and took a deep scratch to his forearm when he failed to notice the sharp remains of his son's arm drag against his skin. A few of the others tried to pull him away but he fought back, and in the end they had to knock him out cold to stop him trying to lift his boy from the ground. Before they knocked him out he kept protesting, "*I need to listen to him! He's trying to tell me something!*" He didn't seem to understand that his son wasn't trying to speak. He was trying to bite.

We left the camp a few minutes later. Nothing could have kept us there, not with that... that cursed *thing* on the ground, still struggling to lift itself up. We didn't know what the hell it was, but we knew it wasn't alive. We knew it wasn't human, and we knew there were probably more of them waiting for us in the forest.

It was a full day's hike back to the trucks. We made it in six hours.

The snow has finally begun to settle on the street outside, and despite the warmth of the restaurant Mike pulls the collar of his *deel* up around his neck. He shivers.

I think they found something beneath the ice. Something that had been waiting there a long time. I don't know if these were the men who started it. I know there were rumors of other strange incidents further to the west, at the deep mines in Krasnoyarsk and the Sakha Republic. I heard about what happened to the container ship that left Magadan for Japan, and the injured men who were airlifted from the mountains near Yakutsk. I don't know if they were all connected, and I don't know why all of these things happened within the same few months, all separated by so much distance.

All I know is that we should not have gone to Siberia. There were things there that should have stayed buried.

●▼●

:::3:::

Batumi, Georgia

The line extends two hundred meters down the street, and in the searing midday sun volunteers hand out bottled water and paper fans to the parents and children waiting to reach the makeshift clinic. In the two years since Georgia was declared free of infection several new, less visible but no less hazardous threats have emerged. Measles, tuberculosis, hepatitis and even polio have made a comeback throughout the Caucasus thanks to low rates of vaccination and a lack of basic healthcare facilities, and whenever UNICEF announces the arrival of fresh supplies all activity in this small town on the Black Sea coast grinds to a halt as parents rush to seek treatment from the team of volunteer doctors working here.

Before the crisis Dr. Kate Willings was the administrator of a WHO-funded pediatric health center in Tashkurgan, a remote town in the province of Xinjiang in China's far west. There she witnessed the start of what is now believed to have been China's first outbreak.

It turned out the locals had been trying to keep it quiet for days. They were terrified of what would happen if word got out. The construction crews had recently broken ground on the new eight lane highway between Kashgar and Pakistan, and the investors had been poking around the town scouting sites for the new hotels. This was supposed to be the turning point for Tashkurgan. They'd waited years for *yi dai yi lu*, the Belt and Road initiative that would see billions of dollars spent on infrastructure projects in the region, and they knew that the slightest sniff of trouble would send investors packing. A quarantine would mean they'd never return.

The villagers only came to us when they finally figured out that they couldn't handle the problem by themselves, when they realized she was far beyond their traditional medicine. The girl had come down from the mountains to the west a week earlier, they said, naked and covered in wounds. They'd tried to calm her down, but when she lashed out at them they decided to lock her up until they could figure out what to do with her. One of the elders told me she was a *jiangshi*, a possessed corpse from some old Chinese myth, and that's when I pretty much checked out of the conversation. I was a doctor. I didn't have time for fairly tales and ignorant superstition.

Just for the sake of an easy life I sent my assistant, Steve Anderson, ahead of me to the village while I held the fort back in town, and before he left I insisted he give me his usual super serious, cross your heart and hope to die ironclad promise to call me only if he found something he couldn't possibly handle by himself. After two years in Xinjiang I was absolutely sick to the back teeth of racing across the province every time someone sprained an ankle or came down with the sniffles. It was as if the locals didn't realize I had an entire clinic to run. As if they thought I just sat around all day waiting by the phone with a bag of aspirin and lollipops at the ready.

My phone rang an hour later, and the first dozen words out of Steve's mouth were definitely not safe for work. "The *effing* lunatic *effing* bit me!" he yelled. "You'd better get down here with some *effing* horse tranquilizer before I kill the *effing*..." Well, I won't say the last word, but it began with a C. Typical Australian. He was the only man I ever knew who used swear words as punctuation.

I was in the car before the call ended. You don't mess around with bites, and this one sounded like it could be a nasty one. Steve told me he'd found the girl locked away in a barn on the outskirts of the village. He said the locals were keeping her in truly horrific conditions, chained to a tractor, and they hadn't even attempted to treat the open wounds on her arms and legs. He said the entire barn smelled like human feces and rot, and the girl was acting completely crazy, snarling and snapping at him when he tried to loosen her ropes. I could only imagine what kind of bacteria would be teeming in her mouth, and now Steve's arm.

Night had fallen by the time I reached the village, thanks to a couple of wrong turns and my awful sense of direction. It was one of those villages too small to even deserve a name, where the directions once you leave the paved road are little more than to take the third track to the right once you enter the shadow of the mountain, then drive straight on and hope for the best. When I finally found it I saw that it wasn't even really a village. It was just a small cluster of a dozen or so yurts around the ramshackle barn, home to maybe two or three families.

The first thing I noticed was that the place seemed to be deserted. Steve's Land Cruiser was nowhere to be seen. There was no smoke rising from any of the yurts despite the temperature hovering just above freezing, and nobody came out to greet me when I honked my horn. I got out of the car and tried to call Steve's phone, and then twice again. Each time it rang until the voicemail kicked in, and it wasn't until the fourth attempt that I realized I could hear a faint ringtone. It was coming from the barn.

Kate looks around to make sure there are no children within earshot.

I saw the tractor as soon as I pushed open the door. The ground beside it was trampled and dark, and when I moved closer I realized it was covered in an ungodly mixture of blood, human waste and some sort of thick black fluid, like old motor oil. The ropes hanging down from the tractor were bloody too. Three of them had been untied, but the final one had been sheared away. I assume this was where the girl had been tied up, but she was long gone.

I found Steve's phone on the ground near the tractor. He loved that thing. He'd saved up for months to buy it on his last furlough to Hong Kong, and he'd sooner leave his pants behind than his phone. I picked it up and walked back outside, praying that I'd find that Steve – or *anyone*, for that matter – had returned. I wanted to call out his name but I couldn't quite bring myself to open my mouth. I didn't know what the hell was going on, but my instincts were screaming at me to stay quiet, get back in the car and go to find help, so that's what I did.

I was about a hundred meters down the track when I saw him. I almost missed him at first. He was down on his hands and knees right at the edge of my headlights, and if it wasn't for the reflective strips on the back of his shoes I would have passed him by completely. I slammed on the brakes, jumped out of the car and started to run towards him before I saw that he was hunched over something. I couldn't quite see in the darkness, but there was something moving beneath him.

Suddenly it all began to make sense. There must have been some sort of accident. Maybe the locals had crashed their old truck, and they'd taken Steve's Land Cruiser to get help while Steve tended to the wounded. *That's* why the village was empty. *That's* why he'd been in such a rush that he'd dropped his phone. Funny, isn't it? The nonsense we can convince ourselves is true just to avoid having to face reality. I think deep down I already knew I was kidding myself. I'd seen the barn. I'd seen the bloody ropes. Something here definitely wasn't right.

I turned back to the car and grabbed my bag from the passenger seat, then ran across the uneven ground towards Steve. I called his name. He hadn't paid any attention to the sound of the car, but when he heard my voice he finally turned towards me.

He was... It wasn't Steve. That was the first thought that came to me. *This cannot be Steve.* It looked like him. It was even dressed like him, but it wasn't him. This was something else. The old woman beneath him stared at me. Her mouth silently opened and closed and her body twitched as Steve turned towards me with a length of her intestines between his teeth. The way he was gripping it... God, it looked like he was grinning at me.

I don't remember running back to the car. One second I was staring at the face of this woman, still alive as she was being eaten, and the next I was behind the wheel, my ears ringing and spots flashing before my eyes, clutching the steering wheel so tight it hurt. I could barely see through my tears. I dropped my bunch of keys beneath the seat and started swearing at myself in rapid fire as I bent double to grab at them with my fingertips. When I finally found them and sat back up I almost had a heart attack there and then.

Steve was standing on the other side of the window, inches away, just staring at me with an open mouth still full of meat. He pressed a hand against the glass as I gunned the engine, and as I tore away down the track it ran down the length of the car, leaving a bloody streak. For the next fifty miles I barely looked at the road ahead. All I could see through my tears was that hand print waving at me from just a few inches away.

The official story was that Steve died in a car accident. That's what they told his mum down in Perth, and that's what I was ordered to tell anyone who asked. There was just too much money at stake. Tashkurgan needed the new trade route to Pakistan. They needed the investors to build their hotels and develop the town as a tourist destination, and they couldn't have some mad English woman causing a panic with crazy stories about cannibals running around the province. I don't know if they won my superiors over with promises or threats, but I was handed my pink slip within the week. They forced me to sign an NDA, and warned me in no uncertain terms that I'd lose my medical license if I so much as breathed a word of what really happened.

Of course I paid no attention. As soon as I was back in the UK I told my story to anyone who'd listen, and of course everyone thought I was a complete lunatic. Well, apart from the tabloid journalists, who thought I was a complete lunatic who could give them plenty of page views.

Within a fortnight my license was suspended. The board said I was 'critically impaired in my capacity to practice medicine according to accepted and prevailing standards of care' due to the loss of a close colleague, and they threw in a prescription medication abuse charge for good measure. After that most of my friends wouldn't take my calls – nobody wants to chat with the mental woman – and my parents tried to get me into therapy. "You've always pushed yourself too hard, love," my dad said. "It's no surprise you'd start to imagine things. Your mum and I saw this coming years ago."

They eventually checked me in to a nice facility in Wiltshire. A spa, they called it, one of those places for middle class parents too embarrassed to tell the curtain twitching neighbors they're checking their kid in to a loony bin. The kind of place with little windows in the bedroom doors, and a masseuse on call who knows five ways to safely restrain someone. They fed me pills by the handful and made me eat with plastic cutlery. They made me sit through daily sessions, trying to make me understand that I hadn't really seen what I thought I'd seen. Trying to get to the bottom of what had made my mind conjure up such a crazy delusion. In the end I almost began to believe them.

Willings lets out a bitter, world weary laugh.

You know, it was almost a relief when the world finally went to hell. I'd already been there a while.

•▼•

:::4:::

Anchorage, Alaska

Charles Joseph Buckley was always something of an enigma in pre-crisis US politics, and an unusual – some might even say radical – choice for Speaker in a House under firm Republican control. The Kennebunkport, Maine native, Yale graduate and heir to the Buckley lumber fortune flirted with the politics of the left in his younger years, interning for liberal Justice Thurgood Marshall through some of the Supreme Court's most contentious decisions.

Rumor has it that Buckley's was the clarion voice behind a scathing dissenting opinion written by Marshall on the constitutionality of the death penalty, a position that incensed social conservatives of the day. It was only in his thirties that Buckley began to grow disillusioned with the left, frustrated by what he saw as a well-intentioned blindness to reality from many of the major players of the time, and began to identify with more traditionally center-right positions.

His internship under Justice Marshall alone would have barred a lesser man from securing a toehold in Republican politics but, as many have since commented, Charles Buckley is no lesser man. He possesses a singular, almost preternatural gift for drawing his political foes towards common ground, deftly reconciling seemingly intractable differences, and speaking in the kind of calm, measured tones that only the most stubborn would describe as anything less than simple common sense. In his own words, "There are more things that unite us than divide us. I'm just good at finding the words that bring people together."

Though now happily retired from politics Buckley remains in Anchorage, occasionally taking on the role of elder statesman – or pro wrestling referee, as he describes it – whenever the old divisions once again threaten to rear their heads. At the age of eighty two he laughs off the idea of a third Presidential term despite the fact that his victory would be almost assured, and despite the fact that a solid majority of both House and Senate have suggested they'd be prepared to repeal the Twenty-second Amendment were he willing to run again.

I join President Buckley – he asks that I call him Joe, a request I politely decline – as he strides with the occasional help of a cane around the proposed site of his Presidential library, a small section of softly sloping hillside at the foot of Flattop Mountain overlooking Anchorage. He takes pains to make it clear that this visit to the site is only a formality. He's already decided that he doesn't want a library, and argues that taxpayers have more urgent priorities than "a glorified vanity project, as if they'll forget my name if it isn't carved into the side of a building."

It was a systemic failure of democracy, is what it was, and the failure was far from limited to the US. We'd all been sailing towards the rocks for years... *decades*, maybe, but those of us on the inside were all so insulated from the real world we didn't see the danger coming until it was far too late to correct our course.

I don't think it's possible to pinpoint an exact moment, you know? There wasn't one particular day when we all suddenly realized *oh crap, this isn't working anymore*. It was just a whole series of events, seemingly unconnected and spread over many years, each of which gradually eroded just a little more of the foundations of our democracy until one day the entire structure came crashing down around our ears.

And you know the really funny thing? The only people who were really surprised by it were us, the politicians. You guys out there in the real world had known the truth for years. You'd tried to warn us that something was deeply wrong – OK, maybe not always in the most constructive ways – but we always found a way to ignore you. It was just... oh Lord, how do you explain two terrible decades with a million moving parts concisely? Forgive me for rambling, but it's really not possible to boil it down to a few words.

Here it is in a nutshell. I'll leave it to the historians to explain it better, but in the years after 9/11 we set ourselves on a perilous path. Just as we'd done several times in our history we chose the politics of fear over hope, simply because we learned that fear was easier to sell. We *chose* to make you suspicious of immigrants, even though we knew that statistically you had little to fear from them, and we *chose* to make you terrified of losing your guns, even though absolutely *nobody* with any power really wanted to take them from you, not even a little bit.

We knew the truth, of course. We knew we were just telling you scary stories, but they were just too good not to tell, know what I'm saying? We knew that it's easier to control people when they're scared. We knew that if we could make voters afraid of their own shadows we could sell ourselves as their protectors, and we quickly learned that this was by far the easiest path to reelection, and the easiest way to squeeze a few extra dollars in donations out of you.

The problem is that we failed to understand that we couldn't hope to *control* this monster we'd unleashed. We didn't understand that we were opening up politics to whomever could most effectively sell their own brand of fear to the voters, and as it turned out some pretty unsavory characters truly excelled in that arena. It was sheer hubris on our part. We were the architects of our own destruction, and by the time we realized our mistake it was far too late to do anything about it.

And the result? We saw the left – the true, *principled* left – completely neutered. They were forced into battles they couldn't hope to win even when they had right on their side, because they'd long ago lost the confidence to win a good old fashioned political brawl. By the end the Democrats were pretty much a spent force, wasting precious political capital just to defend the hard-won victories of previous generations rather than fighting for true progress, but that was nothing compared to the decimation of the moderate conservative movement. We were absolutely *destroyed* as a political force.

Over the course of a decade or so common sense conservatives had become an endangered species in the corridors of power, time and again losing primaries to populists who when it came right down to it really didn't know what the heck they were doing. They were *great* at campaigning, don't get me wrong. They could walk into a local town hall meeting and whip the crowd into a frenzy by playing on the dissatisfaction and disenfranchisement people were feeling in middle America – the very dissatisfaction we in the establishment had consistently ignored for a generation – but once they took hold of the reins of power we realized they simply didn't know how to govern effectively.

Everything just became so damned *partisan*. And yeah, before you bring it up I know I'm on record in favor of partisan politics, and I stand by it. There's nothing wrong with vigorous debate. There's nothing wrong with two guys duking it out on the House floor, each passionately defending opposing positions. Our nation was built on partisan politics, and it's part of what made us great, but this was something else entirely. This was *ugly*. It was *dumb*. It was the willful, self-destructive abdication of common sense in favor of petty point scoring. It was the politics of the schoolyard, and it wasn't doing anybody any good.

The President looks to the sky and shakes his head before speaking again, more slowly now.

I remember this one Congressional breakfast sometime in... I guess it would have been early 2019, back when it was becoming clear that things were getting really bad. It was one of those bipartisan hands across the table things, little more than a photo op with talking points carefully agreed in advance. Nothing contentious was to be discussed. We just wanted to show the American people that we could sit at the same table and pass a bottle of syrup without beaning each other in the head with it.

Everything went fine for the first ten minutes, all nice and polite for the pool spray. No questions, just photos. We fixed our smiles and pretended to laugh at a few bad jokes, and then just after the press pool had been herded out of the room this one guy – Chuck Sheldon, I think, from the Louisiana 6th – broke from the script and started talking about the news reports coming out of Europe. The Paris outbreak was in full swing by then. Hundreds confirmed dead, thousands missing, and we had rolling coverage of the piles of bodies burning along the Champs-Élysées on our screens 24/7.

In hindsight it was perfectly reasonable for him to suggest that we think about heightening immigration controls, just temporarily, just until we could figure out what the heck was going on. He wanted tighter visa quotas, medical checks at our borders, maybe some kind of temporary quarantine for new arrivals. It would have been a smart, sensible move, and who knows how many millions of lives we could have saved if we'd followed through, but in *this* House, at *this* time, with *this* degree of animosity?

He didn't even get the chance to finish speaking before the room erupted. *"How dare you suggest such a thing?"* That was Kathy Lipman from New York. She kicked back her chair, drew herself up and started reciting *The New Colossus*, you know, from the Statue of Liberty? *"Give me your tired, your poor, your huddled masses yearning to breathe free."* She just stood there and trotted out the whole thing, bellowing over everyone in the room. By the time she finished and looked around with this self-satisfied smirk everyone was already storming towards the door, no doubt heading to their favorite journalist to leak their version of the story.

You know what the media reported the next day? I have it memorized. The Times published a scathing op-ed: *Republicans Demand Blanket Immigration Ban*. Lots of 'unnamed sources', lots of the usual 'we're all the children of immigrants' platitudes. It was beautifully written, almost poetic in its structure. Quite moving, in fact. I read the story twice and only found one or two truly accurate facts.

Breitbart was a little more on the nose: *When is Enough Enough? Anti-American Democrats Invite Death to the US.* It was... well, you remember Breitbart, I'm sure you can guess the kind of nonsense they wrote. It was a hateful, paranoid, more-patriotic-than-thou screed that tried its best to draw a straight line between the walking dead and Islamic terrorists, simply because many of the outbreaks in Europe had begun in cities with large refugee populations.

And that was that. Game over. The issue never got a fair hearing, not in Congress and certainly not in the media. Nobody had any inclination to address the actual pros and cons of the proposal. Nobody thought to ask if it might be *good for America*. There were no voices from the sensible center, or what little was left of it. The demagogues just wanted to use the issue to beat the other side over the head, facts be damned.

It was just a couple of weeks later that we lost the Speaker. A stroke, they said, and it wouldn't have surprised me to learn that it had been caused by the stress of the last few months, watching the world beyond our borders fall apart and feeling powerless to do anything about it in the face of the truly epic pettiness and obstructionism from our political class.

To be honest I was surprised when I was nominated to take his place, and I was astounded that there were enough votes to confirm me, though I guess I can see the logic behind it now. The only two realistic choices were me and John Sumner, and despite his popularity with the voters John had made a lot of enemies on the Hill over the years.

I think by then people were beginning to understand that there would be trying times ahead. They were finally coming around to the idea that this wasn't your average flash in the pan health scare. It wasn't Ebola, and it sure wasn't bird flu. In short something *had* to be done, and deep down we all knew we needed to push past the gridlock and leave the politics at the door. So yeah, I suspect I was seen as something of a Goldilocks candidate. Not too hot, not too cold, but just right.

Buckley turns and looks back towards Anchorage, resting on his cane. He sighs as he sees that the smog hanging over the city is thicker than usual today, and only growing denser as the evening chill sets in and half a million wood stoves fire up in the sprawling tent city that leads almost to the foot of Flattop.

Of course we had no idea at the time that it was already too late. We had a conflicted, unpredictable President who'd surrounded himself with sycophants and rejected anything – *anything* – that didn't fit with his worldview. A national media that had long since absolved itself of the responsibility to seek the truth. A fatal degree of suspicion and antipathy within Congress, the media and the population at large. And the living dead banging hard at the door.

We never stood a chance, in the end.

•▼•

Murghab, Tajikistan

Nasreen Bahori greets me warmly at the door of the rusting 5x6m double wide shipping container she calls home, along with the eighteen thousand other residents of Murghab. For our interview she has been allowed to remove her *paranja*, the heavy shroud that covers both her head and body, though her husband Atash insists on chaperoning us throughout. From his seat beside her he exudes an air of ownership I find deeply disquieting.

For her part Nasreen seems equally unhappy with the sharp turn her nation and her own life have taken since the war, though you wouldn't know it from the tone of her voice. Atash speaks no English and the interpreter he requested canceled at the last minute, so Nasreen can speak freely provided she maintains her fixed smile and a cheerful, singsong tone. Every few minutes she turns to her husband and offers a fictional account of our conversation in Tajik Persian, which he believes is related to her work at Murghab's newly built madrasa.

Banned for many years under Soviet rule, Nasreen's coarse, thick *paranja* is now all but mandatory for women appearing in public throughout the formerly secular Tajikistan, and nowhere more so than here in Murghab in the Gorno-Badakhshan Autonomous Region, the heartland of the Islamic Renaissance Party.

At ten thousand feet above sea level Murghab was, before the war, a bustling if downtrodden trading post of four thousand residents at the junction of the only two roads of any consequence in this remote, arid mountainous region: the Pamir Highway, connecting the Tajik capital of Dushanbe to Kyrgyzstan, and the road through the Kulma Pass, the only overland border crossing between Tajikistan and China.

Today Murghab is best known for the twin ornate minarets that tower over its magnificent mosques, from each of which the muezzins breathlessly compete with each other as they sing the call to prayer in the thin mountain air. While still impoverished an effort has been made to present the town as thriving, though one suspects this is more for the benefit of the Chinese across the border than for the residents themselves.

I first met Nasreen in 2014 in the capital of Dushanbe where she worked as a project manager for the United Nations Development Program, shepherding through irrigation projects that were finally beginning to bear fruit after many years of tireless effort. She had for a time been tipped as the future head of the UNDP regional bureau for Europe and the CIS, only to find her career brought to an abrupt halt when the organization pulled out of Tajikistan at the onset of the crisis.

Full disclosure: Nasreen and I were for a brief time romantically involved.

You remember the dress you bought me for the party in Panjakent? The red one, with the lace? They made me burn it. *Not in keeping with accepted standards of morality in modern Tajikistan*, that's how they described it. *Modern.* They don't know the meaning of the word.

Of course that was just the beginning. Even I could see why a backless dress may be enough to incite the confused hormonal rage of these newly emboldened Neanderthals, but t-shirts? Skirts that are hemmed more than three inches above the ankle? Open toed shoes? I'll never understand this mindset. Is there something overtly sexual about my shoulder? Is there some aspect of the back of my knee that could drive a man to lose control of his senses and abandon his devotion to God?

It wasn't this bad in the beginning. I actually welcomed the news when I heard the Islamic Renaissance had taken Dushanbe. They seemed... what's the word I'm looking for? *Dynamic*, I suppose. They had a sense of direction; answers at a time when we had nothing but desperate, urgent questions that had gone unanswered for far too long. I didn't know if they could make things better, but I thought at least they'd address the problems head on rather than burying their heads in the sand. I can't believe I was ever quite so naive.

I don't think President Rahmon understood just how bad the situation had become. For six months he'd been sitting on his hands, ever the Soviet *apparatchik*, waiting for someone higher up the ladder to tell him what to do while his country collapsed around him. We'd lost patience long before they executed him.

I often wonder if he even *knew* what was happening outside the capital. Maybe the party was keeping the reports from him. Maybe it honestly came as a shock when the Renaissance activists dragged him from the Presidential Palace, stood him against those gleaming white columns and consigned him to memory as a splash of red against the marble.

No. No, he *can't* have been ignorant. We *all* knew. Nobody wanted to say it out loud – almost everyone had heard of at least one family that was harboring an infected relative – but by the time the coup arrived there wasn't a man from Khujand to Khorog who hadn't heard the whispers.

Nasreen breaks off to speak at a fast pace with Atash, then turns back to me as her husband nods uncertainly.

I saw my first case months before the coup, back in the early summer. He was the son of a farmer up in Amondara near the Uzbek border. He'd been one of Putin's slaves, those poor boys who fell for all the big promises and ran to Russia seeking their fortune as soon as the borders opened. It seemed like every second man in the country did the same back then, all with the same crazy ideas of coming home with their pockets stuffed with easy money. They all wanted to build their own home, buy a truck, open a store, impress the girls. They were all so *excited.*

Many of them came back crippled and broken, if they came back at all. Six months in the Russian winter playing with tools they didn't know how to use. Accidents were inevitable. What's that thing you used to say? *It's all fun and games until someone loses an eye?* Well, a lot of young men came back home missing an eye, or a leg, or with a few fingers that ended two knuckles short.

Farhad, the farmer's son, came back in one piece, at least *physically*. His father said he didn't speak a word after he returned. Not a single word for a week. He shut himself away in his room and locked the door, and the only sound his father ever heard was weeping until one day Farhad called out and begged him to fetch the doctor. That was when I heard about him. I was working a few miles away in Khyzyldzhar with Gulomov, our staff doctor, screening the villagers for TB. That's where the farmer found us.

Nasreen closes her eyes and shakes her head.

It was a tattoo, one of those ridiculous tribal designs that used to be all the rage in the west. You understand why Farhad was ashamed to tell his father, don't you? Tattoos are *haram*, forbidden by Islamic law. Of course Tajikistan was officially a secular country at the time so he'd done nothing wrong *legally*, but there's little difference between committing a crime against the state and one against your faith. Some might argue that the latter was even more severe than the former.

It seems they were all doing it up there. Lots of long, boring nights, lots of vodka, lots of peer pressure. No TV, no women. Most of them did it themselves, or let a friend do it. They had no idea about hygiene, or of the dangers of reusing needles. I dread to think how many were infected. Just one dirty needle could have condemned hundreds, maybe *thousands*. And the infection was only to the upper layers of the skin, so it could take weeks for the virus to reach the brain. Any of these boys could have been halfway around the world before they even realized something was wrong.

Farhad was delirious by the time Gulomov and I arrived at the farm. He didn't even know who the doctor was as he flipped him over and pulled his shirt away from his shoulder, and he didn't react at all as we pulled back in disgust. The boy had a patch of skin as big as your hand that looked necrotic, black in the center and pink and inflamed around the edges, weeping yellow pus that had glued his shirt to the wound. Leading away from the patch his veins were popped up close to his dusky skin, swollen and dark, like writhing snakes. The doctor prodded at him with a pencil but the boy didn't even flinch, not even when a pocket of pus and watery blood burst and oozed down his shoulder. It was as if his entire arm was dead.

I waited with the boy while Gulomov spoke to his father in the kitchen, taking shallow breaths and trying to ignore the stench, and through the gap in the door I watched the old man collapse with anguish when he heard the word: *amputation*. The infection was too far advanced. If the doctor didn't cut away the dead flesh the poison would only spread, and that meant he'd need to take the arm all the way to the shoulder to save his life. The boy would be a cripple, a crushing burden on this poor man who'd worked his entire life just so he'd be able to pass on his farm when he died.

The doctor left in a hurry, bouncing away down the dirt track in my Land Cruiser back to Khyzyldzhar to fetch his surgical instruments and what few painkillers he had. He'd have to operate on the kitchen table, and quickly. The closest hospital was in Panjakent, three hours to the west on rough roads, and even if the boy was able to wait that long the old man couldn't possibly afford to pay for the surgery. I sat with the father, trying – and failing – to think of some way to console the poor wretch.

The boy died just a few minutes before the doctor returned. We were watching over him when he stopped breathing, and after checking for a pulse I led his father outside to escape the stench and let him weep away from the sight of the body. When Gulomov pulled up outside he jumped from the car with his little black bag and ran for the door, confused as to why we were outside.

I'll never forget the bemused look on his face when I told him the boy had passed, nor the chill that slithered down my spine when Gulomov pointed a finger through the window of the shack and asked "So who's that?"

I stood and turned to the dusty window, and sure enough there was Farhad walking through the kitchen. I just stood there staring at him in disbelief. I'd *watched* the boy die. I'd seen him struggle to take his final breath, and I'd held two fingers against his throat and found no pulse when his chest stopped rising. He was *gone*, I was sure of it, and now he was standing just a few steps away from me, *alive*.

There was something... wrong about the way he was walking, jerky and awkward like a newborn foal, almost as if he was blind. He bumped into the low kitchen table then slid slowly along its side until he found the edge. I should have known something wasn't right. Something at the back of my mind was trying to scream at me, some instinct long ignored by my waking self, but I was too distracted by the father to listen to the warning. The old man pulled himself to his feet the moment he realized what was going on, and before we could take a step he pulled open the door and ran across the room.

Gulomov and I watched through the window as the boy's father took him into a close, ecstatic embrace. I remember smiling as he hugged him tight, tears streaming down his cheeks, and he cried with relief as he squeezed the boy. It was a beautiful moment, despite that little voice at the back of my head that was still crying out a warning. I remember turning to Gulomov and wiping a tear from my cheek, only to feel the breath catch in my throat as I saw the look in the doctor's eyes.

I don't know how long it took me to finally realize

what was happening. I don't know if we could have done anything to stop it. Maybe the boy bit his father in the first moments of the hug, who knows? All I remember is watching the man finally tear himself away. He stumbled two steps backwards and clasped a hand to his throat, and when he removed it his hand came away bloody. He looked confused, as if he didn't know if he should be feeling angry or afraid. He took a hesitant step forward, and then as he got his first close look at his son he suddenly fell back, fear dawning on his face.

By the time we ran into the house Farhad was on top of his father, biting again. I tried not to look, but I couldn't stop myself from staring at the ragged hole where the old man's cheek had been just a moment earlier. I was transfixed by the row of yellow nicotine-stained teeth smiling out at me through the gap, like a row of corn kernels, and I doubled over and vomited on my shoes when the man choked on his blood and sent a spray of red across the stone floor, through the open wound.

I watched Gulomov pull the boy away, and I finally tore my eyes from the old man when the sound of the breath bubbling in his throat became too much for me. It only lasted a few seconds before it stopped, but by then my attention was on the boy. He was trying to twist around to attack the doctor, baring his teeth. His lips were pink with blood and there was a thick strip of flesh hanging from his mouth, and as he snarled at Gulomov it slipped out and landed on the stone floor with a wet slap. I vomited again when I noticed the gray hairs of the father's beard peppering the skin.

The doctor was an old man, you understand, a skinny little thing who'd spent most of his career in Dushanbe treating coughs and colds, tactfully altering the medical records of his patients so nobody would ever know the *real* reason he was prescribing a course of antibiotics. Farhad was a farmer's son, built like an ox. If he wasn't so uncoordinated he'd have easily overpowered Gulomov, but he moved as if he'd forgotten how his muscles worked, like a puppet hanging loose from its strings. He threw himself off balance and seemed to lead with his teeth, and that's the only reason the doctor managed to drag him back to his room and push him through, slamming the door behind him.

We ran – once the doctor took a quick look at the father and realized he was far beyond medical help – and tore away in the car without a second thought. We drove in silence, both too shocked to speak, and it wasn't until we reached Dasthikazy that we found a police station and reported what had happened.

For a while they wanted to hold us. The doctor's shirt was covered with blood, and of course our story sounded completely insane. If I was them *I'd* want to arrest us, but I made a few calls to my government contacts in the capital and made sure we were allowed to leave by sundown.

I don't know what happened to Farhad. I don't even know if the father came back. If his heart had stopped beating before the infection could reach his brain he may have been spared that terrible fate, but who knows? I didn't want to think about what I'd seen. All I wanted to do was get back to Dushanbe, run to my safe, peaceful apartment in the embassy district, lock the door behind me and shut out the world.

So that's what I did. I called in sick for a week, and when I finally returned to work I handed off my assignment to another manager and transferred to the new bridge project at Rushan, as far from the north as I could run. Of course I didn't run far enough. Not *nearly* far enough.

Nasreen breaks off once again, translating her fabricated story as Atash nods.

It was only a few weeks before I started to hear stories from the travelers on the road. Every day we'd hear new rumors about far flung villages from the long distance truck drivers. A local quarantine at Aiwanj, where some kind of unexplained sickness had swept through the local school. In Bolshevik a family of six had been found dead, *dismembered*, and the father was nowhere to be found. We heard that every last one of the guards at Sary-Tash on the Kyrgyz border had vanished in the middle of a snowstorm and left the gates locked, leaving a tailback of hundreds of trucks waiting for days as their cargo spoiled. Dozens of men just vanished into thin air at a border post fifty miles from the nearest village.

And then the stories began to draw closer. Just a few miles away in Pastkhuf, the next village along the road to the south, one night something happened that sent a dozen people fleeing across the river into Afghanistan. Nobody had a clue why they'd do such a thing. Everyone knew the other side of the river was heavily mined, not least the villagers. They must have known what would happen to them. What could possibly be so terrifying that people would choose to run into a minefield to escape it?

That's when the Renaissance began to make noises. They tapped into the anger and desperation that had been simmering throughout the regions for months. Nobody wanted to put a voice to it, especially when the infections went from being distant stories to terrors that were happening right *here*, in *our* villages, to *our* families, but people were angry. They were angry that Dushanbe seemed to be withdrawing from the rest of the country. They were angry at the roadblocks set up on all the roads to the capital, cutting us off from trade, and they were furious that the government seemed to be lying about outbreaks of plague to justify their every action.

When the Renaissance stormed the Presidential Palace I don't think there was a single person in Gorno-Badakhshan who wasn't cheering them on. Finally, we thought, *finally* something will be done. *Finally* they'll tell the truth about what's happening, and someone will come up with an answer.

Well, they did. It just wasn't the answer many of us were hoping for.

They didn't have a name, but I don't think it would be too much to call them death squads. We'd hear of vans rolling into towns at nightfall, filled with a dozen men. Always men, never women, just like the smugglers who sneaked across the border with a car full of heroin. These men weren't carrying drugs, but they were just as heavily armed as the mules.

The first thing they always did was take out the police station. Most of the time it was just a small force, maybe a local sheriff and his deputy who spent most of their time sitting in front of the station playing *peshkadan* with the local drunks. They didn't know what hit them. Most of them didn't even put up a fight. Ours didn't.

Then they moved on to the homes. They swept through each village moving from house to house, killing anyone who seemed sick, or tried to resist, or tried to run. Some they killed simply because they weren't Muslim. There was a Catholic family living in Rushan. Quiet, friendly people. They're not there any more.

Nobody knows how many they killed. Thousands, surely, maybe tens of thousands. And I know I should be judged for cheering them on. I know I'm paying the price now with... with *this*. This husband. That ridiculous *paranja*. This hellish home, and those damned muezzins screaming their call to prayer from their towers. I know I deserve this, but you have to understand what I am. You have to understand why I supported them.

I'm a *Pamiri*, you see. I was born here in Murghab, in the Pamir mountains, in the heart of Gorno-Badakhshan. During the civil war the Islamic Renaissance were our brothers in arms. They fought alongside us, and they suffered just as we did in the ethnic cleansing when the communist old guard destroyed us along with the Garmis. One hundred thousand dead, and the years of peace since then did nothing to heal the old wounds.

They say the enemy of my enemy is my friend, and in the old Soviet *apparatchiks* we and the Islamists shared a sworn enemy. It seemed natural to support them in the beginning. I just wish, if I could go back to the days when you and I were–

Before Nasreen can finish her thought the twin voices of the muezzins begin their warbling call to *Asr salah*, the afternoon prayer. Atash stands, takes Nasreen by the elbow and lifts her from her seat, ordering her to once again don her *paranja*.

The light seems to fade from Nasreen's eyes as she tugs the heavy shroud over her shoulders. The energy and vigor that emanated from her every pore just a moment ago seems to have vanished, replaced with a sadness so profound that I feel tears prick at my eyes.

Atash walks to the corner of the room and reaches down to collect two rolled prayer mats, and in the moment before he turns back I see a

wistful smile flit across Nasreen's face. For a moment I see the woman I once knew, and perhaps – I hardly dare think it – even loved, and as she looks down at her feet I follow her gaze and catch a brief glimpse of something as she lifts the heavy *paranja*. Tied around her ankle I see a flash of color, just for a moment before her husband turns back to us.

It's a scrap of red lace, from a dress I bought her a lifetime ago.

●▼●

:::6:::

Bergen, Norway

Professor Gunnar Amundsen waves me onto his boat with an impish grin, tossing down a rope ladder with one hand while carefully cupping a joint against the wind with the other. As I climb to the deck of the rusting hulk he lets out a chuckle when I pause to notice his unusual attire and the name painted on the side of the boat: *Calypso II*.

Before the war Amundsen was known in academic circles as a colorful character, to say the least, and it's clear that the trials of the last decade have done nothing to sap him of his personality. An epidemiologist by profession, before the war Amundsen was Dean of the Faculty of Medicine at the University of Oslo, a position he clung onto despite the eccentricities that led many to request his removal.

Amundsen was and remains the self-described world's greatest fan of the life and work of French oceanographer Jacques Cousteau. While working at the university he lived in Oslo harbor on a renovated WWII minesweeper named after Cousteau's own ship, *Calypso,* and when in 2004 he saw *The Life Aquatic*, Wes Anderson's part parody, part homage to Cousteau he also decided to adopt as his own the outfit favored by Bill Murray's Steve Zissou: a red wool hat, matching sky blue short sleeved shirt and pants, and a pair of white Adidas sneakers.

While Amundsen's bizarre quirks made him

something of a minor tourist attraction in Oslo harbor in the years before the war, his undeniable expertise in the field of epidemiology made him known around the world as the epidemic finally began its spread throughout the west.

Biting is a ridiculous way to spread a virus, you know. Truly stupid. Just think about that for a moment. Take a look at influenza. It's airborne. It's invisible. A carrier can spread an aerosol of the virus ten feet in any direction with a cough or a sneeze, and it can survive and remain infectious on a dry, non-porous surface – a computer keyboard or subway handrail, for example – for as long as 24 hours. It's an intensely hardy virus, and yet serologic studies suggest that even H1N1, one of the most malign variants we've seen, had an infection rate of just 24% during the 2009 pandemic.

Now imagine that influenza wasn't spread by airborne means or fomite contact but by biting. Imagine you could identify a carrier on sight from one hundred meters down the street. Imagine their skin was sloughing off and they had open wounds and torn clothing. Imagine that to transmit the virus they needed to get within biting distance and physically overpower you, and then imagine that – fully aware you've been infected – you then allowed yourself to pass that virus to others. It's crazy, isn't it? It should never have happened. We should never have had to worry about a virus with such a flawed and inefficient delivery mechanism.

Even a *lyssavirus* such as rabies, which I suppose would be a suitable analog for the zombie virus, isn't something we were ever overly concerned about, even though it was endemic to several continents, transmitted by bite and almost certainly fatal without treatment. And why were we so relaxed about rabies? Simple. It's because human evolution selected for caution. When we see a dog acting in an unusually aggressive manner we back away because we know it's potentially dangerous, and because every living human on earth is the end result of an unbroken millennia long line of ancestors who were too intelligent to put themselves in harm's way.

So why did it happen? How did this frankly absurd, ill-adapted virus sweep so violently across the world when carriers telegraphed their illness from a mile away? How did it succeed when everyone from epidemiologists to thoughtful fans of zombie movies assured us that such an epidemic could never take hold in the real world?

Amundsen kills his joint and tosses the butt over the side.

What we discovered early on in the epidemic was that the... God, I hate calling it the 'zombie virus'. Makes me feel like a character in a B movie. I'll use my own term, if you don't mind, even though the etiology has yet to be conclusively confirmed.

We discovered that *Lyssavirus sibericum* cleverly subverted the usual mechanisms that govern the spread of disease, both in the pathological progression of the virus and also by exploiting cultural conditioning. It... Sorry, it's not easy to communicate these ideas in layman's terms. Not without much more weed, anyway.

OK, first, pathology. Infections with a short latency period – by which I mean direct infections through bites to, say, a major artery – were a different beast altogether. They resulted in an almost immediate acute phase of the infection, but *long* latency infections, what we now call 'slow burns', manifested first as an inflammation of the frontal lobe of the cerebrum, the section of the brain responsible for impulse control, problem solving and judgment, among other things.

Slow burn infections quite literally made carriers progressively dumber. The virus targeted and assaulted the foremost aspect of humanity that had allowed us to become the world's dominant species: our intelligence.

The effect wasn't immediately obvious to observers, you understand. This wasn't a catastrophic symptom but a subtle one, so subtle that even sufferers themselves didn't notice. It diminished a carrier's cognitive functions, making them less able to rationally evaluate the gravity of their own situation or even accept the fact that they'd been infected. For instance, it might lead someone who'd been scratched by an infected individual to believe that it really was 'just a scratch.' 'I feel fine,' they might think, 'no need to worry about it,' without realizing that their cavalier attitude to their own health was actually the first symptom of the infection.

But that's not the most interesting thing. No, the most interesting reason the spread of the virus was so devastatingly successful was thanks to cultural conditioning. It was, and please don't take offense, partly due to the likes of you and others like you who developed and popularized the time-honored tropes of zombie fiction. Unfortunately you helped propagate the disease of false knowledge better than the virus ever could.

Let me explain. A theme common to almost all fictional accounts of zombie epidemics is that infection is virtually immediate, progressing to the acute stage in a matter of seconds or minutes. It's a cheap dramatic device, a sort of get out of jail free card for lazy screenwriters who need visually exciting action scenes and a story that could be neatly wrapped up in ninety minutes. Put simply, protracted illness is both boring and problematic in an action movie, and even those movies that sought to introduce dramatic tension only went so far as to stretch the incubation period to a few hours, allowing infected characters to perhaps say goodbye to a loved one, or agonize over whether to make a selfless sacrifice.

We'd been indoctrinated by these stories for a generation or more. They were baked in to our collective 'knowledge' of zombies, and when the outbreaks began we believed that our experience of decades of zombie-laden media gave us an intellectual edge over the virus. We weren't, like the majority of movie characters, ignorant of the well worn tropes of the genre, and so we made our plans – quite sensibly, we thought – based almost entirely on those tropes. We constructed physical defenses or withdrew from populated areas to guard ourselves against swarms of roving undead. We took every measure possible to prevent being bitten or scratched by infected individuals, and even in some of the most secure sanctuary cities we enforced quarantine periods on new arrivals of just a day or two, a week at most, along with intensive physical examinations.

Reality, sadly, did not conform to common fictional tropes. As the epidemic arrived in the western world it was spread through short latency infections – the classic gore-filled attacks as envisioned by both movies and, indeed, the Tokyo footage – in only a vanishingly small number of cases. We were quite well prepared for outbreaks of this nature. We had plenty of guns and plenty of ammo, and we knew thanks to both movies and common sense to shoot a zombie dead before it could get within arm's reach, and to prevent someone with a bite or scratch wound from entering a secure area.

These short latency infections only came in large numbers much later, once the epidemic was already well established throughout the world, but the initial infiltration came through *long* latency infections.

It was the slow burns that allowed people to get past immigration controls; to board planes, trains and ships, and to carry the virus into the very heart of a country or region before succumbing, sometimes after an incubation period of days or even weeks in the case of, say, the introduction of the virus into a superficial wound, or the absorption of infected blood or saliva through a permeable membrane such as the surface of the eye, or even through sexual contact with a preclinical carrier.

Of course we didn't learn any of this until it was already far too late.

Amundsen takes a silver cigarette case from his back pocket and slips out another two joints, offering one to me. I accept the gift gratefully, if only because it's a novelty to be in a country in which marijuana is legal and readily available.

I was far from the first to suggest that slow burns may be an issue but mine was the first case study published, and the first to conclusively establish the path of infection, so I suppose I can lay claim to the dubious honor as the harbinger of this stealthy apocalypse.

I was initially brought in on the case by a colleague at the Oslo University Hospital, a noted American ophthalmologist by the name of Terrence Kilmartin. He'd been understandably alarmed and quite baffled when he was awoken one morning in the early hours with the news that one of his patients had – completely out of the blue –

succumbed to the virus and triggered a quarantine of the hospital. The patient killed two nurses before she was dispatched, and once the initial panic died down Terrence came to me determined to establish the cause. It was a week before we finally got to the bottom of it, and the chain of events that led to the tragedy turned out to be quite astonishing, and most troubling.

The patient was a young woman who suffered from a condition known as Fuchs' dystrophy, a degenerative disease of the cornea, and she'd been waiting for a suitable transplant donor for several months. That donor came in the form of a motorcyclist who'd wiped out on an icy road near Lillestrom while not wearing a helmet, a terrible accident that had killed him instantly but had, thankfully, left his eyes undamaged. Doctor Kilmartin performed a double penetrating keratoplasty right away.

The surgery went without a hitch and the patient awoke from anesthesia with clear vision for the first time in ten years. There were hugs and handshakes all round, and the young lady was promptly discharged with a clean bill of health. It was only when she returned two weeks later complaining of irritation that Kilmartin discovered an issue, some kind of low level infection around the transplanted corneal tissue. He prescribed a course of antibiotics and readmitted her, if only for her own peace of mind, and didn't give the case another thought. That was the night she passed, and later reanimated.

Two weeks! She'd survived quite happily for two weeks with corneal grafts transplanted from an infected donor, and the truly alarming thing was that the donor *himself* hadn't entered the acute stage before his own death. When his body was exhumed and an autopsy performed there were only small traces of the virus found, predominantly at the site of a piercing his wife informed us he'd received a week before his death.

The news sent shockwaves through the medical field. We'd been afraid of zombies swarming down our streets. We'd been preparing to defend against the obviously infected, against the sort of slavering beasts we knew from the movies, but now it seemed the enemy could be already dwelling within us. It could be festering in the puncture wounds of tattoos, and multiplying beneath skin grafts and in the tissue of transplanted limbs. It could even be lurking, just waiting to be passed on, in our husbands and wives, boyfriends and girlfriends, in our most tender moments.

This is how the virus beat us. This is how it overwhelmed the world, reaching every corner of civilization before drowning us in an uncontrollable, unstoppable tsunami. We'd been culturally conditioned to believe that zombies would come crashing through our front doors, but few considered the possibility that the virus was already lurking within our very blood.

●▼●

Cornwall, England

Martin Rowland shrugs the heavy roll of baling wire from the shoulder of his olive, oil stained Barbour Beaufort and begins to spool out a few yards, snipping off a length with a pair of rusted pliers he keeps tucked in one of his bellowed jacket pockets. He barks an order at me to lift the fallen branches from the fence, then narrows his eyes in concentration as he sets about carefully weaving the new wire into the broken section.

With his weather-worn Barbour, pilled Fair Isle sweater, corduroy trousers and scuffed brogues Martin looks like an English country gentleman straight out of Central Casting, and a Colin Firth lookalike *par excellence*. Few would guess that beneath the graying beard and prematurely lined face was a confirmed urbanite who once famously boasted that he refused to eat in a restaurant until it had won at least one Michelin star.

Despite the icy chill and blustery winds Martin insists on working each day from dawn, patrolling his lonely ten mile stretch of the coastal fence between Sennen Cove and Porthcurno, Cornwall. His fanatical devotion to duty in the reformed Home Guard is all the more impressive – and confounding – when he tells me that in the nine years since he adopted this stretch there has never been a single arrival from the water, and with good reason.

This part of the Cornish coast includes Land's End, the westernmost point of the English mainland, and here the steep granite cliffs are battered by ocean currents originating far out in the Atlantic. There are no lateral currents to drag a body along the coast, and the odds of the living dead not only washing up on these shores, not only surviving the pounding surf, but then managing to climb the jagged, near vertical cliffs are, frankly, so long as to seem absurd.

Rowland seems to understand the utter pointlessness of his job all too well, but he appears entirely undeterred. When I ask him why he bothers to live alone out here, fifty miles from the nearest populated village, and to drag himself out of bed each morning to patrol his lonely stretch come rain or shine, he looks out over the stormy ocean and mutters, simply, "This is my penance."

I used to write for the Guardian. Are you familiar with it? No? Well, it was sort of like... actually, now I think about it you really didn't have any mainstream papers quite so unabashedly lefty as the good old Grauniad. I often forget that you Yanks think 'socialist' is a dirty word, and none more so than those who think it's a synonym for 'communist'.

Not me. No, I wore that label proudly, though I must admit it was often prefaced with the word 'champagne' by my detractors. That's what they used to call us: 'champagne socialists', similar to your own 'limousine liberals.' We were the Labour voting middle classes, the ABC1s. Educated, healthy, wealthy media luvvies who espoused the sort of quinoa eating, virtue signaling, knit-your-own-bicycle left wing views that drove Daily Mail readers up the wall. We were pro-multiculturalism, pro-education, pro-NHS, pro-environment and – above all else, at least in my case – *vociferously* pro-Europe.

The years leading up to the crisis were deeply conflicted for me. On a personal level I was infuriated by the rise of the far right here in the UK, out on the continent and over in the US. Brexit first, then the US election. 2016 was an *annus horribilis* for those of us on the left, and 2017 didn't shape up much better. Right wing candidates like Marine Le Pen and Geert Wilders were gaining ground in Europe, hate crimes against foreigners were on the rise here in the UK, Trump pulled out of the Paris Agreement and then, just to finish off the year with a bang, Putin went even further, tearing up that and every other environmental accord we'd fought so hard to ratify. It was nothing short of crushing to watch society regress at such a blistering pace.

I say these years were conflicted because while I was horrified by what was happening the horror was also incredibly lucrative for me. I'd never been in greater demand. I was bumped up to three columns a week for the Guardian, along with a weekend feature for our sister paper The Observer, and not a day went by that I wasn't invited to appear on some TV or radio panel show to discuss the latest piece of awfulness to emerge. I earned enough to renovate the kitchen in 2016, and by the following summer we could finally afford the deposit on our little cottage on the coast. At a time when newspaper readerships had fallen to record lows I was earning more in a month than I usually earned in a year.

Champagne socialist... It was an unpleasant slur, but I can't claim it wasn't accurate. We weren't really affected by any of this, you see, at least not in any direct sense.

Sarah and I were insulated from the challenges of the real world by our money, and all the creature comforts our immense good fortune had afforded us. We had the townhouse in Primrose Hill, a wedding gift from Sarah's mother, and the cottage in Sennen for long weekends by the sea. I had a nicely diversified portfolio, low risk and spread across a number of ethical investments. Sarah had her little Fiat 500 Abarth runabout and I had the Audi Q7 – the hybrid version, so it was exempt from the London congestion charge. We'd called in a few favors to get Toby enrolled at St. Paul's, and he seemed to be settling in well by the start of the autumn term.

Our little bubble was quite comfortable, thank you very much, and perhaps that's why we were so quick to take sides when people started screaming about immigration louder than ever before. They'd always grumbled about foreigners, of course, because for years the tabloids had fed them a steady diet of such absurd poison that they'd come to believe that Johnny Foreigner was the cause of every last one of their problems. Every time a Syrian refugee was given a council house the Mail would yell about the thousands of Brits who'd been on the waiting list for years, and if your dear old gran had to wait a few extra days to see a doctor about her dicky hip the Express would be up in arms about medical tourism.

Of course they'd never question why the NHS and social housing programs had been so criminally underfunded in the first place, because it didn't fit the narrative to blame the pitiful state of our public services on the government when it was so much more satisfying to blame Abdul the refugee – sorry, 'economic migrant'. Most of the time the stories weren't even true, but you wouldn't know it until these lying rags were forced to publish a retraction three months later at the bottom of page 47, in type so small you'd swear it had been woven by a spider.

It was the Daily Mail campaign that finally spurred me into action. 'Raise the Drawbridge', they called it. Simple and to the point, and emotionally resonant to the sort of small minded, xenophobic Little Englanders who'd always believed that their home was their castle. Every day for a month the Mail devoted their entire front page to stories about the 'European threat', pleading with their readers to tell their friends, call their MP, march on Downing Street... whatever it took to get the government to brick up the Channel Tunnel and cut off our only physical link to France before we found ourselves swamped by refugees fleeing the attacks on the continent.

It was a ridiculous idea. Completely lunatic. For one thing the group that owned the Channel Tunnel was a five billion Euro publicly listed company, not a government operation, and it wasn't ours to close. There was simply no mechanism by which we could seal the tunnel without setting off a major diplomatic shitstorm all around the world. We were already on thin ice with the Brexit negotiations, and we knew that soon enough we'd need to start working on new trade deals with dozens of countries. Closing the tunnel would set back international relations for years, mortally wounding an already struggling economy.

It wasn't really the political or economic arguments that concerned me, though, but the human impact of the campaign that had me up in arms. Around six months earlier the Jungle – the infamous refugee camp on the French side of the tunnel – had been reopened, and there were around four thousand people there waiting to be allowed in to the UK. They were all legally entitled to come here. They all had family here or had been granted asylum, but as usual the government was dragging its feet with the paperwork, because for every new photo of a slightly shifty looking bearded refugee arriving on our shores a few more votes slipped away to Ukip.

I knew that if we closed the Tunnel that would be it. Those poor buggers would be stuck in the camp forever. In essence, by sealing the tunnel Britain would finally be confirming to the world that we'd lost the last scraps of our humanity; that we'd finally stopped even *pretending* to care, and we'd now be turning a blind eye to all the suffering in the world as long as it occurred beyond the white cliffs of Dover.

In any case, the Daily Mail's hateful campaign worked. After a month of relentless attacks on the government the latest polls showed that Ukip, the former fringe party that existed somewhere dangerously far to the right of the political spectrum, had for the first time in its history come within ten points of being the most popular political party in the UK. They were polling at 24%, up from just 6% a few years earlier, and for the first time it looked like there was a good chance the next election would bring a fascist government to Downing Street, if not by an outright majority then at least as part of a coalition with the Tories.

On a Wednesday afternoon in the middle of October the Prime Minister quietly announced that the tunnel would be sealed the following day, and that all rail and ferry travel between the UK and Europe was to be immediately halted. She hid the announcement in the middle of a daily press briefing as if she was hoping nobody would pick up on it, but I was too smart for that. She couldn't sneak it past me.

Within moments of reading the news I sat down at my MacBook and wrote my next column, a rousing call to arms and an earnest plea for sanity and decency in an age of madness. As soon as I uploaded it to the Guardian server I called St. Paul's to let them know I'd be taking Toby out of school for the rest of the week, and by Thursday morning he, Sarah and I were in the Audi and driving down the M20 to Folkestone. I'd spent seven years at the Guardian railing against our shockingly poor record on refugees, and of course I felt it was my duty to do whatever I could to stop this madness.

It was Bedlam down there. There's no way to know exactly how many people joined us for the protest, but by the weekend it couldn't have been less than fifty thousand. We formed a human blockade at the entrance to the tunnel. We sabotaged machinery. We blocked all of the incoming roads with our cars. We sang with one voice in a glorious, exhilarating, joyful rejection of isolationism. We wanted to send out the message loud and clear to our compatriots in Europe and beyond: *we stand with you, friends. We won't abandon you.*

Oh, it was a beautiful sight to see. After years of watching the UK turn in on itself and become cold, twisted and bitter it was heartwarming to see so many good, kind people willing to stand up and fight for what was right. To see them give up their time to stand beside us and refuse to embrace hatred.

For the first time in far too long I actually felt optimistic about the future. *We can win this country back*, I thought. *We can rally the people and turn them away from their xenophobia, their racism, their fear.* The atmosphere was electric, and it only grew more exciting as more people joined us by the hour. By the end of the third day I imagined our voices could be heard all across the country, our message of hope seeping into the hearts of everyone from Folkestone to the Highlands.

Martin pauses for a moment to carefully secure the end of the wire around a fence post, giving it a shake to ensure it's firmly fixed. He slips a hip flask from a jacket pocket and takes a swig, cringing at the harsh taste of whatever bootleg moonshine is available this far from civilization.

The dead arrived early on Sunday morning, just after dawn.

I was sleeping on the rail platform in a little space I'd managed to clear for us beside a bench. Sarah was to my right and Toby was tucked between us, snuggling against me with his little mittens up to his face to keep warm through the night. Such a brave little boy. He hadn't complained once about the cold.

I didn't realize it for a while, but what woke me was gunfire. I'd never even heard it in real life. Each shot echoed across the platform so it was impossible to tell where it was coming from, but it seemed quite distant. When I first opened my eyes I wasn't sure it actually *was* gunfire. I think I must have drifted off again for a few moments, because the moment I heard the first scream I opened my eyes and found the protesters already on their feet, hundreds of them, eyes wide with panic.

I climbed onto the bench and saw that the police were lined up at the far end of the platform, hiding like cowards behind riot shields with their guns poking through the gaps. Real stormtrooper types, kitted out in black with their faces covered in masks so you couldn't look them in the eye. I was shocked. *Shocked.* I knew things were getting bad, but never in a million years did I think the police would fire on citizens engaged in peaceful protest. I mean, damn it all, that's just not British. That's something that – sorry, no offense – we thought only happened in the US and third world states. *This is it*, I thought. *October 17th, mark it down. This is the day freedom dies in the United Kingdom.*

If I'd been alone I might have tried to stay and document this incredible assault, but I could feel Toby stirring beside me and I knew I had to get him out of there. Even if they were only firing rubber bullets or beanbags I'd never have forgiven myself if he was hurt, so I rolled on top of him to shield his body, grabbed him by the hand and yelled at Sarah to get to her feet.

I think I was still only half awake as we started to run, hunched over in a crouch, waiting to feel a shot in my back at any moment. I wasn't really aware of what was going on, but I remember feeling confused. We were pushing our way through the crowd on the platform but we were barely making any progress, and it took a few moments before I fully awoke and realized why.

The crowd was moving in the other direction, *towards* the police line.

I turned around and looked back towards the police, and that's when I finally saw what was really happening. They were allowing protesters to slip through their line. Their guns weren't pointed at us but over towards the rail tracks. I peered through the crowd and saw that there were people down there, their heads and shoulders poking up above the floor of the platform. Dozens of them, maybe hundreds. *That's* who the police were firing on.

They'd come through the tunnel, just like the bloody Daily Mail had warned.

That's the moment it all became real for me. All the panic. All the paranoia. All the fearmongering columns in the tabloids. It felt like a scene from *The Boy Who Cried Wolf*. The papers had spent so many years lying about the dark terrors beyond our borders that I hadn't thought to listen when they eventually told the truth.

The scales fell from my eyes as I saw those creatures march slowly, deliberately onward. They weren't human. They weren't people. They didn't blink an eye when one of their brothers fell to the ground beside them as a bullet buried itself in his skull. They were automata. Mindless monsters. And they were coming for us.

There were more of them coming from the back of the platform, catching up with those furthest back in the crowd and forcing us all to surge forward. I could hear the screams. The platform was hemmed in by tracks on both sides and the living dead had outflanked us. The panic was... it was just insane. Nobody knew what to do, where to run. Thousands of people pushing and jostling, screaming, climbing over each other to get back to safety behind the police line, but there were just too many of us. I saw people tumble over the edge of the platform down to the rails, vanishing in a sea of teeth and grabbing hands.

Through the crowd I caught a glimpse of a young girl who looked to be around Toby's age, just a sweet little girl clinging onto a stuffed Paddington Bear as if she was protecting it from the crowd. She stumbled at the edge of the platform as the adults pushed and shoved above her, and she cried out as she lost hold of the bear. It landed at the edge of the platform, and as she reached down to rescue it a gnarled hand reached up and grabbed her by the hem of her skirt.

The noise of the crowd was far too loud for me to hear it at the time, but in my memory I can still hear the sound of her teeth shattering on the platform as she fell face down. I can hear the sound of her fingernails scrape against the floor as they dragged her down to the rails. Even now I still imagine I can hear the terrified shriek that lasted just a few seconds, and then suddenly stopped.

They must have come at the police from behind. Maybe a group of them managed to sneak past, or maybe some of the protesters had been infected as they tried to escape. There's no way to know, it was all too chaotic, but suddenly the police were firing *back* as well as ahead. Some of them even started to fire *into* the crowd. One man, some middle aged gent who looked like a geography teacher, patches on his elbows and everything, went down with a bullet to the gut. He was just inches from me. God knows how the shot made its way through the crowd and found his stomach.

I turned to look as he fell, and I suppose that's what saved me. The next shot would probably have caught me full in the chest, but instead it buried itself in my arm. I fell backwards onto my ass. I barely felt the shot, but I definitely felt it as someone stepped on my hand a few moments later.

Martin shows me his left hand, the fingers crooked and the bones poorly set.

I didn't see much after that. There were just too many people. Sarah and Toby vanished in the crowd ahead of me. I don't even know if they realized I wasn't with them any more. I don't think it would have mattered either way. There was no way they could come back to find me, not fighting against the human tide flowing back towards safety.

It was all I could do to roll out of the way, to get out from under the trampling feet. I finally found my way to the shelter of a concrete column with a bullet in my arm, a broken hand and a couple of cracked ribs. I could barely breathe, but at least I was alive. I don't know how long I waited there – I think I may have passed out for a moment from the pain – but when the crowd began to thin and I finally heard those dry, rasping groans above the screams I crawled to the edge of the platform. The group down on the rails had moved on to where the police were lined up, so I climbed down from the platform and somehow managed to lift myself up the other side where I had a free run back to the car park and the motorway beyond. I didn't stop until I...

Martin hefts his coil of baling wire onto his shoulder and sets off quickly down the path. He stops a few dozen steps ahead of me, staring out to sea, and I give him a few minutes to collect himself before walking to catch up. His eyes are red, but he looks like he ran out of tears long ago.

They found Sarah two days later during the cleanup operation. Shot, not infected. She was still clutching one of Toby's mittens tight in her hand when I identified the body.

Toby was...

He sighs, and sniffs.

I suppose he didn't have much of a chance in that crowd. Too many frightened people trying to push forward. Too many people screaming to hear a voice coming from beneath their feet. It must have been so easy for Sarah to lose her grip on his little hand.

It was only later we learned that the Prime Minister had known about the outbreak in the refugee camp on the

French side of the tunnel. *That's* why she ordered it sealed. She didn't care about the poll numbers, the Mail's campaign or losing votes to bloody Ukip. She wasn't playing politics, she just knew this was the only way she could protect the country. She tried to do it quietly because she didn't want to cause a panic.

I caused the panic. It was my fucking article, the last one I wrote before I left for Folkestone.

This is a time for heroes, I'd written. *This is a time when all true British patriots must stand and be counted. This is a moment for the ages, a story we'll proudly pass on to our children, and they to theirs, that we numbered among the brave few who fought for the soul of our nation in its darkest hour. That we chose hope over hate, and courage over fear. That we stood atop those glorious white cliffs and cried out in one voice, so loud as to be heard across the globe, that we refused to abandon our European kin.*

I asked all of those people to go with me. *I* asked them to block the workers, link arms and sing our fucking songs, as if we could bring peace to the world with good intentions.

The dead didn't give a damn about our good intentions.

●▼●

:::8:::

Taos, New Mexico

Catalina Alvarado begins by apologizing for speaking to me by video link rather than in person, though an apology is far from necessary. Many in New Mexico speak of the government's efforts to 'handle' Ms. Alvarado in the same way that people once described the CIA's decades-long campaign to take out Fidel Castro.

While it may seem unbelievable that the government would attempt to assassinate a person who is – officially, at least – still a US citizen, and on US soil no less, the recent car accident that left Alvarado confined to a wheelchair has certainly raised questions, and the evasive, conflicted statements from Anchorage in response to the incident have convinced many that the stories surrounding the government's reaction to the popular New Mexico secession movement may be more than just a baseless conspiracy theory.

"What's the plan?"

That was the only thing anyone asked back then, in tones that grew more concerned and desperate by the day. In line at the grocery store, by the watercooler or waiting at the school gates we'd gather in huddles and whisper. "Have they said anything? Are we supposed to be evacuating yet? North? South? *Why the hell aren't they telling us?*" As the weeks went on it became more and more obvious that the reason nobody was telling us the plan was because there *wasn't* a plan, not for us. We were all alone out here.

I've tried to let go of the anger in the years since. I've tried to get over it but it's not easy. It's hard to let go of the bitterness, and it didn't get any easier once the state-by-state plan was leaked. Did you ever read that thing?

I nod. While President Buckley is wildly popular throughout most of the US there are a handful of states in which he'd struggle to poll in double digits were he to run again, and the action plan he commissioned – and legend has it almost single-handedly wrote – is the sole reason.

"We see little tactical benefit, given its climate and paucity of arable land, in devoting significant resources to the defense of New Mexico, with several notable exceptions. If at all practical, relevant areas of the San Juan Basin and Permian Basin regions should be guarded against widespread infection to allow for the future resumption of oil and natural gas extraction. We would also recommend that the WIPP (Waste Isolation Pilot Plant) east of Carlsbad be sealed or collapsed to minimize the risk of radioactive contamination following its closure. Strategically useful military and civilian personnel should be extracted discreetly, where possible without alerting the remaining citizenry.

"Civilian evacuation plan: Not required."

It's hard to get your head around it, isn't it? You spend your whole life working to make America a better place. You pay your taxes, you cast your vote in every election, you sit on the PTA, you even run for city council, because you've been taught since you were a little girl that to be an American means to stand up and do your part for your community. You feel like you're part of the team, and then you read something like that. *Civilian evacuation plan: Not required.* Five little words that condemned me, my husband, my daughter and everyone else I knew to death. Surplus to requirements. Ballast to be cast off when convenient.

And look, I'm not stupid. I know there was no malice intended. I know nobody *wanted* us to die, and I know that trying to save everyone might have meant that nobody survived. I *get* it. I understood Buckley perfectly when he was finally forced to make his famous 'difficult choices' speech a few days after the leak, when he told that dumb story about the lifeboat and the Titanic. If they tried to row back to pull more people out of the water they'd be swamped, and the lifeboat would sink.

I'm a big girl and I understood the logic, but *he* needs to understand why those he left to drown can't ever forgive him. He needs to understand that we don't want anything to do with a United States that proved to be anything but united, and that his government can't just come back and pretend it didn't happen. We survived without their help. *They* left. *We're* America, not them, and that's the way we intend to go on.

"Can you tell me how people reacted when they learned that New Mexico had been abandoned?"

Sure, that's easy. It was unbridled chaos on a scale you'd imagine could only ever happen in the movies. As soon as the President finished his address it started to sink in that we were on our own, and a lot of people took that to heart. We're talking mass looting, armed robberies, profiteering and hoarding on an industrial scale. Albuquerque turned into a war zone overnight.

That's where Jack worked, at the Ford dealership in Signal Hill, and a few hours after the speech the boss called him and told him not to come in the next day. A gang of guys had raided the lot and stolen almost every car. The boss actually knew who did it. He had their faces on the security cameras and he knew exactly where they were keeping the cars, but he couldn't even get through to 911 to report it. That's when we decided it was time to bow out of society and hunker down at home.

Jack and I always loved to watch those apocalypse prepper shows on TV. You remember those shows? You'd get a family who'd spent a decade building some impregnable fortress, and then the experts come in and tell them they made one little mistake that meant they'd be dead in a week. We couldn't get enough of them, and in what little free time we'd managed to grab over the last few months we'd turned our little split level up in Cochiti into a pretty good base for when the shit hit the fan.

I mean, it was nothing special. We weren't *real* preppers, and we didn't have the time or money to plan anything as elaborate as the families on the TV, but we'd done what we could on a tight budget. We had a little vegetable garden out back, and enough tinned food to last six months. We had those fancy new solar tiles on the roof that gave us enough power to run the lights, a mini fridge and an electric stove. We had a backup gas burner, and a gravity-fed filtration system we bought online that would give us as much clean water as we needed.

I also had my little Glock, though I was a terrible shot, and Jack had the shotgun for 'crowd control'. We had a rowboat in the garage so we could fish up at Cochiti Lake. I'd even filled six Jerry cans with gas in case we needed to escape in the Grand Cherokee, and there were well stocked bug out bags for each of us already in the trunk.

We always assumed we were safe in Cochiti. I mean not *safe* safe, not like we were immune from any disaster that might hit the rest of the state. We just felt like it was a nice, quiet community, a little off the beaten track and not an obvious candidate for a place where terrible things might happen. We'd been living there fifteen years. We knew all our neighbors and we'd think nothing of leaving Elisa with any of them. They were good, friendly people, and it never occurred to me for a second that any of them might turn against us when times got tough. It just wasn't that kind of place, you know?

I remember it was a couple of nights after the power had finally gone out, after we'd switched over to solar. Elisa had been having nightmares for a few weeks – she kept watching the news, and she'd heard talk at school from some of the other kids – and she begged me to let her sleep with the light on. I was the good cop of the family so of course she came to me rather than Jack, and of course I said yes. I don't know if that's what tipped them off, but it certainly can't have helped to advertise so obviously to the neighborhood that we were better prepared than most.

It was some time around midnight that Elisa woke me. I'd only just fallen asleep, and I grumbled a little and told her to go back to bed, and then she whispered in that soft little voice of hers. "Mommy, the people in the yard are keeping me awake."

Jack was out of bed before she finished talking, reaching for the shotgun he kept up on the top shelf of the closet. I grabbed hold of his PJs as he walked towards the door and begged him to stay inside. I said the safest thing we could do is just sit tight and wait for whoever was down there to leave, but if they tried to come inside we could go all Wyatt Earp on them.

"We can't let people think we're an easy target, Cat," Jack said. "If we don't stand up for ourselves now what's to say they won't come back for more tomorrow?"

I didn't want him to go, but I knew that look in his eyes all too well. He didn't like to be taken advantage of, you know? I don't want to get too deep into psychology or whatever, but Jack's father had been a mean drunk. He'd watched him beat on his mom and sisters for years. Jack used to provoke him when it got real bad, you know, to take the heat off the girls. Twelve years old, goading a full grown man so his mom didn't wind up in the emergency room again. You wouldn't believe the scars he had on his back from his dad's belt buckle. Back when we first started dating I used to hear him talk in his sleep, and...

Anyway, I don't know, it just turned him into the kind of guy who couldn't help but stand up to bullies, even if he knew he'd take a beating. I couldn't have stopped him from going outside if I'd chained him to the water pipes.

I lifted Elisa up to our bed and told her to stay put while Daddy went to see if he could 'help' the people – "They're probably just lost, honey," I said – then I went through to her room and peeked out through the curtains, trying to stay out of sight as best I could. I knew Jack wouldn't be satisfied if he didn't get to confront the intruders and tell them off.

There were two of them down there, tugging out the little carrots I'd spent a whole afternoon planting months earlier, tossing them into a sack, and when I caught a glimpse of their faces I almost started banging on the window and yelling. I just couldn't believe what I was seeing. It was Jan and Mark Ducey, our more-perfect-than-thou neighbors from just around the corner on Barranca Drive!

I was on the damned PTA board with Jan. She had a son in the same grade as Elisa, and I couldn't abide the woman. She was your typical pain in the ass soccer mom, always going on about her juice cleanses or Mark's latest promotion or how well Ethan was doing in class. You know the type, always parading around in yoga pants. Always coming out with those little "Oh, I wish I could eat whatever I wanted without worrying about gaining weight" backhanded insults. Always sharing some bullshit on Facebook about the wonderful romantic meals Mark cooked for her. A real bitch, you know? And now she was grubbing through the dirt stealing my damned carrots!

I was just about ready to bust when I heard the screen door creak and saw Jack step out into the yard with the shotgun. I was almost *happy* they were stealing from us. I couldn't wait to see Jan drop her sack and start begging for forgiveness. I just wanted to see her fall to pieces and finally admit that she couldn't provide for her family as well as we could. I know that sounds cruel, but the woman had called Elisa 'Lisa' three times in as many months, and I'm almost certain it was intentional. For a mom that's more than enough to start a lifelong blood feud.

I think Jack was just as surprised as I was to see who it was in the garden. I'm guessing that's why he didn't raise the shotgun right away. He just coughed politely, as if he desperately wanted this to be some kind of hilarious misunderstanding, you know? Like Jan might look up and say "Good grief, Mark, this isn't our yard!"

Mark took the shot before Jack could say a word. He was just... calm. Robotic. I can still see it so clearly in my head, playing out in slow motion every time I close my eyes. Mark pulled the pistol from his holster and squeezed the trigger from the hip without a second thought, like you'd see in an old Western, and he'd put the gun away before Jack even hit the ground.

I remember screaming as I watched from the bedroom window. Mark looked up and stared me straight in the eyes without a hint of shock or remorse. Just... nothing. No emotion whatsoever. He took a step or two towards the porch before Jan shook her head, said something and pointed up towards me.

Only it wasn't me she was pointing at. It was Elisa. She'd rushed into the room at the sound of the shot and joined me at the window, and I think that's the only reason Mark didn't kill me. Like it'd be no problem to shoot me dead, but it might be too much effort to chase down and slaughter a kid.

I... I think I must have gone into shock. I remember feeling as if my feet were buried in cement as I watched Jan calmly lift the sack and walk away with Mark at her side. They didn't even have the decency to run.

I don't remember much after that. All I know is that Elisa didn't know what had really happened. Jack had fallen down out of sight beneath the porch so she couldn't see his body. I told her Daddy had gone to help the Duceys with something, then I tucked her up in my bed, locked the door so she couldn't get out, then I walked downstairs as if I was in a trance. There was a shovel by the back door, the same shovel I'd used to till the soil for the carrots, and I dug through the night until the hole was deep enough to bury Jack.

By the time Elisa woke up in the morning I'd packed the Jeep. I poured her a bowl of Cheerios with the last of the milk, made sure she brushed her teeth, strapped her into the back seat and left for the mountains. The only words I said that morning were "Daddy's gonna meet us there." I just kept repeating it over and over, as if it might come true if I said it enough times.

I still had soil beneath my fingernails.

Catalina moves out of shot for a moment before returning with something in her hand. It's her Glock G43 semi-automatic pistol. If the stories are to be believed this is the gun that claimed the lives of all 187 New Mexicans convicted of capital crimes in the years since Ms. Alvarado was elected Governor, though of course the status of her office – and the legitimacy of her criminal court – is unrecognized by the government in Anchorage.

According to official court records held in the new state house in Taos, Mark and Jan Ducey were the first New Mexicans to be executed following their forced rendition from a Colorado refugee camp. There are no records to confirm or refute the claim, but rumor has it that the first to die was actually fourteen year old Ethan Ducey, the son of Mark and Jan, executed in front of his parents. Governor Alvarado fiercely denies the rumors, dismissing them as a smear tactic from Anchorage.

We survived on our own down here. We grow our own crops. We build our own defenses. We bury our own dead, and we enforce our own laws.

When you see Buckley you should remind him of that.

●▼●

:::9:::

Offutt AFB, Nebraska

Dressed down in a short sleeved gray t-shirt stained with the remnants of the Sloppy Joes served up in the noisy, crowded canteen, General Caleb 'Cal' Tolbert cuts an unlikely figure as Commander, United States Strategic Command. Promoted to the role at the age of just 48, even after a decade of enduring the stresses of command the towering 6'5" General maintains an impressive degree of physical fitness. With his broad, muscular shoulders, square jaw and close shaved head it's easy to see why Tolbert's subordinates often compare him to the movie star and pro wrestler Dwayne Johnson.

As we tour the facility a passing Lieutenant Colonel openly refers to Tolbert as 'The Rock', and it's only then that I notice that almost nobody on duty at Offutt is dressed in standard uniform. The General smiles when I raise the issue, informing me that the standards of military discipline expected and demanded in pre-war military installations went out the window many years earlier.

"We were fighting zombies from the bottom of a bunker, son," he says, nodding politely to his secretary as we enter his messy, correspondence-filled office. "We dispensed with 'sir' and 'ma'am' long ago, and if wearing a pair of jeans helps improve morale after ten years under siege then I say bring on the damned denim."

Yeah, the Tokyo outbreak was the long awaited game changer for us. It was the starter pistol firing after months of arguing that the race should already be well underway, and it finally allowed me to march into the White House and demand that we get moving.

I lost count of the number of times I'd requested a seat at the President's daily intelligence briefing, or the number of times I'd sat in the near-empty situation room looking at grainy satellite images and handing out sheaves of intercepted cables to try to get someone – *anyone* – to take the threat even halfway seriously. Nobody at the White House wanted to hear it. They listened politely, of course – hell, we were USSTRATCOM, not a bunch of bloggers spouting conspiracy theories from our basements – but there was always that slightly glazed, disinterested look in their eyes, as if they were politely waiting for me to finish talking so they could get back to their real work.

Finally I understood why NASA Administrator Stofen had always looked so frustrated when I passed her in the halls at the White House. For years she'd been getting the exact same treatment whenever she tried to explain why it was absolutely vital that we increase funding for our Near-Earth Object tracking program. It was that same polite attention she knew would never translate to action. God damned frustrating. The problem is that nobody ever really believes disaster will strike, but when they're finally faced with the asteroid screaming towards Earth they get mad that nobody made a plan to blow it out of the sky. Same thing goes for the undead.

And it wasn't just us getting the brush off, I want to make that crystal clear. The NSA, CIA and even INSCOM had access to the exact same intel we were using to draw our conclusions, and to some extent they'd all entertained the possibility that we really *were* seeing the beginning of something serious, but I think it's fair to say that we were the first members of the US intelligence community who dared put our butts on the line and actually come out and say *"Hey, we're facing a zombie apocalypse here, and we need to start fuckin' doing something about it."* I'm sure you can understand how difficult it was for a serious government agency to go on record with something that sounds so batshit insane.

Tokyo changed everything. For months we'd been working with vague, scattered intel from Dushanbe, Siberia, a few isolated towns dotted around the Caucasus – places with reputations for providing low-confidence data that needed to be carefully considered before we could accept it as valid – but finally we had undeniable, unimpeachable evidence, broadcast live on TV, that the threat was genuine. Suddenly I found myself promoted to the big boy table in the situation room, and I found that I was the only person with an answer when the inevitable question came: *Does anyone have a plan for this?*

General Tolbert hands me a slim laminated volume, no more than twenty or thirty pages thick. The title on the cover reads CDRUSSTRATCOM CONPLAN 8888-11: "Counter-Zombie Dominance", 30 April 2011. He notices my hesitation.

Go ahead, take a look. It's not classified.

"You're telling me the US government had an official plan to tackle a zombie outbreak as far back as 2011?"

That's what I'm telling you. More specifically, *we* had an official plan. USSTRATCOM. This is what we do for a living, son. We spend our days gaming out every possible scenario that could threaten the security of the United States both at home and abroad, and we come up with contingency plans to ensure that we come out the other side in good shape.

OK, OK, you can pick your jaw back up from the floor. CONPLAN 8888 isn't quite what you probably think it is. You're imagining that top military brass sat around a table and devoted serious time to developing a response to a threat straight from the pages of science fiction, but the truth is that even *we* didn't bother to do that.

No, Quad Eight was developed not as an answer specifically to the zombie threat, but to a much more mundane PR problem. You see, back in the day we used a pair of hypothetical war scenarios at the JCWS, the Joint and Combined Warplanning School, to train our recruits in threat assessment, problem solving and strategy formulation. These scenarios were called 'Tunisia' and 'Nigeria'. They were detailed real world response scenarios to threats emanating from those two countries, and as you can imagine there was always a concern about the diplomatic fallout that would result if anyone in Abuja or Tunis ever learned that we were gaming out their deaths, or if, God forbid, the plans themselves were leaked, and some lunatic decided to bomb the crap out of D.C. because he thought we were about to start flying Predator drones over Lagos at rush hour.

That's where Quad Eight came into play. To skirt around the diplomatic minefield we decided to scrap our real world training scenarios and instead game out a threat so bizarre, so outlandish and far-fetched, that no foreign power could ever mistake it for a real world contingency plan. Zombies were an obvious choice because, well, nobody in their right mind could believe we'd ever face such a threat.

So that's how Quad Eight came to be, as a half serious thought exercise designed to be tossed around in a classroom. Of course we never intended for it to be implemented in the real world, but by the time the threat arrived on our shores the origins of the plan no longer mattered. What mattered was that this was the only response to a zombie outbreak that had ever been considered at any level of government, and as luck would have it it had been designed by some of the sharpest strategic minds in US military history.

"So... What was the plan?"

Pretty much what you'd expect from any widespread Ebola-like contagious threat, only with the added twist that not only would we need to curtail the spread of the infection and effectively quarantine the healthy, but we'd also have to deal with the infected – a mobile, physically capable and extremely violent group – after they'd turned.

The details are pretty dry, but the idea was that we'd coordinate multiple military and civilian authorities to maintain our Critical Capabilities – that's our basic infrastructure of road, rail and airfields – and protect our Critical Requirements – our hospitals, power plants, water, sanitation, and so on – while at the same time mobilizing our military forces to aggressively break the chain of infection, stopping the undead in their tracks. You can keep that copy and take a look at the fine detail for yourself, but those are the major bullet points.

I know I'm skimming over the details here, but I can

assure you that Quad Eight was a truly ambitious undertaking. It was a more complex and far-reaching campaign than anything ever attempted in the history of the United States, but all of us at USSTRATCOM – and, indeed, my counterparts at the NSA, CIA and the many government agencies that would be involved in implementing the plan – believed that we could successfully quell the zombie threat and keep our casualties, in our best case scenario, to something in the region of two hundred thousand. We had all the pieces ready to be moved into place. We just needed the go order.

"But none of this ever happened, did it? Why did CONPLAN 8888 fail?"

It didn't fail. It was just never implemented.

"Why not?"

Multiple reasons. If you want the unvarnished truth you should come back and ask me at my retirement party after a few beers, but for now I'll just say that even in the face of such a dire threat to humanity politics was still an enormous obstacle, as it always has been and always will be.

There were powerful personalities involved at all levels of decision making, and even at this late stage there were many who were still looking at opinion polls rather than reality. I'm not here to name names, that's not my job, but when the records of that time are eventually declassified I believe that the history books will need to be rewritten to identify the true heroes and villains. There were a number of great people – honest, honorable public servants – who found themselves in the firing line when the time came to assign blame. Some of them didn't survive, and many of those who did won't live long enough to see their good names restored. It might not be much of a comfort to them, but *I* know they were on the side of the angels.

In any case, the cutthroat politics didn't really make a difference in the end. In order to work as intended CONPLAN 8888 required nine days to fully implement from the moment the go order arrived, but by the time we started moving on the problem we'd already passed the point of no return. We didn't know it at the time, but it was already too late. Before we were ready to implement Quad Eight one of our secondary bellwethers had already been triggered.

"Bellwethers?"

Tolbert searches through the cluttered mess of papers on his desk until, after a spilled coffee and considerable cursing, he finds a poorly Xeroxed file and hands it to me. The cover sheet reads 'Lebanon, Missouri: Mercy-CDC transcript, 10/25.'

It was maybe three weeks after Tokyo that we finally began to put the pieces together, and as soon as we had a firm grasp on the situation we pulled out Quad Eight and began to update the plan to reflect what little we understood of the current threat. I crowdsourced suggestions throughout the base, and it just so happens that a naval ensign on secondment to Offutt approached me with the idea of the bellwethers. Lawrence, I think that was his name. Sharp sonofabitch.

He'd noticed an issue with Quad Eight while batting it

around with some buddies in the mess, and it was this: our response strategy was based on the assumption that the day the go order was given would be the day the outbreak first arrived in the United States. There was no margin for error built in. We'd always just assumed that the danger would become immediately obvious and we'd react right away. That means we assumed that our Critical Capabilities were still secure, and our Critical Requirements were still being met, on Day Zero.

Lawrence argued that this may not be the case. He suggested that the outbreak might not begin as we predicted with a large and visible attack, but it might instead creep up on us, taking us unawares simply because we didn't have eyes everywhere, and so he proposed a system of bellwethers to help us track the arrival and movement of the epidemic.

Our primary bellwethers were the big cities: LA, New York, Chicago, and so on. It was reasonable to assume that a US outbreak would begin in these cities simply because they were the primary ports of arrival from overseas, and – critically – any outbreaks in the cities would mark Day Zero of our nine day countdown. If we didn't trigger our response immediately we'd lose the opportunity, and risk a much higher casualty count than in our best case scenario.

The secondary bellwethers, on the other hand, were small cities and towns far from the usual international routes. We're talking rural conurbations in flyover country, towns more than fifty miles from international air hubs and seaports, that kind of thing. You know, self-contained, insular places that didn't get a whole lot of through traffic. Ensign Lawrence suggested that if the first outbreaks were reported in these secondary locations it would mean we'd completely missed the initial arrival of the infection, and that it may already be too late to trigger an effective response. We picked a handful of towns that fit our criteria and began to monitor all communications closely, including emergency bands, email, phone calls and social media.

Casper, Wyoming. Asheville, Tennessee. Mansfield, Pennsylvania...

"Lebanon, Missouri?"

That's right. Lebanon was our first bellwether to be triggered. We were scanning comms for a range of keywords when an alert was triggered on a call from Mercy Hospital to the CDC down in Atlanta. Some guy, a sales exec for GKN Aerospace who hadn't traveled further than Indianapolis in the last year, had gone nuts and violently attacked his wife in their home. The cops took out the husband at the scene, but the wife was admitted with bite injuries that presented with unusual symptoms. None of the usual strep or staph infections you'd expect from a human bite wound, but something that presented like unusually aggressive necrotizing fasciitis. They worried they might have a new strain on their hands, so they thought it was worth calling it in.

That call was all we needed to tell us we were too late. The CDC doc confirmed that they'd already received multiple reports of a similar infection over the previous week in various locations around the country. He told the doc in Lebanon to quarantine the patient, sit tight and wait for a callback, then he terminated the call.

It was only a couple of hours later that we received our first alert from the CDC. They had their own protocols for this kind of thing, and the reports they'd received had finally reached a critical mass, at which point they sent out a nationwide notice to local and regional hospitals as well as relevant government agencies to warn that we may be facing a potential epidemic.

The General leans back in his chair and sighs.

Game over. This thing had already outrun our capacity to control it before we'd even tied our bootlaces.

We still have no clue how the Lebanon vector was infected. We tracked his movements over the previous two weeks as best we could through social media, telephone records and credit card transactions, and our best guess is that he cheated on his wife while on a business trip to St. Louis a few days before the attack. Maybe a mistress, maybe a hooker, who knows? Maybe he didn't rubber up, or maybe he was into the rough stuff and she liked to bite and scratch. In any case it looks like she had a slow burn infection, and if she was a hooker who knows how many people she infected before she turned? Who knows how long it had been since she herself had been infected?

I don't suppose it really matters. All that matters is that by the time we were ready to implement CONPLAN 8888 the United States was already fatally compromised. The infection was in our streets. It was in our largest cities and our smallest towns. We simply didn't have the manpower or operational capacity to subdue it, and to top it all off we were in the middle of the impeachment proceedings, so nobody up at the top had the first clue who was supposed to be in charge.

You know how the rest of the story goes.

•▼•

The Disputed Territory of Ha Long Bay, Vietnam

With vast tracts of the Vietnamese mainland still overrun and perilous to traverse, my journey to the towering offshore limestone karsts of Ha Long Bay is only possible by sea plane, departing from the fortified city of Hong Kong almost four hundred miles to the east at the end of an exhausting hopscotch trek between sanctuary cities across the continent.

After three days of travel we finally approach Dau Go, an outlying island and home to the unofficial shanty capital of this fiercely disputed territory, and as we circle the tall, jungle topped island I spot the loose collection of makeshift huts built on what little level ground Dau Go has to offer, high above the gentle, turquoise water and protected by steep cliffs on all sides.

Independent travel is still all but impossible in the once welcoming tourist paradises of South East Asia, with each leg of any journey bound in red tape and closely observed by the authorities to ensure that new arrivals don't add to the population of stranded and stateless people the governments of the region universally describe as 'squatters'. My visa for this visit was only approved by the Department of Ethnic Minority Affairs in the new capital of Sa Pa because my interview subject, Karen Walker, has finally agreed to leave Dau Go along with a half dozen of her compatriots when I depart, to be repatriated to the US after several years of often tense negotiations. For this visit I have been officially designated a consular officer by the US Department of State.

Formerly Vietnam's most popular tourist attraction and a UNESCO World Heritage Site, before the crisis Ha Long Bay attracted almost three million foreign visitors each year to its two thousand islets and countless caves. Today the stunningly beautiful region is best known as the home of one of the world's most vocal and troublesome populations of 'Castaways', the self-chosen title for foreign nationals left stranded by their governments while overseas at the outset of the crisis.

Firm numbers are hard to come by, but it has been estimated that worldwide more than thirty million people were on vacation overseas on the day the UN ratified its controversial resolution on the repatriation of international tourists. Aside from those fortunate souls who found themselves stranded in safe zones precious few survived. The seven thousand Castaways still living on the towering karsts of Ha Long Bay consider themselves blessed in hindsight, though they still refer to the UN resolution as 'the Law of Unintended Consequences' after what transpired here.

For thirty minutes we wait, our sea plane bobbing gently on its pontoons, as Karen Walker descends the rope ladders from the heights of Dau Go and climbs into her small rowboat, and it's only as she finally draws near to the plane and tosses out a mooring rope that I notice the unusual design. From the sides of the boat protrude dozens of sharpened bamboo spears, each six feet long and tightly clustered so as to deny any approaching waterborne ghoul the opportunity to climb aboard. Karen pulls the mooring rope taut and extends a plank to one of the plane's pontoons, and she lets out a throaty laugh as I drop to my knees and inch nervously across to her.

The thirty one year old San Diego native has become something of a poster girl for her cause in recent years, arguing that the time has come to dissolve all nations and erase all borders. She claims that the crisis, while tragic, has presented humanity with a unique opportunity to pull together as one and finally draw an end to generations of inequality caused, she believes, by conflicting national interests.

While she has yet to win many converts in government – Vietnamese officials actively oppose her, regularly blocking her satellite signal to stop her pirate TV broadcasts – it's not difficult to understand why she enjoys such popularity among the people. Slim, toned and deeply tanned after years of living on the islands, Karen speaks on television with an infectious enthusiasm completely at odds with the serious, somber government broadcasts that form the standard diet of most official channels. As we row back to shore I find myself nodding along as she speaks.

Did you ever have one of those nightmares where your

parents left you at, like, a fairground or the store or something, and you just chased after them screaming at the top of your lungs as they drove away? Yeah, it was kinda like that, only there were thousands of us, our parents were on the other side of the world, we didn't speak the language and the nightmare was terrifyingly real.

Oh, and there were zombies trying to eat us.

Karen points to the calm waters at the foot of the island, where a handful of small fishing boats bob against a half collapsed wooden jetty before the steeply climbing cliffs.

We were right over there when it happened. See that little dock? That was where our cruise boat dropped us off. There were around fifty of us aboard, most of us Americans and Europeans, all of us keyed up and a little antsy, like we were playing a really high stakes drunk game of musical chairs. We'd all been reading the news. We all knew that countries were starting to close their borders and we were running out of time, but most of us had booked our trips months earlier, y'know? We figured this was our last chance to get out and see the world before it all went to hell.

That boat... *man*, it was like something out of *Caligula*. I mean, this wasn't just our last chance to get out and see the world. It was also our last chance to get out there and screw strange and interesting people, know what I'm saying? Once we got back to the mainland we knew we 'd all be on the next flight home, back to all the interchangeable Daves and Steves in Des Moines, Portland, Houston or wherever. This was our last chance to bang a Pablo from Santiago, or get eaten out by a Jean-

Pierre from Paris.

Ummm, sorry, that was probably a little too graphic. I'm just trying to say it felt like our last chance to be crazy kids out in the world, having new and exciting experiences. We knew things were bad back home. We'd heard about the food shortages and the recession, and we knew the world we'd be returning to would be pretty shitty. I was just nineteen, still a child in many ways, and I felt like I was in the last hour before bedtime, y'know, trying to squeeze in as much fun as I could before mom started pointing at her watch.

Anyway, it happened on the final day of our tour. We'd all woken up with epic hangovers, picked at the breakfast buffet – oh God, thinking about all that food we wasted still makes me sick to my stomach – and went for a quick dip in the ocean beside the boat before they called us back in and told us it was time to go to Dau Go Cave. That's what's at the top of those steps leading up from the jetty over there.

Looking back I know we should have figured out that something wasn't quite right. Maybe if we weren't all nursing killer headaches we would have started asking questions, but at the time we just went with it. They told us that everyone had to get off at Dau Go, all fifty of us. In the three days of the tour so far we'd stopped at four or five different places to swim, kayak, visit pearl farms or whatever, but the stops were always *optional*. We'd never been told one of them was *mandatory*.

And then they went to fetch this one guy from his cabin, this French kid, Florian, who was legit sick, not just hungover. He had some nasty stomach thing and he'd been throwing up since we left the harbor, but they wouldn't even let *him* stay on the boat, even though it was clear he could barely stand.

That's another thing. At every stop on the tour so far our guide, this skinny little Vietnamese guy, Toa'n, climbed off with us to show us around, but this time he stayed behind on the boat with this sad, puppy dog expression. I yelled back to him after we were all off, but he either didn't hear me or just refused to look me in the eye. The captain – I never caught his name, but he was an older guy who wore the same ratty string vest for the entire trip – just pointed at the steps and yelled out to us:

"*You go ap! You go ap stair to cave!*"

And that was it. That was the last we saw of the boat until we reached the top of the steps and caught a glimpse of it through the trees, steaming at full speed away from the island.

Of course we *still* didn't figure out they weren't coming back. How could we know? For all we knew they were just going to, I don't know, top up their fuel or pick up food and beer for dinner that night. We carried on into the cave like there was nothing wrong, leaving Florian propped against a rock with a bottle of water and strict orders to puke in the bushes rather than on the walkway.

I'd guess we were in the cave about an hour. It was really beautiful back then, before we started living in there and totally wrecked the place. It's enormous, maybe a hundred feet from floor to ceiling, with huge stalactites hanging down from the top, lit with colored lamps running off a few solar panels attached to the cliffs outside. It was like some kinda weird cartoon disco version of hell. *Tres* cool.

When we finally climbed back out to daylight Florian was nowhere to be seen apart from a pool of puke he'd left right in the middle of the path, and we figured he'd gone down the steps to get back on the boat.

And that's where we found him, sitting on the dock

with a pale face and a worried expression, surrounded by every last piece of our luggage that had been tossed onto the jetty before the boat left. All of our bags had burst open. They hadn't even been zipped closed before they were tossed, and there were clothes still floating by the jetty. I'm guessing there were also a few iPads and laptops resting on the sea bed, too.

"What did you think had happened?"

Ha, good question. We had no idea, but if I had to give you a description of the conversation for the rest of that day I'd say it was an impressive display of mild to moderate racism. And I'm not gonna claim I was exempt. I think I described the boat people as 'fucking cheating slopes', or something to that effect. There were also a lot of references to 'Charlie' and 'gooks' – these were north Vietnamese, remember, the communists we fought in the war. A few of the guys said we should have dropped the A bomb on this place when we had the chance.

I thought the answer was simple. We'd all paid for the tour upfront in cash, like idiots, so I figured this was just some shitty scam to get us to pay extra. I thought we'd sit around fuming for a couple of hours then an 'innocent' boat would come along to take us back to the mainland for $20 each or something. South East Asia used to be full of tourist scams like that, and to be honest I was more angry at myself than at the bastards on the boat. I thought I was a pretty savvy traveler, not the kind of person who'd fall for dumb shit like this.

I spent the next few hours mentally drafting the review I planned to leave on TripAdvisor. It was gonna be epic. Angry but funny, with just the right balance of righteous indignation and self deprecating jokes to go viral and win me an avalanche of likes and shares. By the time the sun started setting I was almost *glad* we'd been screwed. I figured I could dine out on this story for years. A few of the others had the same idea, and by the time it was dark we were all laughing about it. We lit a fire and started sharing around whatever snacks we could find in the bags. It felt like a good old fashioned camping trip.

The laughter stopped when we saw the body float into the bay, and heard the cries for help.

Karen stops talking as we reach the jetty, and as she helps me out of the boat and towards the first of the rope ladders leading up to the shanty town I notice a long row of crudely carved wooden crosses hammered between the planks of the dock. We both remain silent during the hot, humid climb to the jungle above, and Karen only begins to speak again once we're back under the cover of the canopy at the cliff edge, cooling ourselves with a cold drink of water. The cups are old plastic soda bottles cut in half.

They panicked. The Vietnamese, I mean. See, the UN had this thing called the *Convention Related to the Status of Refugees*. It was one of the old ones, ratified in 1951 before Vietnam became a member, so they'd never signed it, but when the new Secretary-General called an emergency meeting in New York virtually every country agreed to an amendment to reflect the developing situation.

What happened was the UN basically strong-armed the rest of the world by pushing through an update to one particular part of the convention that related to a legal principle called *non-refoulement*. In layman's terms it means that it's against international law to return a legitimate victim of persecution to his or her persecutor. It's the basic principle of all refugee law, and without it everything else falls apart.

What the new amendment said was that every overseas citizen of a nation in which there was a confirmed zombie presence – and by this point that was virtually *every* country – would become *de facto* refugees wherever they were in the world, entitled to housing, healthcare, food, legal representation... every right that refugees are usually afforded in civilized countries. In essence the living dead were classed as persecutors, and with a stroke of a pen it became illegal for any signatory nation to force people to return to their home nations if they had a legitimate fear of persecution. If the threat of being eaten alive isn't persecution I don't know what is.

What's more, the amendment wasn't subject to veto, and any nation that refused to sign would immediately lose all the benefits of UN membership. No emergency aid. No peacekeepers. No access to development funds. No nothing. Basically every country in the UN had two choices: either leave and go it alone at a time when everyone needed as much help as they could get, or accept the burden of a relatively small handful of refugees.

Vietnam signed, of course. They'd have been crazy not to, but they were smart enough to find a loophole. It was just a small clause in the Convention, something the UN forgot to amend in their rush to push it through. You'd miss it if you weren't looking, but the Vietnamese government was looking very carefully.

Here it is: a person could only become a refugee by *requesting* asylum. It wasn't enough to simply be in another country, you had to actually go to a police station or a government office and *ask* for asylum before it became official. Do you see where I'm going with this? Until tourists actually presented themselves officially their host countries had no obligation to offer them so much as a stick of gum.

Nobody knows how many were executed. Vietnam used to get about eight hundred thousand international tourists each month before the crisis, so let's say two hundred thousand were in-country on that particular day. Maybe half of those were Chinese, Laotian, and Cambodian – I heard most of those guys were handed a fistful of cash and shoved back across their borders unofficially – so let's say one hundred thousand were left who couldn't be so easily repatriated.

That's one hundred thousand people who needed to be clothed, housed and fed on the government dime, possibly for a very long time. One hundred thousand who suddenly had access to the kind of legal rights even many Vietnamese didn't have, but *only* if they asked for them. *Only* if they were allowed to get to a police station or a government office.

Now I don't really know the truth of what happened, so don't take this as gospel. All I know is what I heard on the grapevine, but from what I've been told the government quietly put a bounty of ten million Dong on the head of every foreigner in the country. That was a little less than $500 at the time, equivalent to three months of the minimum wage in Vietnam. They didn't make a big fuss about it. Nothing on paper, of course. They just got the word out to the tourist agencies, the hotels, hostels and guides. All people had to do was present a foreign passport to their local police station to claim their reward.

Hell, at least they didn't demand scalps.

"So the body you found in the water..."

Uh huh, we were the lucky ones. Our crew were at least kind enough to just dump us on one of the islands, take our passports from our luggage and head back to the mainland. I don't know if they hoped we'd be able to survive out here or if they were just too squeamish to kill us and decided to let starvation do the job for them, but... I don't know. I don't suppose it matters anymore. They're probably all dead now anyhow.

The body in the water was a young guy around my age, maybe late teens, early twenties. He was... sorry, thinking about it always makes me... He'd been shot in the mouth at close range with a flare gun. It was just one of those small pistols, barely enough force in the projectile to do any real damage, but they'd shot him right in the damned mouth. He was all burned up inside. Black lips and nose, and his throat had collapsed. I just hope he died right away. I hope he didn't have to drown after they pushed him into the water.

As soon as we saw the body someone in our group screamed, and that's when we started to hear yelling from out in the bay. We couldn't see much in the dark, but as they drifted closer I picked out this bright orange shape bobbing up and down in the water. I yelled back to them and jumped in, as far away from the floating body as I could get, and swam out to them.

It was a bunch of tourists, eight or nine of them, all clinging to a bunch of life jackets and trying to stay afloat. A few more from my group swam out, and after a half hour of thrashing about in the water we managed to pull them back to the dock. They were exhausted, close to death. They'd been out on the water since the morning.

It turns out they were from the same boat as the dead

kid. There had been about forty people on their boat, and the captain had ordered them all off at gunpoint out on the open water. The kid who got shot had apparently tried to rush the captain with another couple of guys. It obviously hadn't worked out. Everyone else jumped overboard as the captain reloaded.

Later that night a few more bedraggled floaters showed up one by one, barely alive and desperate for water, and each time we swam out to drag them back to shore. By the morning the living stopped coming, but over the next few days more and more bodies started to float into the bay. Some of them the new arrivals recognized from their boat, but many others were strangers. We counted over a hundred dead by the time they finally stopped floating in.

As far as we could tell most hadn't been murdered. Most of them looked like they'd just slipped away after a couple of days floating under the sun, bobbing up and down in their life jackets, sunburned as hell from the neck up and pruned as hell from the neck down, like your skin gets after a long bath.

We didn't know what to do with the bodies, so we just piled them up on the jetty. Back then we didn't even know why we'd been abandoned. We didn't learn the truth until months later, when the Vietnamese started to flee the mainland. Every day we waited for rescue, and every day it failed to come.

It was a week before we finally burned the dead for fear that they'd pass on some kind of disease to the rest of us. It felt wrong – we still expected a rescue boat would arrive the moment we set them alight, and we'd all end up in jail – but we finally agreed it had to be done.

We were lucky. Up at the cave there was fresh water, and some of the guys in our group were avid climbers.

They managed to make it to the top of the cliffs and find a few things to eat in the jungle, mostly nuts and a few berries. Barely enough for us to survive, but better than nothing.

I think it was about a week before another boat finally arrived, but it wasn't quite what we were expecting. It was a tiny little wooden rowboat that was taking on water almost as quickly as the two passengers could bail it out. As it appeared in the bay we saw they were white, two young Scandinavian guys, and they had something piled up at the bottom of their boat. Four dead monkeys.

It turned out these guys had been stranded with another small group of about a dozen on Hon Chan Voi, the next island about a half mile to the south of us. Over there they had plenty of food – the island was crawling with macaques – but their only fresh water was a muddy pool of rainwater at the peak. The monkeys didn't seem to mind, but the Scandi guys couldn't drink it.

That was our first trade. Four scrawny, sinewy little monkeys for six gallons of fresh water. We helped patch up their boat and sent them back with their water in beer and soda bottles, and a few days later they returned with more monkeys. I wouldn't recommend them, by the way. There's not much meat on a macaque, and they're aggressive at the best of times. When you try to kill them they fight dirty. One girl I know lost an eye.

Over the next couple of weeks another couple of groups showed up, each of them from other nearby islands. One had found an old abandoned boat and the other had lashed together a crude raft from driftwood, but they both came with things we needed. The first group had a bunch of medicine – antibiotics, aspirin and Imodium for Florian, who was still suffering – and the second group not only came with fish but also traded us some lines and hooks they'd made from vines and a few broken keyrings. We ate like royalty after that.

It was kinda weird. We were all still confused and terrified, but after a few weeks most of us had somehow begun to adjust to this new life. We fished in the bay, collected water from the cave, foraged for berries in the jungle and barbecued macaques over the roaring fire we built every night. Nobody ever said it out loud, but I think most of us were actually beginning to enjoy ourselves. It was like the first few chapters of *Lord of the Flies*, when the kids were just having fun before everything went to hell.

We just felt *free*, y'know? Like all the worries of the world were far away, like we couldn't be touched. We were all concerned about our families back home, of course, but I think most of us accepted the fact that there was nothing we could do to help them, and nothing they could do to help us. We just... went with the flow. And look around you. If you were gonna be stranded anywhere in the world can you imagine a better place? Beautiful weather, fresh water, plentiful food and, back then, a bunch of highly sexed twenty-somethings who were just discovering themselves. It was like that old movie, *The Beach*. I'm just amazed nobody got pregnant in those first few weeks.

We lived like that for maybe two months before we realized our paradise wouldn't last.

I was swimming out in the bay one morning, a couple hundred yards out towards the mouth of the bay, where the water was almost shallow enough to touch the bottom with my toes. I'd been out around an hour and I was thinking about swimming back to the dock when I heard a yell behind me, and I looked back to see one of the Scandi guys waving frantically from his boat as it turned in to the bay, shouting at me with this weird, panicked look in his eyes, but he was still too far away to make out what he was yelling.

The boat was low in the water, overloaded with seven or eight people, and water was pouring over the sides faster than they could bail it out, but they turned towards me and started paddling as fast as they could, and finally I managed to make out what the guy was yelling.

Karen shivers despite the oppressive heat.

I'll never forget it until the day I die. The Scandi guy was jabbing a finger towards the water and yelling at the top of his lungs, and finally I made out the words.

"Get out of the water! They're under the water!"

Every muscle in my body froze up as soon as the words filtered through my mind. Without thinking I pulled my arms and legs in close to my body, and seconds later my head went under the water as I began to sink. I panicked, breathing out all my air, and that made me sink even quicker, and just as my toes touched the soft sand I opened my eyes. If I had any breath left I would have screamed.

They were all around me, about half a dozen of them just standing there on the seabed, waving back and forth in the current like kelp. I only caught a glimpse of them for a moment before I thrashed back to the surface, but I'll never forget the way they were all turned in my direction, at least five of them, their arms outstretched towards me and their mouths wide open. The closest was only a few feet away.

The second my head broke the surface I let out a scream that left me without a voice for the next four days. My mind just shut down completely. My body was running on autopilot as I thrashed my arms and legs about and pushed myself towards the boat, and thankfully I only had about ten yards to swim. Any more and I know I would have gone under again, and I wouldn't have come back up.

The guys dragged me aboard just as I felt something brush against my thigh. I don't remember much, but I know one of them gave me a sharp slap in the face to stop me from capsizing the boat as I thrashed around. I went limp and let them pull me in, and I lay there staring up at the sun as they ran their hands over my body to check for bites or scratches. I was certain they'd find something, and instead of taking me to land they'd push me back over the side and leave me to become one of those *things*, standing beneath the surface and reaching out for anything that came close enough to grab.

It was a half hour before I came to my senses. I came to at the back of the dock, as far from the water as they could drag me, and when my vision stopped swimming and I became aware of what was going on I looked around and realized the dock was full. The guys had pulled the boat from the water and set about plugging the holes, and the girls were telling everyone what had happened on their island between sobs.

One of the girls had gone swimming, they told us, over to the other side of their island where they hunted the macaques. When she was halfway across the bay she'd let out a scream loud enough for everyone on the island to hear. They all reached the beach in time to see her thrash back to shore, and she'd collapsed in the sand screaming about something biting her under the water. Nobody really believed her – apparently she had a reputation as a drama queen – until they noticed the wound on her ankle. A bite mark.

This had happened two weeks earlier. They hadn't

dared tell us. They didn't want to tell us that she'd turned quickly after the infection burned through her, or that they'd left her wandering down at their beach while they hid further up the cliffs. They were terrified that we'd be afraid of them, that we'd think *they* were infected, that we'd forbid them from trading their macaques for our water.

The final straw had come when someone – some*thing* – else climbed out of the water and onto their beach, and then another, and another. There were eight of them in the end, shambling aimlessly in the surf or slowly chasing the macaques that danced around them, and with their fresh water supplies running out the group decided they couldn't stay any longer. They climbed down to their boat, jumped on board and rowed to us as fast as they could.

That was the day we started to weave the rope ladders that would bring us up here, high above the water where we knew we'd be safe, and we've been up here ever since. God, though... I remember all those days I spent floating out in the bay, and all the nights I spent sleeping out on the dock. Just the thought that something could have reached up and grabbed me as I...

Oh, speak of the devil.

Karen points down to the dock far below, where a tiny figure reaches up from the water and grasps at a wooden pile. From this distance it's difficult to make out the details, but it looks like a naked Asian woman, the flesh on her arms sloughed away almost to the bone.

I don't know how they're still coming after all these years. Crazy, isn't it?

I watch as a figure – a living, human figure – emerges from the trees at the back of the dock, strides towards the creature still struggling to gain purchase on the slick, slippery wood, and calmly slides a spear through the eye socket. The arms lose their grip on the dock, and as the spear wielder tugs the weapon back the body slips gently beneath the surface. Karen sighs glumly.

You know, I really miss swimming.

●▼●

::: 11 :::

Barcelona, Spain

Even though it has been almost five years since he produced his last video, Gregg Mikolasek is still regularly approached with a combination of awe and gushing praise by fans in his adoptive home of Barcelona. As we find a table outside a bustling bar on a cobbled side street in the trendy neighborhood of Gracia an inebriated patron does a double take, taps his friend on the arm and yells at the top of his voice the word "*utok!*" This translates in Mikolasek's native Czech as 'attack', the war cry peppered throughout all of his videos. Mikolasek takes this moment of recognition with good grace, nodding politely to the beaming drunk.

As sporadic outbreaks cast a long shadow over the European continent the typical response was fear and panic. One by one the cities emptied, and those few that remained populated survived only with a degree of militarization not seen since the darkest days of WWII. Curfews were strictly enforced, and even during daylight hours those who could not escape stayed locked in their homes as much as possible, withdrawing as best they could from public life in the hope that their fragile sanctuaries might protect them from the coming storm. It was under this gloomy, oppressive atmosphere that Mikolasek decided to fight back.

The three time EPF (European Parkour

Federation) champion, avid BASE jumper, martial arts enthusiast and self-confessed adrenaline junkie found himself trapped in the center of Prague as the city fell, armed with nothing but a helmet mounted GoPro camera and his *sibat*, a sharpened bamboo staff he used to teach a Filipino martial arts class in a community hall close to Petrske Square.

While most sensible people would have opted for the quickest and safest route from the city, Mikolasek chose a different path. Wielding his *sibat* he took to the roofs of Prague's Old Town, free running a winding, death-defying path through the city, often descending to street level to violently – and acrobatically – attack the undead whenever the opportunity arose for a spectacular kill.

By the time he finally left the city he had made almost two hundred kills and saved dozens of lives, and every moment of it was recorded in crisp high definition by his GoPro. Within a week of uploading it to YouTube the hour long video had been viewed over two hundred million times, turning Mikolasek into an overnight sensation and a beacon of hope for the terrified citizens of Europe.

While many have since attempted to copy Mikolasek's hyper-violent POV style, likened by critics to Ilya Naishuller's groundbreaking first person science fiction movie *Hardcore Henry,* none have attracted anything close to the same degree of adoration or acclaim.

I wasn't bullied as a kid. I just want to get that out of

the way.

That's what you want to hear, right? Every journalist I've ever met seems desperate to find some cheap pop psychology angle that explains why I took those risks. They want me to tell them I was a skinny little nerd in school, and that when I saw those zombies attacking people I couldn't stop myself from standing up for them. That I subconsciously saw in them every kid who ever beat on me when I was at my weakest, and it made me do something crazy. I'm right, aren't I?

Mikolasek shakes his head.

Sorry, I wish I could help you, but I can't make it that easy for you to win your Pulitzer.

No, I was never bullied. My father didn't beat me, my mother wasn't cold and distant, and as far as I can tell there were no unresolved traumas I was working through by killing the undead. I wasn't even trying to bring hope to the people, to show them we could fight back and we didn't have to be afraid. Not at first, at least.

No, the truth is simple. I killed those things because I enjoyed it. I was looking for the rush. It was just fun to throw myself into the middle of the swarm and see if I had the skills and reflexes to survive. Maybe you can find a psychologist who can tell you what makes me tick, but as far as I'm concerned there's nothing all that complicated about it. I'm just hooked on adrenaline.

When I uploaded the Prague video I wasn't really expecting anything. There were already thousands of hours of footage online by then, everything from TV news reports to amateur video of towns and cities being overrun, and there was no reason to think my dumb movie would attract any more attention than the others.

In fact, I didn't even see the hit count for the first couple of weeks because the generators at the refugee camp in Klatovy were running low on fuel and they stopped letting people charge their phones, and in any case I had more important things to worry about. I was busy trying to find out if my parents and sister had made it out of Prague, so any computer time I got was spent searching the survivor lists the government had compiled from the other camps around the country.

They were OK, thank God. As soon as he heard about the outbreak Dad had taken them across the border to my aunt's place in Dresden, and after a week of waiting I finally found a bus heading up in that direction with a spare seat. When I reached the city my sister picked me up at Bruhlschen Garten, and the first thing she said, before she even hugged me, was "Dad's gonna *kill* you." She refused to tell me what she meant, and after she drove me home she just stood there grinning as I opened the door and saw who was waiting for me.

Dad's face was white. He looked liked he'd aged a decade since I'd last seen him. He was shaking like a leaf as he grabbed me in a huge bear hug, and then he pulled away and shook me by the shoulders before hugging me again. "What the hell were you *thinking*, boy? You think you're some kind of fucking *superhero?* You could have been *killed!*" That's when I noticed the open laptop on the coffee table, and the guy sitting awkwardly beside my mom looking like he wanted the ground to open up and swallow him.

I don't know how, but the guys at GoPro had found my parents even before I had. They'd been trying to hunt me down through social media ever since the video hit a hundred million views, but because I hadn't logged in anywhere since I uploaded it they started reaching out to my family and friends. Finally they found my aunt in Dresden, learned that my parents were with her and showed them the video.

I guess they expected them to be impressed, but they misjudged that to say the least. Mom wasn't so bad but Dad had never really approved of my parkour, and he *hated* the BASE jumping, so the idea of me free running through a city full of zombies was almost enough to give him a stroke.

I had to send him out of the room when the guy made his offer. GoPro wanted to sponsor me to make another video, in Paris this time. There had already been a few small outbreaks on the outskirts around Choissy le Roi and Thiais, so everyone expected it to be the next city to go. GoPro wanted to be on the ground when the city fell, filming it from every angle with helmet cams and drones positioned all around the city.

I won't pretend to understand why they thought this would help market the brand, or even why people still gave a shit about marketing while the world was going to hell, but the guy sold it to me by explaining that my video was giving people hope. He said that all people were seeing on the TV news were casualty counts and reports of more and more towns and cities being overrun; crisis meetings between heads of state that collapsed into chaos because nobody could agree on a way forward. There was nothing out there but misery and despair, nothing to suggest that we could even survive this as a species. All the news was offering was a countdown to our own deaths.

My video offered people another perspective, he said. It made the crisis seem survivable when people saw one guy on his own taking out zombies left and right armed with nothing but a bamboo stick. It turned the zombies into a... well, not a *joke*, exactly, but I think he put it pretty well when he said that the most terrifying monsters were those that live in our imagination. He said that my video helped people look under their bed and see the monsters for what they really *were*, not what they imagined them to be. These weren't superhuman terrors, and they weren't indestructible. We just needed to be badasses to beat them. Then he said that videos like mine would lead to a revolution in Europe, one built on hope rather than fear, and that he wanted it to be remembered as the GoPro revolution.

I still wasn't completely convinced, but then the guy sweetened the deal. On top of the money he promised to pay me – more for a few days of work than I'd ever earned in a year – he told me that if I agreed to make the video GoPro would make sure that me, my parents, my sister and even my aunt got safe passage to Barcelona, which back then was the only really secure sanctuary city on the continent. The Spanish government had closed the entire region a month earlier, and entry permits were changing hands on the black market for two hundred thousand Euros per person.

With that offer on the table it was a no brainer. Even dad grudgingly came around to the idea. I wouldn't say he was happy about it, but we all knew the future wasn't bright for a poor family of Czech refugees now that the EU was collapsing and most countries were moving back to an every man for himself mindset. He knew we'd end up rotting in a camp somewhere if we couldn't find a way out, and... well, I'm sure you know how bad it got at some of those camps. Klatovy was already a mess when I left it, and I'd do anything to avoid seeing my family abandoned there, or somewhere even worse.

"Did you know that the French government had denied GoPro a permit to film in Paris?"

Not when I agreed to do it, no, but I wouldn't have cared if they'd told me. Most parkour videos were already filmed without permits. Besides, BASE jumping was illegal in Paris anyway, as was carrying a weapon like a *sibat*, so I already figured we weren't exactly checking all the legal boxes, you know? I just didn't realize exactly how big a risk we were taking just by being in the city.

Five of us – me, the video director and three drone pilots – spent a week camped out at the Pullman Hotel a block from the Eiffel Tower while the techs moved the drones to their starting positions and I mapped out my route. We'd booked a room but we found the hotel closed when we arrived, so we just broke in through a service entrance and set ourselves up in a suite on the top floor, raiding the mini bar and watching the dead arrive in the street below. There were only a few at first, each of them chased down by the cops and quickly killed as soon as they were reported – the cops in Paris had gotten pretty good at armed assaults after all the terrorist attacks they'd suffered – but as time went on more and more of the locals left, the groups of the dead started to grow larger, and the sirens sounded more and more distant as the cops were dragged in every direction and the infection spread. We started to feel pretty damn lonely up there in the empty hotel.

We weren't all that worried about the zombies. We'd blocked the staircases leading to our floor so there was little danger of being caught by surprise, but on the fifth day the radio started reporting that the Rive Gauche was being evacuated in preparation for a 'sweep and clear' mission. They weren't clear on what that meant, but they suggested the government hadn't ruled out the idea of using napalm or gas to clear the streets. Maybe it was just a crazy rumor, but it was enough to keep me awake at night. That and the air raid sirens that kicked in every couple of hours, for some reason.

That was enough for me. My nerves were shot, and after seven nights of waiting I decided it was now or never. Our plan had been to wait for the swarms to grow thicker at the foot of the Eiffel Tower – we didn't want any 'dead air', where I'd be running through the city without any zombies in the shot – but I hadn't slept more than an hour a night for the last week and I knew that if we waited any longer I'd lose my nerve.

The cameras were all set up and we had the drones fully charged, so I made the call and we all left the hotel room just after dark when the streets looked clear. The director made off in the direction of the Seine to make sure our powerboat was still where we'd left it, and the pilots crossed the river to move within remote transmission range of their drones.

It took a couple of hours for me to reach the top of the tower. The tourist staircase was still open, which took me to around the halfway point, but beyond that the emergency stairs had been completely blocked off, and of course the elevator to the top had no power. I had to solo climb the rest of the way. It was simple enough, but still a little tricky in the dark while carrying gear that could easily snag on the tower's frame. My God, though, it was worth the effort.

I'm sure you've seen the video, but only a fraction of the experience comes across on the screen, even in crystal clear HD. It was an *unbelievable* sight. Paris was dark, as if we'd traveled back in time to before civilization, and the moonlight seemed to turn the Seine into a silver ribbon, splitting the city in two. The only light in the foreground was from the fires that raged out of control, dozens of them in every arrondissement. In the distance the skyscrapers at La Defense stood like a beacon, the only buildings that still had power anywhere in sight. They looked inviting, a safe haven beyond the chaos, and for a moment I even considered changing my route and heading in that direction.

Of course I had no way of knowing that La Defense was the most dangerous place in the city. I didn't know about the plan to lure the dead into the north tower of the *Société Générale* buildings, and I had no clue what was happening when they blew the charges and brought the tower down. I caught every moment of it on film, though. It was beautiful, like the final scene of Fight Club, you know? Would have looked even better with the Pixies playing in the background.

Sorry, I don't want to come across as a dick. It was only much later that I learned that it had gone badly wrong; that they'd set the charges in too much of a hurry, and that instead of falling neatly into its own footprint the building had collapsed into the base of the south tower and destroyed the staircases. They still don't know how many civilians were trapped on the high floors for the three days it took before the building finally came down. Ten thousand, at least, but I know some have said it was closer to thirty.

La Defense, of course, was just a distant backdrop in my video. While I waited for the dawn I was more focused on the glowing line of fire that ran for a mile all the way down the Avenue des Champs-Élysées. I called one of the pilots and asked him to fly a drone to the area, and what I saw horrified me.

There were teams of soldiers burning bodies in huge

pyres, hundreds of them in each one, with maybe half a dozen men around each pile firing jets of flame on them from tanks on their backs, but as the drone flew closer it became clear that the bodies weren't... well, they weren't *dead*. They were writhing as they struggled to escape, only held back by the jets of fire. Our drone hovered over the street for more than an hour before the battery started to die, but in the final few minutes we caught footage that almost made us call off the video and just run.

We decided it was too disturbing to include it in the final cut of the video, but we watched as one of the men got some kind of blockage in his flamethrower. As soon as the jet of flame stopped the pile of bodies he was firing on began to tumble towards him. It was hard to make out the details in the fire, but you could see people – *dozens* of them – stand up and start to walk towards the man, their flesh still burning. He tried to run but he could barely move in his bulky silver fireproof suit. He looked like an astronaut walking on the moon, taking long, slow steps that couldn't outpace the zombies chasing him. When they piled on top of him and tore off his hood... *Jesus*. What a way to die. You wouldn't wish it on your worst enemy.

It all went to hell in a few seconds. It was just... everyone panicked. I think they'd assumed it would be much easier to destroy these things with fire, so they were already on edge after watching them burn for so long without dying. Seeing their buddy die was the final straw, I guess. A few of them started to run, and those they left behind couldn't keep the undead corralled in their pyres. It was a fucking *mess*. Hundreds of burning zombies, some of them little more than bone and charred flesh – Christ knows how they could still walk – roaming around the street, attacking from all directions.

The drone caught a horrifying but beautiful shot of the men panicking and firing their flamethrowers at random. We got a bird's eye view of jets of fire blazing across the Champs-Élysées, crossing each other, bursting against walls, and the dead closing in on the living faster than they could run.

That's when the drone battery died. I have no idea if any of the men survived.

The drunk at the other table calls out cheerfully once again, but this time Mikolasek ignores him.

I didn't really want to shoot the video after that. All the fun had been sucked out of it. If it hadn't been for the promise to get my family to Barcelona I would have quit there and then, but I managed to keep my cool for their sake.

We started shooting just as the sun rose over Notre Dame. We got a beautiful shot of the dawn from the top of the tower. Columns of smoke were still rising from La Defense and Champs-Élysées, a morning mist covered the ground as far as the eye could see, and far below me a small swarm of about thirty were standing around on the Champs de Mars, just staring into space, their arms hanging by their sides. They all turned to stare up at me as I yelled down to them: *Uuuuuutooooook!*

It's almost impossible to properly control a BASE jump. The canopy opens too low to steer with any accuracy so it's more luck than anything, but I came down *perfectly*, right in the middle of the swarm. The chute itself covered five of them as I unclipped and dealt with the rest. I couldn't have planned it better if I tried, and once I was in the middle of that swarm all my nerves vanished. I forgot about everything else and just got on with the job. I turned to the north, crossed the Seine, found the small backstreets and climbed up to the rooftops to begin my run, just me and my *sibat*.

It was three hours before I reached the river again at the old love lock bridge, the Pont des Arts, after my slide down the Pyramide du Louvre. Remember that final shot? A swarm of a couple of hundred were closing in on me from both sides of the bridge, and I dove into the Seine beside the boat moments before they all came tipping over the edge after me. I *swear* that wasn't planned. One of them got so close he took a bite out of my boot. I was sure I'd been infected. The moment I was in the boat I stripped down to my underwear and insisted the director check every inch of me for bites or scratches.

Three hundred and twenty seven confirmed kills in three hours. As soon as the boat left the city I swore to myself I'd never shoot another video as long as I lived.

"So what changed? What made you shoot a dozen more?"

Barcelona. It was the people here. Since Prague I'd been isolated from regular people, first in the Klatovy refugee camp and then in Paris. It had been six weeks since I'd shot my first video, and at that time I'd seen nothing but fear and resignation in the faces of everyone I met. When we finally arrived in Barcelona, though, I found something else. *Hope*. These people weren't willing to lay down and die. They were eager to stand and fight, and as soon as they realized who I was they... well, they turned me into some kind of folk hero.

It was *crazy*. I had people knocking on my door at all hours of the day, begging me to teach them how to use the *sibat.* I had kids telling me they wanted to be just like me when they grew up, a real zombie killer. I had local business owners begging me to show up at their restaurant or bar for a special appearance, and girls throwing themselves at me every time I left my apartment. I felt like a rock star.

When the infection finally reached the outskirts of the city it felt like I didn't really have a choice. Every time I opened my front door there'd be a dozen people waiting for me there. "When are you leaving for the barricade? Can I come with you? Can I be in your next video?" I didn't really want to do it, but... well, I didn't want to stop feeling this way, you know? I *liked* being a hero, and I liked that other people felt like heroes when they were around me. I don't know why they did. I just know they felt brave when they stood beside me. They felt like they could win this, and... I don't know, it just felt *good*, you know?

A few tables from us the drunk raises himself from his chair, knocking over a glass as he stumbles backwards a few steps. When he finally finds his footing he advances on our table, and I brace myself for trouble as he pulls off his jacket. I grab my beer protectively as he looms over our table, and with a sudden movement he pulls up the sleeve of his t-shirt, thrusts his arm in my host's face and grins.

I can just make out the crude, home-drawn tattoo on the drunk's fleshy bicep. It reads *Ejercito de Mikolasek* – 'Army of Mikolasek' – over a skull and a pair of crossed *sibats*.

"Utok," he slurs, breaking into a broad grin and holding his arms wide.

Mikolasek shoots me an embarrassed glance, then smiles back at the drunk and pulls him in for a bear hug. "Utok, kamarade. Utok."

•⁊•

Black Creek, Vancouver Island, Canada

As my ferry approaches the dock I see Officer Rafael Valenzuela waiting at the edge, his shoulders hunched against the driving rain. He clumsily catches the mooring rope and helps tie it to the cleat, and then patiently waits as two dozen visitors file off the small boat ahead of me.

A young cop fresh from the academy at the beginning of the crisis, Valenzuela is still boyishly handsome in his navy blue NYPD jacket and peaked cap, both meticulously clean and well-kept even after so many years. At first he insists the uniform is intended only to protect him from the weather, though as we take a seat at a covered bench overlooking the water he admits that he rarely gets the opportunity to wear the traditional uniform since the department was disbanded. "It's nice to give the old girl an airing every once in a while," he grins sheepishly.

Only two aspects of Valenzuela's jacket are non-standard. The first is the Medal for Valor and Police Combat Cross pinned above the shield on his left breast, both medals awarded – in all but three cases posthumously – to every officer in the NYPD's 10th Precinct. The second is the empty right sleeve, rolled up and pinned at the shoulder to keep it from flapping in the wind. Like almost everyone else at Black Creek, the largest remaining police rehabilitation and convalescent center in North America, Valenzuela carries the physical scars of the war. "I'm a twofer," he chuckles as he tugs up the hem of his trousers to show me his prosthetic left leg.

While Valenzuela is physically and emotionally healthy enough to serve as a volunteer counselor at the center, many here aren't so fortunate. Some are confined to wheelchairs or their beds for want of prostheses and qualified physiotherapists, and Black Creek lacks a single mental health professional of any kind. Valenzuela makes no secret of his frustration about the constant lobbying required simply to keep the center open, and he has a few choice words to say about the fact that the rehabilitation of former cops has been judged a low budgetary priority.

"Even after all that happened we're still short changing those who served," he sighs.

I'll always remember something one of my instructors said back at the academy, in the middle of some seminar about community policing or... I don't know, something like that. It really stuck with me, and I couldn't help but think about it when everything started to go bad. I remember it like it was yesterday. This old captain held up his shield at the front of the class, and he asked us to tell him what it was. A couple of hands went up, and he started pointing to people.

"It's your badge," one kid said. The captain shook his head.

"A City of New York Police Captain shield?" suggested someone else. The captain shook his head again.

"No," he said, and he tossed it on the table in front of him with a clatter. "You wanna know what it is? It's three ounces of nickel. Nothing more, nothing less. I could melt it down right now and sell it for eighty two cents on the scrap metal market. Not even enough to buy a bad cup of coffee."

He looked around the class, meeting the eyes of each and every one of us. "The only value this shield carries is that which is given to it by the people you serve. Not the department. Not the government. Not your buddies on the force, but the *people*." Then he slapped a chart up on the overhead projector that showed the population of New York against the strength of the NYPD. Eight and a half million people versus just thirty five thousand uniformed cops.

"For every one of you kids about to step out on the street in your smart new uniforms there are two hundred fifty New Yorkers, and the only thing that separates you from them are these three ounces of nickel. You're out there, exposed and vulnerable, and when push comes to shove it's not the gun in your holster that'll protect you. It's your shield, and it's only as big as those people think it is."

See, he was trying to teach us that we policed by *consent*, not force. *That's* where our power really came from. We only had authority because the public *allowed* us to have it, and without it we were just a bunch of assholes in costume, know what I mean?

That lesson stuck with me a long time, but it was only during the first days of the collapse that I finally understood just how thin the blue line really was, when Governor Ross issued that executive order banning price gouging after the Prez refused to do it nationwide. Looking back it's obvious the law was completely unenforceable, and it was a dumb idea to tell people to report infractions to the cops, but we did our best to keep the peace all the same. Most of the time we only had to walk into a store and wag a finger before the cheating bastards took the hint, and for the first week or so it went pretty smooth.

The problems started when the store owners finally realized we weren't willing to do much more than issue a warning. I mean seriously, tell me, what else were we supposed to do? Some guy decides to jack up the price of a gallon of milk in his bodega to $10, he refuses to play ball when we go in to have a friendly chat, and then what? What are we gonna do? Are we gonna book the guy? Are we gonna process him, toss him in a cell that's already overcrowded with real crooks? Put a uniform on his door to make sure he doesn't get looted while he's away? Send him to face charges in a crippled court because half the judges have decided to get out of the city? Hell, no! We had honest to God crimes to deal with. We couldn't waste our time playing stock boys, checking price tags all day.

That was it. We didn't realize it at the time, but that was the moment the little snowball started rolling down the mountain, and if we'd known better we might have been more prepared for the avalanche. As soon as the store owners figured out that we wouldn't do shit they started gouging like crazy. I saw one guy in Hell's Kitchen charge $20 for a loaf of bread. Another decided to start selling toilet paper at $5 a roll. The gas stations in midtown started advertising a gallon of gas at $10, so of course the cab drivers raised their fares from $2.50 a mile to $12.

And now we've got a whole new nightmare to deal with. Now we've got people who can't afford to get to work because the cab ride there and back costs them more than a day's wage. Now we've got tens of thousands more hungry, tired, late, incredibly pissed off New Yorkers squeezing onto the subway every morning, and let me tell you they weren't all that fuckin' cheerful at the best of times. Now we've got people reporting cabbies day and night, and nobody at the TLC picks up the phone because they don't wanna deal with the headache. They can't strip the offenders of their medallions because if they tried that there wouldn't be a single driver left in the city, and we can't arrest them all because where the hell would we put them?

And then it got even worse. People started intercepting produce trucks outside the city and buying up their cargo for cash, bringing it into the city and selling it on with a 500% markup. Stores stopped accepting plastic when the machines started to get flaky – I don't know why, maybe the guys at AmEx stopped showing up for work – so there was a run on the banks, then after a few more days they stopped taking cash altogether and switched to barter. Now you've got millions of people who can't feed their kids because they didn't think to stock up on gold Krugerrands, and they don't think it's right to trade grandma's Tiffany engagement ring for a marble rye and a four pack of Charmin Ultra Soft.

You can see the big problem, right? See, the city was a *machine*. It was made up of a million moving parts that all had to fit together perfectly or the whole thing would grind to a halt, and *we* were the oil that kept things running smoothly. As soon as people finally figured out that the cops were just as powerless as everyone else it all started to turn bad, quick. Our shields felt a little lighter each morning. People showed us just a little less respect than they had the day before, and eventually they stopped coming to us at all.

Now that's not to say the city was lawless. We could still arrest people. We could still slap on a pair of cuffs if we actually caught a punk robbing a store or mugging some poor guy, but that's about as far as our power went. We had no way to force people to obey all the little unwritten laws, the unnoticed social niceties that keep a city humming over, and when it comes down to it that had always been our most important job, even though most people never realized it. The job of a cop is simply to *be* a cop; to be visible; to remind people to be good when their own conscience isn't quite enough.

Nobody respects the supply teacher, and that's what we'd become, so people turned their backs on us and instead started looking for protection from the neighborhood watch groups. That was what they called themselves, but they were really just gangs of vigilantes who started staking out their territories, protecting their little piece of the city, and most of those guys didn't play nice. They didn't bother with cuffs and jail cells, and they didn't rely on evidence to make their judgments. They just acted, and we'd find the results bleeding out on a street corner the next morning.

From start to finish it took less than two weeks for the entire system to break down, and this was before the Zees had even arrived. The rest of the country was soldiering on a little better according to the nightly news, but by the time the attacks hit New York we were barely even a city any more. We was just a mass of little self-contained districts, maybe a block or two each, just as much as a few families could defend, bordered by roadblocks built from cars and old furniture. Cops couldn't even get inside most of them without permission, and most people were happy for us to stay on the outside.

And I *got* it, man, I really did. I knew all this was crazy illegal but I understood what was driving people to pull back and defend their space. I lived in Jackson Heights at 83rd and Roosevelt, you know, right by the 7, in one of the blocks so close to the tracks you could hear the sound of the trains even in your sleep, and a few guys had blocked off my own neighborhood. We had three blocks, a pharmacy, a few little bodegas, a Mi Tierra supermarket and maybe fifty families behind our barricades. All known quantities, know what I mean? Good people. No strangers. Nobody who'd cheat a neighbor.

If the rest of the city went to shit we knew we could at least protect our own little piece of it. We could *control* it, understand? And that's what it came down to, in the end. When everything else stopped working we all realized we had to look out for our own, and when your neighbor's *abuela* runs out of her heart medicine you go down to the Rite Aid and you fucking take it. I don't care what the law says, you take the damned medicine, even if it means breaking a window.

I spent a lot of time looking the other way towards the end. I mean, I was still a cop. I still put on the uniform, went to work and did the best I could to keep the worst of it under control. If I caught someone beating on a guy or – God forbid – trying to rape or kill someone I'd shut that shit down and throw them in a cell, but I wasn't about to bust a guy for trying to feed his kids or get hold of some insulin. When things got bad I had to ask myself what it really meant to serve my community, and I decided it didn't mean locking people up for just trying to survive.

Not everyone stayed in uniform, of course. I don't blame them, I really don't, but towards the end a lot of cops left the city, and a lot more laid down their badges and went over the barricades. Maybe some of them had family over there, I don't know. Maybe they just figured they weren't doing any good on our side any more. Maybe they thought it was better to help defend just one little corner of the city rather than try to save the whole thing. Who knows, maybe they were right.

Valenzuela shifts uncomfortably in his seat, looks down at the shield on his chest and polishes at a spot of tarnish with his sleeve.

And yeah, I know some of them went bad. I'm not gonna try to rewrite history to defend them. I heard the stories from Spanish Harlem, and I don't doubt they're true. I know about the officers – and I'm not gonna name names, not now, cause some of those guys have surviving families – who took control of Carver Houses. I heard about the deal they made with the residents, you know, and I know some of those girls are still looking for justice. I hope they get it.

I won't deny any of the stories, or even most of the rumors, but here's something I know for a fact: every officer in the 10th Precinct stayed in uniform. We were the only precinct in Manhattan that stayed at full strength right to the bitter end, even after we learned that we'd been abandoned. Even after we learned there was no military support on the way. No matter what else happened in that place we can be proud of that.

Anyway... As far as we can tell the downtown outbreak started on Pell Street. One of our guys, Cleary, called for backup as soon as he found them trying to break out of their own blockade, but by the time we arrived there wasn't much we could do. Most of the Zees were already in the wind, and we could only save one family who'd managed to find a way out through a few back alleys and over a few walls. They got Cleary, too. Poor guy tried to stop them as they broke through the barrier, and I guess he got mobbed. They didn't leave enough of the body for us to have to worry about him coming back.

Turns out patient zero was an old woman, a grandma who'd arrived from some place back in China about a week earlier, and the family had kept it a secret. They *knew* she was infected. Can you believe that shit? They told the neighbors it was just a dog bite, told them she was strong enough to fight it off. They'd been treating her with all sorts of ridiculous traditional herbal crap for days before she finally turned. Just ignorant, you know? Beyond stupid. Turns out she'd come in on a counterfeit passport, and they wanted to keep her out of the system.

And *of course* she bit a few people when she finally turned, and *of course* the families did nothing but lock them all in a room behind a fucking plywood door, like the morons they were. Nobody even dreamed of calling the cops, not even when the inevitable happened and they broke out. They burned through the entire street before anyone on the outside noticed, and once they got out... *Jeez.*

Downtown New York was the *perfect* place for them to spread like wildfire. A tightly packed population, lots of old buildings full of dark corners, lots of blind alleys, too few cops and not nearly enough guns. By the time we figured out what the hell was going on we were getting reports of attacks all the way from the Battery up to Gramercy Park, and we didn't know how it was spreading so quickly until we figured out that people were getting bitten or scratched and then running as far as they could before they turned, as if they could somehow outrun it.

We lost what little control we had of downtown in less than a day. We spent most of our time running around using that damned Zombie Hunter app everyone was raving about, and you know how that turned out. The attacks kept popping up on the screen, but by the time we reached the locations we almost always found nothing. Of course we didn't know back then that the app was mostly bullshit.

Anyway, that's when we made the call that it was time to get out.

The sergeant holds up a silencing hand as an orderly approaches pushing a man in a wheelchair down the dock towards the ferry, and we sit quietly until they're both out of earshot. Valenzuela nods towards the man in the wheelchair, who appeared catatonic as he passed, his head tilted to one side and his eyes fixed on something unseen in the middle distance.

D.I. Richards from the 44th, up at the Yankee Stadium staging point for the evacuation. I hear he was the guy who gave the order to lock the gates when it got out of control, when there were still maybe four or five thousand alive inside. A lot of the guys turned out that way afterwards, and some of them are still here. Just... checked out, you know? Just broken.

I missed the evacuation to the north, thank God. They had a much tougher time of it than we did downtown. More people, for a start. They were trying to clear everyone north of 72nd Street, and by the time they got to the Bronx the Zees were already ahead of them. It was... well, it wasn't pretty, from what I've heard. A lot of tough decisions had to be made. A lot of weight on too few shoulders. Far too many dead cops.

Compared to those guys we had a much simpler job. Just one job, in fact: get as many people out through the

Holland Tunnel as we could, then block it to stop anything following us. By that point the bridges on the east side had all been barricaded, and they'd already collapsed the Battery Tunnel on the Brooklyn side. It was simple enough to just sweep through downtown and push everyone we could find towards Holland.

We saved thousands. Not as many as we would have liked, and I'm sure a few infected made it through before they blew the tunnel – we didn't have the manpower to check everyone for injuries – but I think we can be proud of what we did. If they'd stayed put those people would all have been wiped out less than a week later when the aerial bombings started. Of course if I'd known about the explosives I wouldn't have stuck around so long.

We had no idea the tunnel had already been rigged with charges. Crossed wires, you know? Too many departments and not enough organization. Nobody warned us that the charges were set on a dead man's switch. They didn't tell us there was a guy at the Manhattan end who had to reset the timer every ten minutes, and since his radio wasn't on the police band he couldn't warn us when his position was overrun.

I got lucky, I guess. I could see the exit at the Jersey side when the charges blew. Another thirty meters and I wouldn't have even been caught in the blast, but I guess I have to thank God at least I got out alive, even if I didn't get to keep all my parts.

Valenzuela looks down at his prosthetic leg and sighs.

I have to remind myself every morning, you know? Every time I wake up and strap this damned thing on. Every time I try to reach out with an arm that's still buried

in a tunnel under the Hudson. At least I got out.
A lot of people didn't. A lot of good men.

●▾●

:::13:::

Puerto Argentino, Las Malvinas, Argentina

US Ambassador to Argentina Art Hollister greets me warmly in the rundown lobby of the Waterfront Hotel – "You're the first American I've seen in six months," he says, and I don't think he's joking – and beckons me up a flight of narrow stairs to the sparsely furnished sea view suite that doubles as both his home and the US Consulate, the only foreign diplomatic presence on Las Malvinas since Argentina seized the islands from the British at the height of the panic. The Ambassador moves a stack of paperback copies of his memoir, *A Stolen Nation*, from the room's only chair and invites me to sit. He remains standing, slowly pacing the small, cluttered room as he speaks.

Hollister is the definition of a modern day political exile. Once a rising star in the Republican party, a former tech millionaire turned Beltway lobbyist turned Senator, he was hotly tipped as a future Presidential candidate when he was named Secretary of State at the tender age of forty five. For a time it seemed as if nothing could stop the momentum of his career, but when the living dead arrived on US shores the game changed overnight, shifting allegiances and leaving him firmly out of favor in the new regime.

For the past ten years, Hollister tells me, he

has suffered the greatest indignity any politician could face – even worse than being implicated in a sex scandal, he insists, since at least they can boost a politician's name recognition. "Just look at Anthony Weiner," he says, shaking his head. "Secretary of the Interior? Seriously? After everything he did back then? The mind boggles."

On the day the former President was ousted from office Hollister was unceremoniously removed from his role, judged guilty by association as the loyal *consigliere* and one of the closest allies of a disgraced Commander-in-Chief, and shortly after President Buckley's inauguration he was offered the Ambassadorship to Argentina with immediate effect. While the position would represent a stumble in an otherwise steadily advancing political career it could, looking at the positive side, give Hollister the chance to bulk out the foreign policy portion of his resume, making him an even more attractive candidate for high office in the future. He had no idea when he took the job that the offer was not as it seemed.

Hollister laughs bitterly as he tells the story.

Buenos Aries, they told me. It was still a safe zone back then, free from infection and relatively stable. It didn't seem like a bad place to hole up for a while. They promised me that after just a year or two in the role I'd be able to return to D.C. and climb out from the shadow of the former President, and in the meantime I could work on my Spanish, drink new world wines and come back with a ten point bump among Latino voters. I'd have the nomination locked down for 2024, so long as...

That's how they said it: so long as... *significant pause*. They didn't want to say this kind of shit out loud, but what they meant was so long as you don't make waves. So long as you don't call it a coup. So long as you just keep your mouth shut and be a good boy, we won't destroy you.

And in any case it was the only offer on the table. My phone wasn't exactly ringing off the hook. My brand was toxic after three years of working so closely with the President. There were just too many pictures of the two of us together in the Oval. Too many shots of me standing behind him as he signed another disastrous Executive Order. Unless I wanted to completely withdraw from public life this was my only option.

So yeah, I accepted the job. I was a good soldier, and while I didn't agree with what was going on I wasn't blind to the danger we were facing. I understood the gravity of the situation, so I took my medicine and got on the next flight to Argentina. It wasn't until I landed that I finally realized it was a one way trip, and a sick joke.

In hindsight I know it sounds stupid, but I didn't really know the geography of South America all that well back then, and in any case when you work in politics you don't worry too much about your itinerary. When somebody points you towards a plane you don't ask questions, you just get on the damned plane. So, when they pointed me towards the jet at Dulles I climbed aboard. When we landed in Rio and transferred to the next flight I didn't think twice, and when the little flight map on my seat back showed us overshooting Buenos Aries I just assumed... Hell, I don't know, I guess I didn't worry about it. Sometimes flights have strange layovers, as you'll know if you ever flew Delta and found yourself stopping in Atlanta for no logical earthly reason.

"Welcome to Puerto Argentino." That's when I

realized what they'd done, when I woke up as we landed, heard that over the PA system and looked out the window to find we were at a tiny little airport that damned sure didn't serve Buenos Aries. I didn't know a thing about Argentinian geography, but you'd better believe I'd heard of Puerto Argentino.

Every few months for years the Brits had pleaded with us to change our neutral stance on the sovereignty of the Falklands. They were desperate for us to legitimize their claim on the islands, and every time they asked we'd send them home disappointed, but not before they forced us to sit through a dull presentation on the history of the dispute. Puerto Argentino was the Argentine name – never officially recognized by the US, of course – of Stanley, the capital of the Falklands.

Hollister shakes his head and gazes out the window over at the low, snow-clad hills on the far side of the Port William Narrows.

President Buckley is a God damned Machiavellian genius. Don't fall for his 'aw, shucks, can't we all just get along?' act, not unless you want a knife buried deep in your back. He was ten moves ahead of the very best, and I'm not ashamed to admit he outfoxed me with ease.

Here's what happened. Buckley knew that the US would need close allies if it was to survive a full blown global pandemic, and he knew those allies might not be the same ones that had served us well during peacetime. For decades we'd counted the UK among our closest friends, and in return the Brits had given us easy access to the European single market and allowed us a lightly regulated English-speaking gateway into the EU.

They were great trading partners, but they were also a

complete pushover. We used to call the UK the 51st state, and with good reason. We loved dealing with them because they'd happily roll over and beg to maintain the illusion of the 'special relationship'.

In wartime, though, they had virtually nothing to offer us. The UK had no manufacturing sector to speak of, and the Brits couldn't even feed themselves without relying heavily on imports. Their economy was built almost entirely on financial services, extremely specialized, and in peacetime they'd thrived as a financial hub. In a world beset by the living dead, though, a country like that becomes a third world backwater overnight. In the newly emerging landscape our close relationship with the UK was quickly becoming a liability.

Argentina, though... now that was a different proposition entirely. Their economy had been in the toilet for years and the peso was still in freefall, but Argentina produced almost everything a country like the US would need in wartime. We're talking maize, wheat, soy, beef, poultry, oil – both crude and refined – along with a laundry list of finished products, from cars and airplane parts to shaving products and vital medicines, all of it produced using cheap labor in a country that was crying out for stable, reliable customers.

In short, Argentina was the perfect trading partner for a United States that not only had to prepare for a sharp contraction in its agricultural capacity but also needed to transition its economy to a war footing. We wanted to be in bed with them, and they only wanted one thing in return...

"The Falkland Islands?"

Yeah, but don't let anyone hear you call them that

.

around here. They wanted *Las Malvinas*. They'd always wanted the islands, because... well, because they're a bunch of small time provincial shitkickers who seemed to think they had a solid claim on the islands just because they happened to live nearby, but that wasn't why they finally made their move. No, they finally pulled the trigger because there are at least a billion barrels of oil beneath Las Malvinas. Argentina wanted all of it, and the crisis gave them the opportunity they'd been waiting for. The UK was too focused on trouble within its own borders to pay attention to its overseas territories.

That's where Buckley came in. In the final days of the impeachment proceedings Buckley was busy making calls. First he got a handshake deal from the Argie government to fast track a new trade agreement that would make the US Argentina's closest trading partner. We'd take virtually everything they could provide, and they'd peg the peso to the dollar to stabilize their economy and create an environment in which we'd both continue to benefit from trade no matter how bad things got. Once that was in place Buckley called the US Ambassador in Buenos Aries and ordered that the consulate be moved to Las Malvinas on the same day the first US warship arrived in the Port William Narrows.

That's where Buckley hit a wrinkle. The Ambassador refused. The man had principles, it seemed, and he knew that virtually every last inhabitant of Las Malvinas wished to remain part of the UK. So of course he had to go, and guess who had two thumbs and was a high profile but politically disposable figure in the US government?

Hollister points at himself and grimaces.

This guy.

Buckley had all the pieces in place before his coup was over, and by the day he was sworn in as President he was ready to go. The moment he entered the Oval Office he made three calls. The first was to redirect the USS Carl Vinson to the south Atlantic. The second was to fire the Ambassador in Buenos Aries. The third was to me.

It was Buckley's second coup of the week. By the time I arrived to begin my long exile in Puerto Argentino the British flags flying over Stanley had being lowered, the forced evacuation of the 3,000 British residents was underway, and the Carl Vinson was anchored ten miles from the coast. Not officially involved, you understand. *Officially* it was taking part in a completely unrelated training exercise, but unofficially it was there to send a message: *Las Malvinas belong to Argentina, because we say so.*

Argentina took the islands without firing a single shot, and I've been here ever since, sitting in this fucking hotel just to serve as a constant reminder to the Brits that Las Malvinas are under the protection of the United States.

"I notice you keep saying that what happened in the US was a coup. Do you mean—"

I mean exactly what I say. It was a *coup d'etat*. An illegal and unwarranted overthrow of the democratically elected President of the United States. I'm saying that for two Presidential terms – throughout the greatest crisis our nation has faced since its birth – the United States of America was under the control of an entirely illegitimate Commander-in-Chief. Did you never read my book?

Hollister picks a copy of his book from the box and tosses it to me. The cover is a simple black

and white image of the Stars and Stripes fluttering in the wind, and beneath it the title *A Stolen Nation: the Death of Democracy and Freedom in the United States of America.*

Here, take one. Nobody else read it either. Buckley had it banned in the States.

In the long and proud history of the United States we had, until recently, only attempted to impeach three sitting Presidents. The first was Andrew Johnson in a politically motivated shit show following the Civil War, an attempt that failed miserably. The second was Nixon, who resigned in disgrace when he saw the writing on the wall, and the third was Clinton, who was eventually let off with a slap on the wrist and a warning to stop screwing his interns.

Now you think of impeachment as a huge deal, right? You'd assume that in order to depose the President of the United States of America, *the leader of the God damned free world*, there must be volumes and volumes of carefully drafted laws to ensure that this immense, world shattering power is never cynically abused. The Constitution must lay out the impeachment process without a single comma out of place, right?

Wrong. The Constitution only defines grounds for impeachment as 'treason, bribery and other high crimes and misdemeanors,' and those final two are vague enough to mean pretty much anything you want them to mean.

Tell me, would you agree that it's right that Congress should be able to define grounds for impeachment as whatever they please?

"Ummm... No, that doesn't sound right at all."

Well, Gerald Ford thought that was just fine and dandy. Back in the day while trying to impeach a federal judge he stated, and I quote, that "an impeachable offense is whatever a majority of the House of Representatives considers it to be at a given moment in history."

Can you believe that shit? He essentially argued that the House can decide to impeach a President for forgetting to tie his shoelaces, and if they could muster a two thirds majority the tightness of a man's bunny ears would officially become legitimate grounds for impeachment. That's *terrifying*, right, that there exists such a dire threat to the separation of powers right there in the heart of our nation's founding document?

What's more terrifying is that Ford was pretty much on the money. There's absolutely *nothing* – apart from the political repercussions it would cause – to stop the House from issuing articles of impeachment against any President at any time, and for any reason. If they can muster the votes they can impeach a President simply because they don't like him.

And that's what happened to the President. To *my* President.

Hollister perches on the edge of his bed and begins to speak in strained tones, as if he's trying to suppress a rage that's been building for a decade.

You think he was impeached for treason, right? I mean, that's what you were told, and you never questioned it? That's what the papers printed, and it's the headline crime stated on the articles of impeachment. For the rest of time the President will go down as the first man who ever sat in that chair to be convicted of treason, and you think it's because he refused to abandon New York because he owned property there, right? You think he put a couple of buildings ahead of the lives of everyone in America, and that's why he was turfed out of office. Am I right?

I nod, hesitantly.

Bull. Shit. I mean God *damn*, I know we lived in cynical times back then, and I know pretty much half the country wouldn't have pissed on the man if he was on fire, but no matter what you thought of his character he wasn't so craven as to put his rental income above the country.

You may not have liked him. You may even have thought he was an irresponsible, unpredictable, narcissistic blowhard who wasn't fit to hold political office – God knows there were days when I felt like that, and I was friends with the guy – but if there's one thing you could rely on it's that this was a man who cared deeply about his own legacy.

He wasn't trying to protect his own buildings. Hell, by the time the epidemic reached New York he already knew his fortune was long gone. His billions were tied up in real estate around the world, and by the time the first undead boots landed on US soil the global property market no longer existed. He knew the economy had fallen so far through the floor it'd take a generation to recover, and by then he'd be long dead.

No, he didn't give a damn about the money. His only crime was that he didn't agree with Charles Joseph fucking Buckley, and the moment he made Buckley an enemy he signed his own pink slip.

For months Buckley had been studying the outbreaks around the world. He'd been speaking to experts and think tanks, chairing endless committees on how to tackle the threat we all knew would eventually reach our shores, and he came to one simple conclusion: the only way our nation could survive was by abandoning the big cities. They were simply too crowded, he said. Too complex. There were too many potential infection vectors – that's literally how he referred to American citizens, as *vectors* – and there wasn't a strong possibility that we'd be able to defend the cities militarily.

Most of all they were economically and strategically worthless in wartime. Nobody needs lawyers, accountants, ad men and hit Broadway plays during a zombie apocalypse, and that's all the cities were really good for when it came to the crunch. What we needed to survive the coming storm were farmers, ranchers, blacksmiths, mechanics. You know, people who work with their hands and produce tangible goods, and those folks sure as hell didn't live in Manhattan.

Buckley has a shard of ice in place of a heart, no matter how warm and folksy he comes across in person. It all came down to numbers for him. How many acres of arable land could be saved. How many bushels of wheat could be grown, how many bullets could be manufactured, and how many citizens could be safely supported given our fixed and limited resources. All of his cold, hard math came down to the same answer. It wasn't just necessary to abandon the cities, but *desirable.*

He determined that the only way to save the nation was to allow the infestation to take hold in the cities while diverting our efforts to preserve smaller towns and farmland, and when the urban areas had become so heavily infected that it became 'politically acceptable' we could safely bomb them into oblivion without the risk of a popular revolution. The faster they were infected the better. It meant there would be fewer mouths to feed.

The worst part of all of this is that the people still love him for it. He condemned half the country to death and brought about the destruction of our greatest cities, and even now the survivors kiss his ass and hail him as the savior of the US. Why? Because the guy's got a way with words. He could steal your lunch and convince you he was helping you drop some weight, and you'd thank him for it and hand him your dinner. And hell, maybe the guy was right. Maybe it really *was* folly to believe we could save the entire country, but we'll never know because he never let us try.

I guess if you had to put it nicely you could describe Buckley as a pragmatist, but I'd use much harsher words.

Hollister calms down, as if he's happy to have finally released his anger.

In any case, Buckley knew the President wouldn't go for it. Right or wrong the Prez was gearing up to fight for every last yard of the country. The VP was in lockstep with the boss, and if Buckley wanted to put his 'screw the cities' plan in action he'd need to get rid of them both.

He also knew it'd be a piece of cake. Everyone in the House and Senate hated each other, but if there was one thing that united the majority it was their disdain for the President and their unshakable belief that he wasn't the right man to guide us through the crisis, so when Buckley maneuvered towards impeachment he didn't meet much resistance. Those few who were still on the fence were mollified by the fact that the Veep would take over – you know, so it didn't look like Buckley was angling for a personal power grab.

He looks out the window once again, grimacing at the hated view.

You want to know the real reason I'm down here? If you try to publish the details I'd expect to read about your tragic 'accidental' death within a week or two, but you want to know the real reason I was quietly shuffled out of the way, far from the public eye, and why I'll remain here for the rest of my life? Lemme give you a thread to pull on, son.

You should ask yourself if it really was just bad luck that the Vice President found himself in Yankee Stadium on that particular day, just a few days after he took charge, and before he'd named his own VP. You should ask yourself how the infection reached the stadium so quickly, and why the National Guard unit ordered to manage the evacuation was diverted to Hoboken at the last minute.

If you want to know what kind of a man Buckley truly is you should ask yourself – really *ask* yourself – who you think gave the order to lock the gates with the VP still inside, know what I'm saying?

•▼•

:::14:::

Port Vila, Efate, Vanuatu

P&O's majestic cruise liner *The Pacific Jewel* found itself docked in the calm azure waters of Efate's Vila Bay on the day the Australian quarantine order was broadcast from Canberra, stranding the liner in the remote Pacific island chain of Vanuatu and giving its 1,200 guests – most of them older couples and young families from Australia, New Zealand, Europe and the US – the questionable honor of becoming the first recorded group of Castaways in the zombie war.

A decade on the adopted islanders have also proved among the most successful of the Castaways, the majority now seamlessly integrated into the local culture, living peacefully alongside the Ni-Vanuatu and offering whatever skills they have in return for citizenship.

Among the passengers were doctors, nurses, teachers, engineers and farmers, and their arrival on Efate, while grounded in tragedy, has come to be seen as a blessing by the locals. As a group the new arrivals are described in almost universally positive terms as *niufala neba*, 'new neighbors' in the local Bislama creole language, and as I arrive in Port Vila I find the Ni-Vanuatu preparing for the upcoming *neba lafet*, an annual festival of intricate body painting, traditional *kastom* dances and communal feasts in villages across Efate to celebrate the contributions made by the recent arrivals.

The Pacific Jewel itself, however, is not quite so welcome. Registered in London, owned by Carnival UK and operated by P&O Australia, like many such abandoned liners this 245 meter leviathan has become the subject of years of legal wrangling between the governments of the UK, Australia and Vanuatu. Since neither Carnival nor P&O still exist it's unclear which country should bear ultimate responsibility for the ship, and the government on Efate grows more concerned with each passing day about the danger of it foundering during one of the tropical cyclones that regularly batter the island chain.

Neither the UK nor Australia will accept the cost of repatriating the liner but both have forbidden the Ni-Vanuatu from dismantling it for scrap before a court can reach a decision. Trapped in an international web of conflicting interests, and without enough diesel to fire up its four enormous MAN-B&W engines, the ship is going nowhere in the near future.

The legal drama is expected to drag on for several years before a suitable court is established to settle the countless international disputes that arose from the war, but in the meantime *The Pacific Jewel* has become an unlikely source of revenue. Its sole resident, the American entrepreneur Sean Pruitt, is rumored to pay the Vanuatu government in the region of $30 million each year to both lease the ship and secure leave to remain in Efate against the strong objections of many islanders, who – until he confined himself to his luxurious lodgings two years ago – spat at his feet and yelled the insult *rabis mit* **at him whenever he ventured under armed guard into Port Vila.** *Rabis mit* **translates as 'rubbish meat', the Bislama term for a cancerous tumor.**

While there are multiple civil suits lodged against Pruitt in countries across the world no criminal charges have yet been filed in the US – indeed, many argue that it's unclear if he even technically committed a crime – and Pruitt is free to return home whenever he pleases. He is, however, unlikely to do so without coercion, especially after several high level government sources suggested that his safety could not be guaranteed were he to set foot in the US.

No, no, no, you've been misinformed. They love me here! I mean sure, there's always gonna be a few jealous pricks who don't understand why I get to live on the big boat while they rot in their little shacks, but that's just par for the course for people at my level. When you make your first billion you soon learn to ignore the envious parasites who suddenly think you owe them a living. It's just background noise, you know? Washes right over you after a while. Most of these guys... well, let's just say they know which side their bread is buttered.

Anyway, I'm guessing you didn't come all this way to ask about my generous contributions to Vanuatu, right?

"No, I'd like to talk about your app."

Bingo. So, what do you wanna know? How about the more than three billion downloads we achieved worldwide, making it the second most successful app of all time after *Angry Birds*? How about the seven million downloads we got on the first day, or the ninety four million in the first week? How about the fact that *Zombie Hunter* more than doubled the opening week download record previously held by *Super Mario Run*, and all without a single cent spent on advertising?

"Whatever you want to talk about is fine. Feel free to–"

It was a fucking *juggernaut*, an unstoppable force of nature that became the number one bestselling app in every country and on every platform in its first month, and once it hit the top of the charts it never gave up its spot for a second until the stores themselves finally went offline. I challenge you to find a single smartphone still in existence that doesn't have a copy of *Zombie Hunter* loaded to it. You can't do it. You just can't *do* it!

Now I know I'm supposed to come across all humble and whatnot in these interviews, but I think we're way past that, right? I'll just come out and say it. I had a stroke of *genius* when I came up with *Zombie Hunter*. That's what it was, plain and simple. It was a eureka moment, just like that Archimedes dude in the bathtub.

Pruitt pours us both a mango smoothie from the jug beside him, but I discreetly set my glass aside as soon as he turns his back. Before arriving on the ship my local guide, Sato Maseng, cryptically warned me that the food and drink delivered from Port Vila may not be entirely 'hygienic'. I cringe as Pruitt takes a long gulp before smacking his lips.

Here's a little background for ya. I'd already been

working with augmented reality for a couple of years before *Z-Hunter*, you know, so I wasn't a noob. I had this one app, *EatSmart*, that helped shoppers pick groceries according to whatever dumb fad diet they were on at the time. Like, if they were on Atkins they could hold up their phone camera to a grocery store aisle and the app would superimpose a smiley face above the products that didn't have any carbs. Complete bullshit, I know, but it was exactly the kind of crap the fatties loved. They'd buy anything that helped distract them from the fact that they were fat, greedy fucks who'd always remain fat, greedy fucks until they put down the pizza and ate a salad.

EatSmart was the app that really put me on the map, even though it didn't make all that much money. I think I cleared maybe three million after tax in the first year once you counted the ad revenue and all the bullshit freemium extras those chubby assholes bought. Y'know, like dumb 99 cent virtual stickers they could share on Facebook to impress all their fat friends. *I've been on a juice fast for seven days, guys! Congratulate me! Validate me!! LOVE ME!!!*

Anyway, once *EatSmart* was out there I could pretty much write my own ticket. I was on everyone's radar, and while I had more than enough cash to develop my own apps I had VCs lining up around the block just drooling for the chance to get in on the ground floor for my next big idea.

I spent the next few months batting around a concept for this great motivational workout app. You know, more opium for the fatties. Here's the pitch: you see a street map of your local area on your screen, kinda like the map you'd see on *Pokemon Go*, you know, but on this map the only features on the screen are the locations of fast food joints. So, let's say you're craving a Big Mac from your local McDonalds but you don't want to feel guilty about it, you tap the icon, select a Big Mac from the menu, and then the app instantly maps out a walking route between your current location and the closest McDonalds that's exactly long enough to burn the calories you'll get from the burger.

Maybe I could have even broken the walks up into individual bites, you know? Like, let's say it takes a dozen bites to get through a Big Mac, you have the app play a happy little *bing!* every time you've 'earned' yourself another bite. Guilt free fast food. The fatties would have eaten it up, if I'd followed through.

"You didn't write the app?"

No, dude, I didn't get the chance before destiny intervened. You remember that guy McIntyre, the CNN asshole with those dumb eyebrows who flushed his career down the toilet when he lost his shit on live TV? That's the guy I have to thank for *Zombie Hunter*. God bless that psycho.

I was meeting with a potential investor for the fast food app in this restaurant in LA, some up his own ass type-A power freak looking for a vanity project to distract him from the fact that his wife was banging the pool boy, I'm guessing. I could have easily funded the whole thing myself with petty cash, but when I figured out I'd need to spend a big chunk on licensed content I decided I should spread the risk a little, so I gave this asshole the chance to hand me a blank check.

Twenty minutes into the meeting the guy was already getting on my last nerve. He seemed to think he was in charge, like *I'd* come to *him* begging for funding. He kept insisting I call the app *CakeWalk*, which was just beyond dumb, so I started to tune out the conversation, y'know? By the time our meals arrived I'd already decided I didn't want to work with him so I started flipping through Twitter on my phone, just to let the guy know he was losing my attention, and that's when I saw the trending news. McIntyre had thrown some kind of hilarious shit fit on live TV, running around screaming like his pants were on fire, and the clip was burning up social media.

I excused myself to the bathroom, sat back on the john and watched the McIntyre video twice, and I was halfway through squeezing out a pipe blocker when it suddenly came to me. *Why are we only learning about zombie attacks on the nightly news? Why are we looking for twentieth century solutions to a twenty first century problem?*

I was so excited I almost forgot to wipe. I ran back to the investor, gave him the quick five minute pitch for *Zombie Hunter,* and I was back in my office an hour later with a handshake deal for five hundred thou seed money and a 10% equity share on a three day ticking clock. The cash landed in my account within twelve hours, and I had the app ready for beta testing in less than a month.

The pitch was simple. You pay $4.99 each month to gain access to the map and play the 'game'. When you see a zombie out in the real world you tag it by taking a GPS-synced photo, with the location instantly uploaded to the augmented reality map, and every week we give cash prizes to the highest performing 1% of players in every country, city, or whatever. So let's say there are a million players in the US, we take in $5 million and distribute one mil in prize money between ten thousand people. The top ten each get ten grand, the next twenty get five grand, the next hundred get a grand, and then we have a sliding scale that goes down until a few thousand people just get their five bucks back.

You see the beautiful simplicity of it all? It was the *perfect* app. First, it allowed people to feel like they were doing their part to protect their country. We gave away free access to every military, government and law enforcement agency that'd take our call, so paid users were helping the cops and the army pinpoint outbreaks in real time, and they were helping the government better coordinate rescue operations and emergency aid. Instant patriotism boner. Second, there was a competitive element. If people didn't get jazzed about saving the world they could get wood about the prospect of winning ten grand, right? Third, it was augmented reality. You could scan your phone camera around and watch virtual heat trails of the routes zombies had taken in the last 24 hours. You could literally *stand inside* one of these heat trails, knowing that one of the living dead had been walking in your footsteps some time in the last day. I swear it'd send chills down your spine. People always got excited about shit like that.

Finally – and this was the thing that *really* got my juices flowing – you couldn't *not* buy the app. What, you're gonna decide to save five bucks because you don't care if there's a fucking zombie two blocks away, shambling closer to you with each passing second? No way, man! People were scared. They were terrified of their own shadows, and for the price of a cup of coffee each month I was giving them peace of mind. It was the *ultimate* must-have app.

That's the thing that really moved units, and that's the reason we added all the little paid extras, y'know? $5 a month extra would buy you an add-on feature that'd make your phone vibrate and sound an alarm whenever a tagged zombie came within your user-set safety radius.

One mile, ten miles, whatever was enough to make you feel safe. $10 would buy you the family package, which would link you to up to five other phones that were running the app – your wife, kids, mistress or whatever – and give you a notification whenever *their* perimeters were breached.

We cleared half a billion dollars in the first month. By the time we hit the peak – just before the Internet started to fail and network coverage got spotty – we were clearing *seven billion a month* in recurring subscriptions, another three billion in paid extras, and that's not even counting the revenue from the paid ads. By the time we hit our peak we'd become one of the top 20 highest revenue generating companies on the planet, but we were the most *profitable* company by a long shot. Once we paid out the prize money, server fees, payroll for the support staff, 10% for the asshole investor and the cut to Apple and Google for using their platforms it was all profit. Billions in profit, *and* we were helping keep people safe. There was even talk of a Nobel peace prize at one point.

"Did you ever directly address the rumors about the app?"

Rumors? Which ones? Every successful app has its critics, and if you wanna make it in the business you learn to tune out the haters.

"I mean the rumors that not all of the tagged zombies were actually real."

How do you mean, not real? You'd really have to speak to the coding guys about that kind of thing. I was the ideas man, but I wouldn't know anything about any technical issues or user error. All I'll say is that you shouldn't believe everything you hear, *especially* when it's potentially actionable, know what I'm saying?

"So do you deny the accusations that 'phantom' zombies were intentionally generated by the system to make users more fearful and boost sales of your add-on services?"

Intentional? Abso-fucking-lutely not. Anyone I've ever worked with will tell you I've always been a straight shooter, and the team I worked with were the best of the best. Never anything short of supremely professional. I'd stake my reputation on the fact that nobody at my company ever – *ever* – generated false attacks. If it was possible to go back and cross check the tags against military and police records I'd volunteer the information in a heartbeat, but unfortunately all that data is long gone.

"I mention it because several law enforcement agencies maintain that at many of the 'outbreaks' they attended no zombies were found. They claim that the *Zombie Hunter* app regularly sent them on wild goose chases that kept them from responding to genuine emergency calls, and some have even suggested that you should be held personally responsible for the deaths of thousands of US citizens as a result of the erroneous information provided by the app."

I'd take that with a pinch of salt, if I were you. I have it on good authority that many of these critics have received payment for their testimony, and my lawyers will make sure their lies don't go unpunished. There are always–

"And one of your head coders, Vijay Chaudhary, recently said that he's willing to provide evidence that you personally ordered the creation of phantom outbreaks in cities where subscription rates were falling."

OK, gimme that fucking tape recorder. *Joel, come take this guy's tape recor–*

•▼•

:::15:::

Tilos, The Aegean Sea

Ebru Demirci shows me a sun-faded, dogeared copy of *Hurriyet*, once Turkey's most popular daily newspaper, and sighs with embarrassment as she translates the cover story. The 2015 article reports that the Syrian refugee population registered in Turkey had topped 2.5 million for the first time. In the final paragraph is a quote from Ebru herself, formerly a hotelier in the popular Turkish tourist resort of Marmaris, complaining that the Syrians should 'stay and fight' rather than impose themselves on the goodwill of the Turkish people. In a further quote she describes those who fled their homeland as 'cowardly.'

"The irony isn't lost on me," she sighs, gesturing towards the seemingly endless rows of canvas tents that still cover much of the small Greek island of Tilos. For years this camp, once filled with refugees from as far afield as Syria, Afghanistan, Somalia and Sudan, has been home to Ebru and almost thirty thousand fellow Turks. "In my defense, many of us thought that way until it was our turn to lose our homes."

The siren arrived almost at the same time as the dead. I didn't even know where it came from. The siren, I mean. It was one of those old wartime air raid warnings, long and mournful, like a funereal dirge, and a sound I never expected to hear in our peaceful little town.

Someone told me much later that it came from Camiavlu Cami, the old mosque in the hills above the town. They said the imams had a sort of... I guess a sort of national emergency network, passing along the alerts from mosque to mosque like signal fires as they were overrun. The swarm arrived from the hills to the north so the mosque was no doubt surrounded, especially when the imam – or whoever it was who sounded that alarm – started making so much noise.

I've often thought of that man in the years since, trapped up there in the minaret as the dead flowed around him like water far below. I wonder if he had some sort of escape plan, or at least enough food and water to last until it was safe to run. Or did he know when he locked the door and climbed the steps that it would be his final act in life? I just hope he didn't feel alone as he watched us escape. I hope he knew how thankful we were, and still are. Whoever it was, he gave his life in return for hundreds, maybe thousands. He truly earned whatever blessing comes after this life.

I was sound asleep when the siren began. I think it must have been sometime around six in the morning. The light outside my window was the ghostly blue of the pre-dawn, and I didn't really wake up until I heard people yelling in the street below, and the sound of breaking glass.

I jumped out of bed and ran to the window just in time to see a young foreigner – an Asian man – climb into the store downstairs and come out with an inflatable rubber ring. I couldn't believe it. Looting in Marmaris! That's the kind of behavior I'd expect to see in those awful places like Ibiza and Magaluf, the kind of vacation spots where young western tourists go to drink themselves into oblivion and take drugs, but Marmaris? No, we didn't attract those kinds of people. Ours was a peaceful seaside town for nice families, not a destination for drunken louts.

I was about to run for the phone to call the police when I looked back down and saw another man follow after the tourist, a young local I knew in passing who I'd always found polite and law-abiding, carrying a stolen surf board over his shoulder. It was only then that my eyes began to adjust to the darkness outside and I noticed all the people out on the beach. It was as if the beach itself was writhing in the darkness, every inch of the sand covered in moving bodies. And then I noticed the movement back on the land, all the... the *creatures* flooding out of all the little side streets, like cockroaches scurrying away from a sudden light.

It all clicked for me in an instant. All those terrible news reports we'd seen in recent months, all the attacks in far off towns on the other side of the country, up on the Black Sea coast or in the far east close to the Iranian border. They'd all seemed so remote, as if they were taking place in another country. Another world. After each new attack we'd sit in the sunshine outside our cafes and sadly shake our heads as we discussed the news. *We'll pray for the dead in Trabzon*, we'd say, or *Baskale will always be in our thoughts*, and then we'd sip our coffee, look out at our beautiful town and the sea beyond and thank God we didn't have to worry about such madness here.

Looking back it seems ridiculous that we managed to live in such denial for so long. That we continued to go to work, pay our bills, buy groceries... That we just continued to live as *normal,* as if tomorrow would always be just the same as yesterday. Finally, when the denial fell away, I couldn't help but feel angry that tomorrow people elsewhere in the country would wake up to the news, sit in their cafes, shake their heads, sip their coffees and tell each other they were praying for the poor souls in Marmaris. For *me*.

I didn't even take the time to dress before I ran out the door, and as I ran out in the street in my nightdress I almost froze at the sight of the madness on the beach. It was so absurd it would almost have been funny, if it wasn't for... well, for everything else. Thousands of men, women and little children were sprinting at full speed into the surf, some of them naked, some in their underwear and many of them obviously drunk and confused, desperately paddling into the crashing waves on bright, colorful inflatables designed for little kids in a calm pool.

Where on earth did they think they were going? Marmaris was in a wide bay choked off at the mouth by two large islands that sat more than a mile out from the beach. Even the strongest swimmers would struggle to make it as far as the islands, and those who did would only find themselves exhausted, too tired to fight against the strong current that ran into the bay, pushing them right back towards the beach. It was madness.

I ran down to the sand and pushed my way towards the shore, yelling like a crazy person, warning them to stay out of the water, but my voice was drowned out in the chaos. It was as if nobody was thinking for themselves. They'd become a *herd*, stampeding mindlessly to the shore and rushing into the water simply because that's what everyone else was doing. Simply because they were thinking more about what they were running *away* from than what they were running *towards*.

I saw a family run past me, a mother clutching hold of a little blonde boy and a father using an inflatable ring to force a path through the crowd. I grabbed hold of the mother's shoulder and tried to plead with her to turn away from the water and follow me. Maybe she couldn't hear me above all the screaming, or maybe she thought I was one of *them*, but she shoved a sharp elbow hard into my nose and I fell backwards onto the sand.

My ears were ringing. All I could see were bright spots bursting in my eyes, and I tasted blood in my mouth. The crowd continued to rush towards the shore, stepping over me, *on* me, kicking me as they passed. I thought I'd die down there, trampled to death by a thousand panicked feet, until someone – I never saw who – grabbed me by the arm and pulled me back to my feet. I cried out to my unseen angel. *Thank you! God bless you!*

I knew I needed to get off the beach before I was carried into the water, but now I could barely move. The crowd was packed so tight that my feet didn't touch the ground, and they only pushed harder when they started to hear the screams from behind them as the dead reached the sand. I felt my ribs creak in my chest and the air forced from my lungs as the mob crushed me. I wanted to scream, but I couldn't even take a breath.

Down where the waves were breaking I could see people trip and fall at the water's edge, knocked off their feet by the current, and as soon as they fell down more people just piled on top of them, climbing over them like rats in their panic, holding them beneath the surface until they couldn't help but take a breath of the salt water. I couldn't believe what I was seeing. When each wave crashed and then pulled back it revealed dozens of bodies, perfectly still, their faces pressed deep into the sand as it sucked around them, and with each second I drew closer to them.

I knew in my heart I'd suffer the same fate. I knew that the moment the water hit me the men behind would knock me off my feet, and I knew they wouldn't even notice me as they struggled to break through the surf. I... I prepared myself for death. I decided to breathe out all of my air the moment the water went over my head. I decided not to fight it, and I prayed that God would allow me to die quickly.

I was just a few steps from the water when He reached down and saved me, in the most terrible way I could imagine. There was a great roar from out on the water, followed by screams, and for a moment everyone stopped and looked out into the blackness.

Someone had managed to find a speed boat from somewhere, but it was clear that they didn't really know how to drive it. The boat was full of people, far too many of them. I saw some of them tumble over the side and vanish beneath the black water each time the boat hit a wave, and the rest fought for the controls as the boat sped forward, scything through the water from side to side as they wrestled over the steering. I watched with horror as it raced towards the shore, bouncing from wave to wave and cutting through anyone who couldn't get out of the way.

It hit the beach just a few feet ahead of me. I felt the wind as it passed by, smelled the hot exhaust burning from the engine, and I screamed as it sliced through the crowd and grounded on the sand with the rotor blade still spinning in the air. I saw a young woman, barely more than a girl, stumble and fall against the blade and...

The crowd suddenly stopped pushing forward when they saw what happened. I thought for a moment that they'd been frozen by the shock of what they'd just seen. I hoped that maybe that terrible sight might bring them to their senses, but then the crowd started to surge towards the beached boat. I don't know what they thought they were doing. Maybe they thought they could push it back into the water and escape, but in any case it finally allowed me to slip out of the crush to where there were fewer people, and then move along the beach until I could make my way back to the promenade. The dead were still there, but suddenly they seemed like less of a threat than the insane, mindless stampede of the living.

I remember weeping uncontrollably as I turned away from the beach and started to run along the promenade to the west, towards the road out of town that curved out to the mouth of the bay. I could taste blood in the tears that reached my lips, and I knew it belonged to the woman who'd been hit by the blades.

All along the beach hundreds of still bodies lay in the sand, crushed and broken. I felt glass cut into my bare feet as I ran but I didn't dare stop to pull out the shards. People – I don't know if they were dead or alive, and I didn't care to check – were still pouring from the side streets, and I just fixed my eyes straight ahead and ran. I knew if I just kept my eyes pointed forward and put one foot in front of the other I'd make it to safety. I barely even noticed that my nightdress had been torn off in the crush, and I didn't care. Fear had destroyed my capacity to feel shame at my nakedness.

I almost stopped, once, close to the end of the beach where I heard a scream from the shore. There were thousands of screams, of course, so many that they broke over me like the crashing waves, but this one was different. It was a child. I guess some natural mothering instinct kicked in, and I found myself slowing down and turning towards the sound. She was just a little thing, maybe five or six years old, naked apart from a set of half-inflated pink water wings on her arms. Her father – or the man who was with her, at least – was trying to pull her into the water, but she was screaming and squirming in his arms. She was terrified, and the man's frantic yelling was only making it worse.

The girl was facing the water. She couldn't see what was approaching behind her, but the father could see them clearly. On the beach behind the little girl a small group of those things, maybe half a dozen of them, were shambling across the sand towards her. They were only a few steps away from her when the father made one last attempt to drag her to the water, but she wriggled out of his grip and fell back to the sand, crying. Her father...

No, it *can't* have been her father. No parent would ever do what he did. How could a father go on living after he turned his back on his little girl and ran away? How could he jump into the water and keep swimming even as she began to scream in pain? How could...

Ebru wipes a tear from her cheek, and takes a shuddering breath.

I just fixed my eyes straight ahead and kept running. I decided to run until I could no longer hear the screams, but I didn't run fast enough. It's been ten years now, and I can still hear them all.

•▾•

:::16:::

Mandore, Rajasthan, India

I join Neelamani Parikh on his daily stroll through the lush, overgrown Mandore gardens, immediately regretting my choice of open toed sandals when I see that the ground is thick with the droppings of the large and boisterous troop of Hanuman langurs that have chosen the gardens as their home. Parikh seems unconcerned as he walks in bare feet, stopping every few steps to chirrup and whistle at the gray, long-limbed monkeys basking in the sun. He allows a baby to clamber up his loose white dhoti, perching on his shoulder and awaiting the gift of a fresh blossom and a small green banana, and he smiles as the wide-eyed langur accepts the offerings with tiny grasping hands.

Before the zombie war Parikh was just another of almost two million anonymous *beghar*, India's homeless, living rough in the labyrinthine alleyways of Jodhpur. Orphaned as a child and blind in one eye, Parikh was twenty three years old when the undead swarmed India. He made a living sweeping floors in a local temple, and by all accounts he should be considered lucky to have survived even the initial outbreak.

It was among the ranks of the *beghar* that the infection first took hold throughout India. An invisible underclass, in the years before the arrival of the living dead the homeless and millions of urban poor of India were marginalized and ignored by the middle classes, and it has since been suggested that this was the reason the country was overwhelmed at such a frightening pace. The infection simmered unnoticed in India's countless slums, in the hidden, invisible spaces beside rail tracks and beneath highways, before finally boiling over long after it was too late to put up a fight.

Parikh reaches into the bag slung over his shoulder and pulls out a handful of blossoms, tossing them out to the gathering langurs while muttering thanks to the saviors of Mandore.

Note: Parikh speaks no English. His words are translated by my often unreliable translation device that struggles with its limited Hindi dictionary. Any errors in the text – especially those related to religious terms – should be considered mine.

You should, I think, understand a little about Hinduism when you talk about what happened in India. You don't need to be any sort of religious scholar, of course – I never received any formal schooling myself – but it's important to know that Hinduism is not a single, cohesive religion. Unlike many other faiths it has no single founder, no central church nor any kind of Papal figure to hand down unbreakable, infallible doctrine.

Rather, Hinduism is simply the name given to the synthesis of cultures, traditions and holy texts of a billion people, each of whom have their own unique interpretation of their faith. For instance, some subscribe to monotheistic belief, that there is one God. Others are polytheistic, believing in a vast Pantheon of Gods, while still more are pantheistic, with a belief that the world *itself* carries a spark of the divine, and that God lives in everything from the trees and rivers to our very bodies. That's just one of the countless ways in which we differ, and it's important to understand that my beliefs – perhaps not at the core, but certainly around the edges – may be almost unrecognizable to the beliefs of, say, a farmer in Tamil Nadu or a Mumbai *dabbawala*.

Do you see what I mean? I mean to say that it's folly to simply describe someone as 'a Hindu', as if that means we all subscribe to the same single fixed set of beliefs, so when you hear scholars talk about the 'Hindu response' to the zombie threat you can be certain their reports will be incomplete at best, and ignorant at worst. There *was* no 'Hindu response' any more than there was a 'female response' or a 'blue-eyed response'. You only have to compare the peaceful, non-confrontational luring tactics of the Kashmiris to the almost absurd violence of the boatmen in the Kerala backwaters to see that we all tackled the dead in our own way.

Hindus do, however, share many almost universal beliefs, and one of those is the principle of *ahimsa*, a central tenet of Hinduism, Buddhism and Jainism. *Ahimsa* means, literally, 'not to injure', and it forbids – or at least strongly discourages – a person from causing harm to another through his actions, words or even thoughts. *Himsa* in this life brings bad *karma*, which may affect our happiness in this life and our future lives, so harm of any kind is to be carefully avoided.

Now I know what you're thinking, and no, *ahimsa* did not forbid us from fighting back against the living dead. We were not compelled to lay down like lambs and placidly accept our fate simply to abide by our beliefs. *Ahimsa* discourages harm but it does permit it as a last resort, after all other avenues have been pursued and found to be blocked.

Or, at least, this is the way many Hindus understand it. But then there are the Jains...

He smiles as a small langur clambers up my body and swings from my shirt. I cringe as the tiny fingers dig like thorns into my skin.

If it hadn't been for the charity of the *aryikas*, the nuns of the Jain Mahavira Temple in Jodhpur, I wouldn't have survived to meet the living dead, and even if I had I would not have enjoyed the sight to do so. They fed me through my youth, and gave me a bed on the harshest winter nights. When I lost my eye to infection they tended to me, and while they couldn't save the right eye they ensured I kept the vision in my left.

The Jains are not Hindus, you understand. They're similar in many ways, but there's little doubt that Jainism exists as a separate religion, though both share many observances. Jains are... shall we say more hardcore than Hindus in many ways. For them *ahimsa* is not just a guiding principle but one of their *mahavratas*, their five great vows, to be honored above all else. Jains are so committed to *ahimsa* that they often wear masks over their mouths to avoid accidentally swallowing insects. Most are strict vegetarians or vegans, and some will not even eat root vegetables for fear that tearing them from the ground might injure the tiny creatures that thrive within the roots. For a Jain all life is sacred, and the idea of killing a human – even a mindless undead creature intent on slaughtering them – was absolutely unconscionable. Life is life. In which form it comes is immaterial.

"You mean they won't kill even when their lives are in danger?"

It can be difficult for a westerner to grasp, I know, but you must understand that for a Jain, and indeed a Hindu, this life is but one of many. Our actions here will echo through all of our lives, and for a Jain to sacrifice himself to avoid *himsa* could be seen as a practical, positive choice from this perspective.

I was at the temple when the dead arrived in Jodhpur, rising in their thousands through the city like the morning mist, and I was only saved from becoming one of them because it was January and the nuns had allowed me to sleep indoors to escape the chilly nights. I awoke just before dawn to begin my chores, as always, and as always I drifted through the temple for a few minutes, rubbing my eyes and stretching my aching limbs before my mind caught up with my body and began to function.

It was only after I'd filled a bowl of water to wash that I noticed the sound. It was the sound of pounding feet coming from the street outside, just loud enough to reach through the temple walls. I spilled the bowl at my feet and rushed to rescue my wet clothing, and when I emerged onto the street I found a crowd of thousands – men and women, old and young – running as one towards Mehrangah Fort, high above the city. I just stood there, staring, until an elderly man slowed and grabbed me by my dhoti. "*Run, you fool!*" he yelled, his eyes as wide as saucers. "Fetch the nuns and run. *They're here!*"

They were planning to fight back from the fort, you see. The government had told us as much in the weeks before, knowing there was nowhere else to safely evacuate the people of the city. They planned to use the solid walls of the fort to protect against the dead while the army led a counterstrike, wiping the streets clean before the people could return in safety. Naturally the wealthiest in the city had already been up there for weeks, waiting for the inevitable in comfortable accommodations, but this was the first time an invitation had been extended to people of my low standing.

I ran back into the temple and yelled out until the nuns were roused from sleep, and – I don't know from where I found the confidence – I sternly ordered them to follow me as if I was something more than a simple unschooled *beghar*, but one of them, Deshna, simply shook her head, laid her hand on my arm and smiled. "That's not our path," she said. "You go on ahead. Be safe, Neelamani."

I didn't understand what she meant until one of the others, Urja, explained. She told me the nuns had decided for themselves that they could not join the fight. They couldn't fire a gun or swing a blade, of course, that much was clear, but she told me they'd decided they couldn't even stand behind those who killed on their behalf.

That was how strongly they believed, to allow themselves to die rather than raise a hand against the oncoming horde. For Jains the *intent* behind an act of violence is more important than the act itself. Do you see? It didn't matter that they would not be the ones to personally wield the sword or pull the trigger. If they knowingly stood behind those who killed to protect them the *himsa* would be just as severe as if they themselves had taken lives, and their souls just as sullied.

I broke down in tears. I never knew my mother, but ever since I was a boy I'd felt as if the nuns had filled that space in my life, and I'd always believed I filled the space their own children would have occupied had they not devoted themselves so completely to their faith. Urja had been the one to bring me to the temple when I lost my eye, and Deshna had been the one who allowed me to stay and work there despite the fact that I was unclean, both spiritually and physically. They had saved my life many times over, and I couldn't believe they thought I'd allow them to die now.

I couldn't believe... I couldn't even *comprehend* the idea that they thought so little of me. That after helping me for so many years they didn't think of me as family but simply another *beghar*; another wretched street child who'd take their charity without believing that a debt was owed in turn. You understand? I know now that they were only trying to help me, but at that moment it felt as if they were asking me to imperil my own soul by leaving them to die. I was angry. Offended.

I ran from the temple, my vision clouded with tears, and after just a few steps I found what I was looking for, as if a higher power was guiding me. It was a gun, an old pistol, no doubt dropped in his haste by a soldier as he ran. I had no idea how to use it. I didn't even know if it was loaded. I'd never even *held* a gun before, but it didn't matter. I had no intention of pulling the trigger.

Across the main road in front of Purana Stadium I found a bus, a bright pink tourist coach with the engine cover lifted to allow it to breathe. The door was closed but the driver was inside at his seat, cowering low behind the wheel as the crowds flowed around him, and I waved my gun until he pulled open the door. I forget what I yelled at the poor man – I'm sure I looked like a lunatic – but whatever I yelled it was enough to scare him into submission. He was so afraid, in fact, that after I ordered him to drive back to the temple he waited, still babbling in fear, as I ran inside to gather the nuns.

Oh, they must have thought I was crazy, running

through the temple, yelling and waving my gun. In that moment I probably was. I certainly wasn't thinking clearly. In that moment the only thing that mattered was that my beloved *aryikas* escaped the terrible fate they'd chosen. They were reluctant to follow me outside, but... well, I suppose they saw the desperation in my eyes.

The driver was frantic when we returned to the bus, and it wasn't until we were all aboard that I realized why. The undead had almost reached us. They were emerging from the alleyways as the driver urged the bus forward. Horrifying creatures, broken and torn, staring at us through empty eyes as we drove out of their reach. The driver, thank goodness, was not a Jain, and when we found our way blocked by a ghoul standing in the middle of the street he didn't hesitate before running it down. I watched it vanish beneath the window, and we all felt the bump as the wheels ran over the body. The nuns cried, and gathered together at the back of the bus to pray for the fallen soul.

We drove north for twenty minutes through the thronged streets of the city, weaving between or just shunting aside the cars and rickshaws that had been abandoned on Mandore Road. Thankfully most of the people had already fled, so we didn't have to worry too much about hitting any living humans. It looked as if we'd make it out of the city unharmed. We'd escaped the dangerous, narrow, traffic choked streets of the center and made it to the broad road leading out to the east, and then without warning a plume of greasy black smoke filled the bus and the engine ground to a halt with a sound like the gnashing of steel teeth.

"I tried to warn you!" the driver yelled, no doubt terrified I'd shoot him. "I told you the transmission was broken!" I could see the terror in his eyes, and I could see that he was even more afraid of me than he was of the living dead. I decided I couldn't take it any more, so I laid the gun down at his feet, begged his forgiveness and thanked him for helping the nuns. He could have picked up the gun and shot me dead where I stood, and I would have deserved it, but I was shocked when instead he turned to the nuns and called for them to get off and follow him.

We emerged from the bus to a terrifying sight. They were approaching from all directions, dozens of them slowly closing in on us and blocking off any conceivable path of escape. I despaired when I realized that not only had I failed to save the nuns but I'd also denied them the peace of spending their final moments in their temple, instead condemning them to a filthy, undignified death in the middle of the street. I almost fell to my knees and wept before the driver grabbed me by the arm, shook me until I calmed down and demanded that I follow him away from the road. That's when I realized where he was leading us.

Parikh gestures to the gardens around him. With their bases now hidden by the vegetation and their walls obscured by thick creepers, Mandore Gardens is the home of a collection of ancient *dewals*, towering monuments to the old Maharajas of Jodhpur. While the cenotaphs are now in a state of disrepair they must once have been an impressive sight, almost like a miniature version of Cambodia's Angkor Wat, their intricately carved red sandstone walls climbing high above the treetops.

The driver understood the cause of my torment. He

could see the strength of the love I felt for the *aryikas*. He knew he wasn't bringing us to safety, but to a peaceful place to die. After all the fear I'd caused him he still performed this act of kindness, helping my beloved family to a place where they could die surrounded by beauty, in the hope that it might remove some fear from their final moments. It was... it was very kind of him.

Parikh coughs and wipes a tear from his cheek, embarrassed by his emotion.

Unfortunately it didn't help my own fear. The nuns were calm and at peace, but I was still terrified. You see, I didn't share their unshakable belief that my soul would soon be reborn in another form. I didn't think of this moment as just another step along my journey, as the *aryikas* believed, but simply its end. I feared these would be the final moments I ever experienced before an eternity of darkness, and they would be filled with nothing but terror and pain.

The dead arrived at the gates as we reached the *dewal* to Maharaja Ajit Singh, and the sound of their gasps and groans taunted us through the trees as the nuns sat on the grass and waited for the end. I felt tears stream down my face as the dead grew closer and louder, and Deshna shuffled over towards me and took my head in her lap, stroking my hair to calm me, whispering that I shouldn't worry. She told me I'd been a good boy, and kind, and that my next life wouldn't be so hard, but I couldn't bring myself to believe her. My tears ran gray from the dirt on my face, staining her clean white robe, and even with the zombies just a few shambling footsteps away I could still summon enough self-loathing to feel ashamed of sending my beloved Deshna to her death in an unclean sari.

She began to sing as the undead drew closer, an old lullaby she used to sing as she was caring for me in the temple. I squeezed my eyes closed and tried with all my might to concentrate only on her voice, to block out the groans, and I whimpered and sobbed as I felt something brush against my shoulder. I gritted my teeth, expecting to feel at any moment the grip of a hand or the sharp pain of teeth digging into my flesh.

And then I heard screams and snarls from all around me, a deafening noise so loud it hurt my ears. Not from the zombies but from something else. Something in the trees above.

Almost on cue a group of a dozen langurs above us break into playful yelps as they chase each other through the high branches, bounding with impressive speed through the canopy. The baby on Parikh's shoulder clings closer to him for protection, turning its eyes warily up to the trees.

To this day I still don't understand why, but they attacked the dead with more ferocity than anything I've ever seen. It's difficult to imagine it now, watching them play up there. The largest of the males only weighs as much as a child, and the females much less, but they make up for it with speed and cunning. They fought like true warriors.

The langurs quickly learned that they could knock the dead off-balance by striking them anywhere in the upper body, and that once they were struggling on the ground they could be immobilized with just a few well-placed bites to the legs. They learned to stay away from the grasping hands, keeping to a safe distance where they couldn't be grabbed, and they learned that the dead feel no pain, and couldn't be warned away with a sharp nip to the fingers.

There were no more than a hundred langurs in the troop that day, but by the time the sun fell and the soldiers finally arrived these gardens were piled with the writhing, crippled bodies of more than one thousand of the dead. In the middle of this ever expanding circle of bodies stood the coach driver, the *aryikas* and me, perfectly unharmed.

They couldn't destroy them, you understand. Their jaws aren't nearly strong or large enough to crush a skull or break a spine, but they didn't need to. Once we learned that the langurs could strike a vicious blow against the dead we learned to use them as surgical strike teams, breaking up the swarms and thinning their numbers ahead of a full attack. We kept them well fed and encouraged them to breed, and by the time the rest of India was overwhelmed we'd amassed a force of over ten thousand in Rajasthan alone. As soon as we reestablished communications and supply lines with the rest of the country we even began to export them, sending dozens, hundreds at a time to all corners of India.

The langurs were truly our saviors, our secret weapon against the dead, and – I only truly began to believe after watching them fight that day – a gift from the Gods.

Parikh grins as we finally reach the centerpiece of the gardens, a four meter tall sandstone statue of a langur standing on its hind legs, teeth bared and arms raised. On its chest it wears the updated crest of the Indian army, two crossed swords over a crimson background with a langur between the blades, and on both arms it carries the two chevrons of the Naik, the Indian

Army equivalent to the rank of Corporal.

I know it's corny, but I like it. Last year we finally convinced the government to agree to give every one of Jodhpur's langurs the honorary rank of Naik. The Jains raised the money to build the statue, and they even got the government to throw in a little surprise for me.

He tugs back a fold in his dhoti and proudly displays the three chevrons sewn into his shoulder.

They made me the Havildar of the Jodhpur Langurs.

Havildar Neelamani Parikh turns out his bag on the ground, emptying a pile of blossoms, bananas and pomegranates onto the grass in front of the statue, and within moments a hundred or more langurs begin to leap excitedly through the trees towards his gift, whooping and chirruping as they go. The baby releases its tight grip on his shoulder, climbing clumsily down his dhoti until she finally tumbles happily into the center of the pile. Parikh looks down at the young monkey and smiles.

Eat up, Naik. Good girl.

•▼•

:::17:::

Portland, Oregon

For the third year running the government in Anchorage has once again pushed back its target date to reinstate the national census to 'no later than a decade from now', and the vast logistical challenges of reestablishing a reliable form of national ID have frustrated officials since the idea was first tabled. Quite simply, the US lacks the necessary technical capacity to undertake such a mammoth task, and the ramifications are far reaching. Property and boundary disputes are rife, accusations of electoral fraud are common, and even today we have no way of determining the population of the United States with any degree of confidence. Estimates range from thirty five to fifty three million, though they are based on precious little hard data.

For some, however, the confusion presents a golden opportunity to do good. Alan Lamb is one of only seven full time employees of the greatly diminished US Census Bureau, currently headquartered on the ground floor of Portland's Waterfront Station Post Office. With the help of a handful of part time and volunteer employees it's Alan's job to comb through the endless stacks of incomplete, fragmented paper records recovered from a wide range of sources around the country, helping to arbitrate everything from boundary disputes to matters of probate.

While the dull, painstaking process of settling

legal battles takes up the lion's share of Alan's time, whenever he can find a spare moment he devotes his energies to a pet project of his. Using the treasure trove of documents at his disposal he helps reconnect survivors with loved ones separated during the panic, a cause close to his heart after losing touch with his own family at the onset of the crisis.

Madness. That's the only way you can describe the exodus from the cities when we learned there was no help coming. It was sheer madness.

We'd spent months preparing our homes for a siege, stocking up on food, water, medicine and whatnot, just waiting for the moment we were all dreading to finally arrive: the announcement that they'd been spotted within our city limits. You'd think people would have fled to the countryside months earlier, right? You'd think the cities would already be ghost towns. I mean, that's the way you always see it in the movies. The smart folks get out long before the poop hits the fan, and the only people left when it all goes to heck are the dumb fools who refused to face reality.

Well, that's not the way real life works, more's the pity. Who had the luxury of quitting their job and decamping with their family to some safe little hidey hole in the woods? Almost nobody, that's who. Few of us could rearrange our lives like that, and especially not on the small chance that the danger would ever reach our doorstep.

No, folks stayed home and just prepared as best they could. We wove it into our daily lives, setting aside a little cash from each pay check to buy... I don't know, like, a pallet of beans or a fifty gallon drum of water. We'd pile everything up in the garage under a tarp and forget about it. Couple Jerry cans, a box of batteries, maybe a bunch of MREs you bought online when you remembered you had a little cash sitting in your PayPal account.

We all kinda thought that if and when the time came it'd be a matter of toughing it out for a few days before the army rolled in and saved us, and that's pretty much the advice we got from official sources. Stay indoors. Don't panic. Prepare to lose power and water. Sit tight and wait for help to arrive. We were told over and over that the absolute worst thing we could do is go running around like headless chickens, blocking up the roads.

It was the day we lost New York and the VP that everything went crazy. They tried to keep it quiet, but it wasn't long before it became crystal clear that the city had been *allowed* to fail. No cops on the street, and no army on the way. Everyone just went nuts, all at once. We all suddenly realized that our homes may not be sanctuaries but death traps, cages in which we'd wait until either the dead broke through the doors or the air force bombed the bejesus out of us.

"And that's how the exodus started?"

Yup. For Sacramento, at least. Maybe other cities got off more lightly.

I was at the office when it happened. Pam was at home with the kids, rearranging tin cans and doing all the other weird little odd jobs that helped keep her OCD at bay. Before I left that morning I told her to keep the TV switched off. She was already a nervous wreck, and the rolling news from New York really wasn't helping anything. She didn't listen, of course. I could hear the set blaring away in the background when she called. Thank

God she'd been watching when they broke in with a local report.

"They're in Carmichael!" That's the first thing she said when I finally picked up on, like, the tenth ring. I had to ask her to repeat herself twice before she slowed down enough for me to understand. Carmichael? *Jeez.* That was only about eight miles from our house as the crow flies. My heart jumped into my throat and my stomach fell out my butt. I looked out the window at the street expecting to see pandemonium out there, but the traffic was moving just like always. I figured word hadn't gotten out yet. Maybe we could beat the rush if we were quick.

I remember thinking at a mile a minute, kicking myself that we hadn't already come up with an escape plan to deal with a situation like this. "OK, hon," I said, trying to keep my voice calm, "here's what I need you to do. Get the kids, load up the minivan with whatever you can carry and head on up to your mom's place. I'll meet you there. I'm leaving the office right now, OK?"

Those were the last words I said to her. Didn't even tell her I loved her.

I was already at the car by the time I hung up the phone. Didn't bother to lock my office door or even tell anyone where I was going. I pulled out into traffic without looking both ways and almost wiped out on the side of a bus before I even reached the street. Stupid. My mind was racing. I kept looking over my shoulder as if I expected to see a bunch of zombies chasing after me.

I guess Pam must have hit the highway before me. I had to battle through the city traffic as word started to spread and people started panicking, so it was a good half hour before I was on the 5 and driving north past the airport. Maybe Pam was already a few miles ahead. Maybe she was just a few *cars* ahead, but there was no way in heck I could pick out an anonymous white minivan from the thousands already snaking out ahead.

It was... weird. I'm sure you can put it a little more poetically than that if you wanna play with the words. I never was all that creative, so that's pretty much the best way I can describe what I saw on the road. Up ahead the traffic was at a total standstill. Thousands of cars, and most of them seemed to have been caught in the middle of changing lanes. I could see plumes of black smoke in the distance up ahead, and I guessed maybe a car had caught fire. *No problem*, I thought. *That explains the traffic. Maybe we're down to one lane.* I think I was still trying to convince myself that this was just a normal day. You know, that people were still acting rationally. The cops would arrive and start directing traffic, and soon enough we'd all be on our way.

I began to worry when I saw people start to drive on the shoulder, and when I noticed that a few cars had found their way to the other side and were tearing away towards oncoming traffic I felt the panic *really* set in. A few trucks were even bouncing through the fields to our left, cutting lines through the crops, but those of us on the highway were pretty much penned in between the median strip and the drainage canal that ran alongside the road. That's when everyone started climbing out of their cars. Not really all that scared yet, but frustrated. You know, shaking their heads, climbing onto the beds of pickups to look out ahead, blaming the crappy drivers who'd snarled up the road.

I was halfway out of the Volvo when I heard the gunshot. Everyone on the road just, you know, *flinched*, all at once. Then another shot rang out, and another, and that's when we realized the shots weren't coming from behind us but ahead. *Ahead?* What the heck? It was supposed to be safe that way!

Everything seemed to go real quiet for a few seconds, like everybody was hoping they'd just imagined it. It was like we were all just holding our breath, praying it wasn't real. We didn't even move when we saw the first person come running back between the cars, sprinting through the traffic with a terrified look on her face. We just... stood there. *Nope. This ain't happening.*

All of a sudden I heard this... this *roar*, kinda like the crowd at a football game. The people up ahead on top of their pickups all turned at the same moment and just started *sprinting* back in the direction of the city. No expressions on their faces, like they just couldn't spare the energy for fear. That's when I jumped back into the car. Don't know why. I was blocked in on all four sides, but I just wanted to feel *safe*, you know? I wanted to feel something solid around me, so I pulled the door closed behind me, locked it, lowered myself into the foot well and shrank myself down as small as I could get, head between my legs and my butt pressed against the gearshift.

I don't know how long I stayed there curled in a ball like a frightened hedgehog. All I know is I heard people running so fast by my car that their screams were like a police siren. Y'know, like the, umm, the Doppler effect. Like *AAAAAAaaaaaaaaaeeeeeeeeooooooo!* Lots of them, maybe hundreds, so many the car shook back and forth as they bumped into it.

After that it went real quiet for a few minutes. I thought about climbing out to see what was going on, but then I got this, like, *shiver* down the back of my neck. Did you ever lay in bed in the dark and suddenly imagine there's someone on the other side of the room just watching you, waiting for you to move, so you just freeze up and pretend to be asleep? It was that kinda feeling. Made me want to hold my breath so I could stay as still as possible.

I heard the first one right about then, just outside the car. It was moving real slow, like it was dragging its feet. I *really* wanted to look up, just to see if it had noticed me, but I just couldn't move. I was frozen. I couldn't even hold on to my pee, I was so scared, and I was even more terrified when I realized my pants were dripping onto the rubber floor mat real loud. Sounded like a drum beat, and I was sure it'd alert the things outside. What a way to go, huh?

I didn't move for hours after that. Every couple minutes I'd hear more of them go by, sometimes alone and sometimes in big groups. Lord knows where they were all coming from. My legs went to sleep and started to tingle, then prick, then the pain got so bad I wanted to cry, but I didn't dare move a muscle until I was sure they'd all gone. I just held myself there, curled up in a little ball smelling my pee as it dried into the floor and tasting the tears running down to my chin. When I finally worked up the courage to move it was dark out, and the only light I saw were from cars on fire further down the road.

I think I walked for... I don't know, I guess five or ten miles through the cars before I saw it, a white minivan with all the doors closed and the driver's side window smashed in. I stood there for about a half hour before I dared go anywhere near it. I didn't want to see, y'know? I know it's dumb, but I figured that as long as I just stayed standing there looking at the van they were still alive, but the moment I walked up and looked in...

It was empty. Well, not *empty*. Dylan's security blanket and Chloe's pacifier were on the back seat, but there was no sign of them. No way to know where they might be. The window was smashed in from the outside, I know that much, but who broke it? Was it an accident, or was something trying to get in?

I look away as Alan removes his glasses and wipes a tear from his cheek, and for the first time I notice what's on his desk beside him: a faded SpongeBob SquarePants felt blanket, and resting on top of it a pink pacifier with a gummy teething ring for a handle. Alan notices, and lets out an embarrassed snort.

Look at me, welling up like a baby. There's gotta be millions of people all around the world who don't know if their families are still alive. I don't know what makes *me* so special.

Maybe they're still alive. I find little rays of hope every now and then, hints in the paperwork about refugee camps that were never officially surveyed. Who knows, maybe they made it to one of them. Maybe Pam didn't make it, God forbid, but the kids did. They were too young to know their surname or where they lived, so maybe they're living somewhere right now with no idea who they really are. No idea their dad's still looking.

It's all I can think about sometimes. Like, what would they look like now? Dylan would be going on fourteen, a real little man, y'know? Chloe would be twelve next month. Hell, I don't even know if I'd recognize them if I passed them in the street.

We both look up as the door to the office creaks open and a middle aged woman walks in. She looks disheveled and flustered, a tissue

tightly clutched in her hand and her eyes red ringed. An assistant rushes over to her, and after a few words directs her over to Alan's desk. Alan collects himself, grabs a loose binder from his desk and stands, suddenly cheerful and full of energy.

Wanna see something cool? This right here is hands down the best part of my job.

The lady arrives at the desk and stops beside me, looking at Alan with a strange mixture of hope and fear. "I'm Susan Robbie. You called my office?" she says in a shaky voice, half question, half statement. Alan pulls a Xeroxed photo from his binder and passes it to her. It's a picture of a young man of around eighteen, smiling and dressed in a smart military uniform.

Ms. Robbie, do you recognize this boy?

She leans against my shoulder for support as her knees buckle. The photo shakes in her hands. For a moment a look of confusion flickers across her face, and her voice emerges in a whisper. "This is my son. This is Kevin, but he's... He was just a little boy when I..."

"Ma'am, I've found him for you. I've found Kevin. He's at the camp in Anchorage. He's waiting for you, Ms. Robbie."

She begins to collapse before Alan catches her, lifting her up and holding her tight as she convulses in long, heaving sobs. Before long Alan joins her, burying his face in her shoulder as the tears stream down his cheeks.

After a moment I feel tears prick at my own eyes, and as I notice once again the blanket and pacifier sitting on Alan's desk I decide to leave them to each other, both weeping for the people they've lost. I walk away, embarrassed and ashamed of myself. As I leave the office and emerge into the sunlight I tell myself I'm late for my next appointment, but I know the truth is that I don't want to be present when Ms. Robbie's tears dry, but Alan's still flow.

•▼•

:::18:::

North Bend, Oregon

By the summer of 2019 the offices of *American Woodsmith Magazine* were on the verge of closure, and the printing presses, paper stock and other equipment were due to be auctioned to offset the eye watering debts of the failing publication. From a mid-Eighties peak of over a million subscribers nationwide circulation had tumbled to a hair under thirty thousand, and as word arrived of the first US outbreaks a cloud hung over the office as the staff prepared for the release of its final issue.

Today *American Woodsmith* – now renamed *Survive and Thrive* – is by far the nation's most popular publication and one of the largest employers in south west Oregon, boasting a staff of nine hundred and distributing almost six million copies to a global audience each month. The expanded operation now includes a radio station, a TV studio equipped for both live and pre-recorded broadcasts, and a small but growing staff to manage the magazine's online presence now that Internet connections are being restored throughout the US.

Marshall Stinson has held the position of Editor-in-Chief since joining the magazine in 2014. A former National Park Service ranger, EMT and long-time volunteer firefighter, it was he who first saw the need for a basic, accessible survival guide for the layperson. We sit in his

office overlooking the busy printing floor, raising our voices above the racket as thousands of copies each minute spit from the presses, and he points to a framed copy of the first post-outbreak issue hanging above his desk.

Ten pages. That's all we could afford to print at first, what with the bank holding most of our paper stock and our ink stores running low. We couldn't get hold of any 60lb gloss text – that's standard magazine grade paper – so the first run we printed on cheap recycled 80lb trash stock. We literally went begging door to door for every scrap before Nick came through and donated enough money for a thousand reams.

Stinson pulls the frame down from the wall and passes it across the desk. The pages are densely packed with text and basic diagrams that make use of every square inch of paper. The title still reads _American Woodsmith_ with _Survive and Thrive_ as a subtitle, but there's nothing at all related to woodwork in the text. Instead the articles relate to all manner of survival techniques, from how to read a mountaineering compass to how to identify edible nuts, berries and leaves.

We published that issue maybe a month or two after the first wave fled the cities, when the real chaos was just beginning. Twenty million people left their homes in the space of a couple of weeks, all of them expecting to live out some dumbass Davy Crockett frontier fantasy, and most of them lacked the common sense and basic survival skills to tie their shoelaces without an online tutorial. It was the largest single migration event in American history, and it was carried out by people whose experience of the wilderness extended only as far as Jack London novels and a few years playing The Oregon Trail as kids.

It was a buddy of mine, Mike Critchley, who first turned me on to the scale of the problems we were facing. He'd been working as a ranger up at Suislaw National Forest when the first wave set up camp, and when the trickle of new arrivals turned into a torrent he asked me to spend a couple of weeks up there to help lighten the load. At first I assumed he just wanted me to help direct traffic or point people towards the latrines. It wasn't until I got there that I discovered just how desperate the situation really was.

When I arrived at the Rock Creek campground the welcome mat Mike had laid out for me was fifty bodies wrapped in tarps, piled up in a heap in the parking lot. The smell hit me as soon as I turned off the coast road. I'm sure you know that smell, right? They'd been sitting there for two weeks at eighty degrees, just baking in the sun, and these bodies hadn't been all that fresh to begin with. Dysentery victims don't leave fragrant corpses.

I remember the wild-eyed look on Mike's face as he told me that something like seventy thousand idiots had descended on the park over the last couple of months. He was right on the edge, close to losing it as he talked about these people like a naturalist describing a newly discovered species, *Homo ignoramus*. He was just beyond baffled that so many people had arrived lacking the most basic survival skills, and what was even more baffling was that these people should have been the *most* capable of the refugees. They hadn't been forced from their homes. They hadn't fled with nothing but the shirts on their backs. They'd *chosen* to leave. They'd had time to pack supplies and prepare to survive in the wilderness, but they just didn't have the first clue what they were doing.

Mike told me the new arrivals had mostly congregated close to the campground, where they could find a spot to dump their cars. They'd ranged themselves out over a stretch of maybe three miles, most of them just a stone's throw from the creek so they could have access to fresh water, but it seems few of them had considered the fact that water doesn't remain all that fresh once a few thousand people upstream have relieved themselves and dumped their trash on the banks.

By the time it reached the entrance to the campground the creek was nothing but milky sludge with a film of motor oil shimmering on the surface. You wouldn't have used the stuff to clean your car, let alone actually drink it, but these people were guzzling it down with abandon, congratulating themselves on their ability to survive out in the wilderness like honest-to-God pioneers.

My Lord, I'd never seen an outbreak of dysentery sweep through a population so violently. I was a Peace Corps kid in my youth and I'd seen this kind of thing before, but at least out in Angola they'd understood the risks and respected the danger. They knew how to treat the sickness and avoid spreading infection, but at Suislaw it seemed like the folks were completely ignorant to what was going on. Thousands of sufferers were crapping out their body weight in diarrhea every day just a few steps from the creek, and to combat the dehydration their loved ones were pouring even more contaminated water down their throats. It was pure madness. It's incredible that the fatality rate was so low.

Poor sanitation was just the tip of the iceberg, unfortunately. Mike took me on a hike through the camp, and over the course of a single afternoon he gave me enough material to write a ten volume series on how *not* to approach a survival situation. Aside from thousands of people digging their latrine ditches just a few steps from their only source of fresh water I saw hundreds of people risking their lives through sheer ignorance.

We found one family camping right in the middle of a poison oak thicket, baffled as to why they were all suffering from painful rashes. A little later we stumbled on a tent deep in the forest that contained three bodies, parents and a young girl, and after just a couple of minutes of scouting we found a bunch of deadly nightshade plants behind their tent, almost picked clean. The berries taste kinda sweet, but it only takes a couple of dozen of them to kill a grown man. I don't know, maybe they thought they were blackcurrants.

Then there were the accidents. One woman had suffered a nasty compound fracture when she tried to fell a backleaning tree from the wrong side and brought it crashing down on her leg. Another guy lost a couple of fingers playing with a chainsaw he didn't know how to use.

We even found one dumbass with a nasty infected wound on his arm, and it was only after we warned him he'd die if it wasn't treated that he told us how it happened. It turns out he'd read an article online that told him to dig pits lined with punji sticks to catch feral pigs. He'd found what he thought was a game trail and dug four or five pits, but he'd neglected to mark their locations and ended up falling into one of them as he fumbled around in the middle of the night looking for a place to take a dump. I didn't have the heart to tell him the closest feral pigs were a couple hundred miles to the east of the park. He lost the arm in the end. I doubt he's still alive.

Stinson carefully replaces the framed copy of his first issue on its hook and sighs as he surveys the lead article on the front page, a set of basic instructions for filtering and purifying water.

Not so many years ago every good parent took the time to raise their kids to be self-sufficient and resourceful, just as all humankind had done for millennia. Learning how to fend for yourself had since time immemorial been just a regular part of growing up, and in recent times we'd even fetishized it as some sort of rite of passage. Hell, I went on my first hunt with my dad when I was eight years old, just me, him and a case of Coors, and I took down my first buck with the old man's Winchester Model 70 at nine.

By the time I was in high school I could light a fire with flint and kindling. I could dress a kill and cure the meat. I could build a basic shelter, identify a hundred edible berries, leaves and fungi, treat a wound in the field, and if you dumped me in the middle of nowhere with nothing but a compass and a simple hand drawn map I'd still beat you home, and I'd have a couple of rabbits skinned and ready to cook hanging from my belt.

In short I could *survive,* and I'd never considered for a moment that this was anything out of the ordinary. I'd always assumed these skills were still being passed on from father to son – after all, they were skills any half competent boy scout should have mastered before his first lay – but somewhere along the way the chain had been broken. Fathers had stopped teaching their kids, and when they passed they took the skills with them to the grave.

We'd become a nation of half men; a generation of helpless pussies that had never faced a greater challenge than putting together a Billy bookcase or scavenging for chia seeds and quinoa at the local Whole Foods. We were happy to store our survival skills on the Internet, and when that began to fail we lost the ability to keep ourselves alive outside of our soft, cushioned Netflix bubble. We'd become so successful at smoothing off the edges of our society that we'd forgotten how to live in the real world, and now our complacency was coming back to bite us in the ass. *Hard.*

The solution presented itself as soon as I returned to North Bend to oversee the final issue of *American Woodsmith.* I was sitting up here in my office, worrying about the millions of people venturing out from their homes without the skills to save themselves, and it occurred to me that the greatest threat Americans faced wasn't zombies. They may have been the most visible and alarming threat, sure, but when you get right down to it they're slow moving, slow witted creatures driven by instinct and lacking any sort of real intelligence. A zombie is just a dumber version of a living human, and nobody with a working brain, a pair of legs and a basic weapon should have to worry too much about them.

No, the greatest threat to Americans was *America itself;* the raw, unvarnished America into which we were all being thrust now the power and water were failing and the local Walmart had been looted to its last roll of toilet paper. Beneath the surface America is wild and violent. It's a country that'll kill you stone dead at the first opportunity, and if people were going to survive they'd need to be able deal with everything America could throw at them, from tainted water to poisonous plants to wild animals to potholed roads. They'd need to know how to change a tire, darn their clothes, stave off the cold and quench their thirst until the government could wrest back some sort of control over the nation, and they needed someone to teach them those skills, *quickly.*

In short, what America desperately, urgently needed was a father figure, and as I looked down on the printing presses at all those men working the machines I saw nothing but fathers. I saw a group of wise old men with calloused hands and active minds; men who'd spent time in the outdoors and knew how to take care of themselves. I also saw a bank of printing presses, and it occurred to me that if we could just get their lifetimes of experience down on paper we might be able to do a little good. Maybe help a few folks get through what was coming.

Stinson points up at the framed copy and smiles.

That first issue ran to fifty thousand copies, right down to our last sheet of paper, and we split them into batches of five hundred and handed them to cops, park rangers, troop transports, and even a few commercial pilots bound for the east coast, with a request that they pass them on to as many people as possible.

Our goal was to get a thousand copies to each state, but we knew we couldn't be picky. We knew most would probably end up thrown in the trash or forgotten in the trunk of a car, and those few that found readers wouldn't go further than a couple hundred miles, but we did our level best to spread them far and wide.

And that was that, pretty much. Once they were all out the door we dusted off our hands, congratulated each other on a job well done and locked the office doors. We were out of paper and our ink had run dry, so we figured there was nothing more we could do.

It wasn't until a month later that the infection finally

boiled over throughout the US, when we started seeing cases in the small towns as well as the cities. You remember when the news networks started running 24 hour coverage of the Peoria quarantine? Remember that interview with the National Guardsman who'd been ordered to fire on civilians? When he burst into tears and said there'd been kids in the crowd rushing the barricade?

Poor bastard. They shouldn't have let him on camera before making sure he wasn't still carrying his weapon. Anyway, *that* was when the real exodus from the cities began, when everyone was terrified *their* town would be the next to see roadblocks set up on the outskirts, and *their* kids locked inside to die. That's when *everyone* began to flee the cities, rather than just the prescient few.

Eugene was already a no-go zone by then. The highway was blocked by a few big wrecks, so the 101 through North Bend had become the only safe northbound route. I was volunteering at an aid station on the road into town, directing traffic up to Portland, Oregon's only sanctuary city. Lots of traffic. Lots of scared people who'd fled their homes without enough cash, gas, food or water. We saw maybe twenty thousand refugees come through town each day, and we worked all hours of the day and night arranging car pools for those who'd run out of gas or broken down along the way.

I'd all but forgotten about the magazine by then. It had been a nice idea, but faced with the scale of the crisis it now seemed more than a little naive to think we could save lives with a silly little ten page pamphlet. To be honest I think I was feeling a little bitter about the whole experience, having spent so much time and effort pissing into the wind when I should have been preparing to keep my family safe. I mean, hell, just the money we spent on the issue might have bought me a small boat, just big enough to get the kids out. Maybe their mom, too, if I could stand to look at her without getting mad about all the alimony I'd paid her over the years.

And then I got in a fistfight.

It was stupid, really. Some rich prick stopped at the aid station one morning to ask about safe routes to the north, and he just rubbed me up the wrong way from the moment he stepped out of his car. Everything about him was just... *punchable*, know what I mean? My fists started to twitch just looking at the guy. You ever meet anyone like that? I've seen one or two in my time, guys who just have faces that seem to be missing a fist.

Anyway, this guy was driving solo in a Mercedes AMG G65 with nothing but a couple of Louis Vuitton suitcases and a few Jerry cans full of gas in the trunk. Now this thing was – bar none – the *least* fuel efficient SUV on the market. It averaged something like 10MPG, and this prick had driven 800 miles from LA without a single passenger. All I could think about when I looked at that smug, sun bed tanned face of his were the hundreds of people he must have passed by along the way, stranded and with little hope of survival, while he coasted to safety using enough gas to take 30 people from LA to Portland by Prius.

Now don't get me wrong, I'm not a hemp pants and sandal wearing tree hugger. I love me a gas guzzler, and a big SUV is gonna take you places a hybrid can't handle, but this guy just pushed my buttons. When I asked him if he'd take some passengers along for the ride he looked at me like something he'd scraped from the bottom of his shoe, laughed, pointed at his rear seats and asked me if I'd allow strangers to scuff up *my* Nappa leather, "If you even *know* what Nappa leather is."

It was hands down the most satisfying punch I'd ever

thrown. It was just... I don't know, it was just months of pent up frustration expelling itself on a single deserving nose. I could feel the cartilage crunch beneath my knuckles, and I followed through with enough force to spread it right across his face. *God*, it felt good. Yoga and meditation can suck it.

Before the guy even hit the ground I reached into the back of his truck and tugged out a suitcase that probably cost more than my car, and I tossed it out on the street as I called over to a group of folks who'd been waiting all day for a ride. The guy cried out as the suitcase burst open on the asphalt and the contents spilled out, and that's when I noticed the paper. I only caught a glimpse of it for a moment before he snatched it from the ground along with his $50 silk socks and whatever other nonsense he'd packed, but I'd have recognized it anywhere. It was my magazine, in the hands of some prick from a city 800 miles away.

He gave it up pretty easily – he flinched as soon as I took a step towards him, the pussy – and I was amazed to see that this wasn't an original. We'd published on 80lb gloss but this was standard A4 copier paper. Someone had actually been Xeroxing it! I demanded he tell me where he got it, and he said they'd been handing out copies for weeks all across California.

"Who's *they?*" I asked.

"*Everyone!* The cops, the army... They're giving out free copies at every gas station between here and Santa Monica!"

I was just floored. I thought at best we'd helped maybe a couple hundred people prepare for the journey out of the cities. In my more optimistic moments I'd thought that maybe – just *maybe* – we'd have saved one or two people from drinking tainted water or, you know, eating the wrong type of mushrooms, but no. As the days went by I found more and more people carrying their own copies from as far afield as Tuscon and Salt Lake City.

I still have no clue how it got so big so fast. I've honestly no idea who was Xeroxing these things, or who was distributing them right across the south west. All I know is that before long people were stopping as they passed through North Bend specifically to thank me.

One woman from down in Medford was in tears as she told me she'd been stuck for a week in the Rogue River Forest with a sick husband and nothing to feed him but raw rabbit meat because she had no way to light a fire. Just when she thought all was lost she dug out her copy and found an article that explained how to light tinder by polishing the base of a soda can with toothpaste until it's reflective enough to concentrate the sun's heat on a focal point. She got the fire started before sundown and her husband got to eat enough to regain his strength, and all because a guy sitting in our office decided to put a good idea on paper. I didn't write that article, but I happily accepted the hug.

It wasn't long after that that the government started to take notice. A couple of troop transports passed through town, and while they were refueling a Major took me aside and asked me to confirm that I was really the editor-in-chief of 'that survival magazine'. When I said yeah he told me to try not to leave town unless it was overrun. Another guy – a Captain, I think – arrived a few days later and told me, pretty damned cryptically, to sit tight. "Just a few more days now, sir. Hope you guys can hold out."

They finally came for us a week later in a long line of Humvees, just as the infection began to arrive in some of the nearby coastal towns. I thought they were kidding when they said they had orders to take us up to Portland,

and when they told us we'd been designated essential civilian assets I almost laughed out loud, but I played along.

I couldn't find everyone – some of the guys had already skipped town, and one had been killed while trying to get his grandkids out of Santa Barbara – but by the end of the day we had most of the team and their families gathered at the aid station. I couldn't believe it when we climbed into the Humvees and, instead of joining the 101, they took us to the parking lot of the local Walmart and loaded us all onto a waiting Osprey. *An Osprey!* You ever seen one of those things?

They were all pretty tight lipped on the flight north. You know, usual military bullshit. "My orders are just to deliver you to your destination, sir," that kind of thing. It wasn't until we arrived in Portland that we discovered what they had in store for us. They'd commandeered the offices of The Oregonian, the city's largest newspaper, and the same Major who'd passed through North Bend a couple of weeks earlier was waiting there to meet us. He sat me down in his office, handed me a cigar and offered us full funding to produce new copies of the magazine "as often as you can get those damned things out on the street."

We were treated like rock stars around Portland from the day we arrived. The Survival Dudes, they called us. They gave us anything we asked for as long as we kept pushing out new issues as fast as we could write them, and lemme tell you we wrote *fast*. We covered *everything*, with regular issues going out weekly along with occasional special editions dedicated to single subjects. Preparing for Winter was a big hit, as were Basic Auto Care and Unusual Foods. You can still find copies of those issues in almost every home in the US.

Most of them aren't originals, of course. We only had the resources to publish maybe fifty thousand copies each week in Portland, and in any case it wouldn't have been efficient to distribute all across the country from up here in the Pacific North West. Instead the copies we published locally were distributed to safe zones throughout the state, while extras flown out on military transports around the country to be replicated locally, like the old Russian samizdat system. Some were even sent out internationally and translated into other languages.

Some of the rarer editions fetch a high price on the collector's market now. Kinda makes me wish I'd held on to more of the originals. You know, someone once told me the Chinese made a knockoff version with a title that translates as *Become Old Man and Make Many Children*, but I think they may have just been yanking my chain.

Stinson points once again at the copy on the wall behind him.

Last year a collector in Anchorage offered me eighty grand for this one. It's one of only twelve known originals of the first issue, and it's gotta be the only one still in mint condition. Like I told him at the time, I took it with me when we moved the office back to North Bend, and I'll take it with me to the grave when the time finally comes.

He looks at his watch.

Hey, I almost forgot. You want to go see Nick? He should be on by now.

Stinson leads me from the office, across the busy printing floor and through to the new wing

of the building that now houses *Survive and Thrive*'s TV studio. I've been looking forward to this since Stinson agreed to the interview several months ago, and I try to contain my excitement as he holds a silencing finger to his lips and pushes open the door. Above it a red neon sign reads 'RECORDING. QUIET PLEASE.'

Beyond the door a cameraman move slowly around a small workshop as the host gathers tools and lays out a stack of tightly bound reeds and long, supple willow branches. The host looks to be around sixty years old, with a plaid shirt straining against his paunch and the trademark bushy mustache still covering his upper lip. He looks into the camera and explains in a terse, authoritative voice that today he'll be teaching the viewers how to build a coracle, a traditional lightweight woven boat used for centuries in parts of the United Kingdom.

"Now you'll want to waterproof the interior before setting it afloat," he says. "If you can get your hands on a waterproof poly tarp that would be ideal, but five or six layered trash bags will do the job at a pinch."

There's something oddly disorienting about seeing a pre-war celebrity in the flesh, something that jars with our perception of reality. The idea that these characters we knew from stage and screen were real people who had to struggle to survive along with us never stops feeling bizarre.

The man standing before the camera is Nick Offerman, the actor and master carpenter who for seven seasons played Ron Swanson in the NBC sitcom *Parks and Recreation*. It was Offerman who donated the funds that made the first issue possible, and it's he who for the last decade has co-managed *Survive and Thrive* with his old college roommate Marshall Stinson. Both have been awarded the Presidential Medal of Freedom, the highest civilian award the nation has to offer, in recognition of their immense contribution to the security and national interests of the United States.

Stinson turns to me and smiles.

Ten years and he's never taken a single paycheck. What a guy.

•▼•

BP Magnus Platform, North of the Shetland Islands

For the past five days the Sullom Voe Oil Terminal has been socked in by a dense pea soup fog, grounding all flights and cutting off the Shetlands from the Scottish mainland, and when a brief break in the weather finally arrives we waste no time. Within the hour my chopper departs for Magnus Platform, the towering rig that looms over the shallow but famously violent sea one hundred miles north east of the Shetland Islands. Strapped in to the seats around me a dozen replacement guards nervously check their weapons as they steel themselves for the beginning of their arduous month long shift.

Magnus is the first and only drilling platform in the North Sea to be pressed back into service since the war, and it has brought new hope to a country desperate for oil to power its reconstruction. The seven wells pumping far beneath Magnus have given the UK a measure of security during its drive to convert its energy infrastructure to 100% renewable sources, though it will likely be at least another decade before this goal is achieved.

As we circle the vast rig in preparation for landing I gaze down in awe at the mammoth swell, the waves mercilessly pounding the thick concrete legs of the platform. On the helipad below a tiny figure struggles to remain upright in the harsh wind as he waves us in. He leans steeply into the gale as his blaze orange windbreaker flaps around him.

We land with a harsh jolt, bouncing twice before we finally settle on the pad, and the guards spring from their seats and out the door, immediately forming a protective perimeter around the chopper. As I climb down behind them I have to grip the door to stay on my feet in the salt-edged gale. The new guards will remain in place for the next hour as they offload supplies, and I have been warned that if I fail to return in time for the scheduled departure I'll be forced to remain with them on the rig until the next shift change four weeks from now. This, I'm assured, would not be a pleasant experience.

As the guards begin to offload refrigerated coolers stamped with bio-hazard warnings from the rear of the chopper one of them breaks from the group and orders me to follow, leading me three levels down a flight of rickety steel steps to the mess, a long, low-ceilinged room harshly lit under fluorescent strip lighting. The guard enters cautiously ahead of me. His weapon is drawn, and he only calls me in once he confirms that my host's feet are shackled to a steel loop welded to the floor, and that his mesh spit hood is securely fastened over his head.

My host's name is Mark Baird, the grizzled Falkirk native offshore installation manager of Magnus, and the man ultimately responsible for all operations on the rig. Like everyone else working this rig he is a prisoner.

In the aftermath of the war Baird and those like him presented the United Kingdom with an almost impossible quandary. What should be done with those who had committed the most heinous crimes imaginable during the crisis? Those whose crimes were so terrible they could never be safely reintegrated into society? With the government and electorate reluctant to employ the death penalty, and with long term incarceration seen as an unforgivable waste of scarce resources, what should become of the hundreds – perhaps thousands – of physically capable, often highly skilled men and women who had taken their own survival to extremes that civilized society even now could not stomach?

Magnus provided the answer, at least for this particular group of criminals. After the public learned of their crimes it was determined that Baird and his team could never again set foot on the mainland, but the skills they possessed were invaluable to a country that desperately needed a steady flow of oil, and so a deal was struck. The men would remain here on Magnus under armed guard, generously fed and allowed to live in relative comfort, and in return they would continue to work the Magnus oilfield for the remainder of their days, or until the oil finally runs dry.

The mess is empty but for two steel chairs, both bolted to the ground and facing each other across a plain wooden table. Baird sits in one, and as I take the other I notice that the chain attached to his feet is just a little too short for him to reach me.

Baird ignores me at first, nervously jiggling his leg and balling his hands into fists as he stares at the guard. *"Fuckin' finally!* **You brought the stuff?"** **he demands. The guard nods, walks to the table and sets down a cooler, and at that Baird immediately relaxes in his seat. He turns to me and smiles warmly, as if noticing my presence for the first time, and begins to speak without introduction in a thick, almost impenetrable accent.**

Seven of them killed themselves, did you know that? I doubt it made the news, but the day we were sentenced seven of the lads slipped away from the guards and took a dive over the side of the rig. That's on top of the dozen who jumped since we were stranded, when they couldn't face looking in the mirror any more.

Baird hugs his arms close around his chest and shivers.

I can't imagine a more bloody awful way to go, to be honest. If they'd jumped in the winter they'd have passed out in ten minutes and been dead in twenty, but this was September. The water would have been around fifteen degrees – that's around sixty Fahrenheit, for the Yanks – and at those temperatures they could have survived more than a day before they finally gave up, if they fought against it hard enough. I don't know. Maybe they had the balls to just go under and take a deep breath of water right away, but even if they managed to summon the courage it's... well, I've heard it's not as easy a death as some say.

So... To what do I owe the honor?

"I'd like to hear your side of the story, if you'd like to tell it. People are curious to know exactly how you survived for so long. They want to know how many really died. The tabloids were a little light on the details, given the closed court hearing."

Ha, really? That doesn't sound like them at all. They're rarely shy about making up their own bullshit details for the sake of a good story. Well, I suppose you should make yourself comfortable. Tea and biscuits? I think I saw some Hob Nobs knocking around earlier.

The guard speaks up to remind me that I've been instructed to accept neither food nor drink while on the rig. Baird shoots him a dirty look, then turns back to me.

Well then, I suppose we shall have to live without tea, if you can call that living. Let's crack on.

It wasn't all that bad in the beginning, to be honest. Most of us were no strangers to delays, what with the shite weather up here. Often we'd be socked in for a few days after our shifts ended, and when a bad storm rocked through we could be cut off from the mainland for a week or so, but BP always paid double time for the overstay so nobody was ever all that fussed. That's why nobody went mental when the chopper didn't turn up on time.

I was here in the mess when the call finally came through from Sullom Voe after a week of radio silence. We'd been watching the news whenever we could get the satellite connection to work, so we already knew everything was going tits up on the mainland, but we were holding out hope that the Shetlands were unaffected. We hoped they'd eventually send the choppers and ferry us all back a handful at a time.

Baird shakes his head.

It turns out that both of the Kazan Ka-62s down at the terminal had been commandeered for urgent civilian evacuations from the mainland. We'd been classified as 'grade B, non-critical', they said, which apparently meant that we were civilians with useful skills but we weren't in enough danger to qualify for priority evacuation. They told us we had virtually endless power and clean water thanks to our desalination pumps, solar cells and fuel reserves, and we had enough food to last another six weeks, by which time the crisis would be over and they could spare the vehicles to take us home. Their advice was to sit tight and ride it out, which didn't sit well with us, not one bit.

I complained to the Major who'd taken over Shetland, some posh English bugger who sounded like he was descended from ten generations of inbred Bertie Woosters, and he told us to stop being such pansies and suck it up. We had warm beds, he said, and no fear of the dead breaking down our doors and tearing us to pieces. He told us we were the luckiest people in the world to be stranded where we were, and we should shut up wi' our whingeing.

I remember I lost my cool and let loose on the guy, yelling at him that we all had families waiting for us back on the mainland. I asked him how he'd feel to be trapped out at sea while his kids were terrified at home, wondering what had happened to their pa, and for a minute he went really quiet. Turns out his two wee bairns and his wife had been killed in the outbreak in Dundee a few days earlier. That shut me up quick enough. Poor bastard.

Anyway, there were 127 of us on the rig the day we were stranded, most of us with years of offshore experience, so there was no real panic. Lots of griping. Lots of worry about what was going on back home, but no panic. Roughnecks aren't emotional types, you see. They're sensible, pragmatic, and steady as a rock until you put a drink in 'em, so we discussed the problem calmly and with no fuss.

A few of the lads wanted to take the lifeboats and try to make it back to land. Seemed like a solid idea, and the boats had more than enough room for everyone aboard, but our coxswain quickly shat on that idea. They were short range only, he said, designed for evacuation and recovery. They only had small maneuvering motors intended to steer the craft clear of flotsam or a burning rig, but over long distance they'd be about as much use as a chocolate teapot.

Up in these waters without any hope of recovery they'd be caught in the current and drift helplessly north into the Arctic, so the best case scenario was that we'd wash up somewhere in the north of Norway or even Svalbard in a few weeks, where we'd either starve or freeze to death, whichever came first.

No, when it came down to it there was really only one sensible option. We'd stay put and ride it out, and trust that the crisis wouldn't go on longer than our supplies held out. Some of the lads kept up their grumbling, but deep down they knew it was the only real choice.

For a while it wasn't so bad, all told. Life went on pretty much as normal. We had the gym, a movie room with lots of DVDs, and even a little library. Well, I say library, but it was really just a stack of Jeremy Clarkson books, five dog eared copies of Bravo Two Zero and a big stack of porn mags some absolute bloody hero had left behind. Once we'd remotely plugged the wells and choked the pipeline back to the mainland there wasn't much work to do apart from basic maintenance, so we just sat around twiddling our thumbs and, ahem, *enjoying* the literature in our cabins.

One thing everyone did at least once a day was come up to the mess and watch the news on the big screen. It didn't make for pleasant viewing. Things seemed to be spiraling out of control back on the mainland. First they lost their grip on the south coast, and then the infection reached the cities and started to spread out into the countryside until eventually it seemed there wasn't a single square mile in the UK that was completely safe apart from the sanctuary cities and a few offshore islands.

That's when we started to let the worry get to us a little. We spent more time on the radio to Sullom Voe, begging for them to come and fetch us, but each time we asked we were given the same response. Not yet. There are people in more urgent need. Sit tight and stop whingeing.

And then one day we finally lost contact with the mainland. I remember turning on the TV one morning and seeing nothing but a blue screen with the words 'signal lost' scrolling across it. I tried all the channels but they were all gone, and the same went for the radio. Just silence and static, or recorded messages playing on a loop, each of them saying the exact same thing they'd been saying for weeks. Stay in your homes. Don't try to reach friends and loved ones. Help is on the way. *Help is on the way.* Joke of the fuckin' century, that was.

It was like a tether had suddenly been cut between us

and the rest of the world, casting us adrift. Until then I hadn't really panicked. I hadn't let the fear get to me, but the day we lost the mainland it just came flooding in all at once. I felt like I couldn't breathe.

And then the food began to run out.

Baird falls silent for a moment, gnawing nervously on a hangnail.

Did you know the average human can survive as long as two months without a single bite of food? Two months. It really doesn't sound all that long when you think about it, eight weeks or so. Difficult, of course, and bloody unpleasant, but not beyond the realms of possibility. Gandhi almost managed a month, and he was a skinny bugger to begin with. I was a fat bastard, so I was starting with a decent buffer.

The truth is that it's worse than you could ever grasp. You can't imagine what hunger *really* feels like until you've gone a month without a mouthful of food. You just can't comprehend it, not *really*. It goes beyond pain. It's *everything*. It becomes almost a physical presence, an obsession, something living inside you through every bloody waking moment. You can't sleep. Can't think. Can't speak. You bite your fingernails down to the quick. You gnaw at the skin at the side of the nails just to have something in your mouth, and you can't stop even when you taste blood.

We started eating paper just a few days after the food stores ran out. Toilet paper was easiest to swallow, but there was no shortage of A4 sheets in the office. By the end of the third week we'd eaten all the toothpaste on the rig, along with every scrap of plant life in the crew quarters. Someone found half an old Snickers bar in one of the bins, and the fight for it got so bad that we had two broken arms and a ruptured testicle in the medical bay.

At the end of the month someone came up with the idea of deep frying a few leather flights jackets we found in the crew quarters. We cut them into small strips and fried them in old chip fat. *God*, they were good, just like the pork scratchings I used to eat as a kid, and once the fat had cooled in the fryers we drank that too, lumps and all.

It was six weeks before we started losing people, and it wasn't hard to guess who'd be the first to die. It was Aarte van den Broek, one of my trainee engineers. He'd been a skinny kid even when he arrived on the rig, but by the time he died he looked like an old man, just skin hanging from bone. Most of us were carrying a bit of weight at the start, but that poor bugger never stood a chance.

Nobody knew what we were supposed to do with the body. We had protocols for this kind of thing, but they were all based on the assumption that there'd be someone back on the mainland waiting to collect it. Some of us wanted to give the lad a burial over the side, but then someone spoke up and said we should keep him in the deep freeze, just in case.

At the time I thought he meant just in case rescue came, so we could take him back to his family.

Baird averts his eyes, his voice falling to almost a whisper.

It was two more days before the next lad died, and the day after that we lost two more. By the end of the week we had thirteen bodies in the freezer, and we all knew we'd soon join them. I'd lost forty pounds. My skin was jaundiced and my eyes were surrounded by dark rings. I could see my ribs for the first time since I was a kid, and I'd cut four new holes in my belt. I barely had the energy to get out of bed in the morning. That's when I started to hear talk from the lads.

I don't want to say his name, but one of the young toolpushers was the first to come to me with the idea. He was a fan of all that weird survivalist stuff about drinking your own piss and living out in the wilderness. He was the same lad who'd come up with the idea of frying the leather jackets. I remember I was trying to grab a little sleep when he knocked on my cabin door and shyly asked if he could have a word.

The average human body, he said, contains something in the region of 80,000 edible calories. He'd read it somewhere, on one of those weird sites on the Internet. Someone had calculated the energy stored in an arm, a leg, a heart. They'd worked out how many calories were stored as fat and muscle, and how much could be found in the liver, kidneys and other organs, all the way down to the bone marrow and the liquid in an eyeball.

We'd already run out of paper by that point, so he wrote out his sums on the wall of my cabin with a marker pen. Thirteen bodies gave us a total of around a million calories, he said. There were 114 still alive on the rig, which gave us a little more than 9,000 calories each, and if we were to ration ourselves to 500 calories a day we could each last another eighteen days. He turned to me and I swear he almost smiled when he said that we'd have even more if a few people refused to eat. He said those who wouldn't eat would only add to our stockpiles, allowing the toughest of us – that's how he described it, 'the toughest' – to last even longer.

We didn't have a brig, but I locked the little fucker in his cabin for the next two days. I'd never been so angry in my life. I mean, these were our *friends*. One of the dead was Matt Whitby, my radio operator. I'd known the guy for eight years. I'd been an usher at the guy's wedding, for fuck's sake! I'd eaten dinner with his wife and played swingball with his son Max in his back garden, and this flint hearted little bastard was casually suggesting I eat him. I mean, how do you even begin to process that kind of thing?

Two days later another man came to me with the same suggestion. This time it was our medical officer. We'd lost four more by then, and he told me that if we didn't start eating right now we'd be beyond the point of no return by the end of the week. Even if rescue came we'd likely be too malnourished to survive. Our organs would have taken too much damage to recover. At least the doc was a little less mercenary about it, but once again I didn't listen. I still couldn't imagine biting into human flesh, even if the alternative was death. It was just... I don't know, I just couldn't do it.

The next morning the doc returned to my cabin after two more lads had slipped away overnight. This time, though, he didn't come to try to convince me. He knew me well enough to know I wouldn't budge. Not without encouragement, at least.

I was sleeping at the time. Unconscious, anyway, and too weak to stand. I woke up as they opened the door, and before I'd fully opened my eyes I heard it close and the key turn in the lock. I tried to lift myself up from the bed, and I almost screamed when the sores on my shoulders – big, raw bed sores from the loose skin rubbing across the bone – tore open.

And then I smelled it.

They'd set a bowl on the floor just inside the room, filled to the brim with some kind of stew. It was...

Baird's voice trails off for a moment, and behind his transparent mask I notice his tongue slide over his lips as his eyes glaze over with the memory.

Jesus, I'd never smelled anything so delicious in my life. I can barely even describe it. The steam that rose from the bowl carried the smell along with it, and it seemed to fill the room with the same kind of delicious warmth I remember from my mum's kitchen as she cooked up a Sunday roast. You know what I mean? You remember that aroma, spreading through every room of the house until it was so thick it felt like you could chew the air and gravy would dribble down your chin? For hours I lay in bed with the sheets covering my mouth and nose, just trying to ignore the smell as I wept. I lay there until the sun set, long after the food had gone cold, but eventually... Well, you know what I did.

I could barely swallow that first mouthful, despite the pain in my belly and every cell of my body crying out for food. As soon as I swallowed it I almost immediately puked it back up, but I persevered. The next day I heard the door open and saw another bowl placed on the floor, and this time I managed to keep it all down. The day after that I was waiting by the door when it arrived, and when I grabbed the bowl with both hands the doctor knew he didn't need to lock the door behind him any more. I was back in command by the next day.

Quite a few of the lads had jumped over the side while I'd been locked up, and a few more took themselves out in other ways. Fewer than I would have thought, given the circumstances, but more than I'd have hoped. Funnily enough, the young lad who first suggested that we eat the dead was one of those who jumped over the side. Turns out he'd lost his bottle at the last minute. Couldn't bring himself to swallow it in the end. *C'est la guerre.*

As for the rest of us, once the floodgates opened there was no stopping us. They say that killers find their first victim the hardest, and each one after that gets a little easier until, eventually, murdering someone is as easy as swatting a fly. Now I don't know if that's true or not, but I know it's true for cannibalism. Once you get past the disgust and self loathing it quickly becomes easy.

After you've eaten a few meals of human meat you stop thinking about a body as a person. The moment they stop breathing you forget that they went to school, got married, had a favorite flavor of crisps and lived entire lives filled with hopes, fears and disappointments. That's what they *used* to be. Now they're just... Oh, I don't know, a nice, thick, marbled cut from the glutes that you can smoke like brisket. Belly fat that can be sliced into ribbons and fried up like bacon. Ribs so tender they fall off the bone as soon as you look at them. They're a carcass that needs to be butchered as soon as possible to keep it fresh and tasty. Warm offal that needs to be carefully removed so the meat can cool before it starts to turn. Cuts that need to be separated according to whether they'll be frozen, cured or cooked fresh. You just...

Baird narrows his eyes and grins.

You're wondering what people taste like, aren't you?

"No! I mean... No, I'm not."

Yes you are. I've seen that look in everyone I've met since. All the guards, too. They're all curious, and I'll tell you what I told them. Trust me, you honestly don't want to fucking know. You don't want to start looking at people like that. You don't want to look at a porn mag and see some girl bent over showing her ass, then realize that instead of dreaming about fucking her you've been wondering if she'd taste better roasted or fried. You don't want to look into someone's eyes and wonder if you could use your thumbs to pop them out of their sockets without bursting them.

It changes you. Once you know what people taste like you don't treat them like people any more. You can't. There's no going back to a time before you knew, before you lost your innocence. We finally realized that when the boat arrived. That's when we realized what we'd become.

"The boat?"

Yeah. The real reason we're all here, and the part of the story that you won't have read in the papers. Didn't you ever wonder why we were the only group of cannibals to be treated this way? Did it never occur to you that there must be millions of people around the world who only survived because they choked down a bit of long pig? No?

I think it had been about four months since we lost contact with the mainland. Most of us were almost back to full strength after eating so well, but the freezer was running low again and nobody seemed set to die any time soon. We'd considered the idea of drawing straws when the time came, but luckily it didn't come to that.

We didn't know about the boat until it was almost at the rig. Nobody was manning the radio any more, so the first we knew about it was when someone went for a walk up top and noticed it drifting about half a mile to the west of us. Bloody hell, it was a surprise. For a moment we thought rescue had finally arrived, until we realized the thing was adrift.

It was a passenger ferry sailing under a Danish flag, *The Margarete*, and apparently it had set sail from Hirtshals three weeks earlier with around two hundred refugees on board. The ferry usually only made the short hop across the Skagerrak Strait to Oslo once a day, so by the time it reached the North Sea and got caught in the current it was out of fuel and helpless.

I remember seeing about forty passengers out on the deck as we sent out the lifeboats for them. They were cheering and waving as our lads steered the boats to their port side and began to shunt them closer. Poor buggers must have thought God had finally answered their prayers.

For three weeks they'd been adrift with no food and just a little rainwater, just waiting to die. It turns out they'd set sail with three or four passengers who'd been infected and turned while they were out to sea. A few dozen were killed in the outbreak and about a hundred were bitten or scratched by the time they got the ship back under control, but the survivors didn't have the balls to kill the infected. They just locked them up below deck, so for weeks the forty survivors had been stuck on deck listening to the groans echo from below. Can't have been much fun.

We put them up in our cabins as soon as they came on board. We gave them as much water as they liked and fed them each a bowl of stew. We didn't tell them what was in it, of course, but we felt they deserved a final meal.

That night we split into groups of two and each went to a cabin to kill and butcher them. We got most of them in their sleep, and the rest didn't put up much of a fight. Mine was an old fella, maybe seventy or so. He was awake as we entered the room, and I think he knew what was about to happen. I don't know how. Maybe he saw something in our eyes. Maybe he'd known since he came aboard. He just lay there as I strangled him. Didn't even try to fight it. He just looked... disappointed.

There were a few women among the survivors, and some of the lads wanted to... well, you know. It had been months since any of us had so much as *seen* a woman. Fortunately they didn't argue when I said no. Killing so we could survive was one thing, but we still didn't think of ourselves as monsters, or at least not *that* kind of monster. It didn't make a difference to our victims, I'm sure. They would have thought we were evil whatever we did, but it's not how I wanted to see myself. I didn't want to... I mean, I wanted there to be a *limit*, do you understand? I wanted to know that there was a line I wouldn't cross. Yes, I'd kill to survive, but I'd never cause needless pain. I'd never rape. I'd never...

Baird sighs and shakes his head.

The things we tell ourselves to help us sleep at night. Doesn't work.

We lasted another two months on the meat from the passengers, but of course eventually we were back to frying up tough, spongy lungs and scraping out bone marrow, rationing the last of the scraps, and we knew we'd soon go hungry again. That's when I realized that we had another option. There was another source of food we hadn't even considered yet.

Baird sees the look of realization dawn in my eyes.

You just figured out why they make me wear this mask, didn't you?

I nod.

I decided I'd be the guinea pig. I didn't want to ask any of the lads, and since I was still technically in charge of the rig I decided it was the captain's responsibility to take the risk.

We had a bugger of a time figuring out how to get one of the dead out from below decks without letting them all out. There were about a hundred of them down there, squeezed up close against the doors, and we couldn't work out how to do it without risking the men. Eventually we took some torches to the deck of the ferry and cut a hole through the ceiling so we could use the lifeboat winch to hook one of them and lift it out, like one of those arcade games with the soft toys and the grasping claws.

I decided to stay on the boat for a week after I ate some of the meat, long enough to be sure it wouldn't turn me. It was the longest week of my life. Not so much because I was worried about infection, but because I couldn't wait to tell the lads about it.

It was the best thing I've ever tasted in my life. Better than human. Better than a crisp bacon sandwich slathered in HP sauce on a hungover Sunday morning. Better than a stupidly expensive blue Kobe steak. It was *unbefuckinglievable*, and we had a hundred of them waiting to be eaten. I don't know why it tastes so good. Maybe it's something in the blood, or maybe the fact that zombies are technically dead helps tenderize the meat and bring out the flavor. I've no idea, but I know I'd step over my own mother for another bite.

Baird sits back in his chair and smiles.

They've run endless tests on us all since then. They poked and prodded us for months after we were rescued. Took blood samples, brain biopsies, spinal fluid and God knows what else. They even made me wank into a cup, and they still can't find any sign that the meat had any physical effect on us. They know we're clean and healthy, but they still make us wear the masks when we're around people.

Baird gives the guard a scornful look.

I think it's really more for their sake rather than ours, to help them believe that we're infectious monsters. They can't stand the thought that we're just like them. That's the only way *they* can sleep at night, by convincing themselves that we're infected. That we're driven by some kind of mad blood lust. That we're nothing but zombies who can still walk, talk and *think*. They can't face the idea that we're only human, and that if they were in our situation they'd do exactly what we did to survive. And so would you.

The guard leans forward and taps his watch, reminding me that I have only seven minutes before the chopper is due to depart for the mainland. I thank Baird for taking the time to speak to me, but he waves me away dismissively. He's already turned his attention to the cooler on the table. Now I understand why the box is stamped with a bio-hazard warning.
As I stand Baird removes his mask and steps towards the table, and I quickly turn away as he

lifts the lid from the cooler. I don't want to know what's in there. I'm already fairly sure, but as I walk from the room and hear the sound of chewing I decide against turning around to remove all doubt.

•▼•

:::20:::

Oaxaca, Mexico

The man sitting at the bar beside me looks like he just stepped off the battlefield, even though it has been three years since he last fired a shot in anger. His shirt is torn at the shoulder. His right eye is swollen shut and a deep purple bruise is blooming across his cheek, and a cracked rib has left him favoring his right side as he gingerly lifts his bottle of Corona, or 'breakfast' as he describes it.

Lieutenant Colonel Rob Mills didn't show up for our appointment yesterday, despite my reconfirming the interview several times, and after a night waiting by the phone in a local hotel I finally tracked him down to the local police station, where he was sleeping off a hangover on the concrete floor of the drunk tank. As I paid his bail the arresting officer explained in halting English that he'd been arrested after losing a bar fight that had apparently stemmed from an argument over an anti-Buckley bumper sticker on the car of a Canadian tourist. The officer explained that he was releasing Mills only because he assumed that an officer of his rank could be trusted to attend his court date should charges be brought. Mills laughs as I tell him this.

Pay no attention to the rank. It's totally meaningless. They handed out battlefield promotions like Pez in the early days, back when none of us really believed we were gonna survive and the desertions were coming thick and fast. You'd struggle to find anyone there from the start who didn't make it to at least Captain. Easy Company rules, know what I mean? Everyone moves up the ladder faster in wartime. One minute you're slogging up Currahee in PT gear, the next they're pinning an oak leaf to your collar and handing you your own battalion.

No, I'm a first lieutenant at best. That's where I was when the shit hit the fan. I would have been more than happy to stay there, keep my head down and just get through it, but it seemed like every other day I'd look around and see another empty space where a soldier had been standing the day before.

Most of the time it was just a private, some snot nosed kid who got scared of the nasty Zees and ran home to mommy, but every so often we'd lose an officer. You'd wake up, shit, shower and shave, and then you'd step out to receive your orders and find there was nobody there to give them. Some of them just ran. A couple ate a bullet. Either way it was an instant field promotion for whoever was next in line.

In my case the entire fucking war was nothing but a long, terrifying exercise in the Peter principle. I didn't know what the hell I was doing most of the time. I didn't know the first thing about command, and there's a sack of dog tags out there somewhere to prove it. I'm sure there are plenty of fast tracked officers who still can't believe their luck – in fact I could name at least two colonels who couldn't be trusted to mop a latrine without falling in – but I never asked for a promotion, and I never wanted one. Who the hell wants to be in command when you're at war with your own country?

Mills takes a sip of his Corona, wincing with

pain as his cracked rib stabs into his side.

Anyway, here I am talking your ear off. You wanted to hear about the campaign, right?

"Yes. I haven't been able to get a comprehensive after-action report from Anchorage."

Well, no shit. There *is* no after-action report worth a damn. It'll be years before anyone takes the time to track down every last company and reconstruct the timeline of the stateside campaign, and even when they do it probably won't be worth the effort. They won't learn anything apart from the fact that we were caught with our pants down. There was no coordination once it all went to hell, no national plan coming down from the top. All I can really tell you is how it played out at Fort Benning, if you're interested.

"Please."

And remember, back then I was just a lieutenant. I spent my days looking down a scope at the sniper school, so I was further out of the loop than the guy who ran the base convenience store. This is just my recollection of events, you understand?

"Of course. Anything you can tell me will be useful."

Well, it was a Goddamn mess from the get go. Seemed like every day we got a new set of orders that directly contradicted those we'd been given the day before.

Evacuate the cities. Protect the farms. Build a refugee camp. Prepare to move south. Nope, prepare to move north. Do a little dance. Make a little love. Get down tonight. Those last few weeks before it all went to hell we didn't know if we were coming or going. It felt like we were just digging ditches by day and refilling them by night. Just spinning our wheels, you know?

I don't know any of the details, but it seemed to me there was some kinda major power struggle going on up top. We had an impeached President who'd ordered us to prepare to defend Atlanta to the last man, a dead Veep rotting away at third base in Yankee Stadium, a new Prez who was telling us that we needed to abandon the big cities, and the Joint Chiefs raving about Quad 8, some mysterious new strategy that was supposed to magically save us all.

Christ knows what that was all about. We never got any of the details apart from some vague crap about guarding hospitals and keeping the roads clear, but apparently this was a tailor made plan specifically designed to fight a zombie incursion. I would have loved to have seen it. Anything would have been better than the shit we had to work with.

As if things weren't already confusing enough we had the added wrinkle of the rogue Governors, about two dozen of them, arguing that Buckley had no legal authority to order the military to sacrifice the cities. Most of them eventually fell in line, but not our guy. Our guy was a stubborn son of a bitch.

You remember Jim Brody, right? Skinny little guy with that crazy white hair, always wore a blue seersucker suit when he went on TV? When we started seeing outbreaks in Georgia he insisted that he should have full control of the military in the state, at least until Buckley was sworn in and had gotten himself settled. He mobilized the state defense force and refused to federalize the National Guard, and suddenly our orders to assist the state forces didn't seem so safe any more.

I mean, who the hell's orders were we supposed to follow? We had Brody actually on base, yelling at us to haul ass to Atlanta. We had the Joint Chiefs on the phone assuring us that they were in command of the military until Buckley was sworn in, and then we had Buckley himself on TV giving that big speech after his state by state plan leaked. And there's us sitting in the middle of it all, thumbs up our asses, wondering what the actual fuck was going on. The whole thing was FUBAR.

Of course Colonel Wright eventually decided to stick by Buckley. Seemed like the safest option, I guess. We were in the middle of a full blown constitutional crisis, and in that situation nobody's ever gonna find themselves charged with treason for following the President, no matter how loudly the Joint Chiefs and the Governors insist there's a legal precedent to put them in charge.

Mills awkwardly leans back and reaches into his pocket, pulling out a half smoked cigar that looks like it's been through the dryer. He strikes a match on the edge of the bar and lights it, then looks sheepishly at me as he exhales a thick plume of smoke. "Sorry. Do you mind?" I shake my head.

Anyway... I always liked Governor Brody. Voted for him a time or two. He seemed like he had his head screwed on straight, and unlike most of those Beltway bastards he actually seemed to give a damn about his constituents, so I felt like an asshole watching him lead nine thousand men towards Atlanta when Colonel Wright ordered him off the base. Christ, what a shower of shit he took with him. Mostly National Guard and state defense force types, know what I mean? Weekend warriors. Middle aged factory workers and office supply salesmen who had about as much discipline as you could expect from two days of training each month, and they were going to face off against tens of thousands of Zees all by themselves.

We met a lot of those guys coming back in the other direction a couple months later, the poor bastards. They were always harder to spot than the civilian Zees thanks to their camo gear. A buddy of mine claimed he took out Brody himself, but I'm pretty sure he was just bullshitting. I never saw the body, anyhow.

Mills drains his bottle, waving it above his head until he catches the eye of the bartender.

Now Buckley's plan for the state was sharp as hell. A little cold, sure, but a stroke of genius nonetheless. Our job was simple: protect farmland, protect the water supply. We were ordered to stake out defenses along the Chattahoochee River from Benning to West Point Lake about fifty miles to the north west, with a five mile buffer on either bank of the river. That gave us five hundred square miles of arable land. Buckley's number crunchers figured this would be enough to sustain about a quarter million civilians over the long term once the food supplies within the safe zone had been exhausted, and there were plenty of farmers in the area to help us get started.

The safe zone gave us a border of one hundred twenty miles. Five thousand men – about a quarter of our total strength, not counting civilians – could easily patrol the perimeter, picking off any Zees that wandered our way and checking newly arrived civilians for infection. The other fifteen thousand from the Benning contingent set to work constructing barracks for civilians and organizing labor for farming and essential manufacturing. The aim was to transform our little safe zone into a self contained and self sufficient nation state, a safe haven for the uninfected and a base from which to retake the country once the infected swarms had been eradicated.

Meanwhile every city with a population of more than two hundred thousand was to be abandoned immediately, with no effort whatsoever made to protect them. We're talking Atlanta, Montgomery, Birmingham, Mobile... All of them just given up for dead. And not just abandoned, either. This was the genius of the plan. Buckley wanted to use them as lures.

The Army Corps of Engineers had spent a couple of weeks rigging up air raid sirens at half mile intervals in concentric rings all around the cities. The Zees would be drawn in towards the closest siren and begin to swarm around it, and then every few hours or so the speakers on each ring would be shut off while the next ring further in continued to broadcast, drawing them in closer to the city, then the next ring would be shut off to draw them in still further, and so on and so forth. They repeated this process every day, and every day a new wave of Zees would be lured in until the cities were crawling.

I actually watched all of this from the command center the Corps set up at Benning. They had UAVs patrolling the skies over Mobile, and we watched the clustered heat signatures move closer to the city whenever they shut off a ring of sirens. It was incredible. For a while it seemed so successful that we thought we might never have to take on the Zees face to face. We thought we could just sit tight and maintain our perimeter as every last zombie in the state got sucked towards the cities and blasted into a fine mist by aerial bombardment.

And then it all went to hell.

"You lost power?"

Yep, we lost power.

The engineers told us we shouldn't have any problems. They'd isolated most of the Georgia grid to conserve power, and while most of our steam-electric and both of our nuclear plants had been taken out of the system we still had plenty of hydroelectric capacity, more than enough to meet the reduced power needs of the state, and hydro can keep generating power for a couple of years without supervision. We should have been made in the shade.

You wanna know what happened? They discovered this just a couple months ago while they were trying to recommission the Oliver Dam plant north of Columbus. A bunch of divers went down to survey the dam on the upriver side, and they all dropped a deuce in their wetsuits when they saw what was down there.

The intake was completely blocked with Zees. Thousands of the fucking things, pinned right up against the grate. Well, I say Zees, but from what I heard there wasn't much left but bones. Apparently the turbine was all gunked up with rotted meat, fat, skin and whatever else could fit through the grate. Nobody even dares touch it now for fear they might dislodge the mass and contaminate the downriver water supply. Whole thing's been sealed up and drained until they can figure out what to do about it.

Anyway, it all went to shit when the power went out.

No more air raid sirens. No more Internet. The UAVs were grounded, so no more bombardment of the cities. It wasn't long before the swarms in Atlanta and Montgomery started to drift back out towards us, and that's when shit got nasty.

Did you ever see a swarm? I mean a real swarm. Not just a couple hundred, but a few thousand of them?

I shake my head.

Trust me, you're better off. That shit sticks with you.

It was the Montgomery swarm that came for us first, maybe a week or so after we lost power. We knew they were heading for Georgia thanks to one of our scouts on highway 85, so we weren't caught with our pants fully down, but still... You can prepare for a swarm, but you're never really *prepared* for a swarm, know what I'm saying?

Now I don't want to oversell it. I know a lot of guys like to get into dick measuring contests about the shit they faced, but I'm not into that. Compared to what we saw a couple years later Montgomery was a walk in the park. Thanks to the layout of the highways most of the Zees in Alabama had drifted up to Birmingham or down to Mobile – they tend to stick to the roads since they can't climb fences – and the boys at Benning had done a pretty thorough job with the bombing raids on the city over the last week or so.

There were only around fifty thousand Zees left in Montgomery when the power went out, and maybe ten thousand of them were headed in our direction. Hell, maybe not even that many. Your memory plays tricks on you, and this was my first swarm. Couple of years later I'd think nothing of facing five times as many Zees before breakfast, but this is the one that really got to me.

The 85 was a real mess, man, a total disaster area. Just west of Auburn some asshole had jackknifed his trailer about a week before everyone started fleeing the cities, and nobody had even made an attempt to clean up the wreck. One side of the highway was blocked by the truck while the other side had hit the same problem people saw all over the country when the cities started to empty out: nobody knew where the hell to go. The road was just a mess of blocked in cars all headed in opposite directions, as if everyone had left their homes without thinking of anything but to get away. They all just thought they'd be safer somewhere else – *anywhere* else – but all they got was stuck in the ass end of nowhere.

I don't want to make light of it – after all, only about half of us made it back – but there was nothing funnier than watching about fifty guys weaving down a blocked highway on tiny little BMX bikes like that bunch of kids in ET. It was the only way to get around, and we couldn't afford to be choosy. One of our guys, Ramirez, could only find a girls' bike, like, pink with rainbow tassels coming out the side of the handlebars. Big fucker, too. I almost fell off my bike, I laughed so hard.

We set up shop on an overpass a few miles west of Tuskegee, at a spot where the highway wasn't too choked with traffic, and we waited maybe four hours until our scout finally reached us. Man, he stank like wet ass. The guy had been out on the road for a couple weeks in the heat, just wandering the streets, you know, reporting the movements of the Zees. Not engaging, just observing.

He looked like he hadn't had a full night's sleep in forever. Apparently he'd been caught napping in the back of a car as the swarm caught up with him on the highway. Poor guy had to sit there hiding under a blanket as thousands of the fuckers walked by, finger on the trigger, then when they finally passed by he had to take the long route through fields and rivers to beat them back to us.

I'll never forget the look of sheer relief on his face when Colonel Wright called in and ordered him to head back to Benning. He seemed like a good kid, but I got the feeling he would have lost it if he had to face that swarm again. He just looked... I don't know, haunted, I guess. I can't say it filled any of us with much confidence.

The bartender sets down a fresh beer, and Mills takes a quick gulp before grabbing his sleeve. "Hey, can I get some peanuts or pretzels? Bar snacks, por favor?" The bartender gives him a blank look. "Me gustaria... ummm... nuts? Shit, I wish I'd learned Spanish. Ah, forget it."

The first of the Zees arrived sometime around 3AM. The real go-getters, you know. Overachieving types, hungry for a meal and quicker on their feet than most. It's lucky the spotters even saw them coming. We were expecting the full swarm to arrive all at once, so we were a little caught out when they started to drift in one by one.

I remember the tension on the overpass. We lay on our bellies, bunched up tight so we all had a clear line of sight down the highway to the west, and our spotters lay beside us whispering our targets and ranges. They didn't really need to whisper – the closest Zee must have been a hundred yards away when they first arrived – but it just felt appropriate, you know? You know that feeling, when your heart's thumping in your chest and your voice just naturally comes out like that?

My first shot went wide by a whole six feet, straight through a car windshield. I almost jumped out of my skin when my spotter laid her hand on my shoulder and whispered for me to settle down, take a breath. "You got all the time in the world," she said, and... well, she wasn't bad to look at and I could feel her breath on my neck. Probably not a technique you'll find in the training handbook, but it worked to calm me down.

I shifted a little, looked down the scope and found my next target. Young guy, maybe early twenties, wavy dark hair. Gray U of A sweatshirt and a pair of torn red basketball shorts. Couldn't make out much more detail than that – hell, I didn't want to – but I felt a chill run through me as I saw his eyes glow white in the scope.

It was the first head shot I ever made. Lucky, too, because I was aiming center mass. His legs gave out and he fell out of sight behind a car. I wasn't even sure it was my bullet until Ellen – that was my spotter, Ellen – tapped me on the shoulder and flashed me a grin. "Now just do that a thousand more times and I'll let you buy me a drink."

After that I got into the groove. They were coming maybe two dozen each minute, and there were about thirty snipers on the bridge with their spotters coordinating targets, so there was no pressure at all. I took out most of my targets at that range with one shot, but whenever I missed the head or spine I'd feel Ellen's breath on my neck and a little whispered encouragement. A couple of times I thought about missing intentionally, but... well, I managed to resist.

By the end of the first hour it felt manageable... mechanical, like a gruesome production line. The bodies were piling up between the cars at our hundred yard marker. Not a single Zee had made it more than a few steps beyond the line, and it felt like none of them would. It felt like we had some kind of invisible forcefield around us, y'know? But then... Jesus, I can still remember the whispers. One of the spotters was moving down the line in a crouch, white faced, whispering as he went. Ellen had her hand on my shoulder, and as she heard him she squeezed, hard.

It felt like... You remember that huge tsunami out in Asia about thirty years ago? I remember watching the video footage as a kid, and for months afterwards I had this recurring nightmare. Man, it fucked me up. I was standing on a beach in Thailand or some place as the water pulled away from the shore. I stared out at the sea for a minute, and then noticed in the distance this wall of dirty brown water race back towards me, filled with little pieces of wood and crap that I realized were fishing boats dwarfed by the wave. I turned and tried to run, but the wet sand was sucking at my heels and pulling me down. Couldn't make it more than a few steps, and behind me I could hear the water rushing towards me as loud as a fucking freight train. I could see my mom screaming at me from way back behind the shore, waving her arms and begging me to run to her, but I just couldn't move. I was stuck in the sand down to my knees and it just kept sucking me down, down, down. All I could do was stand there, crying, just waiting for the wave to hit me. Any second now I'd be swept away. Any. Second. Now.

That's how I felt when I saw the swarm in the distance through my scope. Thousands of Zees. It was the central mass, and from about a half mile away all I could see in the darkness were those eyes glowing white in the scope. I felt like they were all staring at me, like they knew exactly where I was. Man, I half expected to look down at my legs and find they were sinking into sand.

We could hear them coming... just a little, just at the edge of our hearing. It wasn't the groans and cries, though, not like you'd expect from the movies. Zees don't really make vocalizations unless they're attacking. It was just, like, the scrape of shoes against the asphalt. The rustling of clothes as they dragged against each other. Even a few weird sounds you couldn't place until they got closer and you spotted them through the scope. There was one woman with her foot caught in a length of chain link fence, and it made this little tinkling sound as it dragged behind her, like little snatches of applause, you know?

Two of the snipers – I don't know who, and I wouldn't tell you even if I knew their names – got up and ran, and one of the spotters followed right after them. I can't really blame them. Hell, I wouldn't blame anyone who ran from that sight. To be honest the only thing keeping me on the overpass was bravado. I didn't want to let Ellen know I was shitting myself.

Luckily we'd planned for this, so we weren't flying completely blind. About a quarter mile out from our position the engineers had laid out a few dozen shrapnel bombs. Nothing fancy, just little plugs of C4 in glass Coke bottles stuffed with nails and ball bearings. We didn't know how effective they'd be, but the idea was to set them off as the swarm walked over them. Maybe they'd get a few head shots. Maybe they'd just tear off a few legs and thin the herd a little, create a little pile of bodies to slow the rest down and let us pick 'em off. We figured it'd be better than nothing.

Those engineers had balls. They didn't have any remote blasting caps, just short rolls of copper wire leading into the trees beside the road, so they had to stay far too close for comfort to the highway to trigger the blasts. I'd caught a glimpse of them a couple times through my scope, laying low in the tall grass at the tree line peering through scopes of their own. I couldn't imagine sitting there out in the open in the dark, just waiting for the swarm to show. Made me feel like a bit of a pussy up on the overpass, about as safe as anyone in the state could be.

I never found out what happened to those guys. Maybe they ran. Maybe they made too much noise and a couple of Zees got 'em before they could set off the charges. Whatever happened, though, the bombs never went off. We lay there as thousands of Zees marched over the spots, just waiting for the blasts, but they didn't come. I think that's when we all began to really feel the panic. That's when we started to kick ourselves. Why hadn't we used the cars to build a roadblock? Why hadn't we set ourselves up a few miles back so we could have faced them in the daylight? Why hadn't we... well, I don't suppose it mattered.

I started picking off targets at the front of the swarm, increasing my rate of fire from once a minute to once every five seconds. Now each Zee was taking at least two shots. About half of them missed, but now I didn't get the little shoulder pat from Ellen. Now there was an edge in her voice whenever a shot went wild. It wasn't reassuring any more, but panicked. "Fucking concentrate!" she said. "Stop wasting your fucking ammo!" No whispers any more, not now we could hear their groans. We knew they'd spotted us.

Mills finishes his beer and grabs at the next bottle the moment the bartender sets it down beside him. His cigar smolders between his fingers, burned down to a nub.

I was down to one shot every two seconds as they passed the two hundred yard marker, and I was back to one shot kills at this range, but it was nothing to do with skill. It was just because there were too many of them. So long as I aimed around head height I'd take one down, even if it was the Zee behind the one I was aiming at.

Ellen dropped her scope and picked up her M16 as the first of the swarm passed the hundred yard marker. That was supposed to be our signal to evacuate, when the spotters took up arms, but nobody made a move to run. We just stayed on our bellies taking potshots at them, but even as I was firing I could see we were barely making a dent. Every time I took one of them down three more would be standing in their place a moment later, and by the time I took out another one six more would be moving in.

Shit... It was obvious we'd screwed up. We figured thirty snipers against ten thousand Zees should be an easy fight, y'know? Three hundred thirty kills for each of us from a safe, elevated position. Even at a pretty generous ten seconds per kill the firefight should have been over in an hour, but they were just coming at us too fast. We'd expected the shrapnel bombs would create a pile of bodies that'd slow them down and let us pick them off without any pressure, but without the blasts they just surged forward.

The panic didn't really hit me until I realized I was firing pretty much straight down at the road beneath me. I'd managed to keep a lid on it until then, but the moment I was shooting down at the tops of heads... Jesus. One of the spotters tossed a whole grenade belt over the side and the Zees barely even flinched.

I think I'd been hearing the voice through the radio a good minute or so before I noticed it. It was some Major shouting for us to cease fire from his safe little hidey hole about a half mile back from the line. I don't remember the guy's name. Even back then the officers were being replaced so quickly we didn't bother to learn them. I grabbed my radio and yelled something that would have earned me a Court Martial a couple months earlier.

The Major, God bless that son of a bitch, didn't blow up at me. He just calmly explained – in the same kind of patient tone you'd use to tell a dumb kid why he shouldn't touch the stove – that he wanted to try to draw the Zees away from us. I relayed the message across the line, and after about a minute and a hell of a lot of confusion our guns fell silent. We just lay there, pulled back from the edge so the Zees couldn't see us, listening to the groans beneath us and the sound of some kid crying somewhere to the left of me. Shit, I had half a mind to join him.

We all watched as the sky lit up to the east. A red flare shot up towards the clouds, then another, and another. In just a few seconds the sky was full of them, slowly drifting back towards the ground. It was beautiful, but it wasn't a patch on the beauty of the next thing I saw. I crawled across to the other side of the overpass on my elbows, peered over the edge and saw the back of the Zees' heads. It was working! Thousands of the motherfuckers were staring up at the pretty lights in the sky, walking towards them as if they'd completely forgotten we even existed!

Man... I can't explain the relief we all felt. I don't know about the rest of the guys but I was certain we'd all die up on that damned overpass. I thought we'd keep firing until we ran out of ammo, and then we'd have to stand there and just wait for them to come get us. This was like a death row reprieve, you know? A get out of jail free card. I don't know what came over me, but I just grabbed Ellen by the waist and pulled her in for a kiss, and she returned it. Fuck, I'd never felt so alive.

And that's when some dumb bastard let out a scream, and the spell was broken.

Looking back I can't blame the kid, not after I saw what he'd seen. Some of the Zees – maybe just a hundred or so – had broken away from the main group and followed the exit ramp on the highway. They hadn't been fooled by the flares, and now the quickest of them were just a few dozen yards from us.

One of the guys next to the kid who let out the scream grabbed hold of him and clamped his hand over his mouth, but it was too late. The Zees down on the highway had already heard it, and a few of them had already started to turn around. A few seconds later every gun was firing again, and we were right back in the shit.

Ellen and I were on the other side of the overpass, at the very end of the line. We didn't have a clear shot at any of the Zees up on the road with us, so we just started firing down at the highway again. I don't even know why. There was no way we could ever kill them all before they made it up to us, but we fired anyway. If only we'd just...

Mills drains his beer and calls for another. I can see he's already a little drunk, weaving on his stool, and as he reaches for the fresh bottle he almost misses. His stool wobbles back on one leg, and he grabs the bar to steady himself.

They got Ellen.

I didn't even see them coming. We were so focused on the highway we hadn't even noticed a couple of Zees walking up from the other side of the overpass. Quiet fuckers. I turned when I heard her cry out, just in time to see her push the guy over the edge.

I could see it in her eyes the moment she looked at me. You know that look? You ever look into someone's eyes the moment they realize they got bit? When they know they're already dead, but their body hasn't caught up yet?

She didn't need to pull back her jacket. She already knew. I think she just wanted to show me, you know? She wanted me to understand why she... why she did what she did.

It was just a little thing. Barely a nick in her shoulder. It was just a little half circle of red on her skin, little teeth marks. There was no way to tell if they were even cuts. I couldn't tell if they'd broken the skin in the darkness, but she knew. She knew as soon as it happened.

She had the barrel of her M16 under her chin before I could even move. Nothing I could have done anyway. It was either fast or slow. She chose fast.

Mills falls silent for a moment, then sighs.

I don't remember much after that. All I remember is seeing people jump from the overpass down to the highway. Couple of them landed in the middle of the Zees, but most landed on top of the cars and managed to use them as stepping stones until they got out of the mass. Seemed like a good idea, so I joined them.

I got my first promotion when we got back to Benning. They bumped me up to Captain to replace one of the half dozen we'd lost on the mission, and they gave me my first command. I didn't realize until later that it was Ellen's company. How's that for a kick in the balls?

•▼•

21

Lucerne, Switzerland

When the long awaited call arrived from what I took to be one of his household staff, formally extending an invitation to visit the home of Commander Tobias Konstantin Pfyffer von Altishofen, my mind immediately conjured an image of his luxurious accommodations. This man, I thought, the last in a centuries-long line of Pfyffer von Altishofens to take on the role of Commander of the Pontifical Swiss Guard, and the scion of one of Switzerland's most celebrated aristocratic families, must surely live in the lap of luxury.

It's with some surprise, then, that I arrive at the address provided to find the Commander living an ascetic life in the small, windowless basement apartment of a dilapidated concrete tower block on Langensandstrasse, Lucerne, across the street from the gutted shell of an Aldi supermarket, with views over a patch of trash-strewn scrubland leading to the shore of Lake Lucerne.

The Commander lives alone in this cramped, stark space, his only furnishings a single bed, a wooden stool and a small desk on which sits a statue of the Madonna and a well worn set of polished rosary beads. Resting on the bed is a large book I at first mistake for a lectern Bible until the Commander flips it open at random and hands it to me. Handwritten in careful, precise script is a long list of names, dates and crimes, with space left for notes beside each entry:

Vittorio Rossi, March 8, 2022; Murder; Repented.
Gherardo Agosti, March 8, 2022; Blasphemy; Refused to repent.
Lorenzo di Pasqua, March 9, 2022; Theft; Refused to repent.
Karl Schweiz, March 10, 2022; Sedition; Repented.
Teodora Napolitano, March 10, 2022; Adultery; Repented

The book is filled with such entries, dozens to a page and several hundred pages long. This volume alone – just one of many from the Holy See's surviving sanctuary cities – records the executions of more than ten thousand Italians, Swiss, Germans, Austrians and various immigrant travelers since the Vatican expanded its jurisdiction over the fractured, collapsed nation of Italy.

In the years following Barberini's coup, the Commander tells me, almost three hundred thousand were put to death within Italy's borders, each of their fates meticulously recorded in these infamous judicial logbooks. This is the only volume still in private hands. The rest are on display at the Vatican and various museums and cathedrals around the world, intended to serve as a reference to help family members identify lost loved ones but also, and perhaps more importantly, to serve as a constant reminder to surviving Catholics of the darkest days of the Church.

I'm afraid we brought our problems on ourselves, in the beginning, thanks to the nature of our home. Vatican City was a fortress, you see. It was built in a more violent time, designed to protect the Pope and his followers from any number of aggressors, and to the casual observer it appeared all but impregnable, surrounded by walls forty feet high, and so thick they'd withstand everything short of a nuclear blast.

We never tried to discourage this reputation, of course. There was nothing to be gained from absolute honesty in this regard, and we'd always subscribed to the belief that the best way to protect His Holiness was to lead people to believe that he could not be harmed, even though that was far from the case. We were happy to project an air of invulnerability, but the truth was that both His Holiness and Vatican City itself were incredibly vulnerable. Just little white lies, you understand?

This is why so many flocked to the city when the outbreak finally reached Rome. They believed they'd be safe there, kept from harm behind our walls, protected by the same fortifications that had kept their beloved Papa safe for so many years. Thousands of them came flooding in as the attacks spread across the city, Catholics, Jews, Muslims and atheists alike, all of them desperate for our protection.

And of course His Holiness wouldn't turn them away. He was a kind man – far too kind, I thought at the time – but even had he not been a man of such generous spirit he was still the Pope, and it would have been unthinkable for him to order the gates barred, sealing himself safely within while his flock perished at his doorway. He couldn't have lived with that thought, so it was inevitable that he threw open his home to the needy.

By the time the outbreak overwhelmed Rome the

Vatican housed almost half a million souls. They were crammed in like sardines in a tin. They slept in offices, hallways, bishops' chambers and even on the floor of the Sistine Chapel, finding warmth beneath curtains, tablecloths and – oh, it still pains me to think of it – ornate, priceless tapestries pulled down from the walls. It was horrifying for me as a student of history to watch these artworks transformed into blankets and bed sheets, but His Holiness was unfazed. "Great art can stoke a fire in the soul," he said, waving away my concerns, "but of what use is art when the people shiver in their beds?"

We could barely move for the civilians crowding the corridors, and still more arrived each day as word spread that we were offering sanctuary, all of them desperate for food and water from our already overstretched supplies. I pleaded with His Holiness to allow me to take him to the helipad and fly him to safety outside the city, or at the very least to follow me through the Passetto Di Borgo, the protected, once secret passageway to Castel Sant'Angelo. At least there we'd be better able to separate him from the civilians in the case of an outbreak, but he put his foot down.

I remember the force of his words as he stood in St. Peter's Square, surrounded by countless thousands all desperate to reach out and touch him. It shocked me to hear an edge of anger in his voice, usually so warm and soft. "This is my *home*," he said, jabbing a finger up to the dome of the Basilica, "and this is my flock." He swept his arm across St. Peter's Square, and as he did the crowd fell silent. "We will *not* abandon these people in their hour of need."

The Commander smiles softly.

I'd never experienced such an outpouring of love. It's difficult to even imagine it. Half a million souls packed tight in the square, each of them filled with such pure, joyous adoration for one man it seemed enough to carry him to heaven there and then. It was a truly humbling experience.

In any case, it was at that moment that I understood he would never leave Vatican City as long as the crisis continued. His word was his bond, and I knew then that he'd stay and minister to the people as long as they needed his comfort, even if it cost him his life. I also understood that my job, as Commander of the Swiss Guard and the sworn protector of the Pope, had just become infinitely more difficult.

From that day forward he walked among the people without protection. He refused point blank to allow us to guard him as he gave mass, wandered the gardens and spoke to the civilians. He even pitched in and helped construct the barriers at the entrance to St. Peter's Square, unspooling rolls of barbed wire that had been flown in by the army in the days before it disbanded, and as soon as he caught his first glimpse of the undead on the other side of the wire forest he decreed that the Swiss Guard was to be stripped of its official responsibility – our *raison d'être* – to protect the life of His Holiness, and instead charged us with the protection of all those who resided within the walls of the Vatican.

I remember the horror I felt as he made us swear that, if it came to it, we would protect the life of a child over his own life. I know that sounds unpleasant, that I'd be mortified by the thought of protecting a child, but you have to understand it from *my* perspective. I'd spent my entire adult life devoted to the Holy See, guarding the lives of pontiffs from John Paul II to Benedict to Francis himself, and I'd long ago accepted that if given the opportunity I'd happily stand in front of a bullet to prevent any of them from coming to harm, and now His Holiness plucked a young boy at random from the crowd and called out that his protection was to be paramount. That we should sacrifice the life of the Pope if it meant we could save the boy.

He must have noticed my expression as he gave his order. I never was very good at hiding my feelings from him, and when he saw the look on my face he smiled. "I am just an old man, Tobias. If the Lord wishes us to survive He'll need this boy fighting for our future more than He needs me."

The Commander slides his rosary from the desk and runs the beads between his fingers.

In hindsight I think he was already aware of his illness. I don't know how – he certainly hadn't seen a doctor, I would have known – but somehow he knew the cancer was eating away at him from the inside. He knew he didn't have long to live, and before he left us he wanted to ensure that he was leaving the Church in safe hands. That the pieces were in place for what he knew must come next.

He was... well, he was a very intelligent man, and perhaps more attuned to the realities of politics than many who had gone before him. He knew that the Italian government had collapsed – not that it had ever *not* been close to a state of collapse – and he knew that if Italy was to survive someone would have to hold the country together by the seams. He also knew that it may be many years before a new Pope was elected. By the time we learned of his illness we knew of only a handful of

Cardinals left alive in Italy. Only one was present in the Vatican, Camerlengo Silvio Barberini, and while he was...

The Commander shifts uncomfortably.

While he was eligible for the papacy there had always been some... concerns as to his character, even then. He'd never been favored as a potential successor. He was known for a certain hard nosed efficiency and a strong work ethic, but among the Cardinals he was seen as a little too eager. That was always a warning sign. Excessive ambition was a suspicious trait in a potential pontiff, and in the past the Cardinals had always ensured that those who seemed to want the job a little too much were weeded out before they got their wish. They believed it should be a sacred burden, not a career goal.

In any case Barberini could not become Pope without the assent of the College of Cardinals, and there was simply no way to bring enough to Rome to form a conclave while Italy swarmed with millions of cursed souls. His Holiness knew that the term of *sede vacante* may drag on for years, so he was in a race against time to get his house in order, as it were, before he left us.

Pope Francis gave his final mass to a crowd of more than four hundred thousand in St. Peter's Square on a bitterly cold Sunday 'morning towards the end of the winter. I can still see him now, huddled from the wind in the lee of the Obelisk, his frail body wrapped in so many layers it was difficult to tell that there was a person beneath the clothing. His voice was almost gone by then. He struggled to speak in more than a hoarse whisper, so the Guard passed his sermon to the crowd in a sort of relay, calling out his words as we heard them until they reached the edges of the square.

When he finished we helped him limp to the mass of barbed wire at the entrance to the square. It was the first time he'd walked that far in months, since before the winter when he'd been strong enough to help construct the defenses, and for the first time he stood and stared at the fruits of his labor. A thick, tangled forest of wire held back a swarm hundreds of thousands strong, an ocean of monsters stretching out of sight all the way down Via della Conciliazione. He gasped as he saw them – I'm not sure he'd truly grasped the scale of the undead horde that occupied Rome until then – and he stepped forward to the edge of the wire forest and blessed them, forgiving each and every one of them their sins before turning back to me with a weary smile.

"And it came to pass at the end of forty days, that Noah opened the window of the ark which he had made," he said, his voice barely audible over the groans of the dead. "I think I'd like to rest now, Tobias."

The Commander crosses himself.

We found him the following morning, still in his chair by the desk in his chambers, still clutching the pen he'd used to write his final orders. He'd left a sheaf of papers on the desk, mostly personal letters and minor housekeeping notes, but atop the stack was a carefully written sealed letter addressed directly to me, with instructions to take it to the people. The seal was still wet when we found the body. He must only have finished writing it moments before he passed.

The letter was what's known as a papal bull; a decree direct from the Pope to the Church, sealed with the *bulla*, a rarely used lead seal unique to each pontiff. There had only been a handful of them written, six to be exact, in the last hundred years, so I knew even before opening it that this would be of greater import than a final testament or a personal letter.

The cover read in Latin *Papa Franciscus, episcopus servus servorum Dei. Militia Dei*. In English that means Pope Francis, bishop, servant of the servants of God. The final two words were the title of this particular bull, traditionally chosen to mirror the theme of the bull itself. It translated as Soldiers of God.

Militia Dei was an ambitious and far reaching new charter for the Church, laying out the relationship His Holiness intended the Vatican to have with this new and deeply troubled world. It was an edict that declared that the Holy See was to reclaim Italy for God in the absence of a civil government, and to protect the nation until such a time that one could be restored. In the meantime it would become the job of the Swiss Guard, the Gendarmerie Corps and 'any man, woman or child willing and able to bear arms, regardless of faith or lack thereof' to wrest control of the country from the living dead, or 'the forces of Satan', as His Holiness colorfully put it.

He also decreed that I would take on the job of leading the *Militia Dei* from the city to bring some measure of law and order back to Italy. There were no specific orders as to how he expected me to do this – he didn't fancy himself a tactician – but he wrote simply that he trusted me and the Swiss Guard, as loyal servants of both the Pope and the Lord Himself, to 'bring hope to the hopeless, succor to the needy, and justice to those who have been left for too long without.'

Things moved very quickly from there. Within an hour of learning of the Pope's death he was sent to be embalmed, and by the following day his body was exposed for the veneration of the faithful in St. Peter's Basilica, where he would remain for four days before interment in the crypts. It was a truly humbling sight. Hundreds of thousands of mourners flocked to pay their respects, filing in an orderly fashion by the body despite there being no security to hold them back. The love and respect they felt for him was palpable.

I only wish I'd had the opportunity to properly pay my respects alongside them, but Camerlengo Barberini kept us all far too busy to mourn. From the moment he officially announced the Pope's death he assumed command – as was his right, of course, as acting head of state – issuing orders left and right as if he was the Pope himself. For a full week, with only a short break to attend the funeral, my men ransacked the Vatican armory, the museum at Castel Sant'Angelo and every display in the hallways of the city for armor and weaponry, and by the time we finally gathered our arsenal it was clear that the undead of Rome would soon meet their match.

My word, it was a sight to see. Over the centuries the Guard had rarely disposed of arms no matter how outdated they had become. We kept all of our old equipment in storage or on display as museum pieces, and as a result the *Militia Dei* took on an odd, patchwork appearance as each man chose the weapons and armor he felt suited him best. It was... well, let's just say you wouldn't want to see my men approach you in the street on a dark night.

One of my deputies, Rodolfo Massi, a fearsome character who towered over most men, carried a heavy two handed scimitar he'd found in the Sant'Angelo museum. I once saw him decapitate two undead in a single swing, and the blade buried itself in the shoulder of a third so deep that it took two of us to pull it free. One of the men from the Gendarmerie Corps – I don't recall his name now – wore a full suit of Renaissance armor with a plumed helmet and serrated gauntlets, complete with a Heckler and Koch MP7 strapped to each thigh.

I myself lacked the strength to carry such weight – I felt like an old man even then – so I chose light chain mail to wear beneath my dress uniform, with my pockets weighed down with ammo for my SIG P220 pistol. And, of course, I wouldn't have felt like a true member of the Swiss Guard without this...

The Commander lowers himself to his knees beside his bed, and with a wince of arthritic pain he pulls out an object wrapped in cloth, narrow and around four feet long. As he pulls away the cloth I see the edged blade and realize it's the broken remains of his halberd, the traditional weapon of the Pontifical Swiss Guard. The wooden shaft is broken in half but the razor sharp pike blade remains, and at its base the curved ax is blunted and nicked from heavy use.

This is the weapon that saved Italy from the undead. Other armies relied on advanced weaponry and modern military tactics, but for us this simple staff was more than enough. I must have killed five thousand of those infernal creatures before the shaft finally snapped in two.

Many of the men – especially those in the Gendarmerie Corps, who'd never been trained to use it – complained that the halberd was too clumsy a weapon to fight the dead, too cumbersome to guarantee an accurate strike with the blade, and far too long to be useful in close combat. They weren't entirely wrong. It's far from the most efficient weapon, and it takes considerable finesse to use it well, but every last man in our army recognized its utility as we were clearing the area around the Vatican.

The barbed wire forest we'd built to hold back the dead was one hundred meters thick and two meters tall in the beginning, but after months of unrelenting attack the barrier had been narrowed to just a third of its original size. Those infernal creatures simply threw themselves into the mass, twisting and writhing until they became firmly entangled, and after months of this onslaught the forest of wire was a death trap. Tens of thousands of ghouls lay immobilized but still active, their limbs like branches strangled by vines and creepers, and if you didn't cut yourself on the wire you'd be sure to eventually step within biting distance of a writhing corpse.

The halberds were a Godsend. At eight feet long they allowed us to safely and methodically dispatch every last zombie as we carefully cut a path through the wire. We worked in shifts, two hundred men standing just a few steps from the dead, each of us thrusting forward with our halberds to carefully pierce the eye socket of endless ghouls. It was exhausting, backbreaking work, and even when our shifts ended and we pulled back from the front line there was little respite. Before returning to our beds we'd spend hours dragging the corpses into heaps and setting them aflame to rid the earth of their stink. Even today the acrid odor of burning flesh is never far from my mind.

It was two weeks before we finally reached the end of the Via della Conciliazione, and by the time I saw the waters of the Tiber before me the charred remains of... oh, I'd guess hundreds of thousands of bodies lay in our wake. The entire city was shrouded in smoke, plunging us into perpetual twilight, and the ash from the pyres settled on every surface. Everything we touched, every brick, every paving stone, every flower and blade of grass was cast in monochrome, the life and light choked out of our world.

We wrapped our faces with cloth to keep from inhaling the burned remains but we were, if you'll excuse the coarse language, pissing into the wind. The ash always managed to find a way past every defense. It matted in our hair and caked on our clothes. It crept around the masks and found its way to our lips. It mingled with our sweat and clung to our skin like paste, running into our eyes and leaving them pink and bloodshot. I saw men in tears, scrubbing themselves raw with rags long after they'd begun to bleed, and still they scrubbed and scrubbed until someone rested a kindly hand on their shoulder and led them away.

I remember the moment we finally reached the Tiber. I remember climbing down the slick stone steps to the water in a daze, my body caked with ash and dried blood. I didn't even think to check that the water was safe, but thankfully I wasn't punished for my mistake. There were no ghouls waiting to take advantage of my moment of weakness. I wept with joy as I lowered myself into the cool, clear river, watching the ash melt from my skin and flow far away. I felt reborn. It was the first time I'd bathed since the outbreak began many months earlier. I'd forgotten how it felt like to be clean.

The Commander smiles at the memory.

I'd hoped to rest for a while once we'd reached the river, but Barberini pushed us to double our efforts. With Conciliazione finally clear we spent another week extending our fortifications, laying out new wire and barricading alleyways all the way from Via Crecenzia in the north to the Ponte Principe Amadeo to the south. More killing. More burning. More choking ash. I returned to the river daily to wash, which at least gave me something to look forward to once my work was done.

It was exhausting, but more than worth the effort. By the end of the week we'd doubled the area under our control, freeing up breathing room for the half million survivors in the Vatican, allowing them access to both the fresh water of the Tiber and the unspoiled food to be found in the thousands of homes, shops and restaurants we'd liberated.

We were treated like heroes when we returned to the Vatican and finally removed the last of the wire barrier. It was... well, I won't deny it was a pleasant feeling, to receive such adoration. I don't mind saying that my vow of celibacy was difficult to honor, especially as I'd taken mine voluntarily. The Swiss Guard made no such demands of its men, and the woman were... very grateful for our hard work. I don't doubt that many of my men gladly accepted their gratitude.

As for me, I focused on my work, and my dedication was quickly repaid when I found a few survivors out there in the newly liberated streets; poor, wretched souls who'd somehow managed to sustain themselves in their apartments for months without knowing that the safety of the Vatican had only been a few streets away. Some had prepared stockpiles of food and water, and emerged from their hiding places fit and healthy. Others were close to starvation, just skin and bone, like you'd see in old photos of concentration camp survivors. It was difficult to watch these poor souls. Most were beyond the help of our limited medical facilities. Perhaps if we'd found them just a week earlier... Even a few days. It was heartbreaking.

If we hadn't found those first survivors I could have happily returned to my chamber and slept for a month. I was beyond worn out, exhausted to the depths of my very bones – as were we all – but the discovery of people still living beyond the walls of the Vatican lit a fire in our hearts and convinced us to push forward despite our exhaustion. The idea that there may be thousands more in Rome alone, and perhaps millions across Italy just waiting to be rescued... It lent a new urgency to our mission.

I allowed the men just three more days of rest before pushing on from the city. We gathered provisions, paid our respects to the departed Pope and gave confession one final time, and then without fanfare we departed to the north with six hundred men chosen from the Guard, the Gendarmerie Corps and the civilian population.

I had no way of knowing at the time, but it would be almost four years before I once again set foot in Vatican City.

"Four years? Is that how long it took you to hear about what had happened in the city?"

No, I... No. To my eternal shame it took us three years to return to the city after we learned the truth. I'll go to my grave tormented by the thought that we might have saved those people if we'd returned sooner, and I don't doubt they'll be plenty of voices in the hereafter eager to ask me why we didn't help.

The journey north was slow and arduous, taking us across the spine of Italy through the heavily infested regions of Umbria and Tuscany. It was messy, and brutal. Of course we'd expected it to be difficult, but I don't think any of us had truly understood just how hard we'd have to fight for every mile. We knew we'd have to face the undead, but we hadn't even *considered* the other risks. Without proper hygiene we saw men fall to infection from simple flesh wounds. Rabies had torn through the canine population, and not a day went by that we didn't have to tackle a pack of dogs that might kill us with a single bite. Even fellow humans were a risk. Most survivors were delighted to see us, but some... Well, we quickly learned how to judge the character of the men we met on the road.

By the time we reached Bologna we'd lost at least half of the men who set out with us from Rome, but along the way we'd found many more, the toughest and most resourceful of survivors. Good fighters, all of them, and a welcome addition to our forces. We stayed for a month in the city, grateful for the charity of the survivors who'd carved out a life there, and when we finally pushed on we were an army over two thousand strong.

During our time in Bologna we heard rumors that eighty miles to the north east the city of Venice was thriving. It sounded like fantasy to us, but travelers arriving from the region whispered of a city with power. Electric lights. Heating. Air conditioning. Personally I didn't believe a word of it – after all, if you knew of such a place why would you go elsewhere – but I promised the men we'd investigate.

We reached Venice in the early spring after a long, harsh winter. We'd been delayed on the road by the madness of Padua, where a vast swarm had pinned us down for two months and cost me more men than I cared to count. We were exhausted, weak, and at the end of our tether, but our mood brightened when we finally saw the city on the horizon. We could hardly believe it, but sure enough as we approached along the coast we saw electric lights burning out on the islands. I hadn't seen so much as a single working streetlight in two years, and it was overwhelming to see an entire city illuminated in the night. It was thrilling to think that Venice might have heating, ovens and all sorts of creature comforts just waiting for us.

For those last five miles as we approached the city my thoughts were crowded out by the fantasy of finding my favorite little cafe on the Calle Carro still open and serving, a tiny hole in the wall with a couple of seats out on the narrow street, and ordering a *caffe doppio* with just a dash of *grappa* to soothe my aching bones. It had been a year since my last decent coffee, and my pace quickened as the lights of the city grew closer.

We approached from the land through Marghera, which had been looted down to the last scrap, and despite my excitement I insisted we wait until first light to cross to the city. I didn't want to alarm the residents, and if there was anything guaranteed to cause alarm it was Rodolfo Massi arriving in the dead of night with his scimitar strapped to his back. Compared to him a swarm of the undead were little but a minor distraction.

At dawn I ordered the militia to hold fast while I led a party of around fifty men across the Ponta della Liberta, the long bridge that separates the city from the mainland. As was standard procedure with any large populated settlement I ordered everyone to remove their armor and leave behind any weapons too large to conceal. We set out with just a handful of pistols and a few small blades.

The Commander grips the handle of his broken halberd tightly.

The snipers took out three... no, *four* of us before we even realized we were under attack. We were taken entirely by surprise. Firearms were almost unheard of among the survivors, and we simply weren't prepared for the threat of sniper fire. As soon as we realized what was happening we dove for cover behind a bank of overturned cars, too many of us squeezing into too small a space as shots ricocheted from the road just inches from our feet. For two hours we remained pinned down, listening to the bullets hit our cover like a drumbeat, and the sound of one of the injured boys crying as he bled out from a shot in the stomach. We lost three more men and took who knows how many injuries. We were just too many. Every few minutes somebody would be accidentally nudged out from our sparse cover, and the snipers didn't waste the opportunity to strike. They fired at the slightest movement.

It was *intolerable*, the waiting. Our attackers seemed to have an endless supply of ammunition, and it seemed as if they could happily wait until we were driven out from cover by thirst or hunger. I'm not ashamed to say I thought about standing more than once, just taking a bullet to get it over with, but thankfully I wasn't given the time to test my resolve. After two interminable hours an emissary from the city walked out onto the bridge and called out an order for our surrender. I thought I was imagining it at first, and then the voice came again, louder.

I barely found the courage to get to my feet. I was convinced that the moment I poked my head from behind our shelter I'd be picked off by a bullet, and for a long, tense moment I whispered a prayer as the man continued to yell. Finally I found my voice, and the courage to show myself. "We're from the Vatican!" I cried out as I stood. "Please, don't fire! We've come to help!"

The response took me by surprise. The emissary replied that Venice did not recognize the authority of the false Pope, and that no Vatican army would ever be welcome in his city. We should surrender now, he said, or he would blow the bridge and us along with it. I yelled back, dumbfounded, that the Pope was dead. That we did not come as an army but as liberators. His response was... well, it wasn't appropriate for polite conversation, but the message was that every last man in Venice would die before allowing *Barberini's butchers* to cross their threshold.

The standoff lasted another hour before the emissary finally came to believe – or at least saw fit to *pretend* to believe – that I had no idea what he was talking about, and even then he only trusted us enough to allow me alone to join him in the city. The rest of my men remained on the bridge and a squad was sent out to guard the militia on the mainland, and it was made clear that if I dared disobey a single direction the lives of my men would be forfeit.

My hands were bound and I was marched into the city, through the narrow streets all the way to Piazza San Marco. People spat at me as I walked. One even threw something, a rock or a brick, that caught me on my temple and knocked me from my feet. Thankfully the guards surrounded me and restored order before the crowd found the courage to attack *en masse*, but I made the rest of the journey with one eye blinded by a rivulet of blood. It was only when I reached the Piazza that I understood their loathing of me. Or, at least, of what they believed I represented.

They told me that Camerlengo Barberini had taken control of the Vatican. It must have happened not long after we'd left the city, weeks, maybe, or even just *days* after Rome had vanished behind us. He'd gathered a ragtag group of minor officials and called a conclave to elect him Pope, quite illegally. I've no idea if he convinced them with promises or threats, but however he'd managed it they'd elected him unanimously on the first ballot, and white smoke rose from the chimney atop the Sistine Chapel.

From the moment Barberini took the papal seat the fate of the Vatican was sealed, as was the fate of all who lived within its walls. He was a man possessed, issuing edict after edict, each of which seemed to take the Church back in time. Day by day he destroyed the life's work of Pope Francis, a man who'd tirelessly dedicated himself to modernizing the faith, dragging it kicking and screaming into the 21st century.

Barberini's first act as pontiff was to lay down new laws for all territories under the control of the Holy See, and they were the kinds of laws not seen anywhere in the modern world but the most authoritarian regimes. The death penalty – a barbaric practice that had been outlawed in Italy since the fall of Mussolini – was reintroduced, and not only for the most heinous of crimes. Barberini ordered that execution be the first and only form of punishment for rape, murder and theft, but he also ordered its use for adultery, blasphemy, bearing false witness and a number of other minor crimes.

Essentially he instituted the Ten Commandments as the foundation of Italian law, with death as the default punishment for any infraction, large or small. I won't even tell you what he did to homosexuals, but you can be sure it was a punishment that no just God would sanction.

In our absence, the Venetians told me, Barberini had established his own *Militia Dei*, an army of the faithful drawn from the civilians in the Vatican. His army was *vast*, at least fifty thousand strong, and in the year since we'd left the city they'd been responsible for the execution of thousands. As we moved to the north they swarmed through the south like a plague of locusts; two armies marching under the same banner and representing the same faith, but each led by a very different commander. Ours carried a message of hope from Francis, theirs a promise of pain from Barberini.

The Venetians had been fearfully following the progress of the militia throughout Italy all this time, listening in to the few radio stations still broadcasting in the country. Wherever Barberini's army marched they brought with them bloodshed and terror. Just a month earlier they'd taken Napoli, a sanctuary city that had by all accounts fared well in the aftermath of the outbreak. Over half a million inhabitants lived safely behind their barricades, but when the militia swept in the peace was quickly shattered.

With a few days of their arrival the city leaders were thrown from the roof of the cathedral to the Piazetta del Duomo below, as an example to the inhabitants of the city. Their crime? They'd failed to attend mass on the sabbath, and instead had chosen to work the fields to grow crops to feed the city. Barberini's men ordered that the bodies be left to rot where they lay.

The people of the city did not take this judgment kindly. They attempted to rise up against the militia, and the Venetians had listened as Radio Maria, the local religious station, reported that a revolt was underway. A few hours later the announcer reported that the militia had escaped, smashing down barricades all around the city as they left. The dead swarmed in, and by the end of the day the station broadcast nothing but static. No more had been heard from Napoli since.

"Did the Venetians believe that you weren't members of Barberini's army?"

My goodness, no. They nodded and smiled at my claims, of course, but they were *certain* I was lying, and nothing I said could convince them otherwise. My men and I were stripped of our remaining armor and weaponry and set to work as slaves. Half of us were sent to the farms on Lido, and the rest were tasked with maintaining the solar grid that powered the city. This was an ingenious system, by the way, cannibalized from the abandoned cruise ships adrift in the harbor. If I'd encountered it under more amenable circumstances I'd have been deeply impressed, and proud of the resourcefulness of my countrymen.

All of us were fed little more than starvation rations to ensure we lacked the strength to fight, and – with a brilliant cruelty – each group was played off against the other. An infraction by any man would lead to a punishment visited on the other group. If one man attempted to sabotage the solar grid a farmer would lose a finger. If a farmer tried to salt the earth a solar technician would be denied water until he was moments from death. Cruel, of course, but I can't deny it served as an effective deterrent for an army so tightly bound. Nobody would risk sacrificing one of his brothers in arms.

In truth the elders of Venice didn't really need the extra labor force. I suspect they only kept us alive as bargaining chips should Barberini's men arrive, and unfortunately for them this strategy cost the lives of many Venetians. When the militia finally reached the city six months later the elders went out to bargain in a belligerent mood, falsely believing they were in a position of power. I can only assume they were cut down where they stood, and the militia walked into Venice with few casualties of their own.

We were too weak to fight. For the six months of our

imprisonment we'd tilled the soil and harvested the crops that fed the city, surviving on little more than scraps, and when we saw the Basilica di San Marco go up in flames we knew we couldn't hope to resist. I know it was cowardly, but while the Venetians were occupied with the fight I took what men I could find to the north of the island, and from there we swam across the narrow channel to the peninsular.

The channel wasn't even half a mile wide, but we still lost hundreds to exhaustion, and – I suspect, but I never saw – the grasping hands of ghouls beneath the surface. Maybe a thousand men went into the water, and one by one I watched as their heads sank beneath the surface never to return. By the time we reached dry land there were only six hundred of us left alive.

"What happened to the men you left behind in the city?"

Dead. They're in the book, along with the rest. Just like thousands of others in Venice they were tried for sedition and quickly executed. Their bodies were hanged from the streetlights lining the bridge to the mainland and left to rot. I suppose the militia liked the idea of an homage to the Appian Way.

It took us almost two weeks to make our way back to our weapons cache on the mainland, sneaking silently by night from farm to farm, laying low during the day to avoid both the roving dead and any of Barberini's men who might have left the city. Along the way we lost another hundred. Not at the hands of the dead, you understand, but... oh, just wandering away when nobody was watching. Vanishing into the night in small groups. I can't say I blame them, at least not the civilians. They hadn't signed up for this. They'd joined us to fight the undead, not the living. They hadn't enlisted to battle a human army, no matter how illegitimate the Pope may have been, and I couldn't expect them to give their lives for what amounted to a schism of the Church.

The Commander sighs.

By the time we finally made it back to Rome more than two years later we were down to just a handful of men. Maybe there were two, three hundred of us left alive. We were skin and bone, barely discernible from the undead that we no longer had the strength to fight. We'd covered the last hundred miles in darkness, making long detours whenever we saw so much as a hint of the undead, or even the living, and by the time we saw St. Peter's Basilica on the horizon we knew we stood no chance of survival. It was a suicide mission, attacking the Vatican. We knew it would be our final act on this earth but we, the final few faithful, were willing to lay down our lives for the memory of our beloved Pope. For his vision of what the Church *should* be, and against the horrors that Barberini had wrought. We marched into Rome prepared to die.

And then... nothing. We stalked wearily up the Via della Conciliazione, me using my broken halberd as a cane just to stay standing, but we found no army emerge to face us. No roadblocks. No hail of gunfire to repel our approach. All there was was the *smell*. That thick, cloying odor of thousands of corpses that had lain in the sun far too long.

The dead ran into the tens of thousands, almost all of them in military garb. Their bodies had been butchered, just... just torn to shreds, but their weapons lay beside them unbloodied. It's as if they hadn't even seen their attacker approach in time to fight back.

We found Barberini at the base of the obelisk in St. Peter's Square. His body appeared unmarked at first, but then one of the men pulled aside his vestments, and...

The Commander shivers at the memory.

He'd been eviscerated. His... his organs lay rotting in his lap, but even that revolting sight wasn't enough to draw my attention from his chest.

Someone had taken a blade and carved a message into his skin. Crudely and harshly, as if in a rage, so it took me a moment to make out the words...

I am the Lord thy God. Thou shalt have no other gods before me.

Nobody ever came forward to claim the attack, not then and not now. There has never been even the slightest hint as to who destroyed Barberini's army. Nobody even knows why they were all back at the Vatican, after spreading so far across the country. There didn't seem to be any reason for them to have massed there. Rome was clear of the undead, and in years of wandering the country we'd never come across any army strong enough to stand against the Vatican's forces. No army led by men, at least.

Of course some believe that the Lord Himself brought his judgment down on Barberini and his men. They say that He was horrified at the terror carried out in His name. That He came down from the heavens to wipe the stain of Barberini from the Vatican.

"And you? What do you believe killed them?"

Well... I believe...

The Commander runs his rosary beads between his fingers and smiles.

I believe the Lord works in mysterious ways. I'm just an old man. Who am I to question His wisdom?

•▼•

22

Wicklow, Ireland

The heavily fortified N11 motorway running south from Dublin is a tedious stop and start affair, with imposing military roadblocks before every junction at which my papers are scrutinized, though I'm told that in recent months security has been somewhat relaxed. At several of the checkpoints I barely pull to a stop before a bored soldier waves me through the maze of caltrops and sandbags laid down to stop any vehicle that attempts to breach Ireland's modular quarantine zones.

Despite the checkpoints I get the impression that the Irish have finally grown weary of the paranoia and restrictive security. After almost a full year without a reported outbreak they seem eager to finally return to normal life, and only maintain the facade to satisfy the jumpy British government in Westminster, desperate to protect its territory in Northern Ireland from further attacks.

After forty miles and two hours of crawling through checkpoints I take an exit from the N11 and suddenly emerge into a rural paradise. Lush green hills roll to the horizon, broken only by overgrown hedgerows and narrow country lanes. The warm midday sun banishes shade, and in the distance the blue-green Irish Sea sparkles invitingly beneath a cloudless sky. The scene is so welcoming and serene it's hard to believe that just a few miles away, hidden away on an industrial estate south of the Wicklow dock, sits a building in which tens of thousands of human beings – albeit infected – have over the last decade been methodically and systematically slaughtered on camera.

I find Dr. Neve Gallagher waiting for me at a rusting bus stop beside the road at the edge of Wicklow, leaning against her Land Rover and smoking a cigarette with an intensity that suggests she holds a personal grudge against it. As I pull to a stop she crushes the butt against the door, and she instructs me in her thick Irish accent to leave my rental car here and switch vehicles. Only the Land Rover is cleared to go where we're going.

We drive slowly through the silent town and out into the empty suburbs, and I notice a number of hand drawn signs staked into overgrown front lawns, each of them angrily protesting the presence of the lab. There are more by the roadside as we approach the compound, and as we pass the faded sign for the Innotek Environmental Testing Laboratory I notice it's been defaced with colorful language and peppered with buckshot. When I ask why we haven't seen any people Gallagher tells me that most left long ago. Few could stand the noises coming from the lab. Wicklow is now a virtual ghost town, peopled only by the guards and scientists working at the lab.

She leads me through yet more security barriers, five in all, this time designed to keep people in rather than out. In the case of our destination there's good reason for the tight security. Any breaches in the lab's security could lead to a new and potentially fatal outbreak for Ireland.

After passing through the final barrier – a ten foot tall double fence with masses of razor wire sandwiched in between – Gallagher pulls to a stop in a small parking lot beside a sprawling single storey building and pushes open her door. I hear the groans right away. A tight shiver runs down my spine, and I feel my heart thump more quickly in my chest. "Don't worry," she laughs, climbing out of the car. "You'll either get used to it or go mental."

Every instinct tells me not to follow the doctor as she climbs to the top of a high sand bank at the edge of the parking lot. The human race has only survived the last decade by learning to flee from the noises coming from the other side, but I'm comforted by Gallagher's confidence. I steel myself for what's to come, turn away from the Land Rover and follow.

"We call this 'the Pen'," she says, lighting another cigarette as I reach the top of the bank. "Don't worry, they can't get you. Can't even see you, come to that. Most of them have gone blind now. All they've got is their ears, so you'll be grand as long as you keep quiet."

Before me I see a yard around half the size of a football field, surrounded on all sides by a deep empty moat and tall reinforced fences. Within the yard stands a swarm of the undead, most of them naked, many in an advanced state of decomposition. There look to be around five hundred imprisoned in the yard, all of them standing in the relaxed, loose-limbed pose of zombies in their inactive state. Towards the southern edge a gaggle of them are active, and it's only when I see a rabbit bolt from the enclosure that I understand why.

Gallagher slips two fingers between her lips and gives a shrill whistle, and I feel my heart leap to my throat as the crowd turns towards us and begins to groan in chorus. They swarm blindly in our direction, the leaders toppling over the edge of the moat as they're pushed from behind. Hundreds of them slide down the muddy slope and vanish from sight, and before long the yard is half empty, and the pile of undead fills the moat almost to its lip.

"Sorry, I've been warned to stop doing that," Gallagher says, trying to conceal a smile. "The locals used to go crazy when the swarm got excitable, before they all buggered off. We built these sandbanks to try to block the groans, but you know how the sound carries on the wind."

To my relief Gallagher leads me back down to the parking lot and into the building, through narrow corridors to her messy office. Along the way we pass the testing labs, thankfully not in use today. Like most I've already seen the videos of what goes on here, and I'm not eager to catch the live show. Gallagher clears papers from a plastic chair and invites me to sit.

How do we kill them?
That was the question on everyone's lips when they started to appear. Well, that and *are we living in a bloody*

horror movie?

The mad thing was that a lot of people thought we were wasting our time when we decided to find the answer. They thought they already knew because they'd been raised on George Romero movies and, not to put too fine a point on it, daft zombie novels written by the likes of you. For years they'd had the 'answer' drummed into them over and over again. Just destroy the brain, right? They just assumed that the movies were accurate, as if coked up Hollywood screenwriters had any clue about *real* zombies, or had even believed they could exist.

Do you remember those ads for shooting ranges in the States offering courses on how to perfect your headshot? How about that ad for the Beretta 92? *The most accurate pistol on the planet. Headshots every time, all the time... Guaranteed.* That campaign was so successful Smith and Wesson threatened to sue for false advertising.

If you think that was dumb you should have seen the UK, where the strict gun laws meant that advertisers had to get creative. Sales of cricket bats went through the roof after the Folkestone attack. *Shaun of the Dead,* remember? SportsDirect even ran a national ad campaign: *Don't Get Red On You.* Daft. A cricket bat is one of the worst weapons you could carry, as anyone who ever tried to swing one for two days straight would tell you.

There was just so much stupid misinformation being spread it was *scary,* especially when the newspapers got in on the action and started talking about movie tropes as if they had any relevance at all to the real world, and this crap went on for weeks. We were all worried that people would end up getting themselves killed by treating these things like movie monsters, but it was the Telegraph article that was the last straw for the boss.

God, that article. I remember seeing him storm in one morning with the paper clutched in both hands, like he wanted to tear it in two. He threw it down on my desk and showed me a dozen paragraphs of nonsense – in the bloody Telegraph, mind, a proper respectable broadsheet – talking about the relative merits of Simon Pegg's cricket bat and the barbed wire wrapped baseball bat used by that bloke in *The Walking Dead*.

I remember almost laughing at the bit where the journalist argued that while the baseball bat might be easier to swing the cricket bat was far and away the more patriotic weapon for an upstanding Brit. 'Let the Americans keep their gaudy rounders bat,' it said. 'We'll always plump for the traditional and oh-so-British thwack of willow on leather while defending our village greens.' I mean... Jesus, can you even *imagine*? Invoking patriotism in your choice of weapon to defend your bloody family? It was just so far beyond moronic it was untrue.

Anyway, the boss decided that enough was enough. He said if nobody else could be bothered to take a scientific approach to the problem then we'd do it ourselves. We had the lab all ready. We'd just finished running the latest Huawei smartphone through a month of stress tests so the equipment was going begging, and we had a couple of months to wait before our next contract began, if any of us even survived that long. All we had to do was get hold of some test subjects, and there we hit a brick wall almost immediately.

Jesus, the red tape. Ireland was still clear at that point. There'd been one attack up at Dublin airport, some infected bugger on a flight from Beijing who turned just as the plane came in to land, but the police took care of it on the runway before it got the chance to spread the infection. Since then they'd kept a close eye on incoming flights and ships. That's why when we approached the government with a request to actually bring in a few dozen undead we were laughed out of the room.

We spent two weeks banging our head against a bureaucratic wall, and we got precisely nothing in return but trouble. Eventually we got a call from the office of the *Taoiseach* to warn us that we'd receive 'special attention' if we continued to try to procure specimens. Basically they were telling us that the tax man would screw us without lube if we didn't drop it. So... well, we dropped it.

"So what changed? How did you get hold of your first undead?"

Wow, you really didn't do your research before you came, did you? It was the *Emma Maersk* disaster. Did you never read about it? No? Seriously? It was in all the papers. Well, I suppose there was a lot going on back then.

The *Emma Maersk* was a Danish container ship. The largest in the world when she was launched in 2006, in fact. A big beast of a thing, four hundred meters long and fifty wide. She made regular round trips between Northern Europe and Eastern China, calling at Ningbo, Xiamen and Hong Kong to pick up... I don't know, the usual cheap consumer tat they used to turn out in Chinese factories before selling it to us at a massive markup.

Nobody knows how the crew got infected, or even if they *were* infected. All we know is that after leaving Hong Kong the *Emma Maersk* sailed on course for thirty five days. She made it through the Suez Canal and passed through the Strait of Gibraltar, took a turn to the north off the coast of Portugal and set herself on a course for the English Channel. All of this matched her planned route.

She stayed within the shipping lanes, and according to the radio contact she made with the mainland along the way everything was bang on schedule.

It was only when she reached the Channel that people realized something was amiss. The ship should have made an eastward turn just off the coast of Brittany, but instead she carried on steaming north at full speed through the Celtic Sea, on a direct course for the Irish coast. When the Coast Guard tried to reach her by radio they got back nothing but static, and when they sent a chopper on a fly-by the deck was deserted. They couldn't even see anyone manning the bridge. As far as they could tell she was a ghost ship, and there was no way to stop her.

The TV news picked up the story just as the ship ran aground at Wexford. They caught the whole thing on camera from a helicopter. It seemed almost graceful, the way this massive beast of a ship slowed itself on a sandbank at the entrance to Wexford Bay before gently butting up against the harbor as light as a kiss. It crashed better than I can parallel park.

This all happened around midnight and the harbor was empty, so there were no injuries on land whatsoever. I actually remember cheering as I watched it happen. I had no idea what was going on, but I was just over the moon that whoever was piloting the thing had managed to bring it in without killing anyone. It seemed like a rare miracle after all the terrible news of late, and it was one we really bloody needed. The picture cut back to the studio and everyone was all smiles. We could even hear cheering in the background, and then it stopped as quickly as it had started. The screen went to a color pattern for a few seconds, then it cut back to the helicopter.

Those *things* were pouring over the sides. I couldn't

make out what was going on at first because the chopper was too far away, but when the cameraman zoomed in on the deck I can guarantee that everyone watching in Ireland shat themselves. There were *thousands* of them, just tumbling over the sides. Most of them fell straight into the water, but the few that landed on the harbor pulled themselves to their feet right away just as the first of the Gardai showed up. Country police, you know. Unarmed. Poor buggers didn't stand a chance.

There are all sorts of conspiracy theories about what really happened. Most people believe it was refugees trying to escape China. They think they might have been locked in shipping containers with a few slow burn infections, and maybe the crash had burst some of them open. That seems like a fairly likely explanation. Others believe it was a deliberate attack, that the Chinese – or maybe even the North Koreans – intentionally loaded the infected on board and ordered the crew to ground the ship when it reached land. I don't suppose we'll ever really know the truth. Nobody ever found the crew, of course, and after the ship hit we were all a little too busy running for our lives to start an investigation.

Gallagher leans back in her chair and lights another cigarette.

After that we had no shortage of test subjects. Wexford was quickly overrun, and Waterford, and Carlow. The army was caught on the back foot. By the time they managed to get their act together a few smaller swarms had already reached us here in Wicklow. Unlike much of the rest of the country, though, we were prepared.

The Pen was already here when we moved in. It was originally intended to be a reservoir for a desalination plant that never got built, so the only thing we had to do was carve out the moat from the slag heaps and surround the whole yard with fences. As the swarms began to make their way up the coast I rigged up a set of speakers at the back of the Pen, and when the first of those creatures were spotted on the road up from Kilbride I hooked up my iPod, cranked some Kate Bush as loud as it'd go and *voila*, instant test subjects.

The music was like a dinner bell to these bastards. It drew them in for miles around, and they couldn't resist shambling through the gates and trying to get at the speaker. Dumb bastards must have thought there was someone inside singing. Even with the gates wide open they never tried to leave as long as the music kept playing. The buggers just stood there staring at it like... ha, I was going to say like zombies, but I guess that'd be redundant.

Gallagher stubs out her cigarette, half smoked, and waves a hand towards the lab.

And then... all this. The glorious, slightly disgusting wonders you see before you. I'm guessing you've seen the videos, right? They were very popular on the Internet, I'm told, especially the wind tunnel test and the high pressure simulation. I imagine there was a lot of crossover with fans of Eli Roth movies.

Before all this happened we were the largest product testing lab in Ireland, and the second largest in Europe, and we'd grown so big not only because we had great staff but because we had better equipment than pretty much anyone else on the planet. APST, we call it. Accelerated Product Stress Testing. We could take your new phone or your latest washing machine and expose it to the most extreme environments on the planet to discover any flaws before you put it on sale. We could simulate the humidity of the Amazon rainforest, the vibration of a rocket launch or the deck of a ship in a Pacific storm, all from the comfort of our lab.

Remember those smartphones with the exploding batteries? If we'd won the contract to put them through their paces you'd never have heard about them because we would have exposed the flaw on day one. I'm not trying to brag, but we were the best in the business.

When it came to the zombies we didn't really have a tough job, to be honest. We didn't need the kind of pinpoint precision of a regular product stress test. All we needed to do was push a few bodies into the lab, turn the machines up to eleven and take notes as we watched the buggers die. How did they differ from regular humans? Did they have any unusual weaknesses or strengths? Were they more sensitive to the cold than us, or more resistant to heat? Were they affected by humidity or aridity? High or low pressure? Abrasive winds? In short, we just wanted to know the easiest and most effective way to kill the fuckers, quickly and in large numbers.

"And what did you find?"

Well, you've seen the videos, so I'm sure you already know the answer. We found that they're pretty much exactly the same as living humans in almost every conceivable way, setting aside the fact that they eat people and none of them could do a decent book report on James Joyce.

The extreme heat test showed that they start to become sluggish at thirty to forty Celsius, just like us, and that they begin to lose motor functions when they're exposed to fifty Celsius for more than a couple of hours.

Perhaps they're a little more sensitive to heat because they don't sweat, but they balance it out by not producing as much body heat as living humans. Same goes for extreme cold. They begin to slow down around zero, and once they hit minus twenty they begin to exhibit signs of hypothermia, though it's worth noting that they recover more quickly than humans when the temperature increases, because their more viscous blood retains heat a little more efficiently than ours.

We got the same depressing results in every other test we ran. Extreme vibration knocked them off their feet more easily than humans, but that was useless information unless you could figure out a way to induce localized earthquakes or lure them onto a giant trampoline. High velocity dust eventually blinded them because they don't have a corneal reflex, which means they don't blink when something touches their eyes, and at high intensity it eventually flayed the more decomposed subjects, but it took far too long to inflict damage to be of any tactical use, and a zombie missing its skin could be even *more* dangerous than a regular one. Altitude, humidity, salt spray, high and low pressure... We tried everything, and there was just nothing that presented us with any kind of obvious tactical advantage.

We also performed any number of weapons tests. We fired guns at them, removed their organs one at a time, blew their limbs off with grenades, set them on fire and, yes, we even hit them over the head with a cricket bat, but we didn't discover anything groundbreaking. It was just as difficult to kill a zombie as it was to kill a human. It was like the old joke about the bloke who wants to kill a man with a stake through the heart. "But he's not a vampire!", his friend protests. "Yeah, but the stake doesn't care."

It was just so bloody *disappointing*. We'd gone into

this hoping we'd be able to report to the world that we'd found a silver bullet, some easy way to kill them that wouldn't require mountains of ammo and your very own tank, but at the end of months of ceaseless work we came back to the very same conclusion everyone had already known since day one: destroy the brain.

By this point, of course, Ireland was locked down. The military had taken over, and while the local Gardai had so far turned a blind eye to what we were doing here they'd finally lost their patience. They knew they'd be up shit creek if the army discovered they'd allowed us to hold hundreds of living zombies on our little industrial estate, so we were told to destroy the lot of them by the end of the week. Game over.

I'd just finished clearing out a bunch of bodies from the Sahara room – the desert environment simulation lab – when it all went to shit. It was nasty, messy work. We'd sandblasted a bunch of them for an hour at the highest fan setting – almost hurricane wind speeds – and there wasn't much left of the dozen or so bodies but bone and black goo staining the walls. I pretty much scooped them into a bin with a shovel, never a fun job when you're walking around in a bulky isolation suit, then I headed outside to the pit beside the Pen where we burned all the remains.

That's when the power went out. I was standing at the edge of the pit when the floodlights suddenly blinked off. Kate Bush was halfway through Hounds of Love when the sound cut out, and in the sudden silence the next sound I heard was the creak of the magnetically locked gate swinging open. That was the only thing keeping the swarm in the Pen, and as my eyes adjusted to the darkness I saw it was wide open.

There were around three hundred of the buggers in

there that night, and the moment I realized they were no longer locked up I let out the shrillest scream you've ever heard. They all turned towards me, all three hundred of the bastards, staring at me in the dark with those dead eyes. I still wake up in a cold sweat sometimes.

I don't know how long the power was out before the emergency generator took over. All I know is that the fastest of them had enough time to make it through the gate and start powering towards me. I was screaming at myself to run, but my feet just wouldn't listen. I felt like they were buried in concrete for all the good they were. I felt a warm stream of piss run down the leg of my isolation suit, and I realized – in that weird, peaceful, out of body sort of way a lot of people who made it through rough moments describe – that I only had a few more seconds to live.

And then... then I woke up on the floor of the lab, stripped to my undies and covered in piss while some big lummox loomed over me and tried to give me very slobbery mouth to mouth.

Gallagher laughs at the memory, and then pulls aside her hair. Above her left ear a bare patch exposes a two inch long crescent shaped scar.

When I was seven years old I was visiting my gran in Newtownards, a little market town in Ulster, when an IRA bomb went off across the street from the cafe where we were eating lunch. I don't have any memory of it, but apparently I was hit in the head by a collapsing wall. For three weeks I was kept in a chemically induced coma while the swelling in my brain subsided, and when I finally woke up I was left with two mementos: this scar, and a bad case of photosensitive epilepsy.

My kind of epilepsy is pretty rare in someone my age. For most people the seizures die down by their mid twenties, but even in my forties I still get them every few months, jerking all over the place and drooling down my chin like a lunatic whenever my brain gets confused by flashing lights and colors. It's an absolute bleeding pain in the ass.

It was the generators kicking in. Do you see? We had the floodlights hooked up to the emergency diesel rig, and when the lights came back they must have flickered for a few seconds at just the right frequency to scramble my brain and cause me to seize. I was out for the count before I knew what was happening, and it was an hour before I was stable enough to understand what had happened. I'm always groggy as hell for hours after a seizure, and for a while I couldn't figure out why I wasn't dead. Why the hell did the zombies not try to get me? I was the easiest meal they could have hoped for, just lying there like a fish struggling on a dock.

When I was finally *compos mentis* the boss told me that the generators must have been wired up wrong. He said he'd watched as they kicked in, and he'd seen me and most of the test subjects fall to the ground and convulse like we had fifty thousand volts flowing through us. It had been raining and the ground was soaked, so he thought there must have been enough of a current flowing through the Pen to knock them all off their feet just long enough for the lads to bolt up the gate and drag me inside.

I didn't buy it. I knew what had happened as soon as he told me his side of the story.

Gallagher reaches for a remote on her desk, flicks on the TV in the corner and scrolls through

a menu until an image appears on the screen. It shows a brightly lit room, empty but for a naked female test subject standing in an inactive state in the center. She stares blankly towards the camera, her arms relaxed by her sides in what Gallagher calls 'conservation mode', and then suddenly becomes agitated at the sound of the doctor's voice. "Environmental test number 1287. Single subject. Young female, about three months gone. Initiating stimulus at 75Hz."

The lights in the room begins to flicker almost imperceptibly. The zombie briefly looks up at the ceiling but doesn't seem particularly interested. She once again relaxes, and then snarls when Gallagher's voice returns. "No effect at 75Hz. Reducing to 50Hz." The lights begin to flicker again, a little more noticeably this time. Once again the zombie relaxes, and once again she becomes agitated when the voice returns. "No effect at 50Hz. Reducing to 25Hz."

The light begins to flicker even more slowly now. The test subject stares blankly at the camera, seemingly unaffected, and after thirty seconds Gallagher's voice returns with a sigh. "No effect at 25Hz Reducing to..." She falls silent for a moment, and then the voice returns. "*Helloooooo?* Can you hear me, zombie woman?" The test subject doesn't respond. "Hey, Gus, I think we might have someth– *Jesus!*"

The woman suddenly collapses to the ground out of shot. For a few seconds all that can be heard is the sound of feet kicking against a hard floor before Gallagher's voice returns triumphantly. "*I knew it! I fucking knew it!*"

The doctor flicks off the TV and turns to me with a smile.

It seems so obvious now, looking back. We'd spent months trying to figure out how we could kill these things by conventional means. We'd exposed them to every environmental condition we could think of to find some kind of physical weakness we could exploit, but in all that time we didn't give so much as a passing thought to the most important thing about a zombie.

You have to destroy their brain, right? They can keep going without an arm or a leg. They can keep going with half their organs removed. Hell, some of them can still survive for a while after you punch their heart out through their spine. The brain is the only thing they absolutely rely on to survive, and we'd been thinking of this as their greatest strength. It never occurred to us that it might also be the source of their greatest *weakness*.

As soon as she stopped seizing I dissected the brain of the subject, and a dozen more of them over the next couple of days, and sure enough I found exactly what I expected. In every last one of the subjects I dissected I found extensive scarring on their brain tissue.

At the time we knew virtually nothing about the virus that causes the infection. We didn't even know how it managed to turn people into – I'm still uncomfortable using such a silly word – *zombies*. We were flying blind, but this was the first clue we had as to the mechanism of the virus. We found that the infection ravaged the parts of the brain responsible for higher reasoning. It successfully turned humans into mindless vectors for the virus, driving them to pass it to others, but in the process of destroying the higher consciousness of its hosts it wrought such intense damage on the brain that it left itself open to an exploitable weakness: epilepsy.

Gallagher leans back in her seat, lights up yet another cigarette and smiles.

And that gave us our silver bullet.

●▼●

:::23:::

Tsim Sha Tsui, Hong Kong

I've been waiting at the Star Ferry Pier for almost an hour, sweating in the close heat of the city and regretting my decision to tell my contact, Stephen Liu, that he could identify me by my outfit, a gray wool suit designed for a New York fall afternoon rather than the stifling, suffocating humidity of a South East Asian night. My shirt clings to my skin like Saran Wrap, and when a short, elderly man – also dressed in a suit, but seemingly untroubled by the heat – finally approaches with a broad smile and an ice cream cone in each hand I'm relieved when he introduces himself as Liu.

"Best ice cream in Kowloon," he grins, nodding towards the *Mister Softee* ice cream truck that has been a permanent fixture at Tsim Sha Tsui for many years. "You look like you could use something cold."

This is a special night for Liu. He's been invited as the guest of honor to celebrate the anniversary of the innovation that saved Hong Kong, though as we're led to our seats in the raised viewing area set up for the event he shyly whispers that he's not sure why the Chief Executive makes such a fuss every year.

"It's not like I really *did* anything," he insists, modestly. "I just built on Doctor Gallagher's work. Still, I suppose they take some pride in boasting that we were the first." Liu chuckles.

"Between you and me, I think they do this just to annoy Beijing."

Did you know that it isn't actually epilepsy? The legend has taken on something of a life of its own over the years, but in fact Doctor Gallagher's diagnosis of the condition was quite inaccurate. Ummm... I don't mean that to sound dismissive of her work, of course. Far from it. Her discovery of the neurological abnormality was absolutely groundbreaking, and without it I'm sure none of us would be sitting here right now, but the fact remains that her diagnosis was medically incorrect. The undead do *not* suffer from epilepsy.

Liu appears uncomfortable with his perceived rebuke of Gallagher's work, but he presses on.

Of course she isn't a medical doctor but an engineer, so it would be unreasonable to expect her to make an accurate medical diagnosis. And naturally her personal medical history might have led her to jump to the wrong conclusion, while my own experience gave me the insight to reach the correct one, quite by chance.

Now tell me, are you at all familiar with the Bucha effect? How about flicker vertigo, have you ever heard of that? No? Oh, *good!* I never get the chance to tell this story any more.

Liu nibbles at his ice cream as he composes his thoughts.

For a few years as a skinny, awkward young man in the Eighties I served as a cadet pilot in the Royal Hong Kong Auxiliary Air Force. This was many years before the handover to China, you understand, so at that time we were run along the same lines as a British Royal Air Force squadron, with all the curious cultural oddities that entailed. Mostly it meant drinking Bombay gin and tonic in the officer's mess, pretending to know the words beyond the opening verse of God Save the Queen and learning to smile politely when anyone with wings on his collar called me 'old chap', all of which I found quite alien as the son of an uneducated Hakka Chinese fishmonger from the New Territories.

Looking back I've no idea what I was even doing there. This wasn't my world. Not only did I feel completely out of place among the refined British gentlemen and the ambitious *hi-so* Hong Kongers looking to secure their place in the upper echelons of society, but I was also absolutely *terrified* of flying.

I'd never even been in the air before I enlisted, but my father had always dreamed that his son would become one of the brave airmen he'd idolized as a boy during the Japanese occupation. He'd spent years worshiping the pilots who ran bombing missions over Asia. He once told me he used to watch the planes fly overhead for hours at a time, willing them to swoop down and destroy our invaders, and before I was even born he decided that the next time Hong Kong came under threat his son would be there to blast our attackers to oblivion.

Of course I'd always made it clear that I had no interest in flying, but my father was... well, let's just say that he was not a man who enjoyed compromise. Once he made a decision it had a tendency to stay made, and so at the age of twenty, despite my trepidation, I found myself enlisting in an effort to keep the peace.

I trained on an Aerospatiale SA 365 Dauphin 2, the Air Force search and rescue helicopter, and I hated every last minute of it. I wasn't so bad with airplanes – there I could at least close my eyes and pretend I was sitting in a car – but helicopters were a different beast altogether. They plunge. They swoop. They sway from side to side in the lightest breeze, and when you hit a pocket of low air pressure your stomach falls out of your backside while your heart climbs out of your mouth.

Helicopters are *horrible* monstrosities, and over the course of three years I was expected to log one thousand hours as a co-pilot to earn my wings. I managed just seven hundred before the accident, when I finally decided that the fear of my father's wrath on the ground was no longer enough to force me to escape into the air.

It happened some time early in 1985, if I remember correctly. We were in the middle of an unusual cold snap that had sent temperatures down to around five degrees Celsius – almost unheard of in Hong Kong – and of course the first thing everyone did was head out of the city to hike in the wonderful, bracing weather. Naturally a few people found themselves in trouble since most were unaccustomed to such cold conditions, so we weren't at all surprised when we received an order to fly to Lantau Peak to help recover a hiker who hadn't realized that a temperature of a brisk five Celsius at sea level would fall to well below zero at three thousand feet.

It should have been a standard flight with no surprises, so I was given the opportunity to log an easy hour or two as co-pilot under an experienced British senior pilot, a gentleman named Witherspoon who wore the most astonishing mustache I've ever seen, before or since.

We were twenty minutes into the flight and circling the Peak when I noticed that something was wrong. I was scanning the ground for the hiker as Witherspoon took us in a broad circle at around two thousand feet, and then without warning he released the stick. We jerked out of our turn and began to head back out to sea, and I turned to him and asked him what he was doing – timidly, of course, since I was only a cadet, and cadets don't make demands of pilots – but he failed to respond. He just stared straight ahead, as if concentrating on something in the far distance.

I waited a moment and then asked again a little more urgently, and the man finally turned towards me and began to slur unintelligibly, as if he was drunk. Of course that wasn't a rare occurrence back then, in the years before we all worshiped at the altar of health and safety. The experienced pilots had a habit of enjoying an afternoon gin and tonic before taking to the air, and they usually made it back alive and well, but this behavior seemed like the result of much more than just a quick eye opener.

I was about to speak up again when without warning Witherspoon began to violently convulse in his seat, kicking and slapping against the controls as if he was being electrocuted. In fact that's the first thought I had, that something had shorted in the cockpit and he'd come into contact with a live current.

I'd never been so terrified in all my life. In a matter of seconds we plunged five hundred feet towards the mountain. Countless alarms sounded through the cockpit, and the instrument panel lit up like a Christmas tree as the twin engines fell into a stall. I didn't have the first clue what was happening. I didn't even know which controls Witherspoon had hit as he lashed out at the panel. All I knew was that if I didn't take the stick and bring us down safely we'd be dead in moments.

I really don't remember what happened next – the

memory is little more than a blur after so many years – but somehow I managed to transfer control to my stick and pull us out of our dive just in the nick of time. It wasn't what you'd call pretty. We came in almost sideways but somehow, I suspect through blind luck rather than skill, I brought us down to a safe if extremely graceless landing in a clearing at the foot of the mountain. I caught the tail rotor on a tree and one of the primary blades was bent out of shape as it hit the slope, but apart from that there was, quite miraculously, little damage to the craft. Witherspoon suffered a fractured tibia and a concussion, but I escaped with just a few scratches.

Liu takes a bite out of his wafer cone and cringes at the memory.

This was the first time I'd heard of the Bucha effect, but for weeks afterwards – right up until the day I resigned my commission and left that awful place – it was all people talked about on the base.

In the 1950s a doctor named Bucha was commissioned to investigate a very strange and troubling phenomenon. For some reason helicopters all over the world kept crashing, seemingly without any cause at all, and nobody could understand why. The skies were clear, the pilots were experienced and there were no obvious technical faults that would suggest that a crash was imminent, but suddenly the choppers would fall out of the sky as if the pilots themselves had simply steered them into the ground. There were dozens of cases, and by the time Doctor Bucha was called in there was talk of grounding entire fleets.

The only thing that seemed to connect these incidents was that those few pilots who lived to tell the tale reported feeling unwell in the moments leading up to their crash, nauseous and disoriented. Some suffered sudden blinding headaches before losing control of their fine motor skills. Some even suffered full seizures, despite having no history of epilepsy.

It was truly baffling. There were theories that perhaps there was some sort of environmental contaminant in the cockpits – like the castor oil they used to use to lubricate rotary engines, the fumes of which gave World War Two pilots raging bouts of diarrhea – or perhaps there was even some new and terrifying weapon that could disable a pilot at a distance, but nobody could find any evidence to back up these theories. Everyone was completely stumped, until finally Bucha had an epiphany.

Now I'm no doctor so you'll have to forgive the rather elementary explanation, but as I understand it the normal frequency of human brain waves – the sort of brain activity you'd expect in a person who is awake, alert and active – fall between fifteen and thirty Hertz. These are the frequencies at which a normal, properly functioning brain operates. What Doctor Bucha discovered was that if you were to introduce a competing signal into the brain – a signal that precisely matched the brain waves of the subject – you could temporarily block the mental pathways. You could confuse the subject. You could make them feel nauseous or experience headaches. You could even, if you were to get the frequency just right, induce a seizure.

I'm sorry, I know I'm not giving you a very good explanation, but to be honest it's quite beyond my understanding. It was explained to me in layman's terms that the signal acts like a car driving the wrong way down a one way street. When it meets traffic coming from the other direction everything grinds to a halt, or simply crashes. Doctor Bucha realized that *this* is what was happening to the pilots. Somehow in mid-flight they were being exposed to a signal at a frequency that disrupted their mental pathways, and the moment he climbed aboard his next flight he immediately realized where that signal originated.

It was the sunlight shining through the rotors. It seemed so obvious once he'd discovered it, but for months the finest minds in engineering and medicine hadn't been able to see the evidence before their eyes.

As rotor blades turn they momentarily block the sunlight shining into the cockpit below. Of course the light is only blocked for the tiniest fraction of a second at a time, so at regular engine speeds the flicker is virtually imperceptible, but when the hub rate of the rotors – the speed at which they turn – falls below a certain threshold it can create a flicker that precisely matches the frequency of the brain waves of the pilots. This low frequency flicker was disrupting their mental pathways, and *this* is what was causing the crashes.

If any of this sounds familiar, by the way, it may be because many governments, including yours and I suspect my own, eventually began to exploit the Bucha effect as an interrogation technique. At the correct frequency they discovered that they could use strobing lights to disorient criminal suspects, causing them intense discomfort to the point at which they would become compliant. Whether or not it was actually an effective tactic is a question I'll leave for others to answer, but they used it all the same.

Of course as soon as the Bucha effect was discovered helicopters were redesigned so that during regular operation their rotors wouldn't turn at hub rates that could cause the effect, and protective sunglasses or tinted visors became standard issue for pilots. Almost immediately the problem was eradicated, but our case was a one in a million fluke caused by a combination of pilot error and random chance.

Witherspoon was a new arrival, you see. He hadn't trained in the Dauphin, and he wasn't aware that the minimum safe hub rate was much higher than in the Westland Wessex he flew back home, so he was flying with the rotors spinning at a dangerously low speed. As he banked into his turn around the mountain it just so happened that our angle kept the midday sun positioned directly above our rotors, creating a strobe effect at the exact frequency required to cause the Bucha effect. Most pilots couldn't have replicated the conditions if they'd *tried*, and it ended up with us both on the ground and – I don't mind admitting – in need of a clean pair of trousers and a stiff drink.

After I resigned my commission I resolved to never again set foot in an aircraft. I returned home to Tai Po in the New Territories, found a job working as a sales agent for a lighting manufacturer across the border in Shenzhen, married my wife and raised a wonderful son.

Over the years my time in the Air Force became nothing but a distant memory and a colorful anecdote, a frightening story to impress my friends after a few drinks. After many years of hard work I was promoted, and promoted again, and by the time the crisis began I'd become the general manager of the Shenzhen-Kowloon Industrial Lighting Company. It was a good job. A good *life*.

And then the dead came, and overnight our world changed.

Liu falls silent as a voice calls out over a Tannoy in Cantonese, Mandarin and English to

warn that the display will begin in ten minutes. It advises that those wishing to view the show should prepare to don their protective goggles, and others should look away or retreat indoors.

I was at the factory in Shenzhen when Hong Kong sealed the border without warning. It was the worst day of my life. I was working on the payroll when one of my employees burst into my office and told me to turn on the news, and in an instant the ground fell out from beneath me.

My wife and son were on the other side of the border in Tai Po, just ten miles and a twenty minute train ride away from my office. Can you even imagine that? Can you imagine what it feels like to be so close, and yet unable to reach out and touch your loved ones? I couldn't process it. It just didn't seem real. When the news said that the border would be closed indefinitely my mind simply wouldn't take it in. I'd crossed the border just that morning and there had been no indication that there were any problems. Nobody had warned me. Nobody had even *hinted* that perhaps today might be a good day to call in sick, even though I was friendly with many of the border guards. If only they'd... Just a quiet word in my ear, and I'd never have...

In any case, I didn't blame the government, at least not after I heard that several attacks had been reported in the cities to the east. Shenzhen was home to thirteen million people, and even a minor outbreak would have sent countless infected flooding across the border into Hong Kong. I understood that they needed to take whatever measures were required to protect the city, and of course I was relieved that it meant that my wife and child would be secure, but it didn't make life any easier to know that I was trapped on the wrong side. I couldn't help but think of Korea, of all those families torn apart by the Division, separated for life by an arbitrary line on a map. I wondered if I'd ever see my family again, and I'm not ashamed to admit that it brought me to tears.

From the window of my office in the factory I watched helpless for two months as Hong Kong fortified the border wall at the river's edge. I watched it grow to ten meters. I watched it bristle with floodlights and artillery, and then I watched as armed guards arrived to man the lookout points atop it. I spent more hours than I care to remember staring at that damned wall, wishing I was on the other side, and my wishes only grew more desperate as we heard reports of outbreaks in the regions around the city. There was looting. People grew angry and frustrated, and every night I heard gunfire in the streets nearby. That was when the military finally arrived and took control.

For the next six months I remained trapped, separated from my family and surviving only on the charity of my employees. I lived in my office, sleeping on a camp bed borrowed from a local clinic and eating whatever leftovers the wives of my staff could offer.

A nightly curfew was strictly enforced, and the military units that patrolled the streets were jumpy and poorly trained. They were just children, barely out of school. China hadn't fought a full scale ground war for decades and it was clear that most of these young boys had never seen real action. They hadn't had the fear beaten out of them by combat, and they lacked the discipline to keep their fingers off their triggers.

Some of them... well, let's just say there were some *accidents*, and as a result the few of us who remained in the city stayed indoors as much as we could. Even though the streets were free of the dead our safety wasn't guaranteed so we holed up indoors, obsessively watching the news and searching the Internet for scraps of hope to cling onto.

"Is that how you learned of Doctor Gallagher's discovery?"

That's right. I found her videos in the final few weeks before the Internet failed in Shenzhen. They were presented only as entertainment, of course. Doctor Gallagher didn't want to offer viewers false hope. When she uploaded them she made it clear that she'd made no earth shattering discoveries. She shared her disappointment that the tests at her lab had not borne fruit, so I viewed them just as I viewed the videos of the young Czech boy with his stick, and the well armed gentlemen in America, and the seemingly countless videos from Russia, where they'd turned creative zombie destruction into a whole new art form.

I just... I suppose the videos made me feel a little better. It did me good to remind myself that these creatures were not indestructible. They were only flesh and blood. They could be killed almost as easily as *we* could be killed, provided we had the correct weapons and enough resolve.

And then Doctor Gallagher's final video arrived, and I was glued to the screen as soon as I saw the title: *BREAKTHROUGH*. She appeared on screen herself for the first time. She looked disheveled and exhausted, as if she hadn't slept in days, and when I saw the footage of her tests I understood why. She'd finally found a way to incapacitate them!

The video ran for a little more than thirty minutes

after a brief introduction. She showed the initial test, the one with the female in the lab. I watched the subject go into convulsions after it was exposed to a light strobing at 25 Hertz, and then the video cut to the autopsy, and several more afterwards. I saw the scarring on the brains, and I listened to Doctor Gallagher's theory that the undead suffered from epilepsy. She then showed a video filmed outdoors at night, in some kind of caged enclosure in which she tested the 25 Hertz light on a group of a few dozen, but only half of them seemed to respond to the stimulus. The rest remained active and agitated throughout, even as their kin twitched and convulsed on the ground around them.

The Doctor ended the video by explaining that she had no idea why only some of the undead were affected. She explained that she was not a medical doctor, and she pleaded with her viewers to spread the word. Before signing off she warned that her lab would soon be forced to close, and she said she hoped that others around the world would pick up the baton and continue her work.

And that was that. The video ended. Two days later Shenzhen lost its Internet and telephone network. Finally I was completely cut off from the world with no idea what would happen next. That was the day the dead finally overran the outskirts of the city, and the military announced the evacuation to the west, into the hills of Guangxi.

The Tannoy erupts into life once more as the announcer calls out a five minute warning. I look around and see that most of the locals have already donned their deeply tinted goggles. I slip mine on, and look back at Liu in almost complete darkness.

As soon as I watched Doctor Gallagher's video I knew *exactly* what was happening. I remembered as clear as day the moment I'd last seen such a reaction more than thirty years earlier. I was *certain* that this wasn't photosensitive epilepsy. It seemed absurd that it possibly could be; that half of the zombies she tested could have developed the exact same rare neurological illness; that the scarring to their brains could have inflicted such specific damage without killing them outright. It just didn't make any sense.

I set to work immediately. As the military trucks swept through the streets to begin the evacuation I locked the doors to the factory and began to put my plan into action. I had nothing but a theory, and even after many years of working for the company I'd never learned much about electronics, but I was confident that Doctor Gallagher's work had finally given me a way to get back to my family. I was sure that there was a way to force the government to open the border gates and allow me through, to prove that I was too valuable to be allowed to die on the infected side. For the first time in many months I was excited, as giddy as a schoolboy.

It took four days of work to prepare the prototype. I didn't sleep or eat, and by the time I was finished my hands were destroyed, swollen and blistered with solder. I worked from a decades old *Introduction to Electronics* manual I kept in my office, cursing myself for never taking the time to learn the nuts and bolts of the products we manufactured, wishing that just one of my employees was there to help. Any one of my staff could have built the device in just an hour or two – it wasn't particularly complex, after all – but I was slowed down by my clumsy hands, and slowed even further by the fact that I had to keep looking up the meaning of the symbols in the circuitry diagrams I was using.

It was around midnight on the fourth night when the device was finally ready, and the streets were deathly quiet. The evacuation had been completed, and as I unlocked the doors and stepped outside it felt as if I was entering another world. A city that was once home to thirteen million, completely empty. It was... eerie. The electricity was still working in half of the city. The traffic lights blinked from green to red above deserted streets. Enormous digital hoardings at every junction played commercials for fast food restaurants that no longer existed, for Hollywood movies that would now never be seen, and they played for nobody but me. I felt like...

Liu blushes, and lets out an awkward chuckle.

As embarrassing as it is to admit, as I walked through the empty city I felt just like the hero of that American movie, *I Am Legend*. I have to admit that there was a certain swagger in my step as I strode through the empty streets. I'm sure that nobody who saw me would have mistaken me for a movie star, a skinny Asian man in my late fifties, almost bent double under the weight of the car battery in my backpack, but at that moment I felt like the king of the world. It was *intoxicating*. I allowed myself to enjoy the moment. I allowed myself to feel the pride – as yet entirely unearned – of building this device that would win back the cities from the dead.

I'm afraid I indulged myself just a little too much. I was lost in thought, congratulating myself on my achievement like a prideful child, and I didn't notice the men until I almost walked into them. They were standing in a small group about fifty paces up ahead, around a dozen young soldiers with guns slung over their backs, facing away from me. I knew that the curfew was still in place, and now that the evacuation had been completed I knew they'd have orders to shoot to kill. I also knew that if I made any sound I wouldn't have the chance to explain myself before these jumpy, inexperienced boys began firing.

I was completely exposed, standing in the middle of Fu Tian Nan Lu with nothing on either side but sheer walls and locked office doors. The only cover was a row of cars parked along the side of the street, so I shuffled towards them as quickly and quietly as I could, and lowered myself into a squat between two sedans.

I realized my mistake almost immediately. As soon as I rested my weight on the balls of my feet I felt the heavy car battery in my backpack pulling me backwards. I began to fall, and instinctively reached out for something to steady myself: the bumper of the car behind me.

The alarm must have been on a hair trigger. As soon as I touched the car it began wailing an electronic warning loud enough to echo through the deserted streets for miles around. I almost soiled myself with the shock, and my voice cracked as I cried out, "Please don't fire! I'm not one of them! *I'm healthy!*" I waited for either an answering call or the start of the gunfire, whichever came first.

Nothing happened. There were no shots. They didn't call out an order to show myself. Nothing. Just silence. Maybe they didn't hear me over the alarm? I called out again, and again no response came. I could only hear my own breathing, and the sound of my heart thumping in my ears. And then... then I heard the sound of steel on steel. That's when it began to dawn on me that I was in even more trouble than I feared.

The first of them appeared by the side of the car I was

hiding behind. I could see him through the windows. The barrel of his rifle was knocking against the side of the car with each step, but he made no move to swing it from his back. I crept around to the other side of the car as he continued forward towards the noise and flashing lights, then I dropped to my belly and saw more sets of feet, all of them slowly moving towards the sound of the wailing alarm.

I didn't dare stand up. I'd never seen the infected up close, and now I was within spitting distance of them all my bravado evaporated in an instant. I hadn't experienced such visceral fear since that moment thirty years earlier when the helicopter plunged towards Lantau Peak, only now I no longer possessed the foolish courage of a young man. Age had only deepened my fear of death, and it almost froze me rigid.

The first man... ha, *man*. He was barely a teenager. I stared up at him as he walked slowly around the car and realized that he reminded me of myself when I was that age. Just a skinny boy dressed in fatigues two sizes too large because the army didn't make them small enough. The fatigues were bloodied, and at his collar I could see that a chunk had been torn out of his neck. Stringy tendons and loose skin hung from the wound, and his head tilted to the side where the supporting muscles had been torn away. I couldn't take my eyes off him, nor the others as they reached the car. I just lay there, half hidden, staring at these boys and their wounds, until finally it became too much for me and I vomited down the side of the car.

They heard me, of course. They turned to face me all at the same moment, and the sound that came out of their mouths... I lost control of my bladder. I lost control of *everything.* Instinct took over, thankfully, and my body lifted itself up without my input. My conscious mind took a back seat, and adrenaline and terror took me in a straight line to the end of the street and around the corner. I must have ran for a mile. I don't think I was even fully conscious until I reached the border gate. It was only the guns and the yelling that finally pulled me back to the world.

I must have looked like a mess. Crying, vomit running down my chin, drenched in urine, and wearing the same suit I'd been wearing for the last six months. I honestly don't know why they didn't shoot me on sight. They certainly should have, even if they believed I was uninfected, but they simply yelled down an order for me to freeze. A floodlight was turned on me, and the world vanished in the dazzling light.

A voice called down an order but I couldn't make out the words. Then another voice called out, and another, and before long it seemed like all of the guards were yelling all at once, their words crashing together into a single incomprehensible roar. I held up an arm to block the dazzling floodlight and pleaded with them to slow down. I cried that I didn't understand. I begged them not to fire, and when I heard that first shot I fell to the ground and buried my face in my chest.

Time seemed to slow. I seemed to lay there for an eternity hearing the cracks of the rifles ring out above me, waiting for the bullet that would end it all. I even had enough time to wonder where on my body I'd be hit. Would it be a head shot? Would I die before I even knew I'd been hit, or would it be a painful affair? Would I be riddled with bullets and left to die in agony? Only a few seconds must have passed in reality, but in my head it felt like hours. Days. I wanted it to be over. I almost wanted to stand, to bear my chest and give them an easy target.

"*Run!*" That was the first time I could make out an actual word, and for a moment I wondered if I'd imagined it. "Run, you crazy *lou je!* Get the hell out of here!" I realized the voice wasn't in my head. Someone on the wall was calling down to me. There was panic in the voice. Fear. That's when I opened my eyes and finally looked around me. The floodlight was gone. I was curled up on the ground in pitch darkness, and all the lights were turned on something behind me. I almost didn't dare turn my head, and when I finally summoned the courage I wished I hadn't.

There were hundreds of them. Soldiers. Civilians. Old men and young girls, all of them dragging their broken limbs and torn bodies towards the wall. Towards *me*. The soldiers were picking them off one by one, but not nearly quickly enough. They were too panicked. Their shots were going wild, catching limbs or missing entirely. It was clear the creatures would reach me before the guards could take them all down. I looked around for a way out, some way I might slip past the swarm without being caught, but there was nothing. On both sides of the road high concrete barriers blocked my passage, and ahead of me the entire road was filled with the creatures.

I lay there for what felt like an age before I finally remembered the weight on my back. It had completely slipped my mind in my panic, the very reason I was there at the border, but now I moved with purpose. With trembling hands I slipped the backpack to the ground and pulled out the device. After all the running I'd done it was now little more than a tangle of wires attached to the battery, but I somehow managed to pull it out without disconnecting anything.

The first of the swarm was almost on me now, just a dozen or so steps away. I could smell them. I could smell the sharp bite of blood. The musty odor of rot. I could even smell the contents of their trousers, half digested meat that had slithered through their bodies and leaked out from their loosened bowels. It was awful. Overwhelming.

I took a deep breath and forced my focus down to the device in front of me. A car battery, a bundle of wires, a simple circuit board, and a seven thousand lumen LED security light. My hands were trembling as I held the light up ahead of me like some sort of protective talisman, and as I flipped the switch I felt tears streaming down my face and realized I was praying out loud to any god that would listen.

A slow, mournful siren sounds across Hong Kong Bay, and Liu pulls his protective goggles over his eyes. "Here we go," he says, smiling with what seems to be modest embarrassment.

On the opposite side of the bay the skyscrapers of Hong Kong Island suddenly fall into darkness. The siren fades, seeming to drift mournfully away across the water, and then without further warning what looks like every last light in Hong Kong begins to rapidly flicker with a blinding white light. Even through the goggles it's difficult to watch.

The light show has for years been a popular tourist attraction in Hong Kong, drawing visitors from around the world to view the carefully choreographed display as dozens of skyscrapers are illuminated in a rainbow of colors and a dazzling array of patterns. The regular show still takes place every night of the year but one. For just one night each year Hong Kong erupts in a

blinding, strobing visual cacophony to celebrate Stephen Liu's innovation.

This is the light that saved the world; the light that made Hong Kong the world's first truly safe city, and allowed humanity to slowly, steadily retake the planet from the infected. For five minutes the lights of the city shine so brightly they can be seen from low orbit, and then they return to darkness as suddenly as they burst into life. The gathered crowd cheers and bursts into applause as the display ends. Liu raises his voice above it.

You can imagine my fear the first time I switched on that light. I had no idea if it would work. It was, if you'll excuse the pun, a shot in the dark, but I was confident that my theory was sound.

The first few creatures fell to the ground within moments, maybe a dozen of them. The rest kept walking, stepping over their fallen brothers and sisters as they twitched on the floor. For a moment I felt the panic rise, and then a few more fell, then more. It only took thirty seconds before more than half of the swarm were on the ground, convulsing, and by the time a minute had passed they were all down. Every. Last. One.

I didn't count them at the time – I was so terrified I don't think I could have counted to ten without missing a few numbers – but they told me later that I'd incapacitated almost seven hundred of them. The guards on the wall had been able to pick them off one by one as they convulsed.

The next few days were a blur. I lost count of the number of questions I faced, from everyone from the guards on the wall to the Chief Executive of Hong Kong himself. *Who are you? How did you do that? Can you teach us?* I refused to answer anything until they agreed to take me to my wife and son. They insisted. They threatened to lock me away unless I explained what I'd done, or even throw me back into Shenzhen to face the swarms ravaging the city, but I told them I'd destroy the device if they dared. I held it above my head and threatened to smash it on the ground unless they let me see my family. Eventually they relented. I expect they thought I was crazy, and I don't blame them.

"So what was the secret? Why did your device work when Doctor Gallagher's didn't?"

Liu smiles.

You remember the helicopter crash? I'd always wondered why Witherspoon was affected by the flickering light while I remained unharmed. We were both exposed to it, after all, but it was only he who suffered from the Bucha effect. The question had bothered me for years, and eventually curiosity got the better of me and I tracked down a friend of a friend, a neurologist at Yan Chai Hospital. He smiled as I told him the story, and as soon as he did I knew he had the answer.

"It's simple," he said. "You were afraid."

He explained that the frequency of the light flickering in the cockpit had probably been somewhere in the same region as regular brainwaves – maybe around 20 Hertz – which precisely matched those of the pilot, but he told me that my brainwaves *weren't* regular at the time. He said that the brainwaves of those in a state of panic or fear flow at a much lower frequency. They're called Theta waves, and they flow at around 4 Hertz, much slower than anything the rotors of a helicopter could possibly produce. I was saved only by my own cowardice.

Liu removes his protective goggles and blinks in the light.

That was the key to my device. Doctor Gallagher, believing that the undead suffered from photosensitive epilepsy, only thought to test her subjects with light frequencies that commonly affect those who suffer from the condition. *That's* why her tests only affected a portion of her subjects.

The device I built addressed this problem. I wired the LED light to strobe on a cycle within a range of 3 to 30 Hertz, so where Doctor Gallagher's light only affected those few undead whose brainwaves were at a frequency of around 25 Hertz my device cast a much wider net, eventually incapacitating every last damned zombie within view of the light. So simple in hindsight, and yet nobody came up with the answer before I stumbled on it. Just as was the case with Doctor Bucha, the answer was there all along. It was just waiting for someone to make the obvious intellectual leap. Doctor Gallagher made the initial breakthrough, but I gave it that last little push.

Within days of my return to Hong Kong the city swung into action. Every man, woman and child with even the most basic knowledge of electronics was pressed into service to build everything from handheld portable rigs to gun mounted torches to enormous floodlights that could be mounted to cars or even helicopters. Some bright spark even designed an app that would transform the little flash on a cell phone camera into an oscillating strobe.

By the end of the month our soldiers had begun to retake Shenzhen, and once the city had been pacified and the concept had been proved we began to ship lights to all corners of China. Within months all of our cities were encircled with a protective halo that stopped the dead in their tracks, and within two years China was almost completely purged of the walking plague. It was over. We'd mastered the greatest threat to the world since the Black Death.

In the direction of the Star Ferry Terminal the Chief Executive of Hong Kong stands in the center of a crowd of photographers, cheerfully posing for pictures that will adorn the front pages of tomorrow's newspapers. He waves in Liu's direction and beckons him over to join him, but the elderly man pretends not to notice.

China was almost clear of infection before I learned the truth. It was almost a year since I'd built my first device, and after all that time I wanted nothing more than to speak with Doctor Gallagher. I wanted to thank her personally for making the breakthrough that allowed me to find the answer. I wanted to tell her how much her work meant to me, and how deeply I appreciated her efforts. I wanted to tell her that my wife and child were alive only because of her.

It wasn't easy. There was still no Internet, of course, and our telephone network was in tatters. It took three months of patient wrangling before I finally got hold of a working satellite phone – contraband, of course, procured from an old Air Force contact – and another month before I managed to track down the contact details of the doctor. I remember my hands trembling as I dialed the number, and my heart thumping as I listened to the trilling tone and waited for her to answer.

Liu glances over warily at the Chief Executive, still surrounded by photographers and beaming proudly. A grimace flashes across his face for a moment.

Doctor Gallagher had no idea who I was. She'd never heard my name, and she'd never heard of my device. For a moment I wondered if there was some sort of miscommunication. I wondered if my English wasn't as strong as I believed it to be, or perhaps if I was struggling to understand the doctor's difficult accent, but no. There was no confusion. By the end of the call I finally knew the terrible truth.

We hadn't told you. For an entire year we'd been fighting to rid our country of the undead scourge with the most effective weapon anyone could ever hope for, but my government had decided not to share it with the rest of the world. While we celebrated our victory against the swarms that had ravaged our country yours still roamed free. In the west you were still dying in your millions even as life here returned to normality.

They still haven't forgiven me to this day, you know, for telling Doctor Gallagher. Oh, they smile and pat me on the back in public, and every year they invite me here and treat me like a national hero, but they'll never forgive me for stealing from them the opportunity to rule the world. That's why they canceled my patent. It's why the converted my neighborhood in Tai Po into a refugee camp. It's why they pay my pension late every single month, and why it's always only half of my entitlement.

Liu tosses the last of his wafer cone to a pigeon, brushes off his hands and sighs.

Oh, well. At least I can sleep at night.

•▼•

Cheltenham, England

Set toward the western edge of the ten mile wide barbed wire defensive perimeter of Cheltenham, one of only a half dozen sanctuary cities on the British mainland to survive the crisis largely unscathed, the GCHQ building is the only structure within the perimeter that has not been at least partially broken down and scavenged for materials. While the vast parking lot that surrounds it has been converted to a makeshift refugee camp the doughnut shaped building itself still looks as if it was built yesterday, its steel and glass walls gleaming in the morning sun.

It was here that Dan Gosling and his small team of intelligence analysts rode out the war in relative comfort, safely protected behind a high wall of barbed wire and hidden four floors underground. For years they watched the world collapse from their impregnable fortress, voyeurs to the apocalypse, employing a vast network of controversial surveillance tools that were originally designed to sift through the world's communications in search of terrorist threats against the UK.

Now declassified and open to the public I am among the first to witness what was, until the deteriorating global communications infrastructure rendered it near useless, one of the world's most powerful surveillance systems.

"Welcome... to Project Lucius," Gosling calls

out dramatically, raising his arms towards the banks of monitors covering one wall of the large control room. He smiles expectantly as if waiting for my reaction, then slumps his shoulders at the sight of my blank expression.

Bloody hell, I've had ten visitors today, and nobody's got the reference. *The Dark Knight*? Not ringing any bells? Seriously?

Gosling sighs.

OK, so Batman... you know who Batman is, right? Yeah, so Batman needed to track down the Joker towards the end of *The Dark Knight*, but he didn't have a clue where in Gotham he might be hiding so he went to see Lucius Fox – that's Morgan Freeman – who'd developed a method of using mobile phones to send out sonar signals that created an image of... you're not really interested in this, are you?

"No, please, go on."

No, no, I can tell you're not really bothered. I've been down here for years with nothing but the screens and a big pile of DVDs, but I can still tell when I'm boring people stiff. It doesn't matter, it's just a daft movie reference.

Anyway, this is Project Lucius. It may not seem all that impressive from here, but what you're looking at is the control room of the most advanced electronic surveillance network ever built outside the US and China. Right now we're sitting two floors above a liquid-cooled Cray XC40 running 419,000 processor cores at 8.32 petaflops.

That's a computer as powerful as... well, I don't know what to compare it to, but it's faster than Barry Allen being chased by a cheetah with a jet pack. When it was first activated this was one of the top ten most powerful supercomputers ever created, and... you know, now I think about it it may be the only one left in operation. *Christ*, that's a depressing thought.

Lucius is... well, I always liked to think of him as a kind of high tech sieve. He was designed to sift through billions of communications each day, from phone calls to web searches to emails to closed circuit camera feeds to financial transactions, searching through unimaginably large volumes of data for... well, for whatever we told him to search for.

You understand I can't really go into too much detail about our counter-terrorism operations, right? I mean, the existence of the system itself has been declassified, but the details of our operations before the war are still locked up tight until I'm told otherwise, though I'm not sure why it matters any more. All I can say is that if the general public had known exactly how much access we had to their data back before the zombies arrived they would have covered their webcams with so much duct tape there would have been a global shortage.

We had *scary* powers. I'm talking Bond villain levels of power. If I could get the required warrants – and believe me when I tell you that wouldn't have been a problem – you could have given me the name of your first childhood crush, and within half an hour I could have told you the color of the wallpaper in her bedroom, how many times she'd checked out one of your photos on Facebook, and the date she'd purchased her last sex toy.

Lucius was the *ultimate* cyber stalker. He could discover your deepest, darkest secrets in the time it takes to make a brew. Umm...that's not to say I ever crossed the line personally, of course. I always prided myself on my professionalism.

"I'm sure. Did the system help give the UK any early warning of the zombie threat?"

The zombies? Nah, not even the slightest hint, I'm afraid. As far as Lucius was concerned everything was fine and dandy until we told him otherwise.

You see, Lucius is incredibly fast and incredibly smart. If we gave him a pattern to find and fed him the required data he could isolate that pattern faster than you can blink. For example, if we were looking for an upcoming terror attack on British soil we could instruct Lucius to search for suspicious patterns hidden amongst billions of data points, including everything from financial transfers and coded messages between foreign nationals to flight bookings for the family members of those on our watch lists, and he'd handle it like a pro. These patterns were well understood because we, the human operators, knew how terror networks functioned. In short we already knew exactly what we were looking for. Lucius just helped us find it much, much more quickly.

The problem is that Lucius is also, in many ways, incredibly daft. He's an idiot savant, like Dustin Hoffman in *Rain Man*. He's extremely gifted when it comes to recognizing known patterns, but when it comes to unfamiliar stuff he's completely lost. If he doesn't know exactly what he's looking for he has no way of actually understanding what he's seeing, you see, and since he doesn't have any independent intelligence of his own he doesn't even know enough to know what he doesn't know, if that makes any sense. Unfortunately he relies on stupid sacks of meat like us to give him his marching orders. *We* were the weak link, not him.

That's why he was of no use when we found ourselves faced with the zombie problem, because it was a threat that came completely out of the blue. There were no obvious patterns to identify, so as far as Lucius knew the incidents leading up to the crisis were just random unconnected events. I mean he *saw* them, of course. He told us that an unusual number of the workers in the Russian mining programs had died or gone missing. He told us about an upswing in fundamentalist chatter in Central Asia and warned us to expect trouble from the region. He even told us about some kind of panic among the military in Japan a full week before the Tokyo outbreak began, but there was no way for either him or us to connect the dots. In isolation these events didn't seem to have anything in common, and by the time we figured out what was going on it was far too late.

Gosling gently pats a console, as if to apologize to the computer.

It was only after the dead arrived that Lucius really came into his own, and it was all thanks to the emergency budget and a spot of detective work.

It was about two months after the attack on Folkestone when it all started. I arrived at work one Monday morning to find the system almost completely powered down, running at just quarter capacity. That had never happened even once since Lucius had been activated three years earlier, because shutting down almost half a million processors isn't as simple as flipping the power switch. It takes a full day to deactivate such a complex system without damage, and almost a week to start it back up again in a minutely specific order so you don't fry the processors as they take up the load. I couldn't *believe* they'd shut him down without consulting me.

I'm afraid I made a bit of a tit of myself when I stormed into the Director's office ten minutes later. I'd never met the guy and he didn't know me from Adam, so he was a little taken aback when I leaned over his desk and started yelling that he'd killed my baby. It was only when his secretary rushed in and explained who I was that he called off security and asked me to sit. He must have thought I was mental.

After I'd calmed down a little he patiently explained to me that the decision had been forced on him. With over half the country officially at risk we'd been put on a war footing, and the defense budget had been reallocated from overseas threats to domestic security. The intelligence budget had been cut in half overnight, he said, because every pound we spent eavesdropping on ISIS operatives in the desert outside Damascus was a pound we no longer had available to spend on ammunition to defend our cities. He said it just made no sense to continue 'wasting' 12% of the GCHQ operational budget on a high tech electronic surveillance system when we were facing an enemy that didn't even know how to pick up a phone or send an email. It made sense, I suppose, but I still didn't like it.

With Lucius mothballed I was immediately reassigned to the perimeter defense team, helping to roll out mile after mile of barbed wire and set up checkpoints on the roads around Cheltenham, and I wasn't the only one to lose my purpose. Overnight British intelligence was gutted. Highly experienced analysts were sent out to border garrisons and handed weapons they'd never been trained to use. Interpreters were reassigned to airports to help screen new arrivals in the quarantine zones. Even section heads found themselves running soup kitchens and arranging housing for refugees within the new sanctuary cities.

We were neutered, our collective experience and expertise replaced wholesale by that bloody *Zombie Hunter* app. That was the work of some bright spark up at the top who decided that the app provided all the intelligence we'd need to master the crisis. Crowdsourced intelligence, they called it, a bleeding edge solution that could be delivered instantly at virtually zero cost. That kind of bollocks was like catnip to politicians in Westminster, but on the ground we could already see that it wasn't all it was cracked up to be. The Yanks had already started to ask questions about its reliability, and we were fairly certain it didn't work as advertised, but we needed a way to prove it.

A bunch of us started to come in during our down time as soon as we heard about the flaws with the app. Lucius was scheduled to be fully deactivated as soon as the tech staff could pencil it in, so we knew it was a race against the clock to prove that *Zombie Hunter* wasn't up to the task of directing our forces. For a few days we brainstormed ways to use the computer to pick the app apart, and finally I came up with a solution.

Lucius was the key. He had access to closed circuit video feeds all around the world thanks to the backdoors the manufacturers had kindly built in to their systems over the years, and even running at a fraction of his capacity we still had more than enough raw processing power to analyze millions of feeds and match them up with the outbreaks reported by the app. It was an absolute pain in the balls to get our ducks in a row, but after nine days of working without sleep we finally had enough proof to go to the Director.

63%. That's how many of the thousands of reported outbreaks we studied were actually genuine. Sixty three bloody percent. An entire *third* of them were phantoms, and to each of them we were dispatching assault teams who ended up wasting countless hours sweeping empty apartment blocks and turning suburbs upside down in a search for zombies that had never even existed. I didn't know if this was intentional fuckery, user error or just a flaw in the app, and I didn't really care either way. All I knew was that it was an *insane* waste of vital resources and manpower, and we absolutely had to stop using this joke of an app as the only guide for our armed forces.

It took a full day to convince the Director to reactivate Lucius. He wasn't all that technically adept so he didn't really understand much of what we were talking about, but eventually our tenacity paid off. We dragged him down to our sub-basement and made him watch as we matched reported outbreaks with live CCTV feeds. He sat through seven incidents, and only four of them ended with enemy engagement.

Tragically – but conveniently for the case we were trying to make – two civilians were killed by a member of one of the assault teams attending a phantom outbreak while the Director watched the live feed. These were two civilians who would still be alive if the team hadn't been sent on a wild goose chase by an app that simply wasn't fit for purpose, and one soldier who'd go to bed that night, and every night for the rest of his life, with the knowledge that he'd killed a young mother and her son.

Gosling taps a few keys on the closest computer, and a moment later the wall monitors throw up dozens of quickly cycling video images.

Most show cityscapes: concrete shopping precincts, urban apartment blocks, vast parking lots and winding suburban streets. In the corner of each image blinks a single word. For some the word is 'confirmed' in green. On others, 'bullshit' in red. Gosling chuckles and points to a blinking red word.

That was my own personal touch. A little childish, I know, but we had to pass the time somehow.

This is the system we developed in the week it took to power Lucius back up. We worked from dawn to dusk for seven days straight, and by the time the final processor was back online we were ready to go live.

"Exactly what am I looking at?"

This, my friend, is what saved the United Kingdom. You're looking at mobile phone video feeds that correspond with every outbreak reported by the *Zombie Hunter* app. In the space of a week we press-ganged every coder we could find, British or foreign, to design a system by which we could hijack *Zombie Hunter*. We managed to write a simple piece of code that could be pushed to almost every mobile phone in the country – thank God for the Civil Contingencies Act – that allowed us to remotely activate the video camera on any phone using the app.

Whenever a *Zombie Hunter* user tagged a target their phone automatically routed the video feed though Lucius, and we instantly analyzed the footage using DARPA-designed gait analysis software to determine whether there were actually any zombies in the shot. We literally told Lucius to look for figures in each video that walked with that... you know, that odd, shambling walk zombies have, like they're not in full control of their legs.

Within a week of reactivation Lucius had weeded out so many phantom outbreaks that we had a 97% hit rate, which meant that we increased the efficiency of our assault teams by almost 50% in one fell swoop. No more wasted hours searching for attacks that didn't exist. No more civilians put needlessly in harm's way. The only false positives we really came across were blokes who were so drunk they walked like zombies, and we could usually pick those out manually before dispatching a team.

Lucius was an absolute bloody revelation. By the end of his first month in operation we'd already seen outbreak frequency begin to fall, and by the end of the second month we'd started to turn the tide. We saw fewer and fewer outbreaks with each passing day, and by the end of winter we knew the exact location of almost every swarm in the country.

We weren't safe by any stretch of the imagination, of course. Our forces were still on the edge of being overwhelmed every day, and we were facing endless food, clean water and energy shortages – especially in the sanctuary cities, where the situation was growing more desperate each day – but thanks to Lucius the crisis was becoming almost manageable. Thanks to him we were no longer fighting blind. For the first time we realized that we could actually *win* this thing. We could beat these bastards and *survive*. It was... well, it kept us going, you know? Made it worth getting up in the morning.

A tour group of around a dozen enters the control room behind us, made up of equal parts civilians and military officers. They gaze in wonder at the flickering images on the dozens of

wall monitors. Many of the civilians will not have seen an active computer screen for several years, given the careful rationing of power in Cheltenham.

Gosling smiles and excuses himself before jogging eagerly over to the tour group. He stops before them and raises his arms dramatically.

Welcome... to Project Lucius!

His shoulders slump as he's met by a sea of blank faces.

•▾•

:::25:::

Oaxaca, Mexico

Lieutenant Colonel Mills weaves back and forth on his stool, six beers in and hungrily eyeing a dusty bottle of tequila behind the bar. The alcohol has dulled the pain of his broken rib, but his right eye is still alarmingly swollen and the bruise on his cheek is turning darker by the hour. He has resisted my efforts to take him to a hospital, insisting that he suffered much worse during the war without medical attention.

You wanna know what won the war? It wasn't those fancy lights – though God bless 'em, and God bless the guy who came up with the idea – and it wasn't guns and ammo. They all helped, of course, and I would have hated to do it without them, but what really won the war was wire, rope, fence posts, asphalt and good old fashioned testicular fortitude. That's what gave us back America, and it was all thanks to Buckley.

We had a little more than a half million civilians in the safe zone by the end of year four, twice what the number crunchers had told us the land would comfortably support, and the strain was showing everywhere you looked. After four years of struggle the greatest threat wasn't the Zees assaulting the perimeter but the humans within it, hundreds of thousands of them, pissed off, tired and rebellious.

Crime was skyrocketing. We had our fair share of rapes and murders, but it was mostly just petty theft, random brawls and passive aggressive graffiti on every wall near the base. People were blowing up at the smallest things. Some guy takes too long on the john, he ends up with a black eye. One of the moms doesn't pull her weight in the nursery, we'd get a cat fight in the parking lot. Seemed like every day we'd have another dumb, pointless ruckus, another few hotheads threatened with exile beyond the perimeter if they didn't fly right. The MPs were working double time just to keep people from killing each other.

There was just too little food, y'know? Too little food, no AC, and regular assaults on the perimeter that left us constantly on edge. And this was a continuing condition. There was no end in sight, no grand plan to retake the country. People can withstand a lot of privation in wartime, but they have to know that one day it'll end. There has to be some kind of victory on the horizon, or why bother to drag yourself out of bed in the morning? What's the point of living on scraps today if the best you can hope for is a few more scraps tomorrow and tomorrow and tomorrow?

It's no surprise people were getting a little pissed off, and of course this kind of thing hit Americans harder than most. We were accustomed to a standard of living most people in the world could only ever dream about, so when everything collapsed we had further to fall than most.

We'd introduced rationing by the end of our first summer, just as soon as the population hit a quarter mil, and by our third winter things had all gotten a little dystopian, if you know what I mean. For one thing, while we didn't want to outlaw pregnancy outright – we needed people to keep making babies, or this was all for nothing – we *could* place the cost of those babies on the parents, so we instituted our own version of China's one child policy. Each woman was only given extra rations for one new

baby, and for any additional kids she and her husband –
or, in many cases, the random guy she'd hooked up with
for protection – had to take the food out of their own
allowance. A little cruel, maybe, but necessary.

By the time the fourth winter rolled around we were
down to fifteen hundred calories a day for the adults, with
a little more for people with physically demanding jobs,
but even that wasn't enough to keep everyone fed.
Buckley's plan had included leeway for crop rotation and
fallow periods to keep the soil fertile – he was planning
for the long term – but we just couldn't afford it any more.
We were squeezing every calorie out of the ground,
punishing the soil until it gave up its last potato, and it
still wasn't enough.

When Colonel Wright announced plans to reduce the
allowance to a thousand calories per day... Jesus, the riots
got so bad I almost wanted to escape beyond the
perimeter and try my luck with the Zees.

There were eighty seven casualties before we managed
to get the lid on the violence, most of them
quartermasters at the food distribution centers. These
folks were hands down the most despised people in
Georgia. A lot of them had let the power go to their heads
over the years. They were known for slipping their
buddies a little extra, cutting rations for people who
pissed them off, even trading food for sex, so it made
sense that they were popular targets when people finally
lost patience.

Eighty seven dead, more than two hundred injured.
After that the Colonel opened an investigation into the
corruption, and by the end of the month about three
hundred crooked quartermasters had been banished
beyond the perimeter, and a thousand more were
reassigned. On top of that the food allowance was

magically increased to two thousand calories each and the one child policy was immediately scrapped. It was the only way, y'know? The civilians had just had enough of this shit, and we didn't have the personnel at Benning – or the will, to be honest – to put the safe zone under martial law.

Of course that left us facing a whole new problem. We'd made these promises but we didn't have anywhere near enough food to provide two thousand calories a day to a half million people, not over the long term. We were burning through the emergency winter stores just to keep the peace, but we knew it couldn't last. We knew it was just a band aid to stop the civilians from killing everyone in fatigues.

For two months all of us in uniform were walking around on eggshells. I was a Major by then, but I knew my oak leaves might as well have been a bullseye. The rank wasn't a source of pride or cause for respect. It just made me a potential target, and we all knew the day was coming when the other shoe would drop. We'd eventually run out of food, and what then?

And then President Buckley arrived, and everything changed.

Man, what a sight. You met the guy, right? In real life he's only around five ten, but when he climbed down from Marine One I'd swear he was eight feet tall if he was an inch. I don't use the word 'legend' lightly, but I'll make an exception for him.

As he walked towards me from the chopper I felt the weirdest impulse to bow. This was the guy who'd stayed behind with the demo team at Andrews and helped set the charges as the D.C. swarm broke through the gates. He'd volunteered to give up his seat to Anchorage to the pilot's kid, and the Secret Service only got him on the chopper by picking him up and tossing him in like a sack of potatoes.

Knowing Buckley was out there was the only thing that had kept us going through four years of hell. We didn't hear much from the outside world, but whenever a supply drop arrived it brought with it new issues of Survive and Thrive with news from the other states, and there was always something new about the President. Like the time he ordered his chopper to strafe the defensive line at the Abilene camp when it looked like it was about to be overrun, or the time he airlifted an entire company from Duluth to the Apostle Islands on Superior just a few hours ahead of the Minneapolis swarm, even though it left him stranded for a month while he waited for a fuel drop.

Those were the big stories, the heroic rescues, but what really gave people hope were the little things. The kids always talked about the day he dropped boxes of Twinkies and Hershey bars on the camp outside Missoula. Can you even imagine that? Ten months on starvation rations through one of the coldest winters on record, and then one day when you're just about ready to eat a bullet the President tosses you candy from Marine One. That's the kind of thing a man can hold on to, y'know? The kind of thing that can remind a guy that there's still a world out there waiting for him.

Buckley didn't bring us candy, but he brought something much better: hope. As soon as he touched down at Benning we took him on a whistlestop tour of the farms, shaking hands and kissing babies, and when he returned he invited everyone to a speech at the Columbus city cemetery, pretty much the only flat ground in the safe zone that hadn't been cultivated. Colonel Wright announced a public holiday and laid on buses to bring people in from the outskirts. Some even walked all the way from the farms at Lanett and Hills Island.

I'd say something like fifty thousand people were waiting when Buckley finally climbed up on the stage. Fifty thousand people who didn't dare breathe for fear they'd miss a word.

"For four years," he said, "you've been asked time and again to sacrifice. First you sacrificed your homes, and then your comfort, and then the very food in your bellies, and all to ensure that one day we'd be able once again to call this great nation our own. For too long you've suffered, and for too long you've been afraid.

"Friends, the time for fear is finally drawing to a close. No longer will we cower in our camps and safe zones, scraping by just enough to survive. No longer will we fight over scraps and hope for nothing more than to see another dawn. Beyond our walls the nation waits to be reconquered, and after four long years of struggle and sacrifice the time has come to leave the safety of our barriers and reclaim what's ours.

"Right now," he said, resting his hands on the splintered apple crates we'd set up as a makeshift podium, "our military and volunteer forces across the country are preparing to begin their assault. From Raleigh to Midland to Santa Rosa, from the vast plains to the high mountains, from the Gulf of Mexico all the way to the Bering Strait, the bravest among us are pulling on their boots, taking up arms and preparing to show the world what true Americans are made of.

"Tomorrow at dawn I'll march to the western border of the safe zone, and by nightfall I'll be stepping out from the perimeter to take the fight to the undead. I ask you to join me. I won't make any orders. After four years of sacrifice I won't be forcing a single one of you to give even more, but I'll simply extend an invitation. All those with the courage to fight alongside me should join me in the west, and together we'll take our country back.

"God bless you all, and God Bless the United States of America."

Mills takes a sip of his beer and smiles.

Three hundred thousand people showed up at the border the next morning, and by the time we opened the gates and cut the barbed wire another hundred thousand had arrived as the news spread. There were no white feathers handed out that day. The only people who remained behind were the kids and the elderly, along with maybe a few mothers who stayed to take care of a brood. Far as I know barely a single able bodied adult refused the call. Four hundred thousand people carrying shovels, axes and knives. Barely any guns – our ammo stores were almost completely gone after four years – but one on one a shovel can be just as deadly as a rifle.

Buckley's strategy couldn't have been simpler. It was just brute force, overwhelming the enemy through sheer numbers. He and the chiefs had pored over the maps and separated the United States into thousands of zones, each of them bordered on all sides by a highway or some kind of major road, and the objective was simply to fence off each road with barbed wire, lengths of rope, wrecked cars, chain link fence and whatever else could serve as a temporary barrier, and then send in the human hordes to overwhelm the undead swarms in a controlled, isolated arena.

It was something we could have done by ourselves years earlier. We're not talking about advanced military thinking here. It was just a simple, manageable way to retake territory piece by piece, inch by inch. All we needed to succeed was the will to fight, something a lot of us had lost, and President Buckley helped us rediscover it by marching ahead of us out of the safe zone. He led, and four hundred thousand of us happily followed.

After that there were no more complaints about the rationing, no more talk of rioting. We were united. We finally had a purpose. Each morning we'd wake up and take back another mile, another village, another farm. Hell, I don't think many people even noticed the fact that Buckley only marched with us for a few days before leaving for another safe zone. We never thought about the fact that he never really put himself in harm's way, or that he spent most of his time sitting in Marine One eating food most of us hadn't tasted in years.

It didn't matter. Buckley did his job. Once we'd seen him walk out of the safe zone he was with us in spirit. We were Buckley's army, and it felt as if he was leading us every step of the way.

I only saw him once after that, about three years later in the middle of some Godforsaken swamp to the west of Baton Rouge. He was leading a battalion that had marched out of Lubbock, Texas a year earlier. They looked exhausted. Seems they'd had it even worse than us back home. More people, and harsher soil, but Buckley had fired them up just as he had us.

Would you believe he recognized me? Nobody believes me when I tell them, but soon as he saw me he waded through fifty yards of waist deep swamp water, shook me by the hand and congratulated me on my promotion to Lieutenant Colonel. Hell, for all I know it was just the usual politician's bullshit. Maybe he'd called ahead to Colonel Wright and asked for the name of the commanding officer leading the Benning regiment, but I like to think it was legit.

That was the day Buckley declared the south clear.

From Richmond in the East to El Paso in the west humans – living, breathing humans – once again controlled the land.

Of course it wasn't strictly accurate. There were still probably at least a million Zees wandering around the southern states, locked up in abandoned buildings or just roaming the streets undetected, any one of which could have restarted the epidemic, but the point was that the south was safe enough for us to begin farming again. It was safe enough to start reopening factories and restarting power stations.

Within a month the first coal fired stations were brought back online in Louisiana. I remember the night the lights came on in New Orleans. I was in a little bar on Bourbon Street with a few buddies, and we were drinking warm beer when the lights flickered.

Y'know, I didn't even notice at first. It had been four years since I'd seen a light that wasn't run on batteries, and it just didn't register. Then we all stopped talking as the overhead fan creaked, shed a metric shitload of dust and started spinning above us. By the time we'd tinkered with the AC until it hummed into life the beers in the cooler were ice cold, and I felt like I'd been reborn.

That was the day we won America back. The day I sat in a bar and drank a cold beer.

Mills looks at the bottle in his hand and glumly sighs.

I guess I've been trying to get that feeling back ever since.

•▼•

:::26:::

Port Vila, Efate, Vanuatu

The satellite video link halts and stutters, freezing images of Sato Maseng's cheerful smile as he reports the latest news from the island. My Ni-Vanuatu guide has just returned from *The Pacific Jewel*, Sean Pruitt's home in exile.

They came for him this morning, *fren*. Took him away in *hankaf*. He tried to run, but you can't run far on this island.

Maseng's jubilation seems a little misplaced. While the deal to extradite the developer to the US included a provision for the safe removal of *The Pacific Jewel* from Port Vila, nothing will compensate the Ni-Vanuatu for the loss of $30 million in annual revenue paid by Pruitt.

Maseng waves away his worries about the loss of 5% of Vanuatu's GDP, describing it as a price worth paying for the opportunity to finally free themselves from the *rabis mit* parasite squatting in their harbor.

I want you to do me a favor, *fren*. If you see him in the States I want you to tell him I was the guy who *pispis* in his drinks, OK?

•▼•

:::27:::

Ulaanbaatar, Mongolia

Peace Avenue is now hidden beneath a layer of snow, but after just an hour the white blanket has already begun to turn gray, caked in the dust of the dozens of construction projects in the city. Mike flags down a cab and hustles me into the back before climbing clumsily in after me. "Tavan Bogd Hothon, bayarlalaa," he mumbles to the driver, directing him to the newest luxury apartment block overlooking the city.

Do you know what's the big tourist draw now? You won't believe me. *I* didn't believe it myself until I saw it in person, but they're running zombie hunting expeditions to Uvs aimag, up near the Russian border in the far west. When I was young the big thing was illegal wolf hunts. You'd see idiots cruising slowly through Ulaangom in their 4x4s, showing off their kills splayed out on the hood of their car. Now you see them strapping whole human bodies to the roof.

They don't even have to hunt these things. All that's left up there are frozen bodies, and they only run the trips through the winter. From what I've heard they just pierce the eye sockets with long poles. They don't even get up close.

Mike shakes his head sadly.

What do you say to that? You'd think people would have seen enough death by now, but here they are, spending tens of thousands of dollars for the opportunity to drive around in Mad Max cars with bodies strapped to them like trophies.

It's all illegal, of course. They have to dump them before they head back to civilization, but I guess the photos are enough for them. Maybe they passed the war in safety, like us, and feel cheated that they never got to feel the thrill of fear.

Morons. They don't realize how lucky they are.

•▼•

:::28:::

Halong Bay, Vietnam

Karen Walker nervously grips the arm rests of her seat as the sea plane takes off with a jarring bounce. She hasn't flown in almost thirteen years, she says, and the last flight was in a comfortable 747 from Bangkok to Hanoi.

As the small plane climbs and levels off she finally settles, and after a couple of drinks she's finally relaxed enough to look out the window. Our route will take us back to Hong Kong, but the limited range of the sea plane means we'll need to take on fuel in Nanning, the capital city of China's Guangxi Province.

Karen taps me on the arm and points out the window.

See that down there?

Thousands of feet below I see what appears to be a large city split in two by a broad, green river that spreads into a sandy delta as it reaches the ocean a few miles to the south east. The northern half of the city appears normal. In the dusk light streetlamps flicker on in sequence, and even at this altitude it's clear the streets are thronged with traffic. The southern half, on the other hand, is dead. No lights shine, and no traffic moves in the streets.

That's the Chinese border with Vietnam. North of the

river in Dongxing, China, and south is Mong Cai, Vietnam. You watched *La Rive Mortelle*, right?

I nod. *The Deadly Shore* is a favorite of those who support Walker's campaign to eliminate international borders.

Nguyen Le-Huynh spent six weeks shooting on the south shore of the Ka Long, watching as the Chinese mined their side of the river. Each night he filmed the boats as they tried to make it across to the other side, sitting low in the water because they were so overloaded with people, and each night he watched the guards open fire. The lucky ones made it to the other shore, but not a single person survived to reach the city.

He saw hundreds of boats sink. Thousands of refugees die. Why? Because the people on the boats called the river the Ka Long while the soldiers on the other side called it the Beilun. Because they ate different foods and spoke in a different language. Because their passports were a different color. They'd been born on the wrong side of the water, and that meant they had to die.

She shakes her head and grips her arm rest.

The Chinese watched as the Hanoi swarms reached the city. They watched the city's residents run to the shore and dive in, knowing that they'd be killed by the mines before their feet touched land. They listened as one hundred thousand people died screaming, their limbs torn off and their lungs filled with water, and all because the victims lived on the wrong side of the river. They all loved their mothers. They all loved their children. They all looked forward to a good meal at the end of a long day.

They all cheered on their local sports team, and felt their toes tap when their favorite song came on the radio, but they had to die because they were born on the wrong side of the river.

People are people. I don't care where they're from. If there's one lesson we should take from the last decade of hell it's that we're all in this together.

•▼•

:::29:::

Cornwall, England

I find Martin Rowland at his writing desk in the study of his cottage, gazing out in deep thought at the stormy sea, pen hovering over a blank sheet of paper.

I've been trying to write this for three weeks now, but the words don't seem to come quite as easily as they used to.

I ask him what he's writing. He sighs and sets down his pen.

It's an article for the local paper, supporting the vote in favor of resuming freedom of movement between Europe and the United Kingdom.

Back before all this happened this would have been the easiest article I'd ever have to write. It's what Sarah and I believed in almost above all else, and I know she'd still be firmly in favor despite everything. She was born in France, you see. Studied in Italy and moved here for university. She'd be horrified at the idea of keeping the borders closed now the continent is clear, but...

I've been staring at this bloody sheet of paper for three weeks now, and I just can't bring myself to write. I'm just not sure I believe any more. If we'd just closed the borders a little earlier she might still be with me, her and Toby. They might... I just don't know any more.

●▼●

:::30:::

Monroe, Washington

James McIntyre bites into a ripe tomato like an apple, letting the juice run down his arm and drip to the ground. Despite his sickly appearance he seems to be enjoying the day, basking in the unseasonable warmth.

I know it sounds dumb, and I'm damned sure it sounds cold, but maybe this was just what we needed, you know? I mean, just look around. The air's getting cleaner. We're almost completely off oil. I can drink the water straight from my faucet without wondering if some damned fracking company has made it flammable.

Did you see the story about the black bears living in New York? Can you imagine that? Hundreds of them, right there in Central Park, looking up at the shell of my old apartment on West 72nd.

McIntyre looks back at his greenhouse and smiles.

They're welcome to it, as far as I'm concerned. I've got my tomatoes.

•▾•

33792372R00205

Made in the USA
Lexington, KY
15 March 2019